# Sacrificed

## Chanette Paul

LAPA Publishers
Pretoria
www.lapa.co.za

Text: Chanette Paul 2017
© Publication: LAPA Publishers (Pty) Ltd
380 Bosman Street, Pretoria
Tel: 012 401 0700
Email: lapa@lapa.co.za

Set in 10 on 11.7 pt Leawood
Translator: Elsa Silke
Editor: Karin Schimke
Proofreader: Sean Fraser
Cover design: Flame Design
Printed and bound: Novus Print, a Novus Holdings-company

First edition 2017

ISBN 978-0-7993-8183-2 (printed book)
ISBN 978-0-7993-8186-3 (ePub)
ISBN 978-0-7993-8189-4 (mobi)

© All rights reserved. No part of this publication may be reproduced in any manner without the prior permission of the copyright holders.

**Chanette Paul** was born in Johannesburg but grew up all over South Africa. She attended nine schools, studied at five universities and has lived in seven of South Africa's nine provinces.

Chanette writes in Afrikaans, has published in various genres and received several awards.

*Sacrificed* is the English version of her book *Offerlam*. It is the first of her titles to be translated into English and has also been published in Dutch. *Sacrificed* is the first title in a two-part series.

Chanette lives in a lopsided cottage in the Overberg, on the bank of the Kleine River, where her partner operates a riverboat.

When she finds herself in the throes of a serious bout of writing, she goes to her retreat near the southernmost tip of Africa to wrestle with her characters and stories.

For more information about Chanette and her books, visit her website at www.chanettepaul.co.za, her blog at http://chanettepaul.wordpress.com or tweet her at https://twitter.com/Chanettie. She can also be found on Facebook, at https:www.facebook.com/chanette.paul.

Photo: Carine Du Prez

**Main characters in** *Sacrificed*

Ammie Pauwels: Caz's biological mother
Andries Maritz: Caz's ex-father-in-law
Annika: The publisher for whom Caz does translations
Aron: Tabia's nephew who helped Ammie flee the Congo
Arondji: Aron's son
Aubrey: Lilah's love interest

Babette: Shop owner

Cassandra (Caz) Colijn: Ammie's biological daughter/Lilah's mother
César Ronald Bruno Janssen: Ammie's first husband

De Brabander: Detective – Commissioner
Dlamini: Captain in the South African Police Service (SAPS)

Elijah: Ammie's beloved
Ellen: Caz's helper
Erdem: Guesthouse owner
Erevu Matari: Congolese man who follows Caz

Geert Grevers: Detective – Inspector
Gerda Verhoef: Detective – Agent

Hans Colijn: Caz's foster father
Hentie Maritz: Caz's ex-husband

Jacq DeReu: Ammie's second husband/Luc's father
Jan Kuyper: Tieneke and Fien's notary
Jela: Erevu's daughter
Josefien Colijn: Caz's foster mother/Tieneke's mother

Kembo: Ammie's son

Laura Lammens: Luc's colleague
Lieve Luykens: Ammie's carer

Lilah: Caz's daughter
Luc DeReu: Ammie's stepson/Jacq's son

Magdel Maritz: Caz's ex-mother-in-law

Njiwa/Dove: Erevu's grandson

Tabia: Tetela woman who saved Ammie's life
Tieneke Colijn: Caz's foster sister
Tobias: Ammie's third husband

**Other characters**
Alice Auma (Lakwena): A Ugandan psychic and the leader of the Holy Spirit Movement

Joseph Kony: Leader of the Lord's Resistance Army
Kabila: Current president of the DRC
Kamau and Obedele Kambon: Campaigners for reAfrikanization and dewhitenization, both from Ghana

Patrice Lumumba: Congolese independence leader and the first democratically elected prime minister of the Congo. Murdered 1961

~~~~

Foreign Words p. 489
Author's note p. 492
Bibliography p. 495

Oh, what a tangled web we weave,
when first we practice to deceive!

From *Marmion* by Sir Walter Scott

# Prologue

*17 January 1961*
*Katanga, Congo*

The night air reeked of savanna dust, sweat and fear. Of betrayal, greed and the thirst for power. A stench Ammie knew well.

César's left hand gripped her arm. The right hand was clenched around her jaw.

"Watch, bitch," he hissed in her ear. "Watch!"

Elijah stood under an acacia, a hare in the headlights. It was new moon. At the fringes of the pale smudge between somewhere and nowhere loomed the vague shapes of more trees. Somewhere to the left something rustled in the tall grass. A jackal howled in the distance, its mate echoing the mournful cry.

A command rang out, followed by the distinct sound of four rifles being cocked. She wanted to close her eyes but she kept staring as if her eyelids were starched.

Elijah coughed and spat out a gob of bloody mucus. His

vest, once white, was smeared with soil, sweat, saliva, blood. One shoe was missing. He wasn't looking at the soldiers with their rifles. From behind the lopsided spectacles on his battered face his eyes searched out her own. The glare on the lenses made it impossible to read the expression in his eyes.

Another command. Rifles raised to shoulders.

Sweat rolled down Elijah's temples. He strained against the ropes, tried to find some slack around his wrists and ankles but finally gave up. His knees twitched. His calves trembled. His lips were fixed in a stiff grimace.

Everything seemed surreal—what she was witnessing now, as well as the events of earlier that evening.

On her way to Elijah's house to warn him, she had seen the column of smoke from a distance. When she arrived at what had been his house it was clear that nothing had escaped the inferno. Not his desk, with all his documents, nor the shelves with the books he valued so highly. Not the photograph, taken in better days, of Elijah and Patrice Lumumba laughing together. Not even his Immatriculation certificate, the one piece of paper that, only a year ago, had been worth more than gold to every évolué: the passport to a better life.

When a vehicle had pulled up beside her and she was dragged inside, none of the spectators feasting their eyes on the mayhem had lifted a finger to help her.

Now, in these moments before the inevitable took place, Elijah stopped being the eternal student, the teacher, the philosopher. He was no longer Patrice Lumumba's friend, mentor and critic. Or the man who had helped feed, clothe and educate so many orphaned children. No longer the optimist who would simply face the odds and keep going.

He was just a man in a soiled vest, his spectacles tilted at an odd angle. A man who knew too much. Who had too much influence on Lumumba. Who had become a complication.

But more than anything, he was the man who loved her.

Another command. The words failed to get through to her, but the intention behind them was unmistakable.

The vice-like grip around her arm and chin tightened.

Did Elijah, at that moment, still believe in God's will? The will of a God who had saved Abraham when he had been on the point of offering his son, but had not granted his own Son the same salvation? Nor Elijah today.

The sound of gunshots shattered the stillness of the night. Ammie screamed as if it were unexpected. And maybe it had been. Maybe she didn't really believe that these white savages, that César, could be so debased.

Elijah's body jerked, spun to the right, fell against a tree trunk and collapsed in a heap in the shallow grave he'd probably had to dig himself earlier that day. Flesh, sinew and bone serving no further purpose. Blood pumping through the heart one last time colored the vest crimson, hiding the smears of dust and saliva.

César shoved her aside. Pain shot through her knee and elbow as she fell on the gravelly earth, grass blades scratching her arms. César wiped his hands on his trousers as if they were contaminated. For a moment his pale blue eyes met hers before a stream of saliva shot from his mouth and splattered against her cheek.

Dimly she became aware of the sounds of Elijah's body being covered with clods and rocks and gravel.

For a brief moment her world tilted.

"Elijah!" More than a scream, it was a raw sound from a place she hadn't known existed.

The first boot struck her side. The second, her shoulder.

"Whore!"

Somewhere an owl was calling its mate.

The next kick exploded against her temple.

The pool of light grew dim, giving way to the mysterious sounds of nocturnal Africa.

# One

*Monday, September 1, Present day*
*Caz*
*Overberg, South Africa*

Tieneke's voice was as clear as if she were calling from the neighboring smallholding, instead of six thousand kilometers away. The words got stuck somewhere in Caz's ear, their meaning distorted by some tube or bone or anvil. Tieneke? After so many years?

"I said: Mother is at her last gasp," her sister repeated when Caz failed to react. Tieneke was impatient, even in this situation.

Caz remembered that about her. Though she had actually forgotten.

"I didn't know Mother was still alive," she finally found her voice. "She must be well into her nineties."

"Ninety-eight. She's been relatively healthy and quite lucid for her age until just a few days ago, when she suddenly went downhill. But she won't hear of a nursing home. Not that I'd consider it. I've been taking care of her for most of her life, after all. Why not see it through to the end?" Reproach lay like thick sediment in Tieneke's tone.

With unseeing eyes Caz stared at the splotch the Cape robin had left on the corner of the desk. Bloody cheek, eating Catya's pellets, and then shitting all over the house.

What could she say to Tieneke? I'm sorry to hear Mother is dying at the ripe old age of ninety-eight? I'm sorry you never got married—at sixty-five you're probably too old now? I'm sorry I didn't try to make contact again after being chased away like a mangy dog when I needed you most thirty-one years ago?

"Why are you telling me this, Tieneke?" The question sounded heartless. Would have been heartless in any other circumstances. Probably still was.

"Mother wants to see you before she dies."

Everything fell silent—the sound of the wind in the wild olive tree, the din of birds, the soft hum of the computer—as if she had been robbed of her hearing in one fell swoop.

"What?" The word flew from her mouth.

"We don't have much time. You'll have to get a Schengen. Go to the Belgian Consulate. I presume you have a passport. You have to buy your plane ticket before applying for the visa. You probably don't want to waste your time in Dubai or Istanbul, so forget about Emirates or the Turkish airline, even if they do fly to Brussels. KLM has a direct flight to Amsterdam and from there you can take the train to Ghent-Dampoort. It takes about three hours. You'll have to change trains at Antwerp Central. From Ghent-Dampoort you take bus number three. Get off at …"

"Tieneke!" The sharpness in her voice stemmed the flood. Caz drew a deep breath, tried to calm down. "Why does Ma Fien want to see me?"

A deep sigh came down the line. It began in Ghent, traveled through Belgium, across half of Europe, down the length of Northern Africa, Central Africa, Southern Africa, and found its way to the cottage at the foot of the Kleineberg in the Overberg district.

"I don't know. She won't say. She gets terribly upset if I

mention the possibility that you might not come. Is that how you want Mother to meet her Maker? So unfulfilled?"

Why should I give a damn about Josefien Colijn's lack of fulfilment, Caz was tempted to ask. After all, Fien didn't give a damn three decades ago when she turned her back on her month-old granddaughter along with Caz and sent them out into the world to face scorn and humiliation. But this Tieneke knew. She had been there.

The jacarandas had been blossoming in Pretoria. Also the one in front of her childhood home, where she turned for one last beseeching look at the two women on the porch. Stunned that her mother and sister could send her away like that, refusing even to hear her side of the story. Not allowing her to cross the threshold of the house where she had grown up.

The two of them just stood there. Floral dresses stretched tight over plump figures. Tieneke with the first signs of gray in her wispy blonde hair. Fien's hair snowy white, stiffly permed. Longish faces, pale blue eyes, lips pursed over yellow teeth sprouting haphazardly from both sets of gums—a legacy of cruel genes.

Lilah had whimpered in her arms. And just then a jacaranda blossom had floated down and settled on the dark hair. That was how she got her new name: Lila, which later became Lilah when her modeling career took off. Hentie had wanted to call his daughter Johanna Jacomina, after his paternal grandmother, but Hentie's father had forbidden him to have the baby registered. Just as well.

"Cassie, please." These were possibly the hardest two words Tieneke had ever spoken in her life. The image of the women on the porch faded.

"Please what? Why now? Not once in the eleven years before you returned to Belgium did either of you call me or try to find out how I was doing. I had to learn from an attorney that you had gone back to Belgium and were living in Ghent. Not a single word after that either. And now you expect me to drop everything and fly over there?"

"I followed Lilah's career."

Anger robbed Caz of breath. For a moment everything grew dim. "Is that what this is about? Lilah's success? Are you after her money?"

"Don't be ridiculous. We live comfortably. You know we believe in sobriety."

Sobriety? Make that bloody stinginess. Caz had been eighteen before she could choose her own dress for the first time, a dress that wasn't a Tieneke hand-me-down. One that didn't have to be taken in and the hem let out to cater for the difference in weight and height. Caz had been a gangly giant in a family of chubby short-arses.

She took a deep breath. "Sorry, Tieneke, no go. Give Ma Fien my best, but I can't travel halfway around the world just because she's dying. I may be many things, but I'm not a hypocrite."

Silence hummed across thousands of kilometers before Tieneke cleared her throat. "I think she wants to tell you the truth."

"Truth?" The computer's screensaver began its little dance. Multicolored bubbles rolling across the freshly translated text added to the out-of-body feeling that took hold of her. "What do you mean?"

"Come over here and find out, Cassie. Before it's too late. I was only eleven when you were born. Only Mother can tell you."

"Tell me what?"

"Who your biological parents are."

"My *what*?"

"Your birth mother didn't want you, so Mother and Father took pity on you and offered to raise you. That's all Mother said at the time. It's all I know. You can contact us through the attorney to tell us when you'll be arriving. Mr. Moerdyk, in case you've forgotten. In Pretoria. Good day, Cassie."

The line went dead. The silence was pitch black. Like the spots dancing in front of Caz's eyes.

*Ammie*
*Leuven, Belgium*

Eighty isn't all that old, she wanted to say to Lieve, but what would be the use? For the past few years Lieve had been treating her as if her demise was nigh.

"You're eighty-two, Miss Ammie," Lieve reminded her.

Did she say it out loud? That eighty isn't old? Why did she say it anyway? Think it? Of course it's old.

Eighty-two? What had happened to the years between eighty and eighty-two? It had to be a conspiracy. Lieve was trying to confuse her.

"There you go." Lieve stood back. "Your hair is done."

Ammie gazed at her reflection in the mirror. She looked more dignified than she felt. Silver hair in a French roll. A spot of rouge on the cheeks. Pale pink lipstick. She bared her teeth to make sure they showed no lipstick smears. They were whiter than the pearls around her neck and perfectly even. The pearls were real, the teeth man-made.

Was that really her?

Lieve handed her a walking stick and helped her to her feet.

Through the window the day looked dreary. It had been a ghastly August. Not at all summery. And September had fared no better so far.

The rain had been so different in Elisabethville. Pouring from the warm sky and splashing on the warm earth. The weather steaming all through the wet season. The winters were a relief, not something to dread, like they were here in Leuven. Winters without snow, hardly cooler than summer.

Elisabethville. The name had changed. What was it now?

Only yesterday she had remembered it again. That day. She recalled it so clearly. As if it were happening all over again. But she couldn't remember what. What day was it?

"Let's settle you in the living room. I'll bring you a cup of tea before I start clearing up. Okay?" Lieve opened the door for her.

Ammie didn't protest. It was barely an hour since she had got out of bed and she was already tired.

Lieve made her comfortable in a chair before she began to bustle around the bedroom. Ammie closed her eyes.

*January 18, 1961*
*Ammie*
*Katanga*

When Ammie regained consciousness, the first person she saw was a Tetela woman. This was evident from the raised scar tissue decorating her pregnant belly in a complicated labyrinthe design. From this scarification the Tetela people would be able to construe her entire ancestry.

Strange to see a woman in traditional dress. Nowadays everyone wore Western clothing. The hand-woven skirt decorated with cowrie shells sat low on her hips to make room for the distended stomach. The colorful beads around her hips rattled when she moved. Her swollen breasts glistened, the areolas purplish black against the mahogany skin. Her eyes were the color of lychee pips, their expression inscrutable.

Ammie tried to move, groaned. Her entire body was a matrix of pain.

The woman held a tin mug to Ammie's swollen lips. She drank gratefully, but with effort. The goat's milk was cool, yet burned where it touched her cracked lips. It left an herbal aftertaste.

She was lying in a darkened room on a rug made of animal skins. A gap in the wall let in the sun. The filthy panes of the only window were cracked, one corner broken and missing.

Her nose was blocked, forcing her to breathe through her mouth. She could taste rather than smell the stench of sewage and rotting garbage outside. Her eyelids felt swollen and grainy.

"Elijah?" she muttered when the worst of her thirst had been quenched.

"Elijah is dead."

"César ..."

The woman's face contorted with hatred. "Your husband is gone. The dog ran!" Her Congo-French was terse and limited. She chased flies from Ammie's lips. "He thinks you dead. Leave you for tai and fisi."

Ammie recognized the Swahili words, though she didn't speak the language. In the Congo there was enough work for vultures and hyenas to hear them mentioned quite often. She didn't speak Lingala either, the Congo's other lingua franca.

There was a time when she had considered herself a loyal citizen of this country. She might not have been born here, but she had believed it was where her roots lay; it provided her with the only context in which to be herself.

Now she knew she had always been an incomer and would always remain one. She had been as blind as the rest, living in a dream world, where it was considered unnecessary to learn the indigenous languages, get to know the locals, try to understand them. No wonder the Congo had turned its back on them. They were no more than fleas on a dog's back that had to be brushed off.

"Where am I?"

"Elisabethville, but not the one you know. My kitongoji." Her voice rang with bitterness.

Ammie could see and smell the difference between her Elisabethville and this woman's neighborhood. She could hear it as well. Children shouting and laughing. Drums throbbing in the distance. Women's voices.

Cité indigène. A city on the outskirts of a city. A city where white people didn't go. A place to which the indigenous people had to return at night when they had finished their work in the houses and businesses of the whites because they were not welcome in white Elisabethville. At least, that was how it used to be.

"Why are you helping me?" Since Independence, white people were the enemy. Before Independence as well, of course, but now it was official.

"For Elijah. He was good to me. You must sleep now."

As if the words had magical powers her eyelids grew heavy. The herbs, Ammie realized, before she dozed off.

*Ammie*
*Leuven*

"Oh, Miss Ammie, your tea has gone cold." Lieve clicked her tongue.

Lubumbashi. That was the new name for Elisabethville.

Where was Elisabethville again?

Lieve put a crocheted blanket on her lap, tucking it around her knees. "I'll bring you a fresh pot."

"That's kind of you, Lieve. What time will Luc be home from school?" The wall clock was no longer where it used to be. The room looked strange. Whose house was this?

Lieve stroked her hair. "You haven't seen Luc in years. He's a professor now. Just like your first husband. You told me yourself."

No, my second husband. Luc's father was my second husband. Jacq DeReu. César was the first. And after Jacq came Tobias. Three husbands. One great love. The one I never married. Elijah.

This time she kept her thoughts to herself. The pious Lieve wouldn't understand. Jacq hadn't understood either.

"Luc is no longer in Leuven." Lieve's voice came from far away, as if she was coming to the end of a long tale.

"Who's this Luc again?" Ammie closed her eyes and heard Lieve give a deep sigh.

*Caz*
*Overberg*

Damn Tieneke! Spoiled her entire day with her lies. It couldn't be true, Caz had decided after the initial shock. Tieneke just wanted to trick her into making the journey. That was all it could be.

She was the late-born child of Josefien and Hans Colijn. Born in the H.F. Verwoerd Moedersbond Hospital on October 2, 1961. Registered as Cassandra Colijn. Raised in Pretoria. First in Rietfontein, as a baby, and later in Meyerspark, where she went to school and was confirmed in the Dopper

Church. She had been Cassandra Colijn all her life, except for the eleven months her marriage lasted. How could it change now, after almost fifty-three years?

Caz shoved the wireless mouse aside and rolled her office chair away from her desk, annoyed. She had done hardly anything all morning. What was on the screen was pure drivel. She would have to re-do the lot.

The deadline for the translation was still some time away but it was a bloody brick of a novel. And translating from Afrikaans to English always took longer than the other way round. Moreover, the writer occasionally lapsed into the Cape dialect, which is nearly impossible to translate. Not to mention the many instances of humorous word play that made hardly any sense in English and wasn't even remotely funny in translation.

Correct language usage was the easy part. The challenges of translation lay elsewhere. How does one translate the voice of an author, for instance? Another person's take on life? The heart and soul of the disembodied author behind every book?

Word for word and sentence by sentence is how you initially translate. If that fails, you try to find the broader meaning, the author's intention. You try to get inside his mindset, to do justice to the meaning behind the words, the sentences, the story.

Her own present mindset wasn't exactly helping the process along.

Of course it wasn't the complexity of the translation that was paralyzing her brain.

Five words kept echoing through her mind, overriding all other words and their semantic and emotive value in any language. *Biological parents. Didn't want you.*

There was a mindset for you. Here, take this baby. I don't want her, for reasons a, b and c. Good luck with raising a child who doesn't share your gene pool.

Blue eyes. That's what Caz had in common with the rest of her family, though her eyes were a different blue. Darker, with light brown specks. Her hair was blonde like theirs but, while her mother and sister—or whatever they were to her—had straight, thin hair, and her father had been bald for as long as she could remember, Caz had thick, tightly curled hair. She'd worn it long for most of her life in an attempt to make it more manageable. Now that the blonde had turned to gray it was easier, the curls slightly more relaxed. More corkscrew than frizz.

But what set her apart most from her sister and parents had always been her height. Where they were short and plump, she had shot up as if her shoes had been sprinkled with fertilizer. At thirteen she had already towered over her father. She had always been the tallest in her class, until some of the boys caught up with her in their last school year.

Finally at eye level with them, she still couldn't look them in the eye. Her awkwardness in male company was firmly rooted by then and the conviction that she was big and clumsy was an essential part of the way she viewed herself.

When she looked in the mirror she could see her face wasn't unattractive and her figure was well proportioned, despite her being so tall. Yet she felt unattractive. Undesirable. Different.

Not only was she too tall, she also lacked the right background. There was no Boer general in her family tree, no Afrikaner hero who was a distant relative's uncle or grandfather. No grandmother who had survived a Boer concentration camp.

Josefien and Hans Colijn had arrived in South Africa in 1951, when Tieneke was a year old. They knew little about the country's history. It was merely a place where the prospects were better. Where bakeries weren't as plentiful. Where the Second World War hadn't hit the population so hard. The same war that had made Hans leave the Netherlands to end up in Belgium, where he'd met Josefien.

To Josefien, South Africa was the back of beyond.

There were a number of Dutch people in Pretoria, Fien was Belgian—so they were different even in their otherness. On top of which they were Protestants, which distinguished her mother from the other Belgians.

Yet it was because of her distinctive looks that Hentie had noticed Caz, as unbelievable as she had found it at the time.

He had liked the fact that she was tall. "At least I can look you in the eye," he'd said the night they met at the agricultural students' barn dance in Potchefstroom. It wasn't completely true, of course, since he was still a good ten centimeters taller than Caz.

And Hentie was crazy about her hair. He had raked his fingers through her curls that first evening when he kissed her goodbye at her residence. Her very first breath-taking kiss.

He found her reticence endearing. Maybe because he mistook it for timidity and failed to perceive the ire it masked.

She, on the other hand, had been completely blind to the fact that he was simply searching for the best possible mother for his children. A woman with a strong body and a submissive spirit. One who would accept his father's whims and moods.

Physically she was indeed a strong young woman. About the rest, he had been sorely mistaken.

Not that he was the only one who had been mistaken. What she hadn't realized at first was that Hentie and Andries Maritz came as a package. Marry the son and you inherited the father. At Liefenleed, the Maritzes' farm on the far side of the Soutpansberg, they farmed together as the family had been doing for generations.

All she saw at that stage was a big, strong, handsome farmer. One who had fought in the Border War for what he believed in. A real man's man. A pure-bred Maritz.

That first evening, and in the months that followed, she would never have guessed that this "real man" was his father's lapdog. Just as she had never guessed there was a genetic explanation for the difference in appearance between herself and the rest of her family. If, of course, Tieneke wasn't lying simply to get her to go to Ghent.

*Didn't want you.* The words had such a bleak sound.

How could a mother put her child in the arms of another and walk away?

Or did she leave her baby in a cradle and hit the road? A

rubbish bin? On someone's doorstep? Did she turn for one last look?

Did she ever wonder about her daughter again? Remember birthdays? Think of her at Christmas? At her coming of age? Did she wonder about her daughter's wedding day? Whether she had grandchildren? Even great-grandchildren were a possibility, Caz thought, though Lilah had never mentioned such plans.

How could you leave a child and her entire progeny behind—blood of your blood?

She would have to find answers to all these questions, Caz realized. Or she would lose her mind.

She pressed her fingers to her temples. No, it just wasn't possible. Tieneke had to be lying.

Or did it explain everything? Tieneke's aversion to her for as long as she could remember. Ma Fien ... No, apparently not her mother after all. Fien. Fien's increasing aloofness until that moment when she finally chased Caz away. Her father's lack of interest in any of his youngest daughter's exploits. He had been kind, but not interested in his so-called late-born child.

And Lilah, of course. It could explain Lilah.

# Two

*Tuesday, September 2*
*Caz*
*Overberg*

The sleep Caz managed to get was fraught with nightmares. Strangely enough she didn't dream of Josefien or Tieneke. Not actually about Hentie either. Mainly about his father, though Hentie was there in the background—as had always been the case in the presence of his father.

Why Tieneke's shocking news had subconsciously reminded her of Andries Maritz, she couldn't fathom. The dream had been so real that for the first time in years she remembered again how she had felt in her father-in-law's proximity. Almost as if she were married to him, instead of his son.

Caz stepped out on the veranda with her coffee mug, drawing the fresh Overberg air deep into her lungs. There was no wind yet, as was usual before ten in the morning at this time of year. The birds fossicked in the trees. Catya was sitting on the lawn, licking herself as she always did after a meal. A donkey brayed on a nearby smallholding and the neighbors' dog barked in reply.

Everything was exactly as it had been the day before. And yet so different.

Why she had been so desperate to belong in those bygone days she could only ascribe to her feeling of inferiority and the naïveté of youth. It was that very need to belong that had blinded her to the obvious, though Hentie's guile had added insult to injury.

Hentie had been a coward, but no fool. Before the wedding he had made certain that Caz spent as little time as possible with Andries.

Andries was even taller and bigger than his son and an attractive man for his age when she had first met him. For his age? Hello, he was only about forty-seven. Five years younger than her present age. But at the time she had seen him as a much older man.

She'd suspected that with him it would be fit in or fuck off, but after he had given her the once-over, he had actually been quite friendly.

"Good child-bearing hips," he had apparently complimented Hentie with his choice that evening, though she would only find out about it later. After the wedding. Like so many things she would learn about and realize only after the wedding.

Andries was a hardworking farmer. The three farms were big and lay far apart—the main one at the foot of the Soutpansberg, the second near Tshipise and the other one closer to Pafuri.

Caz had had no reason to suspect that Hentie had bargained on her not coming into contact with his father too often during her visits. That was before the wedding. After the wedding it was a different matter. The Maritzes not only farmed together, they lived in the same house as well. She'd thought it would be temporary. It wasn't, and was never meant to be.

She got a foretaste of the implications of this arrangement shortly before the wedding.

After a few canceled appointments, the Colijns were

commandeered to the farm to meet and get to know their prospective in-laws. It was the day after a public holiday, the Day of the Covenant, and two weeks before the wedding, which had been set for New Year's Eve.

It was clear from the outset that the parents in the Colijn-Maritz alliance would not get along. Caz had suspected as much, and had delayed the meeting as long as possible. She had even deliberately sabotaged it during the ten months she and Hentie had been dating.

It hadn't been difficult. The bakery kept Hans busy and Josefien had no desire to meet a pair of backvelders from the wild north, whether her lastborn was set on marrying their son or not.

Finally the meeting couldn't be avoided any longer. Tieneke agreed to see to the bakery and Josefien could think of no further excuse not to meet her daughter's future in-laws.

It was a balls-up—even worse than Caz had feared.

Josefien kept whining about the heat, the dust, the creepy crawlies, and made no effort to hide her disapproval. If she did try to conceal her disdain of the big farmer with the sonorous voice and fearless gaze who was to be her daughter's father-in-law, she failed miserably.

A sweating Hans, on the other hand, tried to impress Andries in his genial baker's way, his apple cheeks bobbing up and down as he chuckled and chattered, running his hand over his ample girth. Andries, however, had no inclination to make small talk with a Dutchman who baked bread and made cakes for a living.

After they had been officially introduced, Andries steered the first conversation toward politics, but Hans admitted he had no interest in the subject. When Andries talked about rugby, Hans shook his head again. Instead, he volunteered a story about a birthday cake he had once made in the shape of a "football."

"I'm afraid you'll have to talk to the wife about that," Andries said bluntly when Hans wanted to explain the fine art of making choux pastries, for which he was renowned in Pretoria.

Maybe things would have been better if Andries had been a wheat farmer and Hans at least a consumer of his product, but Andries farmed with cattle and game. On the Tshipise farm he had a field of tomatoes and some alfalfa for private use, but that was it. His cattle were his passion and his pride, and the game a small goldmine. Perhaps Fien should not have volunteered that the Colijns preferred pork and chicken to beef and venison.

The next day Hans obliged by joining mother-in-law Magdel in the big kitchen. The two of them didn't exactly hit it off. Magdel was too reserved. Or perhaps she had taken offence the night before when Fien had looked down her nose at Magdel's cast-iron pots and declared that they couldn't possibly be hygienic.

Or perhaps Magdel didn't take kindly to Hans's lack of enthusiasm for her homemade bread. Or perhaps because Fien, not quite under her breath, had remarked to Hans, who was about to accept a second helping, that the food was too salty and greasy for his state of health.

Andries Maritz was a bastard and a chauvinist pig, but one thing Caz could vouch for: his loyalty toward his wife and son was indisputable. He could berate and belittle them as much as he liked himself, but no one else dared make a disparaging remark about them.

Magdel must have told Andries about the cast-iron cookware issue. Lord knows why. On the second night, as he lit his pipe after supper, Andries looked his son's future mother-in-law in the eye.

"Well, Josefien, it seems you've survived the unhygienic meals so far," he said.

Fien pursed her lips. "It's just that we do it differently at home. And I do the cleaning myself. Here a maid cleans the pots."

"That may be so, Josefien, but Magdel is an excellent cook and she keeps an eye on her maids. You can eat from the floor, never mind the pot, that's how clean it is. I'm telling you now, you will not insult my wife in her own kitchen. Is that clear?"

Josefien's eyes nearly popped out of her head. Her mouth went slack so the yellowish upper teeth with their overbite were visible.

"Now, now, Andries. Fieneke didn't mean anything by it," Hans tried to intervene.

"I have something to say to you too, brother-in-law," Andries cut him short. "Don't think because you allow your wife to wear the pants in your house she can do it in mine as well. All she has done since arriving here is to look down her nose at everything, and you don't say a word to stop her. Here at Liefenleed we have respect for the institution of holy matrimony as outlined in the Holy Scriptures. The man is the head of the household and his wife is subservient to his wishes. If you choose to play with dough and allow your wife to walk all over you, it's your business. But it won't happen here. That's why I took it on myself to set her straight."

Hans tried to say something, but Andries cut him short. "And just so we understand each other perfectly: your daughter will be well taken care of here. Sandra will want for nothing, as long as she knows her place."

He turned his gaze so suddenly to Caz she almost gasped for breath. "You seem a nice girl, Sandra, but let's get this straight. I don't want any friction under my roof."

He hadn't wanted outlandish names under his roof either, Caz had learned by then. On her first visit to the farm, Hentie had introduced her as Caz, the nickname her roommate at university had given her and which Caz felt fitted her like a glove. Andries asked what her real name was. Cassandra, she said, and since then she had been Sandra to him. It was as though he had stuck her into a box made to his own specifications, labeled it Sandra, and that was that.

Caz sighed and tossed the rest of her coffee over the railing into the shrubs below. Enough now. She had better things to do than obsess about the past. She had been Caz for the past thirty years and that was who she would remain. Whether she was a Colijn or not.

Turning to re-enter the house, she thought she noticed

a movement among the poplars. She scrutinized the area. Nothing moved. It must have been her imagination.

All the ghosts from the past must be playing tricks on her senses. Must be why she was covered in gooseflesh too.

*Erevu*
*Antwerp*

The Samsung tablet had only one purpose: Contact with Jela.

Yesterday there were two messages.

> From: Erevu
> To: Jela
> Ghent connection: Finally phoned SA. After a two-year wait! Use code 4 to decode number: O*#%><O*#%

> From: Jela
> To: Erevu
> Excellent news. Dialing code for Overberg (Western Cape). I'll get on it immediately.

A few minutes ago another message came through.

> From: Jela
> To: Erevu
> Address now known.
> Dove flew to Cape Town last night. Just heard he found the place.

Erevu sighed with relief. At least they had finally found the woman. It was the beginning of their success story. He was convinced of it.

*Luc*
*Damme, Belgium*

"Luc DeReu, good day." His thoughts were still on the assignment he was grappling with as he answered his cellphone. The student's inability to structure his arguments logically exasperated him. And that at postgraduate level. The bloke seemed incapable of figuring out the bare basics of cause and effect. He obviously saw history as a bunch of dates and linear events and didn't understand that history is not subject to Newton's Law. For each action there are a myriad reactions—equal and unequal and not always opposite. Or sensible.

"Bingo! Would you believe it!" An unknown female voice rejoiced in his ear. The accent was Western Flemish.

"Pardon?"

"When Miss Ammie asked for you—for the first time in who knows how long, I must add—I guessed KU Leuven would know your present whereabouts. I must say, they weren't exactly forthcoming. They refused to give me your number. Just said their records showed you had left for the University of Maastricht. There they told me you currently have a post at the University of Ghent. I got your number from their administration. They were much friendlier, thank goodness."

"Who am I speaking to?" he asked, trying to stanch the confusing flow of info.

"You don't know me, but I've heard so much about you, it feels as if I know you. As a child, that is. It's how Miss Ammie remembers you. The name is Lieve Luykens, Professor. I've been taking care of your mother, Ammie Pauwels, for the past five years."

Suddenly Lieve Luykens had his undivided attention. Ammie Pauwels. He had been three when his father married Ammie, but she was the closest thing to a mother he had ever known. Yet one day she had just disappeared from their lives. His father was never the same again. Images of the defeated man flashed through his mind, brought back all the guilt feelings in a flash.

With an effort he brought himself back to the present. "I presume she's no longer living in Doel?" The tragic history of the polder village on the Scheldt was well known. When the residents were forced out of the town to make way for the expansion of the port of Antwerp, he had wondered what had become of Ammie and her new husband.

"No, Professor. It's been years since they lived there. Apparently she tried to hold out, even after 2000, but with her husband gone by then, she finally gave in and moved back to Leuven, where she ran into one of your father's colleagues and heard you had left the university."

Hopefully Ammie didn't find out why he had left.

"Is she still in Leuven?"

"Indeed, Professor, but I'm afraid she's not very well. Her memory increasingly comes and goes. The past she remembers well at times, but she can't always remember what she did yesterday or what she has just said. Her health is also unstable."

"I'm sorry to hear that." What else could one say? Old age spares no one.

"I wondered … She's so lonely, trapped in her own thoughts … I don't know why you are estranged, but she has always spoken highly of you. The way I understand it, the discord was between your father and herself. Would you consider paying her a visit? It might cheer her up. Give her some interest in the present."

Luc remained quiet for a long time. Thoughts and memories turned into a tangle of emotions. To see Ammie again would raise so many ghosts from the past.

"This morning she wanted to know what time Luc would be home from school." There was a plea behind the sad words.

"In that case, she won't recognize me, Mrs. Luykens. What's the point?"

"You never know, Professor. But if it doesn't work, if your visit doesn't do her any good, I won't bother you again. It's just, she's known such hard times in her life. I gathered there were other children as well, but you're the only one I know of for sure. An elderly person shouldn't die alone."

"Die?" Could he live with his conscience if the stepmother who raised him had to die in solitude?

"I don't suppose she's literally dying. It's not that she's actually ill. The problem is she has nothing to live for, Professor. I've been searching for months to find something to interest her. When she mentioned your name again ..." The woman gave a deep sigh. "Oh, well, I tried."

Luc had difficulty keeping up. "Mrs. Luykens, what did you mean by 'other children'?" In all the years Ammie was married to his father, there had never been any mention of it.

"That's the only conclusion I could come to. That there were other children too. You see, when she becomes muddled, she starts babbling about things she thinks I know about or she confuses me with other people."

"Will the weekend suit you? Sunday morning, perhaps?" Luc knew he was complicating his life and he hated complications. But how could he ignore Lieve Luykens's kind intentions? And maybe he could find answers to the questions that had been tormenting him for so long.

"You'll really come? Sunday would be wonderful. I'll get something nice for coffee. The baker around the corner ..."

"Please don't go to any trouble, Mrs. Luykens. I'll be there around eleven. Give me the address, please."

He wrote down Lieve's detailed directions, said goodbye, and gave a protracted sigh. What had he let himself in for now?

Ammie had left when he was twenty-one and no longer living at home. It was 1983, he recalled, just as he could recall the date of almost every major event in his life. It was the curse and blessing of his profession, but also his one extraordinary talent. He suspected he owed his academic achievements to an excellent memory, rather than brilliance.

That day, thirty-one years ago, his father had phoned him in a terrible state and told him Ammie had moved out. Two years later Luc had seen Ammie for the second-last time. It was just before she got married again.

They had met by chance in Antwerp. She told him of her

intended marriage and apologized for everything but explained nothing. Only mentioned she was living in Doel.

He wondered why she had chosen Doel. Ever since the sixties there had been rumors that the polder village would have to make way for the expansion of the port.

The last time he had seen her, or at least thought he had seen her, was at his father's funeral in 1997, but before he could reach her she had vanished into the crowd of university staff and ex-students attending the service.

And now this call.

Why the hell did he agree to go? What hope did a bachelor like him have of bringing any cheer to a senile woman in her eighties? The woman who had destroyed his father's life, besides.

For goodness' sake, he couldn't even cheer himself up.

It was in 2011 that he realized just how boring his life was. Exactly how dull he was as a person. It was the year he lectured in South Africa, a country burning at the hand of its own Nero. Just to step through one's own front door was risky in numerous neighborhoods—but the people carried on with their lives.

Only once had he come to life. Long ago. Before South Africa.

He should have known that a woman like Suri would have an agenda of her own. Why else would a gorgeous young student suddenly start flirting with a nerdy professor? Unfortunately, he never thought further than those ripe breasts, the welcoming hips and his fantasies about where those shapely legs ended.

He might be boring and unremarkable, but he was still a man. Alas, yes, even though he would never see fifty again.

*Caz*
*Overberg*

The translation just wouldn't flow. Her thoughts were all over the place. Tieneke's call. Its implications. Memories of what had been.

Of all things, she remembered again the house in Lillian Street, Meyerspark, where she had grown up.

There had been three terraces and a set of stone steps leading down to the Moreleta Spruit. White stinkwood trees edged the bilharzia-infected stream. Since Hans had spotted a leguan on the bank, nothing could get any of the others there.

To Caz it was a place to escape Tieneke's bullying and Mother Fien's never-ending orders and complaints. She would often climb as high as she could up a tree and sit there, dreaming about the day she would be grown-up.

Once she had been halfway up when she'd discovered the tree was covered in worms. She let go, skinning her knees and arms. She told Fien she had fallen on the steps. Tieneke had teased her for being clumsy.

She'd felt betrayed by her trees, but had learned patience had its own rewards. Weeks later the worms were gone and she could once again escape to her dreamworld.

At Liefenleed, though the farm was vast, there had been no escape. She was bound to a house that wasn't hers, among people she couldn't fathom.

It was in the early eighties. Anti-apartheid saboteurs were regularly crossing the Limpopo. The roads had to be swept for landmines. There was nowhere she could be alone. It was too dangerous.

She had learned about the danger the hard way that night Andries had so harshly reprimanded Fien and Hans.

*December 1982*
*Caz*
*Soutpansberg*

Caz sneaked out through the backdoor after everyone had gone to their rooms. Her emotions were too stirred up to remain inside, her bedroom too stuffy, even though the house was air-conditioned.

Too much was bottled up, too many warning lights were flickering, she had too many misgivings to even think about sleeping.

Outside the heat of the day still clung to the earth, but the fresh air was balm for her distress. She went down the veranda steps to escape from the light and kept walking blindly.

The moon was just a lemon rind in the star-scattered sky, but when her eyes got used to the dark, she could make out the road leading to the gate.

At last she could release her tears of frustration where no one could hear her.

She loved Hentie, but could she deal with his father? His mother, even? Magdel sometimes looked at Caz as if she pitied her, at other times as if Caz was an intruder.

Could she face a life regulated by her parents-in-law? By Hentie? She would have to dance to the tune of three other people. Each with his or her specific expectations. She could never be herself. Or find out who she actually was.

It wasn't the train of thought she should be harboring less than two weeks before her wedding, but she couldn't stop the feeling of dread.

A rustling in the mopane trees stopped her in her tracks. She hadn't realized she had walked so far. She was almost at the gate, a kilometer from the house. Was it her imagination or did she hear whispering voices? No, it wasn't her imagination. She smelled smoke as well. Tobacco of some kind. The workers' huts were far from there.

She whirled round, trying to move quietly but as swiftly as possible. As soon as she felt she could, she broke into a run. A few paces further, with her heart pounding in her ears, she looked over her shoulder. The next moment she was skimming over the uneven surface of the gravel road. Stifling a cry, she struggled to her feet. With her knees and elbows burning like hell, she limped on, a nameless fear propelling her forward.

She had almost reached the back veranda when Hentie came out, the keys to the pick-up in his hand. Seeing her, he hurried to meet her, gripped her arm and hastily led her to a shadowy spot, out of hearing distance.

"Damn it, Caz! Where the hell have you been? I was scared

shitless when I discovered you weren't in your room. I was just coming to look for you."

"I took a walk and went a bit too far."

"Why are you so out of breath? So frightened? And why are your jeans torn? And your shirt ripped?"

"I was just startled. I thought I heard something." With an effort, she got her breathing under control. "I fell when I was running home."

"Darling, you can't just go for a walk on the farm! Especially not at night. There are snakes and wild creatures in the bushes. Not to mention that there could be terrorists in the area! Promise me you'll never, ever do it again."

Terrorists? She hadn't even considered the possibility. Everyone spoke about it, but here, on the farm? If Hentie found out how far she had actually gone down the road, he would have a cadenza.

"Why did you go to my room?" she tried to change the subject.

"I wanted to talk to you. Tell you I don't think the way my father does." He seemed ill at ease. "And I wanted to hold you. Actually, I just missed you." He laid his hand against her cheek. "And now? Why the tears?" he asked when he felt the dampness.

"I don't know whether I'm cut out for this, Hentie. It's such a harsh place, and your father ..."

"Please, Caz, don't even think it. My parents have gone to so much trouble for the wedding ... And what about us? I love you, my darling. Everything will be all right once we're married."

At least she was still Caz to him, and his darling. It soothed her troubled mind. His kiss transported her far away from the farm and her reservations.

Hentie was right, she thought when she finally got into bed. Everything would be all right. Once they were married.

*Caz*
*Overberg*

Caz sighed. She had been so young. So bloody stupid.

Mother Fien and Father Hans had left early the next morning. Hans promised they would be at the wedding, but added that they could not possibly stay until then when it was so obvious they weren't welcome.

Andries and Magdel did not object.

Hentie dried Caz's tears with his handkerchief. Said his father's bark was worse than his bite. A hard landscape produces hard people, but his father was a good and reasonable man. Josefien had just upset him with her attitude.

Shortly afterwards, the Colijns were forgotten. One of the herdsmen had come across a butchered carcass near the gate. A cow in calf. The footprints in the sandy soil, not even a hundred meters from the two-track road, pointed at saboteurs.

Hentie took her aside and looked at her with worried eyes: "See the danger you put yourself in last night? For heaven's sake, Caz, if they had seen you, we would be making funeral arrangements today. You're never going anywhere on this farm again without me or someone who is armed by your side, understand?" He wiped the sweat from his brow. "You can thank your lucky stars my father is none the wiser and you'd better hope and pray he never finds out."

"For crying out loud, Hentie, I went for a walk, I didn't do anything wrong. I understand what you're saying, that it's dangerous, but I didn't commit a crime. I just didn't understand the danger. Now I do."

Two days after Hans and Josefien's departure Andries selected a calf for her and branded it with an S.

"Yours, Sandra, the first of your stud," he said and she realized she would never be Cassandra to him, let alone Caz. She knew he was trying to make up for the quarrel with her parents. Perhaps also for the fact that she had to make an isolated farm, with all kinds of dangers on it, her home simply because she had fallen in love with his son.

She appreciated it, but what she was supposed to do with a calf, never mind her own stud, she didn't have the foggiest.

After that, Hentie never called her Caz again in his father's presence. Both he and Magdel stuck to Sandra. A name that made her feel estranged from herself. As if she had been poured into a fresh mould. As if Andries had branded *her* as part of his domestic herd.

At the wedding, the two sets of parents ignored each other. As a final insult, Hans's towering choux artwork never made it to the dessert table.

That, Caz thought, had been the worst possible slap in the face for Hans and Josefien. Worse than the fact that their request that there should be no dancing at the reception was ignored by Andries. There were two bands, taking turns, and the guests made the most of the opportunity.

Caz sighed and got to her feet. Tieneke's call had opened up a tunnel to the past and she could not find a way to plug the bloody thing again.

# Three

*Wednesday, September 3*
*Caz*
*Overberg*

Exhausted after another sleepless night, and fed up with Tieneke for failing to give her their contact details, Caz got hold of the Moerdyk practice only to draw a blank.

Old Mr. Moerdyk, who had dealt with the Colijn file, had recently been replaced by his grandson. Apparently the grandson was still finding his bearings and the Colijn file was not part of the bearings he had thus far found. Thankfully the secretary remembered Tieneke Colijn's email asking Moerdyk to trace Caz's phone number in South Africa. She undertook to forward Tieneke's email and see whether she could find the Colijn file.

Well, well. Tieneke had a computer and used email. It was probably silly to be surprised in this e-era, but Tieneke and technology just didn't seem compatible to Caz.

The forwarded message landed in Caz's inbox moments

later. It was written in polite, faultless Afrikaans, every comma and full stop in the right place.

Mrs. Colijn's health was rapidly deteriorating and Miss Colijn was urgently looking for Cassandra Colijn's telephone number to inform her. Her last known address was in Sunnyside, Pretoria.

Caz was quite impressed by the secretary who had found her number in the Western Cape with so little information at her disposal. She was also slightly worried that it was so easy to trace her.

On the spur of the moment, she googled her name in the electronic white pages. There were no results for Cassandra Colijn. There were two hits for "C. Colijn." The first was a doctor in Pretoria, whose first name was Colijn. Below that was the entry "L. Colijn" with Caz's landline number and address. Of course, the house was registered in Lilah's name, and the telephone as well.

Fact was, George Orwell's dystopic fiction had become reality. Privacy was an obsolete concept.

Time to make a decision. Go to Ghent or stay. Both options were equally unpleasant. If she didn't go, she would wonder for the rest of her life what Josefien had wanted to tell her. If she went, she would be exposing herself to Tieneke's reproaches and spite, and to Josefien on her deathbed.

For a moment Caz felt guilty. Josefien might have chased her away, but she had also spent two decades looking after Caz to the best of her abilities—limited as they might have been.

Fien had considered herself a civilized woman in a savage country. A skylark among crows. Nothing about South Africa had met with her approval. The Reformed Church wasn't reformed enough. The apartheid government not apart enough. Nothing was ever clean enough, except her own conscience.

On the last night of her parents' visit to Liefenleed, Caz had been somewhat embarrassed by her boring father, who could talk about little other than his bakery and the hard times he had known during the Second World War. But she had been mortified by her mother.

She had seen Fien through Andries's eyes: an unattractive, endlessly complaining woman, unimaginatively dressed, discontent etched into her face.

The contrast with Magdel could not have been more marked. Magdel was attractive and stylishly clad, gentle and agreeable. Or so it seemed.

Magdel's timidity, Caz gradually discovered, was a method of survival. A soft answer turneth away wrath. Turn the other cheek. A virtuous woman's worth is far above rubies. Magdel had deliberately made those adages her own. And she had been rewarded with support, loyalty and a very comfortable life.

Ultimately, Magdel's compliance had stemmed from a kind of selfishness that blindly ignored moral concepts like right and wrong. Her loyalty lay solely with herself and her personal needs and only by default with her husband and child, but especially with her husband. As long as she kept Andries happy, she could do as she pleased.

Caz developed a kind of reluctant respect for Andries. Andries was Andries. You always knew exactly where you stood with him—on the back foot, of course.

With hindsight, Caz now knew her love for Hentie had been reaped too soon. There had been no lack of passion, but there simply hadn't been sufficient gravity in their relationship to face the onslaughts outside the bedroom. Magdel's passive resistance toward anyone who wanted to share her kingdom was no less destructive than Andries's overbearing personality.

Caz looked from the crumbs on the side plate to the coffee ring in the mug, remnants of a sandwich and coffee she truly didn't remember making, eating and drinking.

Relationships. The dynamics between people. That was where her thoughts kept returning. With good reason.

She didn't need a crystal ball to know what lay in her future. She would have to go to Ghent. She would have to try to discover the truth. Before it was too late and she was left

*Luc*
*Damme*

With the dishwasher running and the dishcloth rinsed, Luc poured himself a final glass of wine. Although he had noted that the witloof dish tasted exceptionally good, he had been lost in thought during the entire meal.

He had been too hasty when he agreed to visit Ammie. Why rake up the past now? Ammie was old and senile, Jacq was dead. And did he really want to know what had broken Jacq's spirit?

Some things were better left alone. Life had taught him that. Like the scrap of gossip a so-called friend had thought fit to share with him. "The giraffe," Suri had apparently called him behind his back, telling all and sundry what a boring lover he was.

He couldn't believe it. Didn't want to believe it. Never before had he met a woman who enjoyed sex with such shameless abandon as Suri. With him too. No matter what she said.

A particularly adventurous lover he might not be, but he was a meticulous one. Perhaps because he realized he was no Jean-Claude van Damme. More of a John Cleese—without the moustache, and with a thick mop of hair.

He had shrugged it off as a petty lie Suri had spread out of spite, but the remark kept niggling at the back of his mind.

Still, Suri belonged to the past, painful as it might be. He had lived through it and emerged on the other side. Maybe not unscathed, but not completely shattered either. Unlike his father.

After all these years, Luc was still plagued by guilt. Any idiot could have seen Jacq was in his own personal hell. And it got progressively worse. Especially after Ammie re-married.

Yet what did he do? Did he offer his father a shoulder or

an ear? No, he convinced himself that his father valued his privacy, that he dared not intrude. That his father would exorcize his demons in his own way.

Luc DeReu had simply carried on with his life, lecturing, grading papers, struggling through theses and dissertations, writing articles and academic papers. But his father's once proud, erect posture had become more and more stooped and his words seemed to dry up.

Jacq died a few months after his retirement. Without the students and his status at the university, there had been nothing to keep him on this earth.

His father had not been one for a dramatic gesture. Jacq's hypertension, cholesterol and heart condition were perfectly controlled as long as he took his medication. After his death, Luc came across a number of sealed containers. Jacq had continued to fetch his prescribed medicine every month but had left the containers unopened in the drawer of his bedside table. The dates indicated that this behavior had begun six months before his retirement.

Yes, Jacq had died of a heart attack, as stated on the death certificate. But he had wanted it that way. Because his heart had been shattered thirteen years earlier and no one, not even his son, had tried to help him put the shards together again.

And now that same son was going to visit Ammie? To cheer her up?

*Caz*
*Overberg*

The calculations she made were terrifying. She would have to delve into Lilah's deposits, faithfully made every month despite Caz's protestations. Money actually meant for extreme emergencies.

Caz opened her email program. She felt reluctant to mention the bomb Tieneke had dropped, but with a bit of luck she and Lilah might be able to see each other. Paris was just a stone's throw from Ghent. Lilah was used to travelling all over the world. Unlike Caz who was a house mouse. Travel was not her favorite pastime.

"You don't have a comfort zone," Lilah had once said in despair, "you have a strictly cordoned-off comfort precinct." "Recluse" was another word Lilah liked to use in connection with her mother.

Lilah's reply to Caz's email came barely ten minutes later.

> Fuck it, MamaCaz, you know you don't have to ask about the money! It's yours to do with as you please. How many times must I repeat it? Let me know if I need to transfer more.
>
> It's wonderful news. Not the deathbed part, obviously not, but that you're finally dragging your arse over here again.
>
> The second time in ten years! Hell, we might make a traveller of you yet. ☺
>
> I won't be able to meet you in Amsterdam, unfortunately. No use landing in Paris so I can take you to Ghent either. The timing is off. I leave for a shoot in the Bahamas on September 14 and from there I go on to Morocco and then Dubai. I'll be back in Paris late in the evening of October 7, just in time for my birthday the next day. God help you if you don't spend it with me and stay for at least another week so we can catch up. I'll come and fetch you.
>
> Keep me posted. And, oh yes! Those platform boots I left there last time? PLEASE bring them along. And Mrs. Ball's chutney. And Ricoffy. Will send list later. Also some Afrikaans books and CDs. You know I like the real thing, not the e- and MP3 versions. Not in Afrikaans, anyway. They're not just for reading and listening, they're my most treasured possessions.
>
> Have to run.
> Love you
> P.S. Come to think of it, it's strange you agreed.

Considering the bad blood between you and those two and all that. After all these years. Everything OK? L.

"Those two." Caz sat back and ran her hand over her tired eyes. The grandma and aunt Lilah had never known. The grandma who had refused to know or even recognize her grandchild.

Lilah was eleven when Josefien and Tieneke returned to Belgium in '94 without ever having laid eyes on her. Lilah knew there was conflict in the family but Caz had never given her the details. Just said there were old disputes and that was why her grandma and aunt weren't a part of their lives. She might never have told Lilah that the two had left the country if Lilah hadn't walked in while she was reading a letter from their lawyer.

Caz hadn't cried because she was sad. She was furious. Tieneke and Fien hadn't even deemed it necessary to let her know personally that they had returned to their fatherland. A bloody formal lawyer's letter had to inform her. Not that that was what the letter was about in the first place. A few problems had arisen, which they hoped Caz could help them sort out.

The lawyer said he could do it himself but the Colijns felt it would be cheaper if Caz did it on their behalf.

The so-called problems were trivialities. A quibble about an unpaid municipal account. Someone who had bought their furniture and not paid because something was missing. Some problem with a safe-deposit box, but by that time Caz was so incensed by their audacity that she had stopped reading.

Caz flatly refused. She assumed they subsequently used the lawyer to solve the problems and paid him his due.

She did not tell Lilah any of that. At age eleven Lilah had too many problems of her own to saddle her with Fien and Tieneke Colijn's arrogance and events that took place before Lilah was old enough to understand.

Catya jumped onto her lap and Caz was startled out of her

reverie. For the past few minutes she hadn't been present, here in her study. She had been back in Sunnyside. In the cramped apartment where she and Lilah had been forced to live so that she could afford Lilah's fees at the Waldorf school. It was an astronomic amount, but the alternative was unthinkable.

On Caz's lap Catya coiled herself like an ice cream in a cone until she found a comfortable position. "Well, Catastrophe, now your devout subject needs to find a travel agent she can phone early tomorrow morning," Caz muttered aloud, stroking the cat's head and drawing the telephone directory closer, her stomach in a knot.

# Four

*Friday, September 5*
*Caz*
*Overberg*

The traffic out of Cape Town was moving at a snail's pace. Through Somerset West, it was even worse. Every single traffic light was either red or changing to red just as Caz reached it. Every time she stopped, street vendors descended. Sunglasses, cellphone chargers, junk that surely no one wanted to buy. How did these people make a living?

Going up a windswept Sir Lowry's Pass, she landed behind a pick-up trying without success to pass a truck.

The delay gave her too much time to think. To allow fears to fester.

Not that she could change anything now. She was on her way, her flight booked and paid for. The Belgian consulate just had to get cracking. A Schengen usually took three weeks. But with a dying mother it could be fast-tracked, the lady in charge of visas had told her. If everything went according to plan, Caz would pick up her visa the morning before her evening flight. In less than two weeks' time.

She had to get there as soon as possible, in case Josefien's decline was rapid. The thought of spending three weeks in the same house as Tieneke and Josefien before Lilah arrived was unthinkable, but she didn't have much choice. Even the cheapest accommodation was beyond her means.

Caz had been abroad only once before: four years earlier, when Lilah contracted German measles, of all things, on one of her excursions. The doctor gave strict orders that Lilah wasn't to leave her apartment for two weeks. Caz, who had had the disease as a child and was immune, reluctantly set off for Paris.

As it happened, she did not see much more of Paris than the inside of Lilah's tiny apartment and the route to the closest pâtisserie and superette de proximité, but it was good to be able to care for Lilah and spoil her a little, even though Caz was hardly the nursing type. Nor the motherly type.

Any motherliness she might have had at the outset had to be unlearned in order to raise Lilah strong and independent. There had always been enough love, but from an early age Lilah had had to fight her own battles. Only for the wars could she ask Caz for help.

For those, Caz had the complete armor, modeled on the relentless, non-negotiable belief that her unusual child had the same rights as any other child. And that she had to be treated the same as any other child.

An arsenal of apt, sometimes cutting words in her combat vocabulary enabled Caz to convey this conviction with incisive arguments. Obstinacy, determination, perseverance and her firm refusal to leave a thing alone, saw to the rest.

Caz often had misgivings about her decision to leave the battles to Lilah and fight only the wars for her, but today Lilah was a successful, independent, self-assured woman.

Yet Lilah's success had not come overnight. Caz would never forget the day, nine years earlier, when her child's exotic features had first gazed back at her from the cover of

*Vogue*. Smoldering silver-blue eyes, high cheekbones, and lips that would make Angelina Jolie green with envy.

Subsequently Lilah had often graced the covers of *Elle* and other glossy fashion magazines. Just last month there was an article about her in the Dutch edition of *Cosmopolitan*. One in which she declared it was thanks to her mother that she succeeded where others failed.

Lilah currently lived in a penthouse. Spacious, according to Lilah, but judging from the photos she sent, still too cramped for Caz's taste.

All the years of the cheapest possible accommodation had given Caz a distaste of small spaces and densely built-up areas. That was why she preferred to live on a patch of land outside of town. Even if the house was old. Fortunately it was still safe around there. Not like other parts of the country.

Lilah had already started to climb the ladder of success when Caz headed for the Cape to enjoy her first-ever, proper holiday. En route she came across the village of Stanford. It was love at first sight. After an effusive email, bubbling with enthusiasm for the little town with its Victorian houses and interesting shops and restaurants, Lilah had offered to buy Caz a house there.

Initially she wouldn't accept the offer, but Lilah assured her she could afford it. Now Caz was glad she had swallowed her pride. Soon afterwards property prices went through the roof and it had turned out to be a very good investment.

The place was registered in Lilah's name, so Caz told herself she was actually just taking care of it on Lilah's behalf. Which didn't stop her from doing exactly as she pleased. She had altered and renovated. Made a garden. Lilah had let her have her own way.

Her home was her sanctuary; the hectare or so surrounding it her piece of Africa. There Caz could isolate herself as far as was humanly possible. Once a week she went in to the village of Stanford for the bare essentials. To Gansbaai if she needed a pharmacy or a doctor and once a month to Hermanus for bigger shopping. And to spoil herself with lunch at a place where she could gaze at the ocean and watch the whales in season. For her, these excursions were more than enough connection with the outside world.

No one would even notice she was gone. Except Catya. She would take Catya to the local kennel. They took in cats as well. How the poor thing would cope didn't bear thinking about. The cat was used to her freedom. Catching mice, moles, once even a snake. Luckily just a slug-eater. Birds too, of course, to Caz's dismay. The other day, even a sugarbird had come short. If only Catya would grab the bloody Cape robin that ate her pellets and then shat all over the house, but don't you believe it. The two probably had a treaty of some kind.

At the Orchards farmstall Caz made a pee stop and bought an olive ciabatta. She felt she couldn't use the nice clean bathroom without buying something. Besides, they made delicious ciabattas.

The traffic had thinned by the time she hit the road again and three quarters of an hour later she drove through her gate. It was always lovely to spot the green tin roof through the trees. To know her sanctuary was waiting, the pillow for her head.

As she came driving around the big wild olive and the front of the house came in view, Caz slammed on the brakes. She forgot about the clutch and the car jolted to a halt. Her hand flew to her mouth.

*Ammie*
*Leuven*

"You're hiding something from me, Lieve." Ammie felt good today. The fine weather helped. But Lieve had been scuttling about all day long, and it worked on her nerves. You'd swear they were expecting visitors.

"Oh, it's such a lovely day, I just feel like working, Miss Ammie."

Ammie grunted but said nothing. Lieve was a wonderful carer, but domestic chores were not her strong suit. Neither was lying. And the humming did not occur often either. Fortunately not. Lieve's singing voice was not her strong point either.

The women in Elisabethville's cité indigène used to harmonize so beautifully. Ammie saw a completely different side of them in the weeks she spent in Tabia's slum-dwelling, recovering from the assault by César and his henchman. For the first time she saw them as people, women, instead of mere domestic workers. She tried to understand them better. Even learned to say a few indigenous words, though she could never distinguish between the various languages.

Her sojourn in the cité indigène made her focus more on the similarities between them, rather than the differences. Pain and treachery were pain and treachery, irrespective of skin color and culture; women were women.

The woman with the decorative scarification on her body said her Swahili name was Tabia and that it meant something like "magic spell." She did not disclose her Tetela name.

Maybe Tabia could do magic, because Ammie made a complete recovery from her injuries: the broken ribs, even the broken ring finger, which Tabia had set and put in splints while Ammie had been in an herb-induced trance.

The only thing Tabia was unable to cure with her magic was Ammie's hatred for César. Maybe it was because she and Tabia shared that hatred and thus multiplied it.

*Caz*
*Overberg*

At least there was some advantage to living in a rural area. The police arrived barely fifteen minutes after her phone call. Yet they were long, scary minutes to sit and wait.

Going up the veranda steps in the company of the two policemen, Caz felt dazed. Potted plants lay overturned. The wind chimes she had crafted herself lay in heaps. A clay bowl shaped by her own hands lay shattered. Chairs stood haphazardly all over the place. The precious red-and-blue stained glass panels of the Victorian front door had been smashed.

Inside even greater chaos reigned. Everything that could possibly be overturned lay on its side. Drawers were open, the contents spilling out. Cupboard doors dangled from their hinges. More than one window had been broken. It looked like an act of pure vandalism.

"Can you see whether anything is missing, ma'am?"

Caz looked around the living room and nodded. "My TV and DVD player. The music centre." She groaned and ran to the study. Her desk was empty.

"The bastards!" She gave a muted scream and slammed her fist on the wooden desktop. Pain shot through her hand.

"Your laptop as well?" a constable asked behind her.

She didn't bother to reply. In the drawer she found the external hard drive. Everything was on it except the previous day's work. That she had managed to save her data was more important than the computer. Still, an entire very productive day's work had been lost. She had been so tired the night before she had forgotten about the bloody backup.

"It's the tikkoppe, ma'am. They'll sell anything for tik."

"Well, catch them, damn it!" She rubbed her aching hand and tried to swallow her helpless tears.

The policeman shrugged. "Their numbers grow daily, ma'am, and there are many people who will buy stolen goods. Not just fencers, ordinary people looking for a bargain too. The perpetrators are usually minors. Even if we catch them, they're soon back on the streets. It's a sad state of affairs. You'll have to get in touch with someone who can replace the windows as soon as possible. It's Friday afternoon."

She nodded but made no effort to look up a number or call. "The alarm. Why wasn't it triggered?" She looked at the constable. "Do tikkoppe know how to deactivate alarms?"

"Not usually. They smash and grab. Are you sure you set the alarm?"

Could she have forgotten? It had happened before, but today of all days? The very day the tikkoppe decided to target her place, five kilometers out of town? It was possible.

"You should get a dog. Or several. It's better than an alarm."

"My cat!" she remembered. "Catya?" She shouted so loudly that the constable jumped. "Catya?" She ran out on the veranda. "Kittykittykitty!"

Nothing.

"Catya! Food!"

A thin mewing made her look up in the wild olive. High up. She knew at once her ladder wouldn't reach.

Bloody thieves. Bloody drugs. Bloody New South Africa that was over twenty years old and not all that new.

Maybe she wouldn't use the return leg of her air ticket. Stay over there, even if it was as an illegal immigrant. It could only be better there. Even in prison. At least she would escape from a country where people had to build and pay for their own bloody prisons in an effort to keep the criminals out.

Yes, what she needed, what she craved, was a country where law and order was respected. As far away as possible from all the crime and crap.

*Luc*
*Ghent*

The traffic out of Ghent was a nightmare. It usually took him less than an hour to Damme. He should have taken the E40 instead of the N9. He hadn't thought about it being Friday. Nor that the good weather and the weekend would make everyone converge on Knokke. Despite the fact that the ocean was gray and docile, it still drew people from the cities.

Luc regretted going in to the university that morning, but he had to get his affairs in order for the official opening of the academic year on September 19. He had already spent an hour in this traffic jam, and the turnoff to Damme was still some distance ahead. He supposed he could've switched on his Tom-Tom, but the woman's voice drove him up the wall. Or turned on the radio, but he wasn't keen on getting an earful of current affairs and traffic incidents.

Nothing special was waiting for him at the ancient house he had inherited from a spinster aunt on his father's side a little more than two years earlier, but he enjoyed living there.

Like all old houses, it had its quirks, but it was cozy and full of character. He especially enjoyed spending time in the back garden, the size of a postage stamp. The narrow flowerbeds bordering the fences, the potted herbs on the patio and the small greenhouse where he grew hydroponic vegetables for personal use were his pride and joy. It kept him busy in the evenings and over weekends, especially during the planting and growing seasons.

In winter he listened to music, read more than usual, watched DVDs or reread the pages he had written over time, in the probably vain belief that they might one day become part of a historical novel.

Now and again, when the weather was favorable, he spent a weekend at Zandbergen, where his houseboat lay at anchor. The green meadows, swift flow of the Dender River and brisk walks in the forest made a pleasant change.

But this weekend his routine had been completely upset. He regretted it more by the minute that he had allowed himself to be persuaded by Lieve Luykens to undertake the hour-and-a-half-long drive to Leuven. And he had no idea how he would be received.

No, he would much rather have stayed at home. He had bought the latest Luc Deflo novel the previous day. His namesake certainly knew how to entertain.

Reading crime novels provided an escape from his boring life. While he was reading, Luc DeReu became Dirk Deleu. Or Lee Child's Jack Reacher. Connelly's Hieronymus Bosch. Rankin's Rebus. Or whoever the hero might be in the books of a specific author.

His life was uneventful but it was peaceful. He could do with a warm female body, but the accompanying complications would probably not be worth it.

Perhaps he would have been a more exciting person if he had stayed on in South Africa. Now *there* was a country that made the blood course through a man's veins. The people use every possible opportunity to get out of doors. They climb mountains in shorts and sneakers. They swim in a sea that isn't just an enormous lake with barely an attitude;

it does its best to swallow you. They fish, the most prized catch being a galjoen. They dive for crayfish and the large periwinkles they call alikreukels. Barbecuing, known locally as a braai, is almost a national sport. It was probably all the vitamin D that made them live such effervescent lives.

But his year-long contract had not been renewed. Possibly because he was never able to elicit much more than stifled and less stifled yawns from his students.

Maybe they were numbed by the crime in the country. And the country's history. The so-called white guilt. Maybe that was why a class with mainly white students, as was then still the case, showed hardly any interest in the affairs of the rest of colonial and postcolonial Africa—past or present.

He had been in Stellenbosch just long enough to begin to understand these white South Africans' dry sense of humor and their obsession with rugby. Just long enough to want to see more of the sunny country in all its diversity.

Of course he had noticed that people buried their heads in the sand. Endured what would never be tolerated in Belgium: the almost relentless, almost *casual* violence that all too often went unpunished by law. But then, South Africans were from Africa, not Europe, their mindset far removed from what he knew and understood as part of his daily life.

Who was he to criticize? He had not been born a white child in Pretoria or Bloemfontein. Or a colored child in Mitchells Plain. Or a black child in Soweto or Gugulethu.

He often wondered who or what he might have been if he had been born and raised in Africa. He also wondered what his life would have been like if he had stayed on in Stellenbosch for another year or so. But such speculation was an exercise in futility.

In the end you are the victim of your own comfort zone until you are forcefully jolted out of it. And even then, you hang on to what is familiar until there are no other options left.

At least in Belgium he wouldn't be hijacked. Or bashed over the head for his cellphone. Or get his block knocked off because he happened to be shouting for the wrong team, or had made an error of judgment in traffic. It was a consolation. So was living an unchallenging, comfortable life in a country where you don't have to feel guilty because you are white and speak your mother tongue.

Right now he had to concentrate on getting Sunday's trip over and done with. Getting past the ripple Ammie was temporarily casting on the tranquil waters of his boring life.

*Ammie*
*Leuven*

Ammie was relieved when Lieve left. The apartment sparkled and smelled fresh, but the bustle had exhausted her. Usually Lieve came for a few hours in the mornings, and returned in the late afternoons to fix Ammie's supper and get her ready for bed. Today Lieve had been here almost all day. It was exhausting.

Ammie knew something was afoot, but Lieve refused to say what she was planning. Worrying about it exhausted Ammie, though she had felt much better all day, more lucid, as if she had a renewed grasp on the principle of cause and effect and could distinguish between what is and what was.

She hoped Lieve wasn't bringing someone from the church round again. Surely not. Lieve had been thoroughly embarrassed when Ammie had unceremoniously got rid of the previous one.

The only person she had ever voluntarily discussed religion with had been Elijah. It was the one thing they had never agreed on.

Elijah, who grew up at a mission station. Whose hand was never far from the Bible. Yet neither the Bible nor his unshakable faith could put an end to the love between them.

"If a clever man like Solomon could not fathom the ways of love, who am I to try?" That was what Elijah said to her the first time she lay in his arms after they had finally surrendered to their feelings. It had happened so unexpectedly, that first time. So unplanned. But it had been so right. Or so they believed.

She had known she belonged with him the day, almost a year earlier, when she had looked into his wise greenish-brown eyes and had seen a reflection of herself. Not only her likeness, but also her soul.

In the background, Patrice Lumumba was shaking hands with people who had come to hear his views on the future of an independent Congo. Nobody could have predicted then that the honor and responsibility of the position of prime minister would be bestowed on Patrice barely a year later, only to be taken away from him in a matter of months. Neither that he would be murdered only a few months later.

In that moment, however, Patrice was forgotten. The future of the Congo faded into insignificance in the presence of the lightning bolt that had simultaneously struck both her and Elijah.

It was as if their love had existed even before they themselves had seen the light of day. As if they only had to find each other to confirm it.

Two months after they had lost the battle against the inevitable consummation of their love she realized she was pregnant. She feared the child might be César's but when it was born, the paternity was clear. Only the midwife was with her and she bribed the woman to tell César it had been a stillbirth. And to find a wet nurse.

She was heartbroken when she placed her son in the arms of another young mother, saw the little mouth search for the plum-colored nipple and hungrily begin to suck at the full breast. At least Elijah could keep an eye on the child at the children's home he helped run at the mission. About that they agreed. Their child would grow up with other children who had been orphaned by hatred and emotional callousness—just as Elijah as a child had been orphaned due to prejudice and intolerance.

Ammie understood that she had made a liar out of a man who irrefutably believed in truth, honesty and integrity. Denied him his fatherhood. But there had been no other way. She knew César would destroy them, and there was more at stake than love.

There was the battle Elijah was fighting, along with Patrice Lumumba, in the MNC, the Mouvement National Congolais. The time was October 1959. Patrice was arrested after an anticolonial riot in Stanleyville in which thirty people died. The date for the conference in Brussels to finalize the future of the Congo had been set for mid-January 1960.

In the streets, the Congolese were insisting on their independence with sporadic chanting: "Dependa! Dependa! Dependa!"

At that point the fight to throw off the colonial yoke, but especially to replace it with something workable, had been more important than personal happiness.

César had stood on the political sideline, had trimmed his sails to the wind. He didn't give a damn about the Congo's independence. In his arrogance, he believed it wouldn't make the least difference to his life. The wealth of the Congo still lay there for the taking and, as a businessman, he was in a position to make use of it.

How he had managed to remain in Moise Tshombe's good books was unclear, but Ammie knew César could get at Elijah by stirring up Tshombe's hatred of Patrice Lumumba and the Lumumbists. Whether for personal or political reasons, they could under no circumstances afford for César to find out about her and Elijah.

He didn't find out. At least not until a little more than a year later.

She had sacrificed her son and the chance to find happiness with Elijah in vain.

In June 1960 the Congo was declared independent. The MNC won a convincing victory. Kasavubu became president and Patrice Lumumba prime minister—only to be kicked out by Colonel Joseph Mobutu a few months later and flung in jail.

In the second week of February 1961, she and Tabia heard that Patrice Lumumba and two of his faithful supporters, Maurice Mpolo and Joseph Okito, had been murdered by the residents of a small settlement a few days after their escape from the military prison in Thysville.

Of course everyone suspected that the story wasn't true. What Ammie and Tabia didn't know was that Patrice and his two confidants had been gruesomely put to death the same night as Elijah and not too far away from the place where Elijah had died.

César had planned his revenge very carefully, knowing that the atrocities committed that night and in that vicinity would be kept a secret at all cost.

It would be decades before the particulars of Patrice's murder were disclosed. Elijah's death was never mentioned. He was just one of thousands who lost their lives at the time.

If only Patrice had listened to Elijah and not delivered that inappropriate address during the independence celebrations, insulting the Belgians and particularly the Belgian king. If Patrice had followed Elijah's advice and not involved the Russians, would things have turned out differently? Would the history of the Congo have gone in a different direction?

Futile questions. One might as well say, what if Kings Leopold II, Albert I and II and Boudewijn had treated the people of the Congo well, instead of humiliating and abusing them? What if they had invested in the country, instead of taking from it as much as they could? Would the country's history have been different then? So much wealth. Copper, uranium, barium, diamonds and who knows what else? So much potential. But it was exactly that wealth under the crust of the earth that awakened greed and megalomania. Followed closely by cruelty and inhumanity. Especially in a country where violence was the rule, rather than the exception.

Ammie gave a deep sigh. According to Lieve, she was becoming very forgetful. She remembered very little from the last few years. Goodness knows, she would give anything to be able to forget the entire past.

Actually she hated lucid days like today.

*Erevu*
*Antwerp*

Erevu read yesterday's message again.

> From: Jela
> To: Erevu
> The opportunity arose. Dove was unable to find objects at address. Nor any luxury articles. She seems not to have the goods. She did not sell them.
> Managed to get information. Still going through rest of computer but e-fax was sent to Belgian consulate—motivation for expediting visa. E-mail: Booking for September 17 on KLM flight to Schiphol confirmed.
> Over to you.

He had answered immediately.

> From: Erevu
> To: Jela
> Good work. Sorry it could not be wrapped up sooner, but nothing worthwhile comes easily.
> Dove should fly here 16$^{th}$ latest. We'll take over from there.

Just now Jela gave him the good news.

> From: Jela
> To: Erevu
> Dove's flight arranged. Lands 15$^{th}$. Schiphol.

The answer came quickly. *100%. Will make arrangements.*

It was twelve years since his mother had confessed on her deathbed—told him at last where he came from. Gave him what was his due. Told him there was much more.

A year after his mother's death, he had persuaded his uncle to give him more information. Names. Places.

Two years ago, when his cousin had drunk too much beer at his uncle's funeral, he had learned about the nkísi, the two woodcarvings occupied by his ancestral spirits and imbued with special powers.

Since then, he had been trying to follow the tracks that had been covered by time and cunning.

Through guesswork and a lot of determination, Jela had found out the Colijns' last known address in Pretoria. The old woman and her eldest daughter had long since gone back to Belgium, and the old man had died. Evidently the youngest daughter had remained behind on her own but they hadn't been able to track her down. And now, this link to her.

For the past two years he had been hot on her heels. He had gone to Belgium for four months at a time. He had found the old woman and her daughter in Ghent. Pretending to work for the telephone service, he had attached a device to their landline that relayed the numbers they dialed to his cellphone.

Now it was almost time. Nothing was going to stand in his way. Nothing and no one. The nkísi had to be found.

The timing was excellent. Their holy calling was bleeding to death without the power of the ancestors. And the nkisi were the vessels of that power.

# Five

*Sunday, September 9*
*Caz*
*Overberg*

At last Catya had calmed down after her fierce battle with the poor policeman who had rescued her from the tree. She had eaten her first proper meal and stopped running helter-skelter at the least sound or movement. Caz understood how the cat felt. She was a bit skittish herself.

Thank goodness for Ellen. Caz literally fell into her char's arms when Ellen responded immediately to her call and offered to sleep over on Friday and Saturday.

Not only was Ellen kind; she was also a miracle worker. Alone Caz would not have managed. As it turned out, it took them all of Saturday to get the house back in order. But it was Ellen's empathy that meant most and helped Caz get over the worst of the shock.

Now she was alone again, and still living in fear. That, and the rude invasion of her sanctum, annoyed her most. TVs and computers could be replaced and one could probably get used to a Victorian front door without its original panes, but she doubted that the dread and the feeling that her sanctuary had been contaminated would ever vanish completely.

She was too bloody scared to water her garden. To sit on the veranda. To open a window. She jumped at every sound, every movement she saw from the corner of her eye. She didn't go anywhere without the damned panic button in her hand.

How dare a frigging tikkop who was no use to society change her life like that? What was more, the bastard had got away with it. And she was one of the lucky ones. She had only been robbed, and thankfully she hadn't even been home.

She couldn't begin to imagine the fear of people who had had much worse experiences. People whose loved ones had been murdered, people who had been the victims of armed robbery, hijacking, rape. Farm attacks.

The windowpanes were replaced late on Friday afternoon. That same evening, the security people tested the alarm system and declared it in perfect order. But not before telling her off for not phoning them at once.

"And it's no good if you don't switch it on, ma'am," she was told. "Even when you're at home, understand?"

She thought of asking whether she was to be confined to a single room at a time for the rest of her life, taking every movement into account, calculating where the sensors would pick her up. She said nothing however. It would serve no purpose. In South Africa you had to accept that criminals controlled the lives of good citizens, and made their lives a misery. That you had a better chance of being raped than getting a promotion at work.

She could only hope the insurance people wouldn't refuse to pay out on the grounds that she had apparently failed to switch on the alarm. It would be the cherry on the icing on top of the terrifying cake.

One consolation was that the computer guy in Stanford knew what he was about. She would fetch the new laptop she had ordered the next day and he would help set it up. It would save her a trip to Somerset West. She'd just have to take the knock and pay with her credit card, though she hated running up debt. Hopefully the insurance company would pay out before she left.

But the pragmatic implications were the least of her problems. The solitude she had always cherished here on the smallholding had now become a hazard. She could go out to places where she'd be among people, but she still had to return. Sleep alone.

She would have to learn to face her fears, get used to moving around fully alert and the panic button around her neck like a talisman.

A dog. She should probably get one again. Though she had sworn never again. Having Rufus put down in April, after he had been her constant companion for twelve years, had broken her heart. For weeks she had moved around in a daze, her emotions fluctuating between self-reproach and grief.

Maybe she would find the courage when she returned from Belgium. If she ever returned to this lousy country.

*Luc*
*Leuven*

Ammie's apartment was on the ground floor in a quiet street facing a park. The woman who opened for him was short and round with a ruddy complexion. Her hair was streaked with gray and had clearly recently been styled. The dress looked new and the shoes were serviceable, but shiny. Around her neck was an ornamental cross. Evidently Ammie was not dependent on state care. It was hardly likely that employees of the state would be allowed to openly display religious symbols.

Instead of letting him in, she stepped outside and shut the door behind her.

"Professor DeReu? I'm so glad you kept your word. I know you must be very busy." She hesitated. "Miss Ammie doesn't know you're coming. I didn't know how to tell her. I was afraid it would send her into a tizz. She had a lucid day on Friday but yesterday the veil came down again."

Couldn't she have let him know before he came all this way? "In that case, maybe it would be better to try again another time, Mrs. Luykens." Hypocrite. If he walked away now, he wasn't coming back.

On his way over he had convinced himself he wasn't trying to bond with Ammie again. He merely wanted to hear what had made her leave her husband and stepson high and dry. He was not sure he was ready to hear the answer, though. What if it was something dreadful that threw an entirely new light on his youth and his parents?

"Oh no, Professor. Please don't go without seeing her. I'm hoping she will be brought back to reality when she realizes who you are." Lieve wrung her hands.

"Fine," he agreed after a short pause. He was here anyway and if she wasn't of sound mind, little harm would be done. At least he could soothe his conscience if she passed away, tell himself that he had tried. "I can't stay long."

"The pastries are ready, I'll just make the coffee."

He sighed. Evidently coffee and eats were non-negotiable.

Lieve took a deep breath and exhaled audibly before she turned and pushed open the door. Her nervousness rubbed off on him.

A door in the hallway led to a living room. Lieve stopped in the doorway.

"Miss Ammie," she said with a cheeriness that sounded slightly fake.

"Who was it, Lieve? Who bothers us on the holy Sabbath? People with leaflets again?"

Over Lieve's head he saw Ammie sitting in a chair by the window. Her snow-white hair was fixed in a loose bun. She was still an attractive woman, though the years had left their merciless mark on her face.

"No, you have a visitor, Miss Ammie." Lieve stood aside for him to pass.

Luc entered the living room and crossed over to where she sat. He bent down and held out his hand.

"Good day, Mother Ammie. It's Luc. Jacq's son. Do you remember me?"

Ammie's eyes widened, swept across his face. "Jacq!" She pushed his hand away and tried to hoist herself to her feet by pushing on the armrests of the chair, but sank back down again.

She stared at Luc, bewildered. "I was at your funeral!" Her eyes searched for Lieve. "Lieve, hold up your cross!" She grabbed her walking stick and swung it in Luc's direction.

Luc ducked but the stick struck him on the thigh.

"Miss Ammie! It's Luc. Not the professor." Lieve grabbed the walking stick and wrapped her hand around Ammie's. "I mean, he's also a professor, but it's not Jacq. It's his son, Luc."

Ammie let go of the walking stick and sank back in the chair. "Luc?"

Luc nodded. "It's me, yes."

"But you're an old man?"

He grinned. "Fifty-two, Mother Ammie."

"A professor?"

"Of history. Like Father." Except that Father had stuck to medieval history and I didn't, he thought, but he doubted whether Ammie would be interested. His own students were barely interested in his field of study, never mind anyone else. Colonialism and postcolonialism aren't the most exciting subjects in the field of history.

"A professor as well. Who would have thought. Jacq would have been proud of you."

Hardly. He'd never quite lived up to Jacq's expectations. "I'm glad you think so, Mother."

Luc cursed his inability to make small talk. To talk, period. He guessed he could ask how she was, but it was evident that Ammie was losing the battle against age.

He could ask about her life in Doel, but what could she tell him? That she had been cruelly forced to sell her house before it was expropriated? He knew that. She was one of many.

Never mind Doel. The only thing he actually wanted to know was what had happened between her and his father. But even he, socially inept as he was, realized that he needed a preamble.

"Shall we have coffee?" Lieve asked when the silence lingered.

"That would be nice, thank you, Mrs. Luykens." Just let it be over.

"Please, call me Lieve. Miss Ammie likes café latte. What do you prefer? I could make a macchiato?"

He had never been able to fathom the Starbucks coffee religion. With a little, a lot or without milk. Cappuccino or espresso. That was all he understood. He preferred coffee with lots of milk; it was all he ever ordered. "Koffie verkeerd is fine. Thanks."

"Two café lattes then."

Koffie verkeerd is latte? Now he knew too.

"What are you doing here, Luc?" Ammie asked bluntly. "You're not here to visit an old woman out of pure kindness. With or without koffie verkeerd."

Luc was caught off guard.

"Miss Ammie ..." Lieve tried to step in.

"Go make the coffee, Lieve. The man is a professor, I'm sure he can speak for himself." Ammie suddenly looked surprisingly lucid for someone supposedly living behind the veil of the past.

With an apologetic glance at Luc, Lieve obeyed.

"I want to know why you divorced my father and just left us. Never contacted me again," he blurted out tactlessly.

For a moment Ammie gazed at him in silence. "I didn't just leave you. Your father told me to move out and never contact him or you again."

He was caught on the wrong foot again. "But why? What was it about?" He was probably being rude, but after his first undiplomatic question, the damage had been done. "I know he loved you."

Ammie's expression was neutral. "He found out that we weren't legally married."

Luc stared at her, astounded. "I beg your pardon? After a marriage of eighteen years?"

"I've just told you, there was no marriage. The ceremony wasn't legal. We're not divorced either, because we were never married. The woman he loved didn't exist." She turned her face to the window. "There was a lot about me he didn't know. He had no idea that I was never sure whether my first husband was alive or dead and that I was possibly a bigamist."

Hell and damnation! His father, who always kept to the straight and narrow, would definitely not have been in a forgiving mood after a bombshell like that. His world was black or white, with no gray in between. Right or wrong, without any nuances. He would have been shocked to the very depth of his Catholic soul. But had it been enough grounds to make him react the way he did? Enough to shatter him like that? Perhaps. Because to Jacq DeReu two things were more important than anything else: his good name and the respect he enjoyed. Moreover, his belief in law, order and social structure was without compromise.

"How did he find out?"

Where she had been quick to reply a moment before, she now took her time. "Does it really matter?" she asked at last.

Probably not, he had to admit.

"I presume you confirmed afterwards that your first husband was no longer alive? Or divorced him? You got married again, after all."

"Tobias and I weren't officially married. We just pledged ourselves to each other during a personal ceremony. Unlike with Jacq, I was honest with him. More or less."

"Why didn't you? I mean make sure, or get divorced?"

"I didn't dare leave a trace anywhere. I couldn't risk my first husband finding me. Nor his daughter." Her gaze went past him as if she had stepped into a different world. "I cursed her. No one will ever believe her. Even if she finds out."

"Cursed?"

"The day she was born."

"You were present at your husband's daughter's birth?

Cursed her?" How did that make sense? An illegitimate daughter?

Lieve stopped on the threshold. She looked as taken aback as he felt.

"Of course I was present. Go away now. I'm tired. Lieve …" Something happened in her eyes, as if a membrane was pulled over them. "Who is this man, Lieve? Did he bring leaflets? How many times must I tell you …" Her eyes closed.

*March 1961*
*Ammie*
*Katanga*

"You are better now. You must go." There was no expression on Tabia's face.

Ammie was quiet for a long time. Where would she go? "Give me a few more weeks, Tabia. Please. To make plans. To try to get help. How will I get away on my own?"

"There is no time. It will just get harder. You can't have the baby here."

"Baby?" Shock surged through her. Yet she knew at once that Tabia was right. The signs were unmistakable. Perhaps she had just refused to acknowledge them.

"Your other child, he is safe at kimisionari. He is protected. This one is not good here. This one is msichana. We mean nothing."

"How do you know it's a girl?" Ammie felt dazed. Tabia's words hardly made sense.

"I know. Maybe you are hurt inside. When they kicked you. You need daktari, not mganguzi. The ancestral spirits do not work for white people. My brother's child will take you tomorrow. It's a long walk. To the Angolan border. The road to Northern Rhodesia is not safe."

Tabia got up from her haunches, disappeared into the hut and came out with a canvas rucksack in her hands. Ammie recognized it. It was César's.

She took out a dress that belonged to Ammie. It was creased, but clean. "My brother's child go to your home."

Ammie's eyes widened. "César?"

"He is not there. Brother's child watched the house a long time. Nobody there. The dog is hiding. Or left country. Or he is dead. Gendarme looking for him."

Tabia had been trailing César the day he murdered Elijah. She had watched the whole horrifying tableau on the savanna from behind a clump of bushes. She saw the other vehicles speed away when César started kicking Ammie. Only one helper stayed and joined in. And she saw them leave Ammie for dead and drive away.

Tabia waited until they had disappeared in the direction of Elisabethville before going to Ammie's aid. When she saw Ammie was still alive, she wanted to seek help at a nearby villa. A young boy stopped her when she was still some distance away. He told her terrible things had happened in the house that evening. Tabia talked him into helping her get Ammie to the nearest populated area. Somehow she persuaded a resident to help her. She left Ammie there and went home where she had again found someone to help her get Ammie to her dwelling.

All for Elijah's sake, Ammie had learned from Tabia. Elijah, who helped Tabia after she was raped by a Belgian soldier and almost bled to death. Elijah who stopped her from taking revenge. Tried to teach her about forgiveness and the liberation it brought.

Tabia did not go in search of her rapist to stab him in the heart as had been her plan, but forgiveness was too much to ask. Though she was considered beautiful, and her lineage was pure, no Tetela man would ever look at her again. Not after she had been violated by a white man. So there would be no dowry for her family. That was why she had come to Elisabethville to become a white man's whore. To stay alive and send money to her family. Until her pregnancy began to show a few months earlier and the man no longer wanted her. It was the end of her meager income.

All these things Tabia had told Ammie over the past weeks. Without visible emotion, her eyes pitch black and unreadable. But she did not tell Ammie how she had happened to be there on the savanna that fateful evening. Or why she had been trailing César.

Tabia was entitled to her secrets, Ammie had decided at first, but now she wondered anew. Tabia was right about one thing, however. Ammie couldn't stay and bring her child into the world there.

She'd never thought she could be more terrified than the night Elijah was murdered. Now she knew that her terror of what lay ahead was even greater. Fear of the unknown is worse than fear of death. It's an immeasurable fear, precisely because the outcome is unknown.

But even this corrosive apprehension did not overshadow her other worry. Whose child was she carrying? Elijah's or César's?

# Six

*Wednesday, September 17*
*Caz*
*Cape Town*

Caz stared in disbelief at the scale on which she had placed her lilac suitcase and its much smaller companion. She raised her eyes to meet the unsympathetic gaze of the KLM ground stewardess. "You can't be serious."

It was clear that the woman was dead serious. "I'm sorry, ma'am, it's clearly stated on the e-ticket. Only one piece of luggage in the hold. Maximum twenty-three kilograms. Hand luggage no more than nine kilos. You can take the vanity case as hand luggage, but I'll have to weigh all the pieces together. Please remove the vanity case from the scale."

Despondently Caz obeyed. The e-ticket had been on her stolen laptop, and she hadn't made a printout. She'd had no idea there was a single-piece-of-luggage rule.

She already had so much to carry. How would she manage yet another item? Lilah could read Afrikaans books on her Kindle, but no, she insisted on the real McCoy. To touch and to treasure.

"Your case alone weighs more than twenty-three kilograms," the stewardess announced. "It will be a hundred dollars for the excess weight."

"A hundred dollars?"

"Ma'am, if you don't want to pay the hundred dollars, I suggest you take your luggage to the empty scale over there and re-pack. There's a long line behind you. By the look of things, you'll have to do something about your hand luggage as well."

The "things" being looked at consisted of a bulky coat, a backpack containing her new laptop, a handbag, and a bag of books. If she added the vanity case, she would make a pack mule smile.

Caz sighed, dragged her bag off the scale onto a trolley and headed for the empty scale. How did people manage to travel so light? Take that stylish young woman taking photos with her cellphone, for example. One medium-sized suitcase and a handbag.

But then she probably didn't have to pack for a month. And she almost certainly didn't have a daughter who was desperate for Afrikaans books, and Ricoffy, and Mrs. Ball's, and a bottle of jerepigo. One who had left her favorite platform boots in South Africa during her last visit and simply had to have them back.

Caz gritted her teeth when the cellphone was swung in her direction to take a photo. It would probably be posted on Facebook with a comment like "What was this woman thinking when she packed for her trip?" Or was someone confusing her with Antoinette Kellerman again? It was the hair.

A woman had recently tapped her on the shoulder in Hermanus. Her broad smile faded the moment Caz turned.

"I'm sorry, I thought you were Antoinette," she muttered, embarrassed.

Caz must have looked slightly bemused .

"Antoinette Kellerman ... the actress? Hannah in *Song*

*vir Katryn*. From the back, your hair looks just like Antoinette's. All silver and curly. But your face is younger. Different. Sorry."

Blushing, the woman turned away. Caz didn't know how to make her feel less awkward.

Miss Traveling-light who had just taken another photo would also soon discover her mistake.

By the time Caz had placed all her belongings beside the empty scale, she was dripping with sweat. She took a deep breath. Time to be practical. The plane was leaving at five to twelve and it was only nine.

Her best option would be to phone the company where her car was being stored while she was gone and pay them extra to come and fetch her excess baggage. What a bloody schlepp.

Caz gritted her teeth again. If that damn woman pointed that cellphone in her direction one more time she was going to slap her bloody face.

*Luc*
*Damme*

What was it about humans that made them find the unknown so much more interesting than the known? Or rather, why did they want to ferret out things that had nothing to do with them?

Luc could not explain his behavior. He only knew that he had been upset by his conversation with Ammie. That he wanted to know more, to understand.

He had enough self-discipline to open the email from South Africa only after he had washed the few supper dishes.

Exactly how much time Ammie had spent in South Africa after fleeing the Congo he didn't know. But from her stories when he was a boy he knew she had been there. At least South Africa was an easier place to start than the DRC.

A short note explained that the attached document was all they had been able to find on one Annemie Pauwels who had entered South Africa as a refugee in 1961.

The "attached document" was a jpeg copy of a sworn statement by Annemie Pauwels, declaring that she'd had to flee the Congo hastily during a state of emergency without being in possession of the necessary travel documents, which she suspected were destroyed in a fire. She had been smuggled across the borders of more than one country, faced many ordeals, and lost the baby she was expecting. She implored the embassy to help her travel to Belgium. She was traumatized and wanted to be reunited with her family. She appealed to them on humanitarian grounds. As soon as she was back in Belgium, her family would help her get the necessary documents. The handwritten date was illegible but the year was 1961.

It was hard to believe that the embassy had complied, but she seemed to have had her wish granted. Perhaps the authorities were more obliging fifty-three years ago than they were today.

Ammie hadn't spoken much about her personal life in the Congo, but she often spoke about what it had been like to live there. The political and social chaos. The hot weather. The tropical rains. The multicolored butterflies. The shrieking monkeys in the trees. The verdant vegetation, sweet-smelling flowers with sweet-sounding names, like frangipani. A place where bananas hung in huge bunches on the trees, and coconuts and avocados were plentiful. A place where people boiled and ate poisonous roots. Manioc, or cassava. When Luc asked how it was possible to eat poisonous things, she laughed and pointed out that he loved tapioca. It was from the same plant, she said, and only poisonous in its raw form.

After that, he had never eaten tapioca again. But he was keen to find out more and Ammie readily obliged. Her stories made him wonder how people from a civilized country could move to a place where there was chaos. Yet it sounded incredibly exotic.

Once Ammie spent a lot of money on an avocado just so that he could taste it. Another time she added tinned coconut milk to an unfamiliar dish. Luc's eyes had watered and he was afraid his mouth would burst into flame, but he tasted another world. Far from Leuven and Antwerp and Knokke—the only three places he'd known as a child.

Ammie had also spoken about the ways the Congo was different from South Africa, and yet there were similarities. She spoke of mountain ranges vanishing over the blue horizon. Soutpansberg. Magaliesberg. And of the blue, blue sky and the harsh sun, even in winter. Of a city swathed in a lilac haze in October, when the pavements were carpeted in lilac and jacaranda blossoms burst under the soles of your shoes. Jacaranda—the very word had a lilac sound to it.

Luc deliberately detached himself from the memories. Last week's visit to Antwerp had left him with more questions than answers. From the copies he had made at the archives and elsewhere—under the pretense of doing research for an article he was writing for a genealogical magazine—it was clear that something was amiss.

The name Annemie Pauwels was not in the register of births and deaths in Antwerp where, he had always understood, she was born. He remembered her saying she had lived in Antwerp until she was five before moving with her parents to the Congo.

He could only assume her birth certificate had been issued under another name. But he couldn't find any proof that she had legally altered her name to Annemie Pauwels. The South African document confirmed she had entered the country under that name.

Even if her first husband were dead, her marriage to Jacq would still have been illegal because she had used an assumed name. His father would never have forgiven Ammie for that. For eighteen years he had lived with her, under the impression that they were married. Even though he had been oblivious of the fact that the marriage was invalid, in his Catholic eyes it would still make him a whoremonger.

Luc couldn't even begin to imagine his father's reaction to the possibility of bigamy as well.

Obviously Ammie must have got hold of some kind of identity document, but he knew she didn't have a passport. She had always refused to accompany his father to foreign countries. It was probably too risky for her to apply for travel documents.

But there had to be documents somewhere, from the time before she began to use the false name.

Luc took out his handkerchief and polished the lenses of his new glasses. Presumably Ammie hadn't lied about her date of birth. He put the spectacles on and turned to the printout he had made of all the births and deaths from 1930 to 1939. He hadn't read it yet, except to search in vain for Annemie Pauwels's name.

Ammie had laughed when he'd pointed out that she had been born on the day of the Reichstag fire. "A young historian, just like your father," she had said.

February 27, 1933.

According to the official document, four babies were born in Antwerp that day. Three boys and a girl. The girl was named Amelie de Pauw.

He felt himself getting excited until he read on. Date of death: January 16, 1961, at Elisabethville, Congo.

Still. Annemie, Amelie. Pauwels, De Pauw. Aside from the date of death, there were just too many correspondences pointing toward Ammie having been Amelie de Pauw in an earlier life. If she had been Amelie de Pauw, what on earth had happened? Why was she declared dead? Had Ammie done something terrible and made sure that she was thought to be dead?

Potverdorie! He should never have gone to see her. Instead of finding a satisfactory answer to a single question, he now felt as if he had stuck his head into a hornet's nest.

He threw the list aside. He needed to switch off his thoughts.

A book wouldn't do the trick. A movie perhaps. Yes, one of his trusted Jean-Claude van Damme standbys.

He definitely didn't want his students or anyone else to find out he was a fan of the Belgian movie star—not because of his acting talent but because of his karate skills. And he especially wouldn't like anybody to know that he immersed himself in Van Damme's heroes to such an extent that, after watching one of his movies, he felt as sure-footed and strong as Jean-Claude himself.

Pathetic, but that was how it was.

*Caz*
*Cape Town*

By the time Caz had dealt with the luggage fiasco, she felt as if she had run a marathon. Worst of all was the mortification she felt at her own stupidity. She wondered how many people had been watching her frantic scurrying.

But at last she was on her way with a case that had weighed in at exactly twenty-three kilograms. She had scored an aisle seat to boot. The check-in attendant must have felt sorry for her. There was still half an hour before she had to board. Just enough time for an ice-cold draft. To hell with the midnight hour.

She was on her way to the country with the largest variety of beers in the world, after all.

The past ten days had been crazy. Fighting with the insurance company, a spat with the police because they hadn't taken fingerprints. Catya demonstrating odd behavior, like peeing inside. Hopefully she had calmed down by now after the wails and moans the night before when Caz had taken her to the kennel.

But nothing in the chaos of the past two weeks had been more disruptive than the loss of her laptop. Besides a day's work, she had lost all her emails and recent email addresses as well.

To crown it all, she'd had to upgrade to a new Word program. What a doozy!

Thank goodness she could convince the publisher to give her a month's respite for the translation. Annika understood that the circumstances were exceptional. Hopefully she would figure out the new program while she was in Ghent. She might even get a little work done.

But first she had to get there. She wasn't looking forward to the flight. She didn't know what was waiting on the other side, or how she would be received. Tieneke had written to give her directions from Amsterdam to Ghent, adding only that Josefien's condition was rapidly deteriorating.

Still, Caz was relieved to get away. She hadn't had a proper night's sleep since the burglary, and she was permanently on edge by day.

Luckily there had been no further signs of intruders on her property. Ellen considered it an isolated incident.

"There are plenty of naughty kids in the township, but this doesn't look like their work. Maybe it was just a few skollies passing by," she said.

Ellen had promised to check on her home twice a week and water the garden and the plants on the veranda. Dear, dear Ellen.

Chill. That was what she had to do now to be ready for tomorrow. The train trip from Schiphol to Ghent-Dampoort was a prospect she certainly wasn't looking forward to. Facing Tieneke and Fien even less.

*Erevu*
*Antwerp*

> To: Jela
> Photos received, thanks. Quality good enough. Will be able to identify CC.
>
> From: Jela
> To: Erevu
> Just learned of an enquiry at the embassy in SA about a refugee from Congo, 1961. Annemie Pauwels.
> No record of Annemie Pauwels in Be though the enquiry came from Be. Person enquiring a professor writing article for genealogical journal.
> Will try to find out more about him.
> Old lady's alias? Could mean she's not dead. If not, she must be in her eighties.

The network Jela had built up over the years was at last yielding dividends. It was good that Dove was here. It meant they could be in two places at the same time.

The professor might be a problem, but the possibility of the old woman being alive overshadowed all else. He hadn't managed to track her down anywhere, so he'd assumed she was dead. That was why he was following the Colijn route. But if the old woman could be found, it would simplify matters. If anyone knew where the nkísi were, she was the one.

# Seven

*Thursday, September 18*
*Caz*
*Schiphol*

Of course the bloody lilac suitcase was the last one to emerge from the jaws of the baggage carousel. Apart from the obvious link with Lilah, she had specifically chosen lilac in the hope that it would make the bag easy to spot. She had just been proved wrong. About five other lilac travel cases had already rolled past.

The thought of Lilah reminded her to switch on her phone. She had put it on roaming in Cape Town. A few messages about the roaming procedure came through. She sent Lilah a short message, telling her she was at Schiphol. Lilah replied almost at once that she was flying to Miami in an hour.

*Timing sucks, but see you soon, MaCaz.*

Five kisses ended the message.

Pushing her luggage trolley, Caz aimed for the green exit. Surely Mrs. Ball's didn't have to be declared.

Her hand luggage was a nightmare. By the time she found the trolley, the bag of books had numbed her fingers. Her coat kept dragging on the floor and the strap of her handbag kept slipping off her shoulder. Only the backpack was manageable, though it seemed to be getting heavier by the minute.

The arrivals hall was a huge moving, waving, greeting throng. Schiphol was even bigger than Caz had imagined. And much bigger than she remembered Charles de Gaulle.

She knew Fien was on her last legs, but hell! Couldn't Tieneke have made an effort to meet her? It would have been so much easier. It's only two hours by car, after all: the same distance as Cape Town International from Stanford.

Now she had to find the train station. Tieneke had sent a detailed message yesterday morning. Caz had to make sure not to take the expensive high-speed train, Thalys. She should buy a ticket at a vending machine at the station. To buy one on the train was much more expensive.

What Tieneke obviously didn't know was that Caz had a dire relationship with vending machines. Drawing money at an ATM was about as far as her skills went. But in Stanford, where there wasn't a single traffic light in a radius of twenty-five kilometers, there was no pressing need for mechanical skills.

According to the website, the station was directly below the airport. Searching for a staircase seemed a good place to start. She read the noticeboards. Metro? Was that what she was looking for? She wished she wasn't such a bloody useless traveller. Perhaps she should take a moment to regroup. Gather her wits. Focus. She could see the exit and she longed to breathe air that hadn't been recirculated until it smelled like a vacuum-cleaner bag.

It was much warmer outside than she had expected. Warmer than Cape Town even, where it was supposed to be spring. Too warm for the sweater she was wearing, but there was no way she was carrying that as well.

The smokers huddled together and plumes of smoke rose up in the air. For the first time in years she longed for a cigarette. Not for the taste, but for that feeling a non-smoker could never understand, one that has nothing to do with nicotine or tar, and everything with addiction.

Even if the air outside was almost certainly polluted by much worse substances than cigarette smoke, it was still better than the air in the plane and the airport. She drew a few deep breaths.

Water. She had to get a bottle of water. One more thing to carry, but she was parched.

She turned the trolley round to go back inside.

"Ma'am?"

Caz looked over her shoulder and realized she was being addressed. The voice belonged to a well-built youngster of about eighteen in tight-fitting jeans and a crisp white T-shirt. Adidas on his feet. His red backpack looked reasonably new. On his cap was a Blue Bulls emblem, the light blue in sharp contrast with his ebony skin.

It took her a second or two to realize that the Blue Bulls were a complete anomaly in the place where she currently found herself.

"So sorry to bother you, ma'am, but I'm in a bit of a fix." The boy's English was faultless, though he spoke with an accent.

"My name is Njiwa and I'm a student. I want to buy a train ticket, but I'm five euros short. I'm not a beggar, ma'am." His brilliant white teeth gnawed at his lower lip. "Truly, I'm not. If you give me your phone number or email address, I'll make sure you get your money back. My grandfather will refund it with pleasure. He's meeting me at the other end."

The boy sounded genuine. The product of a good school, she guessed. It would explain the stilted, almost affected English. Embarrassment probably accounted for the bashful expression in his eyes. "Blue Bulls?" Caz asked, pointing at the cap.

He gave a shy smile. "Where I come from, it's a rugby team, ma'am."

Caz hesitated only a moment. "I'll tell you what. I have to catch a train as well. If you push the trolley for me, get me to the right platform, and show me how to buy the ticket, I'll give you five euros."

The smile broadened. "It's a deal, ma'am. Why don't you put your backpack on the trolley as well? It looks heavy."

It was a relief when he helped her slide the backpack off her shoulders. He turned and headed back inside, pushing the trolley.

She fell into step beside him. "You look as if you know your way around?"

"Yes, ma'am. I've been to Amsterdam before. But this time Schiphol is just the first leg of my journey."

"Something to drink?" she asked when they passed a kiosk. She took her wallet from her backpack.

"A Coke would be nice, thanks, ma'am." He looked somewhat embarrassed.

"Call me Caz." She bought a cool drink for him and a bottle of water for herself before they set off again.

"And your final destination is?"

"Ghent, ma'am. Ghent-Sint-Pieters to be precise." He tilted his head. "You don't happen to be South African as well? The accent is familiar."

"I am indeed. Coincidentally, I'm also on my way to Ghent, but to Dampoort."

He stopped and stared at her, surprised. "No way!"

"Yes."

Njiwa shook his head and resumed walking. "I've heard of this kind of coincidence when you travel. My grandfather once met a random stranger in Berlin and they found out they lived about ten houses apart in the same street in Sandhurst. It's hard to believe."

"It's a massive coincidence, yes." Caz couldn't fathom why the boy made her feel uncomfortable. He was well-spoken, polite and smart. He could very well have a grandfather who lived in Sandhurst and was waiting for him in Ghent at this moment. Had her reclusive lifestyle made her suspicious of everything? Or was it still the aftermath of the burglary?

That was what it was, she concluded when Njiwa continued to help her with her luggage and settled her on the train even after the machine had spat out the ticket and she had given him the five euros.

"I won't intrude any further, but I'll be in the next carriage if you need me. I'll come back to assist you when we reach Antwerp. Thank you for coming to my aid. I really appreciate it."

"You've already earned every cent. Thanks, Njiwa, you're very kind."

He raised his index and middle fingers to his cap, and smiled.

*Luc*
*Damme*

Amelie de Pauw, Annemie Pauwels. Luc was haunted by the two names.

His research skills and access to sources were handy, but very little information was forthcoming on Amelie de Pauw. He did find out that her father, Albert de Pauw, worked as an accountant in Leopoldville, as it was known at the time, for the business conglomerate Société Générale de Belgique.

Her mother was Hortense Baert. No profession. Died of blackwater fever in 1952, when Amelie was nineteen. A little more than a year later her father married Hortense's sister Constance.

A few months before her father's death three years later, in 1956, Amelie married César Ronald Bruno Janssen, a businessman of Leopoldville. The nature of the business he conducted was unclear. Early in 1957 their address changed to Elisabethville.

The cause of Amelie's father's death was simply given as an aircraft incident near Bakwanga in the Kasaï-Oriental province, which also claimed the lives of Constance and the pilot.

Luc's chair creaked as he leaned back.
Annemie, Amelie.
Pauwels, De Pauw.
Congo, Congo.
The same date of birth.

Annemie: No paper trail.
Amelie: Death certificate.
Annemie: Lived in Elisabethville.
Amelie: Moved from Leopoldville to Elisabethville.
Interesting. Very, very interesting.

*Caz*
*Antwerp/Ghent*

Caz couldn't imagine how she would have managed without Njiwa.

He had to wake her for the change and here, at this vast station in Antwerp, she would never have made it in time for the first train to Ghent if he had not found the right platform, saving her another hour's wait. And that was above and beyond his indispensable help with her luggage.

An angel must have pitied her and sent the well-mannered boy.

There wasn't much time to appreciate the grand station building. She got a vague impression of an enormous vaulted ceiling and impressive architectural features.

The train was almost full, but Njiwa helped her find a seat and arranged her luggage around her before going off to look for a seat in another carriage.

The nap before Antwerp had done her good. For the first time she felt alert enough to take in the scenery.

What she had expected she didn't know, but she'd never imagined that Belgium would be so green. Or that there would be so many small farms. Or maize fields.

Around the stations it looked like it probably looked near stations everywhere in the world. But the rest was lovely.

At Ghent-Dampoort, Njiwa stepped out of the train to help her get to the main exit of the station. When she protested that he would now have to take a later train, he shook his head.

"Not a problem. I just wish I could return your five euros."

"You were worth much more to me, don't worry. Actually..."
She unzipped her handbag.

"No, no, please, ma'am," he protested when she took out her wallet. "I don't need money. My grandfather is a wealthy man and he looks after me well. It was just a misjudgment on my part. I bought him a present on the plane without realizing I'd be five euros short for the train. Really, I'm going to be very embarrassed if you give me any more money. We're compatriots, after all."

Reluctantly Caz put her wallet away. "Njiwa, you're too good to be true," she said, smiling. "Well, off you go."

He nodded, then paused and took his cellphone out of his pocket. "I know my grandfather will want to call to thank you. Would you mind giving me your number?"

Caz got the same uncomfortable feeling she'd had earlier. She didn't like handing out her cellphone number, but the boy had certainly saved her a lot of trouble and misery. "There's no need for him to call. I can only receive messages anyway."

He lowered his eyes and nodded. "Okay."

Now he thought she didn't trust him. What the hell was wrong with her? She wasn't in a crime mecca anymore.

"Oh, very well." She gave him the number and he keyed it in so fast that the two slim thumbs looked like one.

"Let me put my number on your phone as well. Then you can call me if you run into a problem. I'll help if I can. You never know what might happen in a strange country." He held out his hand. Reluctantly she gave him her phone. Deftly he repeated the procedure.

He frowned and brought her cellphone closer to his eyes. "I see your WhatsApp wants to update. Shall I give permission?"

Were today's young people born with cellphone manuals embedded in their brains? "Okay." Lilah used WhatsApp, but Caz had never bothered to find out how it worked.

After a while he looked up and handed back her phone with a broad smile. "There you go. Goodbye, Caz. Maybe we'll run into each other again here in Ghent. I hope you enjoy your stay."

He took off his cap and held out his hand. A cool hand, Caz noticed.

"Njiwa!" she called after him as he began to walk away.
He turned.
"Your name ... it's unusual."
"It's Swahili. A nickname, actually."
"What does it mean?"
He laughed. "My grandfather says I'm the peacemaker in the family. He gave me the name. It means dove." He raised his cap in a final greeting and jogged down the steep staircase.

Suddenly Caz felt completely alone. One more bus ride and she would come face to face with the two women she hadn't seen for thirty-one years.

# Eight

*Caz*
*Ghent*

By the time Caz got off at the Ghent-Brugge bus stop, she was completely fed up and on the verge of tears. The struggle with her luggage was a nightmare. First she didn't know where to wait for Bus 3. Then she almost headed in the wrong direction. Toward the city instead of the suburbs. And then she didn't know where to get off the bus. Fortunately, she remembered the street name.

She was exhausted, her feet ached, her arm felt numb and her shoulder muscles were cramping painfully.

When the bus drove off, she put everything down on the pavement and sent Tieneke a message. *Please fetch me at bus stop. Too much to carry. Exhausted.*

After a long moment the answer came. *It's just a short walk. One street block and a few houses. Look at the numbers.*

Caz felt like smashing the phone against the first available wall. *No,* she typed. She had no strength for anything more.

She turned her case lengthways and sat on it the way she had last done as a schoolgirl. She would stay there until someone came to help her. Yes, she knew it was her own fault, but damn it! Couldn't Tieneke be a bit more accommodating?

There was movement lower down the street where there seemed to be a shop, but none of the people looked as if they could be Tieneke. Caz closed her eyes and hung her head. Why the hell had she saddled this wild horse? Why had she answered the damned phone that bloody day Tieneke phoned? She didn't usually answer her landline when she was working.

"Cassie?"

Caz looked up slowly. Tieneke looked as if she had been destined to be sixty-five since birth. She had lost weight and her skin was pale but relatively wrinkle-free. Her hair was snow white and short, but the color and style suited her. She looked chic in navy slacks and a loose-fitting floral top. She'd had something done to her teeth as well.

"Tieneke, you look fabulous!" Caz got to her feet with a slight groan.

Tieneke's gaze swept over her. Perhaps she was also wondering what the appropriate form of greeting would be. A handshake? A peck on the cheek?

Neither, it seemed.

"You look as if you've been through a mangle. What were you thinking, dragging along all this luggage?"

Caz gritted her teeth, but kept her voice steady. "Hello, Tieneke."

"Yes, good day." Tieneke picked up the coat and the vanity case as if she instinctively knew they were the lightest of the lot. "Come, I don't want to leave Mother alone too long."

So that was what you did when you hadn't seen each other for thirty-two years. You instantly fell back in the old ways.

Caz adjusted her backpack, picked up the bag of books, pulled out the handle of the case and followed Tieneke.

It was indeed not far. Only a few minutes on foot. The

silence between them was even heavier than the case Caz was dragging.

Tieneke unlocked the front door, but before she pushed it open, she turned to look at Caz. "Aren't you interested to know how Mother is?"

Caz sighed. "Tieneke, you told me she was dying. What's the good of asking? Should I ask how far from dying she is?" It was an awful thing to say, but Tieneke had always managed to bring out the worst in her. Now Caz understood why. With Tieneke, she was always on the defensive.

Tieneke frowned. "Your flippancy is uncalled for. For your information, she has better and worse days. Dying isn't a constant thing."

"Tieneke, can we go inside, please? I'm about to fall down. I was up at five yesterday morning to get my visa in time and I've only managed a few short snatches of sleep in between. I'm hungry and I'm parched. Can I just regain my strength before you continue taking me to task? You can tell me later how Mother is feeling today and how it's different from yesterday and the previous days. Okay?"

Tieneke gave her a grim look and pushed open the door. To the right of the gloomy entrance hall was a steep, narrow staircase, and to the left a passage led to the rooms on the ground floor. There was a smell in the air that, incredibly enough, she remembered from the Meyerspark days, but it was mixed with something else. Something medicinal.

"Your room is upstairs."

Caz looked at the staircase and closed her eyes. She lowered the bag with the books to the floor and grabbed the handle of the case with both hands.

"Shh, you'll disturb Mother," Tieneke whispered when Caz reached the third step.

Caz couldn't manage a reply. She had to focus all her strength on hauling the case from one step to the next. The thing might weigh twenty-three kilograms, but it felt like a ton. An eternity later she stood on the landing, sweating.

"Where to now?" she panted.

"Another one up."

Caz looked at Tieneke in disbelief. The staircase continued upward, even steeper and narrower than before.

"We have only two bedrooms. I was going to find you a room next door, but it didn't work out. A boarder moved in last week. You'll have to sleep in the attic. I've made you a bed there."

Caz looked her in the eye. "Tieneke, I'll sleep in the attic. I'll lug the suitcase up there, even if it's the second-last thing I ever do, but after that I want a beer. A very tall, very cold one."

"We don't keep liquor in the house."

"I didn't think so, but we passed a shop on the corner of the street and I saw a poster advertising Stella Artois. It's beer, in case you don't know."

"Mother won't ..."

"Then I'm taking over your bedroom." Caz made for a closed door leading off the passage.

"Verdorie. Fine, I'll fetch you a beer while you haul up your luggage. Everything. I don't want to fall over any of your stuff."

"Not one beer. Bring at least six. And all of them cold. Ice cold." Why had she assumed it would be any different from when they were living together? They were still trying to get the better of each other. Even after three decades, nothing seemed to have changed.

Tieneke threw her a last look before she went down the stairs.

By the time Caz reached the top floor, her arms and wrists felt ready to snap.

The attic was almost completely dark. She grabbed hold of a dangling string and pulled it. The light came on.

Attic room? An ironing board, laundry hamper, washing machine and tumble dryer testified to the fact that the room, which was no bigger than her pantry at home, served as a laundry. At least she could stand up straight in her pantry. Here the ceiling sloped, so she would have to keep ducking her head.

There was a skylight of clear perspex, but the accumulated dirt on the outside didn't allow much light into the room. The bed was an inflatable mattress. Single. Covered by a down comforter.

A comforter in this airless sauna?

Caz sat down on the top step and lowered her face into her hands again, struggling to hold back the tears.

No. You're not going to crack now, Caz Colijn, she admonished herself. Look on the bright side. It's a beautiful comforter, even if it is pink.

*Erevu*
*Ghent*

> To: Jela
> Dove did a brilliant job.
> Any news on the professor?

> To: Erevu
> From: Jela
> Great!
> Request for information on Annemie Pauwels made by Professor Luc DeReu. Ghent University. Still working on it but his trail is relatively clear. Unfortunately I have to work backward and it takes time.
> CC's laptop didn't yield much. Nothing of note in the inbox. Small nest egg in the bank, but that's all. Not worth taking risks for.
> But she remains the key.

Erevu nodded as if Jela could see him. He had made the right decision sending Jela to Belgium for her last few years of school. Just like his mother had done with him. There were times when he had been unsure whether it was such a good idea, especially since he had to do things he wouldn't have done if he hadn't needed the money for her schooling.

But look now. Graduated from university. A good job. A girl to be proud of, even if she did arrive unbidden. He had only been eighteen, still at school here in Belgium. If Jela's mother hadn't died shortly after her birth and her parents hadn't refused to have anything to do with the baby, he would probably not have played much of a part in his daughter's life. He had taken her to the Congo and left her with his mother while he completed his training.

History repeated itself when Jela gave birth to Dove at the age of seventeen. But best of all was that they shared a dream. A dream that had come a long way.

Jela was only seven or eight in 1986 when that dream came into being. When he had gone to Uganda and met the spiritual medium Alice Auma Lakwena in person. What a remarkable woman. She was the one who had finally given his life direction.

Erevu had first heard of Alice Auma during church services at the mission where he went to school. The missionary, Brother Jonathan, told him about the Ugandan woman possessed by the spirit of an Italian captain who had drowned in the Nile during the First World War. She called the spirit Lakwena, the Messenger, and said he used her to communicate with nature and that nature responded.

He had asked Brother Jonathan *how* nature responded and the old man rattled on about the woman being possessed by demons because she misused the Bible while still worshipping ancestral spirits.

Erevu had remained silent. White people didn't understand. Wasn't Yeshua an ancestral spirit as well? Only one who was world renowned? About whom one read in the Bible?

No one had written about Motetela—the great ancestral spirit of the Tetela, he at whom one may not laugh—but he was a spirit every bit as important as Yeshua.

Erevu decided he had to know what the answer was that nature had given Alice Auma and he proceeded to find out. With great effort and at great cost, he crossed the border.

The price was high, but for the first time he truly understood his calling and realized there could be only one logical outcome. An outcome now in sight. He, Erevu, would be venerated as the architect of the ideal Congo. Jela would be his right hand and Dove his foot soldier.

Jela's view on how to realize the dream had since changed. But whichever way they turned their dream into reality, Cassandra Colijn had to lead them to Amelie de Pauw or, if the old woman happened to be dead after all, to the nkísi that had been taken unlawfully from him and from his progeny.

*Caz*
*Ghent*

Caz couldn't remember when last she had downed a beer so fast. Tieneke looked on with disapproval, but at least she had made her a somewhat dry ham-and-cheese sandwich.

When Caz took a second Stella from the fridge, Tieneke rolled her eyes to the ceiling.

"So tell me," said Caz, pushing away the plate. "How's Mother?"

"Her mind is reasonably sharp, but she's physically weak. She tires quickly, even from talking. You woke her with the racket you made with your suitcase, but she's asleep now. She seems calmer, now that she knows you're here. I think it would be best to give her until tomorrow before you meet with her. She needs to rest."

And what if she dies during the night? Caz couldn't help wondering. Then all would have been in vain. "I'll wait until she wakes up, but I'd like to see her today."

Tieneke gazed at Caz's empty plate for a moment, then sighed. "We'll see how she feels. What would you like to do in the meantime?"

Unpacking was not an option. There was no wardrobe, or even a chest of drawers. She would have to live out of her suitcase. "I'd like to take a shower, if possible."

"Of course, but try not to use too much water. I'll bring you a towel. The bathroom is …"

"On the first floor. Yes, I know, I've already found it. Had to pee, you know. Thanks." She swallowed down the last of the beer, put the plate in the sink and tossed the two empty bottles in the bin.

"No!" Tieneke clicked her tongue and took out the bottles. "We recycle. Flanders has been named the region with the most successful recycling program in all of Europe."

"Just show me where, and I'll recycle, but right now I'm going to fetch my bathroom things and a change of clothing."

"And please put the dirty dishes in the dishwasher. After you've rinsed them, of course."

Caz nodded patiently. "I will. Next time."

Thighs protesting and knees aching, she climbed the steep stairs. But the battle in her mind blocked out the pain she felt. A battle between reason and revolt. Between exhaustion and the rush of adrenaline.

You'll have to keep your wits together, Caz Colijn. Not be so touchy. It's no good. You have three more weeks ahead of you. Let reason prevail.

Well and good, O Sane One, revolt taunted her, but perhaps you should hide the razor blades. For your own sake. And stay away from knives and scissors. For Tieneke's sake.

*Erevu*
*Ghent*

Erevu jumped when his tablet pinged.

> From: Jela
> Dove must be at the Ghent University campus tomorrow and pretend to be a student. It's the start of the academic year. There will be a procession to the Aula.
>
> He must watch out for Luc DeReu in the procession. Tall, lean man, thick gray hair. Glasses.
>
> I attach a photo but it's not very clear. No contact for now, including eye contact. Just identify him and make sure DeReu notices him. Dove will be conspicuous, but once DeReu re-

> gards him as a student he'll keep doing so, even if he sees Dove repeatedly.
>
> DeReu is Plan B to get to the old woman if CC fails. Don't know yet how they are connected but he wouldn't have enquired in SA for nothing. Somewhere there must be a link. The year proves it.

Erevu smiled. What would he do without Jela?

*Caz*
*Ghent*

"You get your way. Mother wants to see you, but you're to greet her and that's all. She's tired. She's usually better in the morning. We'll have to see." Tieneke was no more morose than usual, but Caz got the idea she was reluctant to have her see Josefien today.

Did she have misgivings? But why? She was the one who had all but blackmailed Caz into coming, after all.

"I'm just going to the bathroom first." She was suddenly very nervous about facing Fien.

She pushed her fingers through her curls and made sure her mascara wasn't smudged. For the first time in a long while she took a good look at her face in the mirror. Not only to make sure she was presentable, but to see what she looked like. To others.

After the incident in Hermanus when the woman had confused her with Antoinette Kellerman, Caz had googled the actress. The woman had been right. The hair was the same. Her face was softer, though, the features not as strong as Kellerman's. And yes, Caz was considerably younger.

But the face at which she was staring now did not look young. It looked frazzled, and afraid. It was true, she *was* afraid.

Fien had never raised a hand to her. There had been no need. Her words hurt like no whip could. But Fien's sharp tongue was only one of the things Caz feared at this moment. What she feared most was what she was about to hear about her origins.

Caz took a deep breath. Surely she was strong enough to face up to an old woman just short of a hundred? A dying old woman, besides.

Tieneke opened the bedroom door. "Speak loudly and clearly. Her hearing is not very good."

When the door clicked shut, Caz was alone in the room with Fien.

If she hadn't known it was Fien, she would never have recognized her. Nothing remained of the full-figured woman with the sharp gaze. The deeply wrinkled cheeks were sunken, the face and hands bony. The watery eyes glinted, even paler than before. A few tufts were all that was left of her hair. In fact, the hair on her scalp seemed to have migrated to her chin. The teeth, grinning macabrely from a glass on the bedside table, accounted for the slackness of the mouth.

The woman she had feared just a moment ago was no more than a living cadaver. Yet she still carried an aura of authority. How it was possible, Caz couldn't fathom.

"Hello ... Mother." What else could she call her?

"Cassandra." She raised her hand slightly and beckoned Caz closer with a crooked index finger.

Caz obeyed.

"I don't have much time. Been waiting for you." She coughed drily and pointed at a glass of water next to the one with the teeth.

Caz held the glass to her lips, wiping the drops from the corner of her mouth when she indicated she'd had enough. Was it tenderness she felt? No, she wasn't that magnanimous. What she felt was more a sense of letting go.

Fien in the throes of mortality was not the woman she had known. She couldn't be angry with her. One quiet hateful thought seemed enough to push her over the edge.

"Your mother bribed me." She gasped. "To take you in." Another gasp. "I didn't realize. No amount. Of money. Is enough." This time a sigh. "To raise. Another woman's offspring."

Caz swallowed. Did she hear correctly?

"You destroyed. Our family." She gave another dry cough. "Never again. A happy family. Since Ammie Pauwels. With her big belly. Arrived." She closed her eyes, drew a shuddering breath.

Ammie Pauwels. The room tilted briefly. Caz's ears rang. Her birth mother had a name.

Caz was startled when a rattling sound came from the bed. She feared Fien was coughing or choking, until she realized the skin-clad skeleton was laughing.

"What's so funny?"

"Ammie. Who left you. And then Lilah came." The laugh became a cough, then turned into an anguished wheeze.

The door flew open and Tieneke rushed in. "Out, Cassie!" Tieneke grabbed an oxygen mask, turned on the tank and placed the mask on her mother's face.

Caz stood rooted to the spot. "What do you mean 'and then Lilah came'?"

"Verdomme! Can't you see you're upsetting her? Calm down, Mother, calm down. Out, Cassandra! Out, I said!"

Caz turned and left. Not because she was following Tieneke's orders, but because she couldn't stand the sight of the creature in the bed a moment longer.

She's old. She's senile. Forgive and forget. She's old, she's senile ...

Over and over Caz repeated the words to herself, like a mantra, but it didn't stop what she was really feeling. A stabbing pain. A dagger being turned and pushed in again.

Go ahead, fuck with me all you want, you old witch, she wanted to scream, but leave my daughter out of it!

# Nine

*Luc
Damme*

Tomorrow was the opening ceremony of the academic year. Every year it was a great to-do, which the first-years probably found exciting, but Luc just wanted to get it over with. Lectures commenced on Monday. His preparation had been done; the postgraduate students' assignments had been graded. One last blissful free weekend lay ahead.

He was going to use it to relax, but today he might just make a call or two.

For the time being he was assuming that Amelie de Pauw and Annemie Pauwels were the same person. Despite the death certificate. If it weren't the case, he would find out soon enough.

Discovering that their marriage was illegal, or even worse, possibly bigamous, would have been a huge blow to Jacq. Luc had found the answer to his initial question, but a series of new questions had ensued. Why hadn't Ammie divorced her first husband? Why had she left him? Had any children been born from their union?

If so, what had become of them?

And these questions were only the tip of the iceberg.

It would be preferable to get the answers from Ammie herself but he didn't want to upset her again, like the last time. Besides, he strongly doubted she'd take a call from him, never mind allow him to see her again. And then there was the matter of her memory that came and went.

That left Lieve. Why would she think there were other children? How much did she know? How much had she figured out from things Ammie had said when her memory was doing its veiled dance?

Only one way to find out.

"Lieve Luykens, good day?"

Luc sat back in his chair. "Good day, Lieve. Luc DeReu here."

"Professor?"

"I just want to know how Ammie is."

There was a short silence. "She's furious with me, Professor. I don't think I should even be talking to you. I need the job and your mother and I have come a long way. I don't want …"

"Ammie doesn't have to know, Lieve. I won't put your job in jeopardy. I give you my word. I'm just worried about her." It wasn't completely untrue.

Lieve gave a deep sigh. "I understand, but what I don't understand is why you're suddenly worried about her now, after all these years."

Lieve might not be a rocket scientist, but neither was she stupid. Proceed carefully, DeReu. Do you yourself even know why?

"I blamed her for the way she treated my father, Lieve. When I heard she was getting married again, well, what can I say? Besides, my father would never have forgiven me if I'd remained in contact with her behind his back." True, yes, but actually he was just a wimp who had wanted to get on with his life.

"Professor, I don't think there would be any point in developing a conscience now. I'm sorry I involved you. It was a desperate attempt to give Miss Ammie some purpose in life. It didn't succeed."

"Lieve, at my age one regrets a lot of things. Ammie haunts me. I would like to understand her better. I might get through to her. Perhaps I can think of a way to make up for abandoning her when I was an arrogant youngster. You must remember that I was barely twenty-one when she disappeared from my life, without warning or explanation. I was hurt. I couldn't discuss the matter with my father. He refused to talk about her and fell into a deep depression." The admission was unexpectedly painful.

Perhaps he could finally admit to himself that his anger hadn't been only about his father. He had been deeply hurt on a personal level as well. Ammie might not have been his biological mother, but she was his mother in every other sense of the word. He couldn't understand how she could turn her back on him with such ease. Maybe he had been too afraid to try to find out what had happened to her. Why she had left. Afraid of being hurt even more. Or was he just making excuses?

"What do you want to know?" Lieve asked after a long silence.

"You mentioned other children. I'd like to know more. Perhaps the answers are there. Are they still alive?" He gnawed on his lower lip while he waited. It was make or break.

"Me and my big mouth." She was quiet again. "I think there were two. Whether they're alive, I don't know. Remember, these are just assumptions I made while she was rambling, mistaking me for someone else."

"I understand, but anything could be important."

"Sometimes she calls me Fien. That happens when she's very confused. And out of sorts. It has something to do with a letter. Recently she gave me a furious look and said something like: 'Did you have to mention Cassandra? I don't want to know anything about her. Do you hear me? I don't want to know anything about César's spawn. Do you get that, Josefien Colijn?' And then she said: 'She might have come from my body, but not from my soul. She's nothing to me. I paid you to take her and raise her. You were greedy enough to agree. I don't owe you anything.' It was awful. She looked at me with such venom in her eyes. That's probably why I remember it so well."

César. Amelie de Pauw's husband was called César.

Cassandra. The prophetess who received her gift of prophecy from Apollo and, when she wouldn't return the love he felt for her, was cursed by him. No one would ever believe her prophecies.

Bingo.

Ammie's claim to have been present at the birth of her first husband's child made sense to him now. She was the mother. Could a mother really cut herself off from a child so completely? Evidently, she could.

"And the second child?"

"She mentioned another child only once. She called me Tabie … no, Tabia. Said I must make sure Elijah's child is well. When he's grown up, explain to him why his mother was forced to leave him."

"Elijah? I thought her first husband was called César?"

"I don't know who Elijah is. Maybe she was more confused than I had thought. That's all I know about the children. If I understood her correctly, mind you."

"César's last name?" Janssen might be a common name, but César wasn't. If he was César Janssen, at least there was less doubt that Ammie had once been Amelie de Pauw.

"I don't know."

"Do you happen to know where this Cassandra … I presume her last name is Colijn … was born?"

"Miss Ammie once said something about Fien being in South Africa. But I really don't think I should say anything more, Professor. I'm betraying someone I work for, but worse than that, someone I really care about. Good day."

There was no chance to say goodbye, or to try to keep her talking a little longer. Still, it had been a fruitful conversation.

Josefien Colijn. Cassandra—perhaps Colijn. César—perhaps Janssen. Tabia. Elijah. He wrote the names down, one below the other, and folded his hands behind his head.

South Africa. In her affidavit she had referred to a baby she had lost. Not true. She had paid one Josefien Colijn to raise the child.

Grote, gulle Griet.

Where in South Africa did this happen? Jacarandas. Ammie once showed him pictures in a magazine of jacaranda trees in full bloom. *Panorama*. The name of the magazine. The city was Pretoria.

She had also mentioned people who had helped her return to Belgium, but she was always vague about the details. She was ill when she arrived here, she had said. Was taken by ambulance directly from the plane to the hospital. He couldn't remember her ever saying what the illness was. Could it have been malaria? She'd contracted it in the Congo and had suffered relapses for years. The last time, if his memory served him correctly, shortly before he went to school.

Fine, what did he have? A thousand questions, but one overshadowed all the others. No, two. What had happened to Cassandra, presumably Colijn, presumably from Pretoria? And why did he want to know?

Because he wanted to understand Ammie, and the rift between her and his father. But that wasn't all. He was curious. The eternal student. Besides, his life was so incredibly dull that others' lives inevitably seemed more interesting than his own.

Curiosity aside, if his father had found out that Ammie had lied, not only about her name and marital status, but also about a child she'd fobbed off on someone else ... No wonder he had been shocked to the core. To a man who put honesty and integrity above all else, it would have been a fatal blow to hear what his "wife" was guilty of. A wife who had been a mother to his own child. Was that why he had forbidden her to make contact with any of them?

Ammie was never motherly in the true sense of the word, but she was good to her stepchild. He had never wanted for anything. She tended to his cuts and abrasions with kisses and plasters and always saw to it that he had had enough to eat and drink and that he slept warm.

In his teenage years she often defended him when his father was too strict. After he had left home he was always welcome to drop in and stay as long as he wished.

She was a good mother to him. But their relationship lacked true intimacy, real mother-son affinity. He could speak to her about most things, but it was as if her mind was elsewhere. As if she forced herself to seem interested, but never really was.

The conversation about the birds and the bees had never taken place. To his relief at the time. But when he looked back, it might have been a symptom of something that was lacking.

Of course his father had been hopeless with the father-son relationship. He was an introvert, caught up in his studies, his professorship and academic duties. The academic world was his universe, Ammie the morning and evening star in his personal constellation and Luc a comet that claimed sporadic attention.

He presumed Jacq and Ammie had sex but he never saw signs of it. For all he knew, his father could have been a eunuch and Ammie a virgin.

But she wasn't. She had given birth to at least one child—before or during 1961. There were probably only a few months between himself and the daughter who was given such an unfortunate name.

Lost in thought, Luc sipped his coffee, scarcely noticing it had grown cold.

Why had Ammie been scared of her first husband? Of her daughter? So scared that she remained in hiding for more than half a century? Three more questions Luc would like to learn the answers to.

Okay. Start at the beginning. Ammie was Amelie de Pauw, married to César Janssen. Political unrest broke out and she had to flee.

Had it really been only political unrest, as everyone had assumed? Or had she fled from her husband?

Why? How? He couldn't remember her ever telling him who had accompanied her. Her parents were long dead. Her mother died of blackwater fever when Ammie was nineteen and her father and stepmother four months after her wedding.

He looked at his notes. In an aircraft incident. An unusual way to die. He typed "Bakwanga" in the search box.

It was the original name of the town known today as Mbuji-Mayi, he discovered. Bakwanga was also the name of one of the biggest diamond mines in the DRC, formerly Zaire, and before that the Belgian Congo.

Luc read on, but what followed was merely an anecdote about a girl who had discovered an enormous diamond in a pile of mining waste in the Mbuji-Mayi district in the eighties.

Luc closed the internet page. He was wasting his time. The Congo was full of diamond mines and in the primitive circumstances of those years plane crashes were probably not unusual.

The question remained: How did Ammie travel from the Congo to Pretoria? Surely she couldn't have embarked on a weeks-long flight across a large tract of African soil on her own?

Another thing: How did she pay Josefien Colijn's bribe money? The money couldn't have come from a bank account. There was a document that certified her dead. She was living under an assumed name.

Cash? Had she carried it with her without being robbed? And what would Congolese francs have been worth in South Africa? Next to nothing. Belgian francs, not much more.

It didn't make sense. Raising a child was a lifelong task and, if Lieve's memory served her right, a task that a greedy woman had been prepared to take on. A greedy person wouldn't do it for a pittance.

*Ammie*
*Leuven*

"I'll see you tomorrow morning."

Ammie looked up at Lieve. For the past week she had deliberately been ignoring the meddlesome woman.

Lieve nervously wrung her hands. "Miss Ammie, please, can we make peace? I'm sorry the professor's visit upset you so much."

"Too late now." How dare Lieve disturb her equanimity like that?

"I was trying to do something good." Lieve seemed on the verge of tears.

Ammie gave a deep sigh. Lieve was right. They couldn't go on that way. "I know, Lieve, but talk to me first the next time you get a sudden urge to do something like that."

Relief showed in Lieve's eyes. "I will, Miss Ammie. Good day then. Until tomorrow."

"Good day, Lieve."

When she closed the door behind her, Lieve looked a good deal more cheerful than she had during the past few days.

She had reason to be upset with Lieve. Since Luc's unexpected visit the memories had been more persistent than ever. The worries as well. Why on earth did she tell him what had caused Jacq to chase her out of his life? But when Luc asked her so bluntly the answer simply popped out.

Not that she told him the whole truth. Only the bottom line.

Ammie closed her eyes, tired of fighting against the memories she tried to keep at bay.

When Tabia told her to get out of the country, to go to Southern Rhodesia or South Africa, Ammie didn't think she would survive the journey.

She was not only afraid of what might befall her along the way. She was afraid César would be waiting for her. Or track her down. He'd had more than enough reason, after all. And with his contacts, there was every chance that he would learn that her "body" had disappeared. He would reach the logical conclusion, though he might not guess that Tabia was the one who had saved her and robbed him.

Tabia. The woman with magical powers. The woman who knew things. Sometimes because she was shrewd and sometimes in ways Ammie couldn't understand. Her grandmother was said to have been a nganga.

Was Tabia still alive? There couldn't be an age gap of more than two years, either way, between the two of them, but life expectancy in the Congo was short. Especially for women.

*Ammie*
*Katanga*

"In Angola people will help you. But you must pay."

Ammie lowered her head into her hands. "With what, Tabia?" She peered through her fingers. "With my body?"

"La!" Tabia clicked her tongue. Ammie could see she was insulted.

"How then, Tabia?"

Tabia put her hand in César's canvas bag and brought out a bulky linen pouch. She held it out to Ammie.

Ammie's hands trembled when she untied the drawstring and opened the bag. She tilted it and shook out a number of stones in her hand. Even uncut, the dull gleam told her what she was holding.

When she looked up disbelievingly, Tabia nodded. "Almasi."

"God's truth, Tabia. Where did you find these?"

"I steal them." She smiled for the first time. "From César."

"How did you know? That César had diamonds? Where he hid them?"

"I know."

"Tabia, if he should find out ... He'll kill me."

"He will kill you anyway. I give you protection." She entered the hut again and came out with two wooden objects. The mask, Ammie noticed immediately, resembled her own face, but with scarification on the cheeks. The figurine looked like Tabia, highly pregnant and with the same scarification patterns she had on her body. But the proportions were wrong. The head was unusually big, though smaller than the swollen belly. The chief focus was the pregnancy. The breasts were distended, the legs oddly short. In all, the figure was about thirty centimeters tall. The craftsmanship was exceptional.

"Who made it?"

"My brother's child."

A boy of about eighteen, who had stuttered on the few occasions he had spoken to her. Whom she often caught gazing at her with soulful eyes until she grew uncomfortable. His name was Aron.

Ammie tried to stop Tabia when she put the two objects in the backpack. "What will I do with them?"

"Carry it in bag. The mask makes you strong. Tabia's baby keep your baby safe. It is the work of the nkísi. They also look after almasi."

"But the almasi ... You need them too. For your child."

She smiled. "I keep some for my child. There is enough." She grew serious again. "You will walk far. You must give them one by one. Never show more than one. Keep one in cheek. Always one with you. Suck on it. It takes thirst away too."

"I'll need my passport at the border," Ammie suddenly remembered.

Tabia shook her head. "My brother's child searched. He did not find it. People will help you. For the almasi. Keep nkísi with you. Always. Even if they are heavy. Nkísi keep you safe."

Ammie nodded, but she knew the kind of fear she felt could never be driven away by a talisman or two.

*Caz*
*Ghent*

"Mother has calmed down. She's asleep now."

Caz looked up when Tieneke entered the living room. The roughest edges of her anger and humiliation had been smoothed over. Only the feeling of powerlessness remained. She was looking for answers and she wanted them as soon as possible. Even if the woman who knew the answers was the one person Caz would prefer never to see again.

"I see Mother upset you as well. Tea?" Tieneke's expression was surprisingly sympathetic. As sympathetic, anyway, as Tieneke was capable of.

"Thanks, that would be nice." Caz followed her to the kitchen.

Tieneke switched on the kettle. With her back to Caz, she leaned against the counter and lowered her head.

"Your life must be hell." Caz involuntarily lifted her hand to place it on Tieneke's rounded shoulder, then dropped it again.

"She wears me out." Tieneke's blue eyes were watery when she turned. "I wish she would die and be done with it. I wish she had died ten years ago and got it over with. No, twenty years."

Caz stared at her, astounded.

"There. I've said it." Tieneke pulled a paper towel from the roll, dried her tears and blew her nose.

"No one can blame you for feeling that way, Tieneke. Least of all me. I would have lost my mind."

Tieneke's lower lip trembled. "Don't be nice to me. I hate you and that's not going to change."

"Hate is a strong word."

"Not nearly strong enough for what I feel towards you."

That bad? She hadn't realized. "Why do you hate me? Get it off your chest." Caz folded her arms.

Tieneke nodded. "Very well. It's come a long way, I must warn you."

"I have enough time."

"I was eleven when that woman came," she began. Her eyes were shut, as if the events were being re-enacted behind her closed eyelids. "She was highly pregnant. Worn out from suffering. Yet she was beautiful, despite everything. The gash on her forehead. The cuts and bruises covering her arms."

"Where did she come from? How did she end up with you?" The person Tieneke was talking about was her birth mother, yet to Caz she sounded more like a storybook character.

Tieneke opened her eyes. "She fled from the Congo. Through Angola and Rhodesia. In Nylstroom she stayed with people who helped refugees, but they could only take her in for a while. The man was a Dutchman and a baker, like Father. He knew Father from somewhere, contacted him and asked whether they could take the woman in, just until after the baby was born and she was able to travel. They were already putting up another refugee family, relatives of theirs, and couldn't keep her any longer. He told Father she could pay for her stay. She had means.

"Father discussed it with Mother. Initially she wouldn't hear of it, but the bakery wasn't doing well, even then, before there were shopping centres in the suburbs. There was a good bus service and people went to the city for their weekly or monthly shopping. And the well-known Hatfield Bakery was still the favorite, even though it was further away.

"Anyway, Father persuaded Mother. It was only for a few months and the extra income would be handy. Besides, the woman was Belgian and she was in trouble. Those were Father's arguments.

"Mother didn't care about Ammie Pauwels's Belgian roots, but the extra money would make life easier. At the time they didn't realize that 'means' and money weren't necessarily the same thing."

Caz frowned. Means? After fleeing through Africa?

"Ammie moved in," Tieneke continued. "Mother wanted to know when and how much she would pay, but Father said it had been sorted out. Father still had a say then. It was before Mother turned into the harridan she later became.

"Ammie kept to herself, but our privacy was affected, the household was disrupted. Mother began to change. I think the turning point was a conversation she had with Ammie. I overheard them talking in Ammie's room. Ammie was crying bitterly. When Mother came out, she was different. After that she was aloof toward Ammie and Ammie kept to herself even more.

"When her time came, Father took her to hospital. You were born. In those days women stayed in hospital much longer, and there were complications as well. You were born by Caesarean section and Ammie underwent a hysterectomy."

Caz felt reluctant sympathy for the woman. She must have been a wreck by then. The woman. It was her birth mother Tieneke was talking about, but she was still struggling to get used to the idea.

"The baby—you—were discharged a good while before Ammie. Mother had to take care of you. In the meantime Ammie fell into a deep depression—probably what's known today as postpartum depression. One day the hospital phoned. Ammie had disappeared."

Tieneke paused but Caz sensed there was more to come. And it wouldn't be good, just as nothing about this story was good.

"A day or so later she came home. Mother thought she looked feverish. Ammie denied it. She said she had to go back to Belgium but she couldn't take the baby along. From the canvas bag she had with her when she arrived and had left behind when she went to hospital, she took five diamonds. Uncut. Each about as big as a man's thumbnail."

Caz closed her eyes. She wasn't sure she wanted to know what was coming, but she steeled herself and looked at Tieneke.

"Mother could have the diamonds if she helped Ammie get to Belgium and undertook to raise you. Mother refused. What was she to do with rough diamonds, she wanted to know. Ammie laughed. 'Ask your husband, Mrs. Colijn,' she said. 'He has already sold two smaller ones quite profitably.'"

Caz didn't want to hear the rest, but she didn't stop Tieneke from describing in detail how she had been bartered as a baby. She just wanted it to be over.

"Mother phoned Father at the bakery. He dropped everything and came home. Well, you know how it ended. You stayed. As did Ammie's canvas bag, containing two appalling wooden objects and a few more diamonds. Father drove away with Ammie. How he succeeded in getting her to Belgium without documents, only he and she would know. I guess somewhere a diamond came into play. Back then the laws weren't nearly as stringent as today."

Caz wasn't sure whether Tieneke was referring to diamond dealing or procedures to leave the country. It didn't matter. Both, presumably.

"Of course the neighbors knew Mother was never pregnant and they must have seen Ammie around. There was a lot of gossip. One rumour was that you were Father's love child. But shortly after Ammie left we moved to Meyerspark, where no one knew us and everyone assumed you were the late-born child of the Colijns. We could buy our own house. Father opened the bakery at Silverton. The rest is history."

"And *this* is why you hate me? Because this Ammie woman made it possible for us to live more comfortably?" Caz asked when Tieneke stopped talking.

"No, because everything was different after you came," Tieneke said, ignoring the sarcasm. "Father and Mother were never the same again. They didn't trust each other, and they argued a lot. Father withdrew from us more and more. I used to get all the attention, but now you were there. Our family life changed completely and it wasn't for the better."

"I don't suppose the fact that none of it was my fault makes any difference," Caz said.

"I was a child. You came and changed everything. That's all I could see. Later I hated you because you were smart and pretty and didn't even appreciate it. Just took it for granted. I struggled at school. You barely opened a book, yet you fared well. By the time you went off to university, I had been working in the bakery for seven years."

"I got a scholarship," Caz reminded her.

"After Father's death," Tieneke continued as if she hadn't

been interrupted, "I got rid of the bakery, but I still had to look after Mother."

Hans's death shortly after Caz found out she was pregnant had been a shock. Neglected diabetes seemed to be the cause, but at the funeral she realized she was also being blamed for Hans's death.

"No man ever looked my way," Tieneke interrupted her thoughts. "At the time of Father's death you, on the other hand, had been married for a few months to a rich, handsome man and you were pregnant as well."

"Yes, and of course the marriage had a fairy-tale ending." The words tasted bitter in her mouth.

Tieneke switched on the kettle that had switched itself off some time ago.

"You had everything a woman could dream of—especially an old maid like me. And you threw it away. Why didn't you just admit you were raped? They would have come to terms with it."

Caz breathed deeply to try to remain calm. "And allow them to send away my child? Over my dead body."

Tieneke gave her a pensive look. "That's why I hate you most. You gave up a wonderful life in the lap of luxury and the love of a handsome man for a life of hardship with your child. Despite all the foreseeable consequences, you did the 'right' thing."

Caz shook her head. "A mother doesn't think of right and wrong, of rich and poor. A mother thinks only of what would be best for her child. I couldn't accept that the best thing for Lilah would be to be sent abroad and raised by strangers." That had been Andries's solution. Of course Hentie had agreed. She never found out what Magdel had thought.

Tieneke gave a derisive chuckle. "Are you telling me Ammie Pauwels was thinking of her child's welfare?"

Caz was silent for a long time. "Maybe she thought she was doing the right thing."

"But she wasn't, was she?"

"Evidently not. Goodnight, Tieneke, never mind the tea."

The walk up the stairs to the attic was a long, wearisome journey. Physically and mentally. She had been bartered for a few uncut diamonds. Wow. She supposed it could have been worse. Like being betrayed for thirty pieces of silver.

# Ten

*Erevu*
*Ghent*

It was the second night he couldn't sleep. But not because of the hard mattress in this miserable place where he had been staying for a while. The excitement was too much. For so long he had simply kept going. Trusted they would be successful—one day. That Yeshua would show him mercy. That Motetela would look after his descendant. And now it looked as if he was on the brink of success. As if "one day" had finally arrived.

He realized now that he had been a doubting Thomas. No longer.

The nkísi would give him the power he needed. Not only the power the nganga had invested them with, not only the forces activated in them to protect him and make him prosper. The scarification on the nkísi depicted his family tree, provided clear evidence that he was a direct descendant of Motetela.

This proof, together with Yeshua's order-creating commandments and the purification processes advocated by Alice Auma, would make him the ruler of the Congo and from there his influence would spread to the rest of Africa. And further.

And the spirit of his ancestor, N'Gongo Leteta, would be with him. Gongo, who had been tied up by white people and fired at all day without being injured. It was only when the traitors called in a Luba magician that they could kill him. And only because the man told them to take Gongo's nkísi from him and shoot him in the ear.

Like Gongo, he would be impervious to bullets, because he would have the power of the nkísi and his ancestors behind him. The blessing of Yeshua. The wisdom of Alice Auma.

He wondered whether the woman he was renting this room from would remember—when his success became known—that for a week or two she had harbored the mightiest African leader in the memory of mankind.

Would she still look at him with such disdain? So clearly consider him her inferior?

Perhaps he should not judge her so harshly. In her presence he played the role of a humble man from Africa.

She'd been reluctant at first to rent him the room. She was suspicious, but only until Jela transferred the money for a full month's rental. Amazing what people were prepared to do for money.

But she had still put him in the attic, charging him the same rent as for the other two much more comfortable rooms in the tall, narrow house. Even though both rooms were vacant when he arrived. Dove had offered him his room when he moved in this afternoon, but it suited him up here.

Maybe the roof amplified the sounds, for a while ago he had heard movement on the other side of the dividing wall between him and the house next door, where the woman had put her so-called sister.

He wondered if Cassandra Colijn knew her sister owned the neighboring house and rented out the rooms.

To think that only a wall was separating him from the woman who was going to help him assure his future. His own and that of the Congo.

*Ammie*
*Leuven*

Today the hours were melting into each other.

She kept dozing off. Her dreams were filled with tropical images.

During her waking moments memories assailed her, taking her back to that dilapidated hovel in the cité indigène.

The morning of her departure she discovered another reason why César would not allow her to live.

*March 1961*
*Ammie*
*Katanga*

Before daybreak Tabia helped Ammie put the canvas bag she had packed for her on her back. Two big portions of fufu—the doughy dish made of cassava and wrapped in banana leaves—and a bunch of bananas were her rations for the road. What she would live on when they were depleted remained to be seen.

"I did not want to tell you, but you must know. My brother's child also find this." Tabia held out a document. "Aron is a clever boy. He can read and write."

Ammie took the paper and read by the light of the candle. She had to read it three times before she realized what she was holding.

"My death certificate?" She looked at Tabia, mystified.

"The date is day after he try to kill you."

"I see that. Also that some doctor signed it and said I died of multiple injuries sustained during a riot." Slowly the implications got through to her.

There would be a copy of the certificate. It would have been submitted to the relevant authorities.

She no longer existed. Not here, nor in Belgium. She was standing here in the early morning darkness, breathing, but she was dead. Born in Antwerp, died in Elisabethville. Rest in peace. Live in hell.

Taking leave of Tabia was not an emotional moment. Fear dominated all other emotions Ammie could possibly feel and Tabia was clearly relieved that her duty as a Samaritan was over. In the end they remained two women from two totally different worlds.

"Go well," Tabia said.

"You know I'm grateful. Very grateful."

Tabia nodded.

Ammie hesitated, then asked. "Why? Really."

"You know." Tabia looked her in the eye. Challenged her. Rubbed her extended belly pointedly.

The truth dawned on Ammie. It didn't shock her as much as she would have thought.

"You go well too. I wish you the best." Even though you are carrying my lawful husband's child. Even though the child was obviously fathered before he found out about Elijah and not meant as punishment for me. You were César's whore, for who knows how long.

That was how Tabia had known where César lived. Tabia had probably lain with him in the house Ammie had considered hers. But how Tabia had found out about the uncut diamonds was a mystery. César would not have told her. Had Tabia or one of her relatives spied on him? Spied on them both? The thought sent a shiver down her spine.

The irony was blatant. César's whore saved the life of César's whoring wife. Not for Elijah's sake after all, but out of hatred for César. Because he had rejected Tabia when she had fallen pregnant and robbed her and her family of an income.

That was the greatest irony. César had tried to kill her, but indirectly he was responsible for the fact that Ammie was still alive. Despite the death certificate issued for her.

*Caz*
*Ghent*

Had she done Lilah a disservice by defying Andries Maritz? Caz wondered as she tried to get comfortable in her bed.

Yes, Lilah was a lovely young woman. Yes, she was super successful. But wouldn't she have been that anyway? Just achieved it more easily?

Possibly. But in the days following the birth, Caz had firmly believed she was doing the right thing for herself and her child. In the midst of her despair, she had known she was choosing a hard road. Just not how hard.

Though she often wondered in those first few months of her marriage whether she had made a mistake, there were good things besides the frustrations.

The Maritzes had been popular people in the district. Andries was a well-respected man and Magdel a queen bee. The farming community had welcomed Caz as the newest member of the Afrikaner elite, even though there were envious looks from a number of young girls. Hentie had been regarded as quite a catch.

For the first time in her life she began to feel she belonged, even though it was as Hentie's wife, and Andries and Magdel's daughter-in-law, and not in her own right. She eagerly soaked up the Afrikaner identity that she'd inherited from the Maritzes. Before, she had been neither Belgian nor Dutch, and had not felt herself to be properly South African either.

There was much that she questioned about the Afrikaners, but having to forfeit her opinions in order to belong seemed a small price to pay. Besides, she'd never had very strong opinions. At least not at first.

Andries was a true Afrikaner and until that year he had been a staunch Nationalist. The year 1983 was a year of landmines and car bombs. Arson too, at Pelindaba and elsewhere. Farmers beyond the Soutpansberg drove around in bombproof pick-ups, especially on the road next to the new border fences on the near side of the Limpopo River. In shopping centres countrywide every handbag was inspected, and customers were body-searched for safety reasons.

When Prime Minister P.W. Botha announced he was going to ask the nation for a mandate to institute measures of reform and power sharing, Andries joined the Conservative Party, though he had no time for either of its kingpins. Power sharing was not an option. Whites ruled over everyone who wasn't white, and that was the end of it.

Yet Andries treated his farm workers well. For those days, anyway. No one went hungry. Staple food was provided, they could grow their own maize and occasionally he shot an impala and shared out the meat. On Sundays there was a church service in an old barn. Andries called at their huts on a regular basis to bully the people into relatively orderly living conditions but also to find out whether they had any problems.

Magdel did a lot for the women. She helped with nearly every childbirth. She nursed the sick, brought them medicine and made sure hygienic standards were kept up.

She taught the women to knit and after a while launched a project providing the children of the district with sweaters. Which was slightly ironic, because in the far north day temperatures below thirty degrees Celsius were rare and considered cool. In winter the temperature could plummet at night, but it seldom went below ten degrees. By that time the children were in bed, snug under blankets provided by Andries and Magdel.

All was well in Andries's kingdom. And when Hentie, after they had paid a secret visit to the gynaecologist in Louis Trichardt, announced that their honeymoon had yielded a profit, everyone was overjoyed.

An heir was on its way. A boy would be first prize, but a girl was also good. Time was on their side, after all. Sandra was young and had good hips and full breasts that could provide for many children. She was indeed an excellent incubator.

When Magdel thawed out in the joy of the moment and confessed to Caz that now she could at last stop feeling guilty for having given Andries only one son, Caz understood why Hentie had had to take a wife whose fertility seemed beyond question.

Andries arranged an ox braai and just about everyone in the Soutpansberg district was invited. Whites only, of course. Caz didn't have much part in the celebration. The aroma of barbecuing meat confined her to the bathroom.

But for the first time in her life she had made someone proud. Andries was even prouder than Hentie.

Caz realized she would have to think wider than herself and Hentie and the marriage she had dreamed of for them. She would have to close her eyes to Hentie's inability to stand up to his father and her own growing anxiety about what being an Afrikaner might ask of her. She had to consider her child's future. As a Maritz, it was bound to be a bright one.

Hans's unexpected death when she was five months pregnant came as a shock. Hentie took her to Pretoria, where they stayed at a hotel. Every morning Hentie dropped her at the Meyerspark house. In the evenings he fetched her without being invited in. Fien's insinuation that the tension caused by Caz and her in-laws had contributed to Hans's premature death was hurtful. But she would shake it off, once she was back at Liefenleed. Life went on.

Back in the north, Caz settled in and gradually began to feel more at home. Once the baby arrived, she thought, the last few irritations would disappear. As a mother, she would be too busy to pay attention to Andries's quirks, Hentie's servile attitude towards his father and Magdel's silences. She would also have more bargaining power, especially if the baby was a boy. Maybe she could even convince Andries that she and Hentie should have their own home. A baby would complicate their present living arrangements.

Rain was scarce in the remote bushveld, but on the afternoon of October the eighth there was a heavy thunderstorm. A cloudburst. Within minutes the dirt roads were impassable. The storm blew over, but the rain kept pouring down.

At seven that evening Caz's waters broke. By that time the Nzhelele River was in flood and so were the tributaries that were usually nothing but sandy riverbeds. The farm was cut off from the outside world. There was no other way; the baby would have to be born on the farm.

Caz wasn't worried about where the birth would take place—Magdel was an experienced midwife, after all. But she *was* afraid of giving birth. It seemed impossible for a child to be squeezed all the way through her pelvis—good hips or not.

But the hips proved to be good after all. The labor went as smoothly as was possible with a first delivery. Just before twelve the baby slipped out, wet and miserable-looking, at the very moment the rain stopped rattling on the tin roof.

The silence was deafening. Magdel looked at her grandchild, horror-struck. She thrust her into Caz's arms and fled the room. Exhausted as she was, Caz was the one who had to help the baby take its first breath.

The muscles in Caz's chest contracted as always happened when she remembered that night. A night that should have brought a double blessing. Good rains and the birth of a first grandchild at Liefenleed.

But the rain did huge damage when a dam wall broke in the early hours, and the heir was not only unwanted, but an abomination in the eyes of her grandfather. She saw that in Hentie's eyes, she was guilty of the worst betrayal a woman could commit. Especially an Afrikaner woman.

*Ammie*
*Leuven*

Ammie wasn't sure whether she had woken up and remembered or whether she'd been dreaming. She was no longer in her dark bedroom in the early hours of morning. Neither was she in Katanga. She was back in that awful suburban house in Pretoria, with its smell of boiled cabbage and burned rice, the night her waters broke.

She had been dreading the birth, but she also felt relieved that the time had come. At last she would know whether she would love or hate the child.

During her flight she had endured a lot. She and Aron had

lived in permanent fear. They'd had to trust complete strangers. Mostly it had worked out, but sometimes not. The shelter they could find was mostly in appalling locations. Hunger and thirst were their constant companions. It was a miracle that she hadn't lost the child during their journey.

She didn't remember the details. One day merged into the next. By the time she arrived at the Colijns, the journey was shrouded in a haze of suffering.

What she did remember about those terrifying days was the inner conflict she endured. On a physical level she had fled so that César could not get hold of her. On an emotional level she hovered between fear that she wouldn't survive and fear that she would, only to find out that César was the baby's father.

That night she realized that the moment of truth had arrived.

Fien handed her the prepacked suitcase and Hans took her to hospital.

The night was endless. It was a difficult delivery. Much more difficult than the first one. Probably because of internal injuries caused by César—as Tabia had predicted. At last the doctors decided on an emergency Caesarian section, followed by a hysterectomy.

The pain and discomfort when at last she regained consciousness after the operation, the utter exhaustion and empty feeling faded before her eagerness to see the child.

"A perfect little girl," the midwife said, smiling, and held out the crumpled little creature.

It took only one glance to see the baby was César's. The child of a murderer, a monster. A child that had already mutilated her body and would go on to crush her spirit, just as César had.

Repelled, she turned her back on the midwife and began to sob as if she would never stop. The doctors attributed it to depression after the difficult birth, the operations, the pain she was suffering and the knowledge that there would be no other children.

But none of that mattered to her. The physical pain was

overshadowed by the pain of the knowledge: the child for whose sake she had suffered countless ordeals during her flight, the child for whose sake she had kept going way past her true physical and mental capabilities, was not Elijah's.

She had been forced to give up her first child because it was Elijah's. She couldn't bear to look at this one because it was César's.

She knew she would have to sacrifice blood of her blood. Because of César's blood. She knew she could never love the child. Knew she would do the child a grave injustice if she kept her. It was no excuse, it wasn't honorable, but it was a fact.

"Ma'am, we have to put your baby to the breast," the sister reprimanded her when she kept refusing to touch the child.

"My milk will poison her. It's filled with hatred," Ammie said and believed it.

The result, other than the sister's shock and incredulity, was an injection. One that mercifully put her to sleep for a very long time. They didn't bring her the child again but evidently gave her to Fien. She didn't care where the child was, as long as she didn't have to see her.

And she didn't see her again, not even when she was negotiating with Fien and Hans. Just heard the mewling sounds from the room that had formerly been hers.

The child had probably been laughing at her, knowing vengeance would be sweet. By the time Ammie landed in Brussels she had mastitis and was delirious with pain.

# Eleven

*Friday, September 19*
*Luc*
*Ghent*

Ghent was a madhouse, as always this time of year. The tourists hadn't left yet and the students were pouring in, filling up every nook and cranny. Fortunately, Luc had a reserved parking spot. One less misery to contend with.

He washed his hands and rinsed his face in the restroom before he headed for the Commissiezaal. There was a press conference at a quarter to two and the academic procession would start along its planned route at a quarter to three.

He had to push all other matters aside. Focus on today and forget about Ammie, the daughter she had left behind in Africa and the mystery of how she had paid Josefien Colijn to raise her child.

The walk from the Universiteit Forum to the Aula would be a sweaty affair in this unseasonable heat, even though it was only half a kilometer. And the Aula wouldn't be much cooler.

His father would probably have had a few things to say about the program. A female rector would have been bad enough, but two female professors were acting as speakers. In fact, all the other speakers, except for the Governor of West Flanders, were women.

It didn't bother him. Women in the academic world were often more proficient, more dedicated and a lot less egotistical than their male counterparts.

He hesitated on the threshold of the room. There was a buzz of voices and the occasional sound of polite laughter. Somewhat reluctantly he joined the throng.

The gathering in the Commissiezaal had nothing to distinguish it from similar occasions in previous years. He had to duck out of the way a few times to avoid the video camera. He had no desire to be on film.

The procession was a jolly affair with roadside kiosks and street musicians, yet it was still ceremonious. Leading it were two scepter bearers in white bibs, followed by the rector, Professor Anne de Paepe, and the highest office bearers. Then came the ordinary professors, followed by the rest of the staff, adhering to a strict academic hierarchy.

Of course there were a few students brandishing banners to protest against the increase in registration fees, but that was part of the tradition. One of the banner-wielding fellows lost his footing on the steps just as Luc walked by, but soon righted himself.

With his finely chiseled features and well-proportioned frame, the youngster was sure to be a hit. Women students tended to go crazy for male students of exotic origin.

In the Aula there was the buzz of muted voices, the sound amplified by printed programs fanning faces. But when Professor De Paepe began to speak, the noise died down.

Though the rector delivered an inspiring message, Luc found his mind wandering back to the young man with the banner and from there to the year he had spent at Stellenbosch. The students there had been so much livelier and bolder—in their body language, the look in their eyes, the sound of their voices. But aggression was swifter and harsher over there. You saw that in their eyes and their body language too, and heard it in their voices.

No, Stellenbosch lay far behind him. Let him focus on the speakers of the moment instead. His fascination with Africa and especially South Africa was hopelessly romanticized anyway.

*Caz*
*Ghent*

Caz feared she was losing her mind. It was afternoon and she was still trapped in this place Tieneke called a home. It was a cage, furnished in somber dark-wood furniture, the windows draped with heavy, dark curtains. A cage that smelled of cooking, antiseptics and disease, and felt damp because it lacked fresh air and sunlight.

In Fien's room on the floor above, the angel of death was waiting with ancient patience while the grandfather clock in the living room ticked audibly toward the final hour.

Caz wanted nothing more than to flee, but she couldn't leave Tieneke, who had been up all night, trying to relieve Fien's shortness of breath.

Caz had washed the dishes, done the laundry, ironed, swept and dusted where there was hardly a speck of dust. She had texted Lilah, composed an email that she couldn't send because she didn't have an internet connection and didn't want to bother Tieneke. Made tea. Made coffee. Fixed lunch. Washed dishes again.

She went upstairs. "Tieneke?" she called softly at Fien's door.

Tieneke came out, closing the door behind her. Her eyes were red, the eyelids swollen.

Caz felt guilty but pressed on. "I have to get out for a while. Is there something I can get you from the corner shop?" It was no good offering to relieve Tieneke. For one thing, she didn't know what to do and, secondly, Fien would have a fit. In a manner of speaking.

Tieneke rubbed her eyes. "Milk. Butter as well. I'll just get my purse."

"I've got money. It's the least I can do. No improvement?" She nodded in the direction of the door.

"Slight. The intervals are getting longer."

Caz nodded. "I won't be gone long."

"If I were you, I wouldn't come back."

Caz looked at her, surprised.

"Go now." Tieneke made a shooing motion with her hand. "And you don't have to hurry back. There's nothing you can do here."

Caz didn't hesitate a moment longer.

The air outside might not be unpolluted, but it was a good deal fresher than the air inside the house.

She walked past the shop. Past the next block of houses. At the bus stop she turned left and walked another street block or two. She had to stretch her legs. Draw air into her lungs.

Back at the bus stop, she saw a man and a woman, each dragging a big suitcase, come to a halt some distance ahead of her. More people who didn't know how to travel light. It made her feel slightly better about her own inability.

The man pressed the doorbell of the house on the corner. Moments later the door opened and a man in his early thirties came out.

He greeted them cordially in Flemish, took the woman's suitcase and motioned them inside.

The door closed.

A guesthouse? There was no sign. It looked like every other house in the row, slotted together like Lego blocks.

Caz sighed and walked on. Even if it was one, she couldn't afford it, no matter how desperately she wanted to escape from Fien and Tieneke's aura.

At the shop she bought milk, butter and splashed on a bottle of wine. She wouldn't even try to work out what five euros were in rands. At this moment it was the medicine she needed, whatever the price. She bought chocolate for Tieneke.

There were no shopping bags. Not even for sale. She walked back with the items she had bought in her hand and the bottle of wine tucked under her arm.

She took a deep breath before inserting the key. For a long moment she stood motionless, looking up into the grayish blue sky.

A movement in the house next door drew her attention. A curtain stirred, as if it had just been drawn. Nosy neighbors, she decided. You find them everywhere.

Tieneke stood in the kitchen, holding a cup of tea.

"Is she better?" Caz opened the fridge and put away her shopping before she turned.

Tieneke's face seemed carved out of wax. "It's over."

"Over?" It took a fraction of a second before she realized what Tieneke meant, but still she could not take it in.

"I've just phoned the undertakers. The hearse is on its way." Tieneke's shoulders began to shake. Caz reached out to comfort her when she realized that Tieneke wasn't crying. She was laughing. She threw back her head. "It's over. Oh, thank heaven, it's over!" she said.

Caz closed her eyes. She understood Tieneke's relief. She also understood that the laughter might be hysteria—the result of pent-up tension—rather than happiness. What she didn't understand was why she had to come all this way just for Fien to scotch her quest for the truth.

How the hell was she going to find out more about her birth mother now? Whether she was still alive? Who and what she is or was? Ammie Pauwels. That was all she knew. Belgium might be a small country but it still had more than eleven million residents.

Good grief, how callous could one get? The woman who had raised her was dead and all she could think of was how it would complicate her life. But she would be lying if she told Tieneke she was sorry for her loss. Or sympathized. Fien was too old and decrepit for anyone to see her demise as anything but a relief. To Fien herself, but especially to Tieneke.

Tieneke's laughter vanished as suddenly as it had come. "I loved her. In spite of everything. Really. Except for the past five years. It's been hell." A sob erupted. "I couldn't carry on anymore, Cassie, I just couldn't." She looked at Caz with tears in her eyes. "I must thank you. You gave me the courage to do it."

Caz turned ice-cold. She gulped. "Do what, Tieneke?"

Tieneke avoided her gaze. "When I heard the door close behind you, I switched off the oxygen cylinder. Left the room. Shut the door, went outside and sat in the garden. That's all."

"And then?" Caz wasn't sure she wanted to know, but what else could she say?

"When I went back in, she was gone." Tieneke sighed. "For five years I've been wishing she would die. And it took only twenty minutes. So easy. So quick."

*Luc*
*Ghent*

After the official proceedings were over, the guests gathered around tables laden with refreshments and a counter where pints of beer and wine by the glass were available. Luc made his way through the crowd, looking for the exit. This wasn't his kind of thing. Besides, during the speeches he had thought of a plan to find out more about Cassandra, presumably Colijn.

Someone grabbed his arm. "Had enough?"

He looked down at his colleague Laura Lammens, smiled and nodded before trying to ease out of her grip.

But she held on. "How about a drink at the Graslei? We could discuss the VGK program."

His instinctive reaction was to refuse. He wanted to get home. But he and Laura would be working together this year and he would have to stand in for her for a few months while she was away on a research trip. They would have to talk sometime.

Anyway, he would have to take care that finding out more about Ammie and her daughter didn't become an obsession. Especially not at the start of the academic year. He had to focus on the students and his other commitments and decide on a topic for his next academic article.

"Fine. Shall we walk?" Their destination was about four hundred meters from the Aula. He could take a tram back to his car.

Laura nodded and fell into step beside him. She was a rather plain but likeable woman in her forties. They got on well at work but had no social contact, other than the occasional small talk at a compulsory cocktail party or an event of the Vlaamse Geschiedkundige Kring, to which they both belonged. This year they were both serving on the VGK board.

The cafés at the Leie River waterfront were crowded but they managed to find a table at De Witte Leeuw. Boats filled with tourists cruised up and down the river. Students laughed and chattered. Visitors took photos.

Luc felt stuffy in his suit. He loosened his tie and was on the point of pulling it over his head when he remembered he was in female company.

"Do you mind?" he asked.

Laura laughed. "Of course not. Remove your jacket as well, if you wish. The weather is so lovely."

Gratefully he complied, and rolled up his sleeves. There, now he could think again.

While they were waiting for the kriek beers they had ordered, they talked about Anne de Paepe's speech. When the cherry-red drinks arrived, they spoke about the student representative who had stood her ground in front of the formidable audience.

"In my day I wouldn't have dared," laughed Laura. "I was much too reserved."

"Yet now you face hundreds of students every day."

"That's different. I don't have to impress anyone, just share my knowledge, give guidance and hand out assignments. They're children, compared to me. The student representative had to address her superiors."

It was not what could be considered a riveting conversation, yet the companionship was pleasant. At least it got his mind off the mystery surrounding Ammie, which was exhausting as well as frustrating. "Another one?" he asked as she drained her glass.

She smiled. "Don't mind if I do." Was it his imagination or were her cheeks a little flushed?

*Caz*
*Ghent*

"There's nothing you can do here, Cassie. You'll just be under everyone's feet," Tieneke said when the hearse stopped in front of the house. "Take a bus and explore the city. It's such fine weather. It will take your mind off things."

Relief washed over Caz. "Are you sure?"

Tieneke nodded. "I've been handling Mother's affairs for years. I'll handle this last one as well." For a change, there was no reproach in her voice.

"Where would you suggest I go?" asked Caz as the doorbell rang.

"Ask the bus driver to drop you at the Korenmarkt stop. From there you can walk in almost any direction. There are beautiful old buildings all around, and hundreds of street cafés. The most popular ones are at the Graslei. Have something to eat. I'm not cooking tonight."

Caz didn't have a clue what a "lei" was, let alone one made of grass, but anything seemed like a good option if it meant she could get away for a while. She hurried upstairs. When she came back down with her handbag over her shoulder, she heard voices coming from Fien's bedroom.

She was through the door before Tieneke could change her mind. She knew there was a bus every ten minutes. Two people were waiting at the stop. She recognized them as the couple she had seen earlier, entering the house on the corner.

"... and the bathroom is lovely. And clean! We were really lucky," she heard the woman say.

"I told you sharing the facilities wouldn't be so bad." The man smiled. "Not at that price."

"Excuse me for interrupting, but that place where you're staying, is it a guesthouse?" Caz asked in English.

The woman gave her a friendly glance. "No, not quite. My husband found a website where you can find lodgings at a reasonable price because you're staying in your landlady's home and don't have a private bathroom. Air B&B. Less than thirty euros per night, and we have a large roof terrace as well.

The arrival of the bus put a stop to the conversation.

"Thanks for the information," Caz managed to say before they got on. She fumbled in her wallet to find the two euros she needed. The bus pulled away while she was still zipping up her handbag and she sank down in the first available seat.

Hardly an hour had elapsed since Fien died and she was playing at being a tourist. The thought made Caz morbid. How was it possible that Fien's death had so little effect on her? It seemed unreal. Yes, for decades she had borne a grudge against the woman who had raised her, but that wasn't all. Fien's death left no gap in her life whatsoever. Except for the missed opportunity to find out more about Ammie Pauwels.

She wondered how Tieneke felt. How she would feel when reality struck home. Not only about Fien's demise but about the fact that Tieneke had helped her cross over.

Strictly speaking, it was probably not murder. Caz would have been surprised if Fien had lived another week. But it wasn't euthanasia either. Tieneke had done what she had done, not to release Fien from further suffering, but for her own sake. Tieneke had always been impatient, keen to finish what had to be done. But expedite her own mother's death?

Speeding up her death was the least of it. Caz couldn't believe that Tieneke had simply closed the door and gone outside. Left Fien to battle the angel of death on her own. Made her go through the valley of the shadow of death alone. Or whichever cliché could be dredged up to say she had left her mother to her own fate. Okay, Mother, die now and do it on your own. No last words of comfort, no last whispers of love, no final squeeze of a hand. Just a closed door, you, and death. All alone and deliberately orchestrated.

The thought itself was bad enough, but now that she knew how Fien had died, did it make her an accomplice? She could report it, of course. Where? What would she say? My sister who isn't my sister moved forward the death of my mother who isn't really my mother by a few days, at most. Throw her in prison, even though she sacrificed her whole life for the bitter, demanding old bitch.

It wouldn't bring Fien back to life.

Besides, was Tieneke's action any worse than Fien's heartless decision to raise a child in exchange for diamonds? Was it any worse than Ammie Pauwels's resolve to barter her own child out of her life, heart, and mind?

She supposed she should be grateful Ammie Pauwels hadn't left her at the door of an orphanage. Or dumped her in a garbage bin. Well, thanks for nothing.

And thanks to Tieneke, she wouldn't find out anything more. All she had heard from Fien was how she regretted the barter, and the name of the woman. Tieneke could have told her the name on the phone.

Tieneke knew more than she'd been willing to admit at first. She had gained more information from Tieneke than from Fien.

"Korenmarkt, Mevrouw," the bus driver interrupted her thoughts.

Caz got out hastily. She was certainly not much of a tourist, she admitted to herself. She had been so wrapped up in her thoughts that she had not learned a single thing about Ghent since she got on the bus.

Enough of that. She was going to focus on her surroundings and forget the past.

When she looked around her, she began to realize where she was. Six thousand miles from home. But that wasn't the point. She was not only in another country; she was in another world. A world with buildings erected long before Jan van Riebeeck established his little refreshment post at the Cape of Storms.

She wandered, amazed, without noticing where she was going, where she turned left or right. She marveled at the Oude Vismijn with Neptune towering over the gateway, trident in hand. At a row of buildings, nestled snugly side by side, yet none of them similar. At a medieval castle whose bulky turret could be seen behind the gables of houses that looked as if they had been drawn on graph paper.

She bought "echte Gentse neuzen" at an odd wooden cart and got only a few of the cone-shaped sweets for two euros. The soft filling under the brittle crust had a raspberry taste—extremely sweet, but delicious.

At the Café 't Galgenhuis Caz sat down and ordered a beer. A pilsner, to be on the safe side. She had no knowledge of the myriad beers available.

From there she wandered on. Around the next corner she came across the Graslei. Not a blade of grass to be seen. It turned out to be a street forming a quay on the right bank of the Leie River.

It was crowded. There were boats on the river that looked more like a canal, people under umbrellas, a street musician with his guitar case open at his feet, waiters weaving their way between countless tables. She walked across the bridge decorated with baskets of flowering geraniums and petunias. Flat-bottomed boats crammed with tourists passed under the bridge. To the right she spotted the turret of the medieval castle a street or two higher up, keeping vigil over the colorful display. She couldn't take her eyes off the scene.

Never mind another country, it felt as if she were on another planet.

*Luc*
*Ghent*

Strange that certain people are just so much more conspicuous than others.

Some for obvious reasons. Like the bearded young man with the guitar on the harbor wall. Or the woman with the shrill, irritating laugh a few tables away. But then someone comes along, like the woman with the long, curly gray hair crossing the bridge at that moment, her head tilted back, her gaze moving from one gable to the next.

The hair was unusual and she was quite a bit taller than average, but that was not what had caught his attention. Neither was it the slim figure and the pert breasts. It was the visible wonder, the pleasure she took from her surroundings, that made him notice her. As if she was taking everything in, absorbing her surroundings, not just looking around and mentally ticking off sights on a list.

There was something else too, something he couldn't quite put his finger on. Something about the way she walked. As if she moved more freely, with a lack of restraint, as if her shoulders were attached more loosely to her body than those of other people.

He was sorry when she disappeared around the next corner.

Opposite him Laura was talking about the Eerste Bach- en Ouderavond the VGK was planning for October 1, to provide first-year bachelor students and their parents with information on history as a field of study. It was a follow-up to her story about the VGK's Godparents' Evening on September 30. Before she could launch into a story about whatever the VGK was planning next, he ordered their third kriek. The last one, he told himself.

"What made you decide to specialize in colonialism?" Laura asked, the subject of the VGK mercifully exhausted.

"My father's field was medieval history. Contemporary history was the furthest I could get away from that, so I chose it. My stepmother spent a large part of her life in the Belgian Congo. It interested me, hence colonialism."

Laura kept the questions coming. He answered where he could and as much as he was prepared to. From the corner of his eye he saw the woman with the long, curly hair return from the direction of the Gravensteen Castle. As his gaze drifted away from Laura, he noticed a young man behind the tall woman. One who looked a lot like that afternoon's banner carrier.

Was it his imagination, or was the guy following the woman? When she stopped, he fell back. When she walked on, he moved forward as well.

The woman moved off in the direction of the Korenmarkt and the young man followed.

Jean-Claude van Damme might have known what to do, but Luc didn't. There was no script. And no reason to interfere.

Opposite him, Laura prattled on.

# Twelve

*Caz*
*Ghent*

Caz jumped when someone tapped her on the shoulder.
"Good afternoon, Caz. It's just me. My apologies if I frightened you. I didn't mean to." His formal way of speaking still surprised her; the smile was still gleaming white.

"It's fine. I was lost in thought. What a coincidence …" She searched her mind for his name.

"Njiwa," he helped her. "Not really. When the weather is like this, all of Ghent is here at the Leie. It's the best place to be. Did you manage to find your way after Dampoort?"

"Yes, no problem." She wasn't going to bore him with the details of the exhausting final leg of her trip. It felt like years ago instead of only a few days. Hell no, not even days, she realized, just yesterday.

Nijwa dug in his pocket and took out a five-euro note. "I've been looking out for you. I hoped I'd run into you." He held out the money.

Caz shook her head. "I told you, you earned every cent."

He returned the note to the pocket of his jeans. "Okay, at least I tried to repay you."

"I never asked, what are you doing in Ghent? Just a visit to your grandpa?" Caz asked when he made no attempt to leave.

He laughed. "It's going to be a long visit. I enrolled at the university. First year. Today was the official opening of the academic year."

"Why here?"

"My mother went to school in Ghent and studied here as well before she got a job in South Africa. She was only seventeen when I was born, so my grandpa decided to send her here. Lubumbashi isn't a good place to get an education, and she was smart. He also wanted to get her away from my father, who didn't have much ambition. He later died in the civil war. In 1996, when I was barely a year old."

"That's very sad."

Nijwa shrugged. "My grandpa was there for me. He raised me until my mother could get her life back on track. A process that included a brief marriage here in Belgium."

"Where is Lubumbashi?" She steered the conversation away from his tragic past.

"In the DRC. It's where my grandpa is from. His father was Belgian. It was in the time when it was still the Belgian Congo, or shortly afterwards. His mother, my great-grandmother, belonged to an indigenous ethnic group."

The Congo again. Yet it was understandable. Belgians were historically linked to the Congo. "How did you end up in South Africa?"

"After her studies, my mother got a job at the DRC Embassy in Brussels. It helped that she could speak Lingala and French. Besides Flemish, of course, which she learned over here.

"Anyway, after a year or so she wanted to return to Africa. Anywhere but the Congo. It was rough there. As a Belgian citizen, she was transferred to the Belgian Embassy in Johannesburg. She brought me from Lubumbashi when I was about ten and I continued my schooling there. Luckily we both missed the whole apartheid debacle." He winked. "But wait, I was actually looking for a friend."

Caz nodded. "Well, a first-year student has a lot on his plate. What are you studying, by the way?"

"I'm starting with a BA, but my real interest is politics." He grinned. "Someone has to knock the Congo into shape. It might as well be me." He gave one of his mock salutes and, with a "have to run," he vanished into the crowd.

*Luc*
*Ghent*

Luc gave a wry smile. He had definitely read too many crime novels and watched too many action movies. What did he think was happening, here, among hundreds of people?

As it turned out, there had been nothing sinister about the dark-skinned fellow following the attractive woman. She clearly knew him. Her friendly smile while they were talking was proof enough, even though she had been visibly startled when he tapped her on the shoulder.

And off she went. A pity. He'd enjoyed watching her— the way she walked, taking in the scenery, the way her hair moved. He'd been trying to discover what was so different, so fresh about her.

Verdorie. If anyone was guilty of anything, it was he. Of voyeurism.

Perhaps to make up for his secret indiscretion, he suggested to Laura that they should eat something. They both ordered waterzooi, hers with chicken and his with fish. At least he wouldn't have to cook and wash up at home.

Thinking of which, he still had to drive. He would have to stay on the wagon from here on, even if he was dying for a glass of wine with his supper.

*Caz*
*Ghent*

Caz headed off in a new direction, not quite sure what she was looking at. The buildings she passed spoke of the craftsmanship of centuries ago. One was obviously a cathedral, there were statues and fountains to pick and choose from, but she didn't know what a single one was called or what it represented.

She should have picked up a map of the city with details of the various tourist attractions, but in a strange way she enjoyed not being able to attach names and functions to the city's architectural treasures.

Tomorrow was another day, as was the day after. For now she was just enjoying the spectacle of human genius. So many visual images to absorb, so many impressions, lines, angles, arches, textures to take in.

Around her was a throng of pedestrians and cyclists, but they seemed remote. She was alone with her inner camera. Her cellphone was hardly state-of-the-art and she had left her camera in the attic room. A sure sign that she was not a dedicated tourist.

While she was enjoying the scene, she thought about Njiwa. Why did she feel so uncomfortable in his presence? His behavior was impeccable. He was evidently well educated. Yet...

He reminded her of a poorly translated paragraph. The words and sentences were exactly right, but as a whole they failed to convey the message.

It was as if his eyes never really made contact. As if there was the Njiwa who was talking to her and the one who was an onlooker—measuring and reflecting on everything that was being said and placing it in another, secret context. As if he were testing every reaction and allocating marks.

She tried to push the thoughts aside. Surely she was imagining it. The exhaustion of the trip, Tieneke's behavior and Fien's death had made her overly sensitive. Or maybe she was just suffering from typical South African paranoia.

And maybe low blood sugar as well. She had to get some food inside her.

*Erevu*
*Ghent*

"Why did you tell her so much?" Erevu felt like shaking his grandson.

"If you mix the truth with the lie, the lie is more credible. Now she believes I have a good reason to be here. Besides, I had to think of something. The professor was there too. I think he noticed I was following her. I had to do something to set his mind at rest. I couldn't just say hello."

"I thought they didn't know each other?" Erevu ran his hand over his shaved head. Dove mustn't spoil things with his youthful indiscretion. When he let Dove know the Caz woman had boarded the bus, he could only guess she would be heading for Ghent's tourist hub. Dove was supposed to follow her to see if she met anyone, not make contact with her again.

"They don't know each other. She never once looked in his direction. He must have been watching me after he recognized me."

"You're playing with fire, Dove. The time for games is over. The old woman is dead. The hearse came earlier. Things can start happening now."

"Like what, Nkoko? Surely we must find out first where the other old woman is?"

"She, this Caz, will hopefully look for her. The old Colijn woman probably told this Caz where she actually comes from. Approaching death and fear of what lies on the other side work like truth serum. My mother, too, unburdened herself on her deathbed.

"We must just stay on the Caz woman's trail. We don't know who has the nkísi, or who knows where they are. One of the two old women must know. If it's the one who has just died, it will soon become known. One of her daughters will inherit them. If it's the other old woman, we'll get it by staying one step behind this Caz woman, wherever she goes." If he kept believing it, it would be true.

*Ammie*
*Leuven*

Ammie gave a sigh of relief when the door clicked shut behind Lieve, glad that they had managed to clear the air. What was the use of staying annoyed? It wouldn't change anything. Only complicate things between her and the carer she couldn't get along without. A dear woman with the patience of Job.

It wasn't Lieve's fault that she had made such a mess of things.

When she was writing Fien that letter, she had known she was making a mistake, but she had to find out what had become of the wooden mask and figurine. Tabia's nkísi. If, for some reason, Fien had held on to them, she couldn't run the risk of having them lying about in Fien's home. Not after she had become aware of their value.

The article had been in the *Gazet van Antwerpen* Jacq subscribed to. Aron Matari, an artist from Zaire, was exhibiting his work in an art gallery, Ammie read. The year was 1982, and Mobutu was still in control of the country she had known as the Belgian Congo.

The name struck her like a thunderbolt. Aron Matari. Tabia's nephew.

Aron, who had made the mask with Ammie's features, and the figurine of the pregnant Tabia. Both with the scarifications so typical of the Tetela.

The same Aron who had taken her over the Angolan border, later to Southern Rhodesia, to Bulawayo, where other Belgian refugees from the Congo had agreed to take her to South Africa, to Nylstroom, where they had relatives.

During their flight Aron had looked out for her safety. Found her food and water. Bandaged her injured feet when they had to walk long distances before he could arrange some form of transport. On donkey carts, trailers, once even a bulldozer. Sometimes they managed to hitch a ride on a train.

During all that time he never spoke to her, except when absolutely necessary. Maybe because he stuttered, or maybe he simply had no wish to speak to the white woman in his care.

Just before the people from Nylstroom sent her to Pretoria because they had no room for her in their home, Aron found her again and asked her to help him find work. The Nylstroom people refused. She gave him her address in Pretoria and told him to ask for work there, promising she would try to help.

But she couldn't. When Aron turned up in Pretoria a few weeks after her own arrival, Fien wouldn't listen to reason, though she tried to explain that she owed Aron her life. No black savage would be tolerated on her property, Fien had said.

She should have expected it after she had unwisely confided in Fien, sharing her fears about the birth with her. About who the baby's father might be. The confession had completely changed Fien's attitude toward Ammie.

Ammie had never heard from Aron again. Then she read the article in the *Gazet*.

A few days later she went to Antwerp. Though there was no sign of Aron at the gallery, his art did the talking. His touch was mature now, more artistic. In a distinctive nkísinkondi style, he told the tale of a country where violence was the norm. There were also two smallish sculpted harps. The soundboxes were in the shape of full-breasted women, their backs arched, the strings attached to their heads and feet.

His artistry was undeniable, and the gallery realized it. The prices took her breath away.

On her way out, someone held her back by the arm. When she turned, she thought at first it was Aron himself, but then she realized the young man standing before her had to be at least twenty years his junior.

"My father sends message," he said in broken Congo-

French. "He asks if his mask and statue protected you. If it brought you blessing."

"It must have. I'm here, aren't I?" she replied.

He was silent for a moment. Pensive. "He wants to know what you did with Tabia's gift to you."

She had left it with Fien in South Africa, along with her baby and her conscience, but that would be the wrong answer. "It's in a safe place," was all she could think of saying.

"He says you must look after it. Very carefully. The spirit of mask and statue are very strong. Keep it close. And look out for Tabia's son. He asks a lot of questions about almasi. He knows there are more almasi than his mother has."

She stood frozen to the spot while he walked down the street. By the time she wanted to call him back, he had vanished into the crowded Antwerp street.

Ammie went back inside the gallery but the woman in charge couldn't help her. "Aron sent his son after you, but then he left. I understand they'll be returning to Zaire soon," she said. The woman didn't know where the two were staying. All she had was a price list of the artworks and the details of a bank account in Lubumbashi.

It had been more than twenty years since Ammie had left South Africa. Fien might have got rid of both objects. Yet she felt obliged to try and save what could be saved. Not only because the two items were so valuable. Aron's son had made her ashamed of her casual treatment of Aron's handiwork. Works of art he had specifically created to protect her. And there had been an urgency in the words of Aron's son that seemed more than an idle warning. Something that stirred up a deep anxiety. Especially the last part: look out for Tabia's son.

He wasn't only Tabia's son. He was César's too. African magic, genetically combined with European hunger for power.

Against her better judgment, Ammie wrote to Fien. It was as if a force beyond reason was driving her. She still had the Rietfontein address, but after the letter was forwarded a few times, it miraculously reached Fien.

There was something to be salvaged after all. Fien had kept the mask and figurine in the garage with a load of other stuff she couldn't throw away, yet didn't want in her home.

Fien reluctantly agreed to take the items to a bank for safekeeping, as long as Ammie paid. They agreed that Ammie would send Fien the money.

The first annual payment, for 1982, went without a hitch. For some reason the 1983 payment did not reach Fien.

Fien wrote a sharply worded letter. Something to the tune of: I had to pay the bank myself. As if it's not enough that I had to care for your ungrateful brat for so long. The so-called payment I got for raising your child didn't nearly make up for the trouble she caused. She even insisted on going to university. What for, I ask you? She's out there in the wilderness now, doing what with her precious degree? But thank God she's married, even if her husband is a young twerp with an oaf for a father. And for your information: you're going to be a grandmother. Make sure I get the money at once.

Ammie would never forget the expression on Jacq's face when she walked in and found him with the letter in his hand.

It was a terrible, yet liberating, moment.

"You have a child?" was all he asked. She told him everything.

Jacq could accept the fact that she had been married before, but not that she had committed adultery, especially not with a man like Elijah. He was dumbstruck when she told him she had never divorced her first husband and that she didn't know whether he was still alive. But to Jacq, the worst thing by far was that she had abandoned her child.

It had been careless to leave Fien's letter lying on her desk. Later she would wonder whether, at a deeply subconscious level, she had wanted Jacq to see it. Wanted him to find out. She could no longer live the lie.

The revelation steered her life in a new direction, but she had devastated a good man. She could not have predicted that Jacq would be unable to get over his distress.

She sometimes wondered what her life would have been like if she had torn up that letter like the ones before.

If Jacq hadn't found out about her past, she might have stayed in Leuven, trapped in a soul-destroying marriage that wasn't legal but, because Jacq didn't know it, was as binding as a legal one.

Jacq was a highly intelligent man and took good care of her, but he wasn't exactly exciting. He was far too fixated on sin.

Would a life with him have been better than the one she had lived in the end? She didn't think so. She would have liked to be a part of Luc's life and follow his career. But in the end, she suspected, as a grown man he was just as tedious as his father had been.

She knew she was coldhearted. Perhaps even without a conscience. Africa did that to you. That and other things. It taught you to deceive, to hate, and how thin the veneer of so-called civilization was. All that was deep and dark floated to the surface so much more readily there.

In Africa forgiving and forgetting didn't come easily, if it ever came. If César ever found her, she could expect no mercy. That was the shadow she had been living under for more than half a century. It had determined everything she had done.

César would be an old man, if he was still alive. Eighty-seven.

He had at least one son. With Tabia. And he had a daughter. Born from her own body, but belonging to Fien. Evil of the kind found in César couldn't help but be genetic. It was too strong to be diluted by blood that was less evil.

"Elijah," she muttered. "Elijah, if only things had been different."

*Caz*
*Ghent*

Caz felt guilty when she returned to Tieneke's house after nine.

It was silent as the grave. Only the hall light, which burned day and night, was on. Tieneke was probably asleep. She had to be exhausted.

Because the sun went down so late, Caz hadn't realized what the time was when she had ordered her food after a long wait to be served. Though she had chosen one of the smaller, cheaper restaurants off the Graslei, it was still bustling.

The stairs creaked, no matter how softly Caz tried to tread.

Tieneke's door opened just before Caz reached the second flight. "Cassie?"

"Yes. Sorry to bother you."

Tieneke came out, tying the girdle of her dressing gown. "I thought I'd drop off immediately, but it seems exhaustion is not enough. Shall I make us some hot chocolate?"

"Yes, please, if you're having, but don't make it specially for me."

"I wouldn't have offered if I didn't want some myself." Tieneke brushed past her and went down the stairs to the kitchen.

Meekly Caz followed.

When she had put the milk on the stove, Tieneke turned and folded her arms. "So, Mother is dead and life goes on."

Talk about stating the obvious. Caz nodded. "Are you okay? I mean in the circumstances?"

"I feel strange. Removed from reality. It's weird not to be listening for sounds from the bedroom all day. Not to be on standby. I feel restless." She turned to the milk on the stove, then back to Caz. "Mother wanted to see you this morning. I refused. I didn't think it would do either of you any good."

Caz gritted her teeth. She hadn't particularly wanted to see Fien herself, but now she'd never know whether Fien had wanted to tell her more. How dare Tieneke make the decision on her behalf and her mother's? But of course Tieneke had made other important decisions on Fien's behalf as well. Like when to die.

"Mother said she knew you only came because I let the cat out of the bag about your biological parents but she still appreciated your coming."

Caz gave her a sceptical look.

"She got upset because you look so much like Ammie. You're much taller, of course, and Ammie had straight hair, but even though you're quite a bit older than Ammie was at the time and not as breathtakingly beautiful, your features are very similar."

Talk about a backhanded compliment. Or maybe no compliment at all.

"She wanted to tell you about Leuven and Doel."

"Pardon?"

"Leuven is a city and Doel a town here in Belgium. Places where Ammie lived."

Caz drew out a chair from under the tiny kitchen table and sank down on it, her legs suddenly shaky.

Just in time Tieneke saved the milk from boiling over. In silence she made the hot chocolate and sat down opposite Caz.

"You see, Ammie contacted Mother. By letter. Years ago. You were pregnant with Lilah. The postal address was Leuven. It's a university city and capital of the province Flemish Brabant. Not far from Brussels."

"She asked about me?" So she hadn't been forgotten after all.

"No, it was about the two awful African objects. Apparently they have some value and she asked if Mother still had them and, if so, would Mother put them in a bank for safekeeping."

So two African curios were more important than her daughter. Well, life was full of surprises.

"It's not important now. The point is, she was living in Leuven at the time."

"Not any more?"

"No, she and her husband separated when he found Mother's letter. The one in which she mentioned you and your pregnancy. We learned of it when he wrote to Mother a few months later. He asked if we thought you would want to make contact with him. Said he might not be your father, but he felt you'd been treated unjustly and he wanted to let you know he hadn't been aware of your existence. If he had, he would have contacted you long ago. He also wanted to find out more about you."

At least one person had been concerned about her welfare, no matter how briefly and superficially. "Mother Fien refused." She didn't ask.

"No, she didn't refuse, she just didn't answer. She tore up the letter and wrote 'address unknown' on the envelope of the next one, and returned it without opening it."

"Was that after Lilah's birth?"

Tieneke nodded.

"And Mother Fien didn't think I might have benefited from someone actually caring about me? Even a stranger in a strange country, one who didn't know me from Adam? A man who might have been able to tell me where I, and especially my daughter, come from? Or at least where Ammie Pauwels was so that I could find out from her what the hell was going on?"

"Be reasonable, Cassie. Mother would have had to spill the beans. We're talking about illicit diamond trade. And she was still upset about Father's death. And of course about Lilah and you and everything."

"Reasonable? Tieneke, she never wanted to see me again. She told me so in no uncertain terms and kept her word until a few weeks ago. Anyone's interest, even a stranger's, would have been welcome. I could have found out about Lilah. It's not my fault that Father traded diamonds illegally. Do you have any idea how alone I was, how overwhelmed, how confused? I had to find a place to stay and a job. Try to survive on so many levels. In the meantime I had to figure out how to look after a baby."

Hentie had given her five hundred rand behind his father's back. Magdel two hundred. Later, when he had cooled down, Andries had deposited a thousand rand into her account. Seventeen hundred rand was a lot of money then, but it could only stretch so far, no matter how careful she was. And that was only the financial side of things. At times she had thought she would lose her mind—usually when Lilah whined and wailed as if she would never stop.

"Let's not open up old wounds. We can't change any of it now. There's another reason why I'm telling you about the letter. There was a letterhead."

Caz looked at her expectantly.

"KU Leuven. Katholieke Universiteit Leuven. Ammie's husband must have worked there. I don't remember the initials, but his last name was DeReu. The university's admin might know where he is, if he's still alive. And he might know where Ammie Pauwels is, if she's still alive."

Caz allowed the possibility to sink in while she sipped her hot chocolate. A starting point. That was all it was, but at least she had one now. "And Doel?" she asked.

"I found out about Ammie's connection with Doel only this morning. It was what Mother had wanted to tell you. I said she could tell me, and I'd tell you. I didn't want a repeat of yesterday. For both your sakes."

Caz waited while Tieneke sipped her chocolate.

"Doel is a town on the Scheldt—the river—in a district known as the Land van Waas," Tieneke continued. "In East Flanders, same as us. About fifty, sixty kilometers from here. It's a ghost town today, but Ammie lived there for a while after she left Leuven. Around 2000 or 2001, Mother recognized her in a photo in the newspaper. The residents had yet again been told to leave the town to make way for an extension of the port of Antwerp and she was one of the protesters. Only a few people live there today. One of them might be able to tell you where she went from there."

"Fourteen years later?"

"I take it it's the diehards that are left. People who have been living there for years and years. They must have known Ammie. It was a small town, even before what happened put it on the map." Tieneke took the two empty mugs, rinsed them and put them in the dishwasher.

It made sense. If Ammie had been one of the protesters, at least one of the so-called diehards must have known her.

"You have at least two starting points: Leuven and Doel. I'll write down the wifi code tomorrow, and you can do some research. Just don't spend hours on the internet or download large files. Now I'm going to bed. Sleep well, Cassie."

"Goodnight, Tieneke, sleep well. And thanks."

Caz sat staring at the kitchen table when Tieneke had left. She had both ends, now she just had to look for the sausage. Where that silly thought had sprung from, she didn't know. Maybe from a proverb she vaguely remembered? But it wasn't important. What was important was whether she was going to embark on this crazy search or not.

Did she—if Ammie Pauwels was still alive—want to look her birth mother in the eye? The woman who had been more concerned about objects you can buy in a curio shop than her own flesh and blood? Did she really want to do that to herself?

Caz sighed. Sleep. She needed sleep. She just had to connect her cellphone to the charger again. She couldn't believe how quickly the battery ran out. She charged it last night and had scarcely used it since. She hoped there wasn't something wrong with it. But she couldn't worry about that as well. The day had brought more than enough of its own troubles.

# Thirteen

*Saturday, September 20*
*Caz*
*Ghent*

"I have to get to the undertaker and go and see the minister," Tieneke said tersely after a breakfast of bread, jam, cheese and a boiled egg. "Let people know about Mother's death and so on. Can I drop you somewhere?"

Tieneke's accommodating attitude of the night before had vanished. Caz had noticed it the moment Tieneke had given her the wifi code with barely a greeting.

"Is there anything I can do for you? Help you with?"

Tieneke shook her head. "You don't know anyone, and you don't speak Flemish or Dutch. How did you think to help me?"

"I don't know, Tieneke, but if there's anything, just tell me. Babette, the woman at the shop down the street, understands me quite well, by the way. I speak Afrikaans to her because she doesn't know much English."

"That may be so, but I'll manage. I want the funeral to be

as soon as possible. I'm thinking of Tuesday. If I can manage it, there should be no reason for you to stay after Wednesday. You don't have to go to the notary's office with me. I'm familiar with the contents of Mother's will. Everything comes to me."

As if there could have been any doubt. What bothered Caz more was that Wednesday was the twenty-fourth. Fourteen more days until Lilah returned. Two weeks without accommodation.

"Look, Tieneke, I understand you'd like to be rid of me. There's no further reason for me to stay. But I'd like to ask you a favor. You know how much luggage I have. A lot of it I brought along for Lilah, but I won't see her before October the eighth."

"October the eighth? I'm sorry, but you can't expect me ..."

"Hang on," Caz stopped her. "I had a look at Google maps. After the funeral I want to go to Doel and then to Leuven. But I'd like to leave most of my luggage here and travel light. I don't know how long I'll be away, a few days at most. As soon as I return I'll think of something else."

Tieneke thought for a moment. "Fine, I can lend you a smaller suitcase. Just stack all your bits and pieces neatly so that I don't fall over them."

Caz nodded. "Thanks, Tieneke. And yes, you can drop me in the town centre. Please. I'll take the bus back." Tough luck if Tieneke didn't want help, but she was definitely not going to stay here alone. The place was suffocating. It was as though Fien was still hanging around in ethereal form.

"I'll get the car. Wait at the front door."

Caz was surprised when an almost-brand-new Polo drew up with Tieneke behind the wheel. It was a very snazzy car for such a stingy person.

"Nice wheels," she said when Tieneke pulled away.

"A woman on her own needs a reliable car." Tieneke kept her eyes on the road.

"Mother Fien agreed?"

"Mother was an invalid long before I bought the Polo. Quiet, I have to concentrate."

Caz grinned to herself and wondered how many other things "Mother" had never known of.

*Luc*
*Damme*

When he woke up this morning Luc knew he had opened a door that should have stayed shut.

Laura had definitely read more into their outing than there could ever be. It was clear from the way she had kissed his cheeks when she said goodbye. Not like a colleague. Surely it was enough to air kiss only one cheek? But no, left, right, left the kisses had come, the last one a lingering one. Definitely not an air kiss.

Not that he could do anything about it at the moment. He would just have to keep his distance in future. She would realize soon enough they could never be more than colleagues. She was a nice person, but the thought of two equally boring people together was simply unbearable.

Which meant, of course, that any hope of finding a woman to share his life with was futile. He had no interest in boring women, and interesting women didn't like nerds. So why was he thinking these thoughts in the first place? He'd made peace with his bachelorhood a long time ago and he certainly wasn't looking to complicate his life.

It annoyed him that the image of the woman with the long gray curls kept popping into his mind. The subtle sway of her hips. The arch of her back when she had looked up at the gables. The way in which she had shielded her eyes from the sharp light, the little finger slightly raised above the rest of the slender hand.

Surely he had more important things to occupy his thoughts?

He went through the house with feather duster, vacuum cleaner and polisher, made sure that the water supply to the hydroponic system in the greenhouse was in order, watered his flowerbeds, pulled out a few weeds and tidied up. He swept the small patio and wiped down the outdoor furniture.

Eventually he gave it up as a bad job. Even while his hands were busy, his thoughts kept returning to all the unanswered questions that had been plaguing him since his conversation with Lieve. He made himself a cup of coffee and put the note with the names on the table in front of him.

Josefien Colijn. Cassandra—maybe Colijn. César—maybe Janssen. Tabia. Elijah.

No use trying to find out more about Tabia and Elijah. But Cassandra Colijn was a different story. Social media, he had realized yesterday in the Aula, held the answer.

Though he was registered on Facebook and Twitter, he did not use social media himself. He had liked the webpage of Ghent University and that was about it. It was just not his thing.

He entered Cassandra Colijn's name. There was only one hit. A woman in Holland. He glanced briefly at the photograph. No, she was in her twenties. A daughter, maybe? But in Holland? He found a Cassandra Collin and a Cassandra Clare. Those were the only Cassandras whose last name began with C.

He fared no better on Twitter.

South African women took their husbands' last names, he remembered. At her age she would surely have been married at least once. It was hopeless.

He was about to close Chrome, when he paused and went to LinkedIn. It was the only other social media platform where he was registered. He couldn't quite remember why. Someone had pestered him on email to join, if he remembered correctly.

A number of Cassandras, but none from South Africa seemed a likely candidate.

A few Sandras showed up when he scrolled down. Cassies too. He typed Sandra Colijn in the search box. Thousands of Sandras, but no Colijn. He typed Cassie. No Colijn. Right at the bottom a Colijn. Caz.

He clicked on the link.

Caz Colijn. Stanford, South Africa. Translator. English to Afrikaans, Afrikaans to English. Editor and proofreader of fiction—Afrikaans and English. A BA degree in languages from a university in Potchefstroom and a string of diplomas for translation, editing, advanced language courses and so on. Mostly through Unisa. No photo. Numerous recommendations.

Should he send a request to join her network? No, rather not. Not now. First he had to consider whether he wanted to stir up another hornet's nest. If it turned out to be her.

He went back to Facebook and then to Twitter, but there was no Caz Colijn. No photos. Except for a presence in her professional capacity on LindkedIn, the woman was as private as could be.

Could this Caz be Ammie's daughter? As he had no idea how old she was or whether her full name was Cassandra, it was impossible to say. But it did seem significant that she was from South Africa.

In the course of his studies he had discovered that fact, background information and intuition often went hand in hand. Reliable information and extensive knowledge were at the top of the list, of course, but academic intuition and the odd stroke of luck sometimes played a significant role.

His intuition told him he had found the right Cassandra. But empirical evidence was all that counted. And that never came easily.

Luc closed the lid of his laptop and got up to make more coffee. He considered reading his book, but in the end he sat back down at his desk with a sigh and again studied the note with the names. As if it could make him any the wiser.

Fine. There was a Caz Colijn in South Africa, but was her real name Cassandra?

Josefien Colijn, if she was still alive, was probably also still in South Africa. He doubted that she would be using social media.

César Janssen might be dead, but at least he was Belgian. Would he have returned here, like Ammie? Left a trail?

He opened his laptop again and searched the name César Ronald Bruno Janssen. Moments later he drew a sharp breath.

More than four hundred and fifty thousand hits. Verdorie, couldn't César have had a less familiar last name?

Most articles were about Pierre Jules César, the astronomer who had discovered helium, among other things. And then there was Ronald Janssen, the murderer who had confessed to three, but was suspected of fifteen murders, dating back to 1991, as well as twenty rape counts since 2001.

But he had been born in 1971. At best he could be related to the César Luc was looking for. Which was irrelevant.

If there was any information about César Ronald Bruno Janssen among this multitude of hits, it was going to be a near impossible task to find it.

César was probably older than Ammie. Though Luc doubted that Twitter or Facebook was an option, he gave it a try. Who was to say a man in his eighties couldn't tweet?

There was a César Janssen after all. His profile was not visible but, judging by the few photos, he was young. There was also a Ronald Janssen in Holland—evidently a dog lover, who believed Sinterklaas's assistant, Zwarte Piet, should remain black, despite the debate about racist implications that was currently raging. This Ronald appeared to be in his forties, at most.

Out of sheer desperation he entered "Josefien Colijn" on Facebook. Nothing. He erased Josefien and left Colijn. Cassandra Colijn, the same one from before, the one who was too young, and lived in Holland. Geertje Colijn, a housewife from Beverwijk in North Holland. Looked to be in her late sixties or even older. Tieneke Colijn, from Ghent, as it happened, could also be in her sixties, but the photo was blurred. The rest had Colijn as a first, not as a last name.

Geertje, he saw, had had a birthday on March 23. No one called Josefien had congratulated her.

The settings on Tieneke's Facebook page were private. A few links shared by friends were all he could see. While he was looking, a new message appeared. A picture of a floral bouquet, with the message: *Just heard of your mother's passing. Sincere condolences. Please inform us of the funeral arrangements.*

Okay, that was one time in your life when you didn't deserve to get inquiries from strangers. He closed the page.

It was a lovely day he was spending indoors, poking his nose into other people's tragedies. There were better ways to enjoy his last free weekend before the start of the academic year.

Yet he didn't get up immediately. If Tieneke Colijn was in her sixties, her recently deceased mother had probably been in her late eighties. Could she have known the Colijn family who had emigrated to South Africa so many years ago?

He brought himself up short and got to his feet. Too late now, the old lady had passed on.

*Ammie*
*Leuven*

For the umpteenth time Ammie wished Luc had never visited her. Since then everything felt more muddled than before.

As if it wasn't bad enough that she was haunted by the Congo, Jacq and Tobias's ghosts had also risen again.

She kept dreaming of them. Dapper Jacq, dressed to the nines. The gray goatee trimmed just so. Every hair in its place. The tailored suit perfectly dry-cleaned, the tie precisely knotted. A weakness for Italian shoes.

And then there was Tobias, with the unkempt hair and bushy beard. Overweight in faded denims and plaid work shirts. His big hands, rough and knobbly, that betrayed how he earned his bread.

Tobias had been a skilled cabinet-maker, but not a brilliant one, while Jacq had been a renowned professor, an expert in his field.

Initially she had admired Jacq's intellect and could listen to him for hours. But to Tobias she could talk. Jacq was a gentle, careful lover. Tobias was passionate and enthusiastic.

But there was one quality the two of them shared. Neither had a drop of malice in their nature. Both were men with integrity. That was the difference between them and César. Probably between them and herself as well.

Combined, Tobias and Jacq represented the qualities she had loved in Elijah. When Elijah was on his way to a meeting, he was always impeccably dressed. At home he spent his time in khaki shorts and sandals. She could both listen and talk to him. Sometimes their lovemaking was gentle, sometimes passionate.

But Elijah was more than just a combination of Jacq and Tobias. He had a deep-rooted kind of wisdom that had nothing to do with academic knowledge. He was without pretension, yet a fully rounded person. There was something noble about him. He loved her with all his being, not just when it suited him.

His only failing was that he was so incredibly naive. That he believed in the goodness of humankind and God. That he could not see that some people were evil to the core and that God didn't give a damn about the human race.

For that he had paid a heavy price. And so had she.

He almost had her convinced that everything would work out for the good. Especially after Patrice Lumumba became prime minister. And look what had happened.

If there were a God who cared about his creatures, he would have allowed Elijah to realize his potential. Patrice as well. Or He would at least have seen to it that the child she carried was Elijah's.

And then Lieve wondered why she wanted nothing to do with God or the church.

# Fourteen

Tuesday, September 23
Caz
Ghent

Protestant churches are in short supply in Belgium, Tieneke told Caz, as it is chiefly a Catholic country. The church Tieneke and Fien belonged to, where Fien's memorial service would be held, was beautiful from the outside, with stained-glass windows, but inside it was without ornamentation and not very big either.

There was another Protestant church in Ghent, Tieneke said, the Rabot Church, but she and Fien hadn't liked it when they returned to Ghent years ago and were looking for a spiritual home.

Fien disliked the fact that there were a number of black congregants, and especially that the church was in partnership with a church in Sharpeville. Evidently, anti-apartheid sentiments in the congregation had run high before 1994. Caz could imagine that it would have bothered Fien. She had been apolitical, but a racist.

The sober lifestyle advocated by the church they did join must have fitted her like a glove. To Fien, it was not just a case of cleanliness being next to godliness. Sobriety bordering on stinginess was the pinnacle of virtue and piety.

Years ago, Caz's engagement ring had been a bone of contention. Extravagant and wasteful, Fien proclaimed when Caz proudly showed it to her. Ironic, if one took into account the barter agreement involving diamonds she herself had entered into.

The church was virtually empty. Only she and Tieneke, the minister, the undertakers, the notary and seven women of Tieneke's age attended the service. Fien had survived all her contemporaries. The hymn they sang sounded thin, as if the domed ceiling were absorbing the sound, instead of amplifying it.

Caz could follow most of the service. With dry eyes she listened to the minister's version of Josefien Colijn, the devout, humble Christian.

There was no sign anywhere of a sob or a tear.

After the sermon Tieneke thanked various people and said a few words about Josefien. She spoke about the good mother she had been and the good wife to Hans Colijn in earlier years. She made no mention of Caz, who was relieved rather than affronted.

After the service coffee and refreshments were served in a smaller reception room, but with so few mourners it was soon over.

When everyone had left, Tieneke came up to Caz. "The notary has some time to spare, as the service was so short. He has just asked me to come to his office for the reading of the will. Would you like to go home and pack? I can give you the key. You can take a bus."

"I've just about finished packing. I'll come with you and take a walk while you speak to the notary. You can text me when you've finished."

"Fine. It's close to Sint-Baafsplein and a number of other tourist attractions."

When she got Tieneke's message, Caz was sitting at a

restaurant overlooking a fountain, with the impressive St Bavo's cathedral to her left. She had just ordered a beer. Actually she was longing for a glass of wine, but a single glass cost as much as an entire bottle in the supermarket. It wasn't Fien's kind of tight-fistedness that held her back, but the fact that from the next day she would have to pay for her board. Her budget had taken a turn for the worse.

She sent Tieneke a message that she was at *'t Vosken*, and realized the damn battery had to be charged again. It had become a daily nuisance.

From the way Tieneke came walking round the corner, Caz could see she was impatient.

"I want to get home," she protested, sitting down opposite Caz.

The waiter appeared at once.

Tieneke looked at Caz's almost full glass and chewed on her lower lip. "Kriek, please," she decided, her cheeks slightly flushed.

"Kriek?" Caz asked.

"Cherry beer," Tieneke answered tersely, wiping the sweat from her brow with a linen handkerchief.

Beer? Tieneke? Caz suppressed a smile. Only two hours after Fien's funeral, and the new Tieneke had made her appearance.

"It was a nice service, don't you think?" Tieneke remarked.

"Very nice." Full of lies, unless the minister hadn't known Fien at all. But she would rather not say it.

The waiter placed a goblet filled with deep-red beer in front of Tieneke.

She took a substantial sip. "Don't look at me like that, the alcohol content is very low." Caz noticed the slightly flushed cheeks again, as if the liquor was reflected in Tieneke's face.

"May I have a sip?" Caz knew she was being deliberately annoying. It had been drummed into their heads during childhood that tasting another person's food or drink was unhygienic.

Surprisingly, Tieneke nodded.

The beer was lovely. Not nearly as sweet as Caz had expected. "Wow, I think I've found a new favorite." She wiped the rim of the glass with a napkin and pushed the glass across to Tieneke.

"Refreshing on a hot day," Tieneke nodded.

"Did everything go according to plan at the notary's office?"

"I saw to it that Mother's affairs were in order a long time ago. It was just a formality. Once he was satisfied that you have no claim against the estate, the man wanted to reminisce about the old days. His grandfather and Mother's father had known each other. His father assisted us when Mother inherited the house from my grandmother."

The house Tieneke lived in at present, Caz assumed. The fact that Tieneke had said "my grandmother" didn't go by unnoticed. Caz vaguely remembered there had been grandparents in Belgium. Also that Fien had taken a trip to Ghent to visit her parents when Caz was in high school.

What Caz found more interesting was Tieneke's remark about the claim. Was that why she had wanted to make certain Caz knew she wasn't Fien's biological child? So that there could be no claim? Well, well, well.

Tieneke dug in her handbag and produced an envelope. "This is for you."

Caz's eyebrows shot up.

"It's the key to a safe-deposit box and the details of the bank where it is kept. Apparently Mother gave it to the notary for safekeeping years ago. Don't get too excited. It only contains two awful African curios. A horrid mask and figurine. The things have been a nuisance since Ammie started nagging about them. You can take over now. I don't want to be bothered."

Thanks for nothing. African kitsch was her share of the inheritance. A consolation prize for being unable to stake a claim against the estate. Yet, many years ago her birth mother had held those objects in her hands. Fled through large parts of Africa with the artefacts and a number of diamonds in a canvas bag, and her daughter in her belly.

"Do you happen to know why Ammie brought them along from the Congo?" Caz asked pensively.

Tieneke frowned. "I remember Mother saying Ammie believed they would protect her. Or something like that. Superstitious nonsense."

Maybe it worked. Ammie had survived, after all. Pregnant or not. "Anyway, thanks, I guess." Caz put the envelope in her handbag. "Where's this bank where they are kept?"

"Pretoria. Silverton."

Pretoria. A lot of help that was. When would she ever get there?

"You're going to Doel tomorrow?"

Caz nodded. "I see on the internet I have to change trains a number of times. I wouldn't have managed with my big suitcase."

"Well, at least we *have* trains, and they run on time."

Caz knew it would be no good pointing out that her words weren't meant as a criticism of the Belgian transport system. She allowed the jab to pass. After all, Tieneke wasn't wrong. South Africa's rail service *had* just about ground to a halt.

The waiter interrupted to ask whether they would like to order anything else. Tieneke shook her head. When the bill arrived, she made no effort to reach for her wallet. Not that Caz minded, but hell. Most of the inheritance that Tieneke came into today originated from the diamonds Ammie had brought from the Congo. Caz had no doubt about it. Hans had been a good baker but a poor businessman.

On the other hand, he appeared to have been quite skilled at selling illicit diamonds without being caught. Every person has his own talents, it seemed.

*Wednesday, September 24*
*Caz*
*Ghent*

"No time for breakfast this morning, Caz, I have to be at the hairdresser's. I have a standing monthly appointment to have my hair cut. There's yoghurt in the fridge, help yourself. Just hurry, my appointment is at nine-thirty."

Caz took the plain yoghurt from the fridge and wondered whether Tieneke had arranged the funeral so that it wouldn't interfere with her "standing monthly appointment." The container felt light. "My first train leaves just after two this afternoon from Sint-Pieters. I plan to leave here at about one and take the bus and train to Sint-Pieters. I'll wait for you." The night before, eyes drooping, she had googled the timetable and tried to make sense of it. She had written down the times and names of the stations, but she would like to take her time studying it this morning.

There were hardly more than three spoonfuls of yoghurt left. Caz finished it straight from the container. It wasn't worth using a bowl.

Something about the public transport timetable didn't quite make sense. On the last leg of her journey, the bus from Sint-Niklaas arrived at Doel at twenty-one minutes past five, while the last bus left Doel at fifty-seven minutes past six. It would give her slightly more than an hour to spend in the town. There had to be another option.

Tieneke shook her head. "I have shopping to do and things to take care of. I won't be back before you leave. You'll have to go when I go."

"I can take your extra key. Surely you won't be needing it before I get back?"

"And if you lose it? No, I'm not taking a chance."

Caz knew it wasn't the true reason. Tieneke just didn't want Caz around while she was not at home. Caz threw the yoghurt container in the recycle bin, though Tieneke had told her it could not be recycled.

"Hurry up, get your suitcase. I don't want to be late and cause the hairdresser to rush." Tieneke fished out the yoghurt container and threw it in the garbage without a word. Caz took it to mean that she'd do anything to get Caz out of her house as quickly as possible.

Caz adjusted her significantly lighter backpack on her back, hooked the strap of her handbag over her shoulder and pulled out the handle of Tieneke's suitcase. It was barely big enough for three or four days' clothing and toiletries, but it made her more mobile.

"I'll drop you at Dampoort," Tieneke offered unexpectedly. "It will save you the bus ride."

"Thanks, that's kind of you." Tieneke probably wanted to make sure she was indeed on her way. Presumably she gave no thought to the fact that Caz would have to while away more than five hours before she could catch a train to Doel.

Oh well, she could take the train to Ghent-Sint-Pieters, wander around, and do some sightseeing in that part of the city.

Waiting for Tieneke on the pavement in front of the house, Caz noticed the curtains move in the neighboring house again. This time on the ground floor, at the narrow window beside the front door, which was identical to Tieneke's. Whoever had been peering at her had drawn the curtain again, just in time.

Tieneke stopped and opened the trunk. Caz put her bag and backpack inside and got into the front passenger seat.

Caz couldn't help noticing again that Tieneke's Polo was brand new. She had considered buying a new car herself a while ago and, if her memory served her correctly, the most basic Polo cost more than two hundred thousand rand. She'd had no other choice but to have her ten-year-old secondhand Camry repaired yet again the next time it broke down. Fuel guzzler or not.

It was none of her business how much money Tieneke had, or how she spent it. Fair was fair. Fien had earned her money, raising Caz.

"Your neighbors are a nosy lot, I see?"

Tieneke gave her a brief glance. "How's that?"

"They watch from behind the curtains. Do you know them?"

Tieneke shook her head. "They come and go. The rooms are rented to people who need accommodation for a week or more. It's cheaper than paying per day."

Exactly the kind of accommodation she was looking for, but certainly not next-door to Tieneke.

"Cassie." Tieneke sounded hesitant. "When I called you ... I thought Mother regretted sending you away when you had nowhere to go. I thought she wanted to ask for your forgiveness. I still think so."

Caz gave her a sceptical look. "If she had wanted forgiveness, I don't think it was because she was sorry. She might have been afraid of what lies beyond death. Chaff and wheat, goats and sheep, heaven and hell, you know ... that kind of thing. Whatever her motive, she didn't handle the preamble very well."

"I know. I eavesdropped. I think when you stood there in the flesh she became flustered. Or she simply couldn't break the old pattern."

"And you? Do you find it hard to break the old pattern?"

Tieneke nodded. "Yes, but so do you. Don't argue. I'm not trying to justify what Mother and I did to you. But like Tijl Uilenspiegel said: The whole world hates me, but I'm the cause of it."

"*I* am the cause? How the bloody hell could I have caused you and Mother to reject me? Especially on account of something that was never my fault in the first place?"

Tieneke gave her a sidelong glance. "Not?"

Caz sighed. "No, and if you still don't believe me after all these years, there's nothing more I can say. Hentie is Lilah's father. There was no other possible candidate. As I kept telling you at the time."

"But you caused a lot of it through your attitude, Cassie. You always considered yourself better than the rest of us."

Caz looked at her in shocked disbelief. "Now I've heard everything."

"Maybe you didn't mean to, but that was what it felt like." Tieneke switched on the indicator and turned in at the station. When she had parked the car, she looked at Caz. "I also caused most things that happened to me. It's not really Mother's fault that I'm an old maid at the age of sixty-five. I was afraid of life. Maybe in a warped kind of way I found pleasure in being the aggrieved sister. I enjoyed making you feel guilty."

Caz gave a slight laugh. "One thing I can say about you, Tieneke: you're not afraid to call a spade a bloody shovel. I appreciate that about you, even though it's not nice to be at the receiving end."

Tieneke rolled her eyes. "We're not going to try to be sisterly now, Cassie. We don't like each other—never have and never will. I just wanted to clear the air."

"See what I mean?" Caz turned to her. "But for what it's worth, thanks for telling me about Ammie. About Doel and Leuven and the letter. You could have kept it to yourself."

"I wanted to at first, but then I realized if I want to leave my old life behind, I have to get proper closure. That's what I've been trying to do. For my own sake. And, yes, you've probably guessed it: initially I contacted you to make sure you knew you had no grounds for a claim against the estate when you found out about Mother's death.

"I finally have a life of my own to look forward to. I have a good ten, maybe fifteen years left. It's not a lot, but it's something. I don't want to spoil it with reproaches and remorse. I want to make the most of it. I want to know when you leave here I never have to see you again, never have to wonder about anything from the past. I'm buying my freedom, that's all."

Caz opened the door, and then paused. "Maybe I can learn something from you. I'm also merely existing most of the time, instead of living."

"Okay, okay. Enough now. I really don't want to know about your life. I hope you find whatever you are searching for on this journey, but whatever it might be, it is no concern of mine. I'll see you when you fetch your things and that will be the end of it."

Caz nodded. "Suits me. But, Tieneke, I really hope you enjoy the last stretch of your life. That you'll make the most of it." She rested her hand very briefly on Tieneke's knee before she got out. The trunk was open by the time she got there. The lid had barely shut again when Tieneke pulled away without a wave or a final greeting.

Caz stared after the car as it drove away. They had never been sisters; they would never be friends either; yet something between them had changed.

Maybe that was why she had to come so far. Not for Fien's sake, not even to find out the truth about her birth mother, but also to get closure. On more than one level.

But, she thought as she headed for the station building, now she had embarked on yet another search.

What did she hope to find? Not necessarily a person in the flesh. Not even answers to all the secrets. Maybe just resignation. Making peace with the idea that life was a mystery.

Or maybe she was searching for herself.

*Erevu*
*Ghent*

Couldn't the woman have taken the bus! He had been ready to ride his bike to one of the next stops and get on the same bus so that he could find out where she was going. Judging from the luggage, she was certainly not on a mere sightseeing trip.

Now he was on the bus and guessing she was going to be dropped at Dampoort, which was the closest station. He hoped and prayed he would be in time to see which train she was taking.

Erevu made certain he was the first one out when the bus stopped. He paid no attention to the clicking tongue of a fellow passenger as he pushed past. Heading for the station building, he broke into a jog.

*Caz*
*Ghent*

Caz stood at the departure board and tried to make head or tails of it. According to her notes, she had to get to Sint-Pieters and board the Lokeren train. Yet, according to this timetable, she could catch a Lokeren train from Ghent-Dampoort in less than half an hour.

"Can I help you?"

Caz turned. A tall black man of about her own age gave her a friendly smile. He was neatly dressed, his head shaven.

"The timetables can be very confusing if you're not familiar with them." His Flemish had a strange accent but was completely understandable.

She returned his smile. "Thanks, but I think I'll manage." She hoped.

Caz dragged her case to the refreshment counter and bought a bottle of water and a packet of crisps. The man bought a sandwich, she noticed as she walked off in search of Platform 9.

The train was on time and fortunately not full. She found a seat and sat looking through the window. She saw the tall man get into the next carriage. She might as well have asked him about the route, as he seemed to be traveling in the same direction.

Caz closed her eyes and lay back against the headrest.

Talk about a wild-goose chase. What did she think she would learn about Ammie Pauwels in Doel? Why did she want to find out anything in the first place, if it was so clear that the woman wanted nothing to do with her?

It was a bit like Everest. People say they climb the mountain because it's there. It's the only reason they need. Unfortunately she didn't know where her own Everest was or whether it even existed.

*Ammie*
*Leuven*

Someone was crying.

"No! Oh, no! Miss Ammie, open your eyes. Please!"

Lieve's voice.

"The doctor is on his way. Just open your eyes, my dear Miss Ammie."

It was peculiarly difficult to open her eyes, but she managed. "Lieve?" Her voice sounded odd. It took a great effort to articulate. Her tongue had become lazy.

"Miss Ammie! Thank God, thank God."

She heard the distant sound of a doorbell.

"The doctor!" Lieve moved out of her sight.

Ammie closed her eyes. So tired, so incredibly tired. Woozy.

People spoke, but she was too tired to try to make sense of the words. Only one word got through to her. Stroke.

"Who …" No, too tired to think.

"Elijah," she muttered.

# Fifteen

*Caz*
*Kieldrecht*

What a disaster. It had been easy to get to Sint-Niklaas, but there was only one bus to Doel and it only left at five past five. Kieldrecht, she had found out when she asked about the nearest town to Doel, was about ten kilometers away.

So here she was at Kieldrecht. There were two buses to Doel per day, but she had missed the first one, and the next one would also be leaving at five past five. She would arrive at Doel at exactly the same time she would have if she'd caught the train at Sint-Niklaas. There was no taxi service to Doel, as she had hoped.

She would have to while away three hours here and she'd have only an hour and a half to spend in Doel before the only bus back departed. She could have spent the three hours so much better in Doel.

If she didn't have the bloody suitcase to drag she could have walked the ten kilos, but she wouldn't have saved much time anyway. She wasn't exactly Caster Semenya.

Caz sat down on a bench and rested her forehead on the handle of the case. It was madness. What was she hoping to achieve anyway?

If she hadn't been so keen to see Lilah on her birthday, she would have changed the date of her return flight to South Africa and forgotten this whole escapade. Although for months to come her credit card would remind her of this wild-goose chase.

"Ma'am?"

Caz looked up. A sturdy girl with black-framed glasses and a pink streak in her short pitch-black hair stood in front of her. She had noticed the child earlier. One couldn't really miss her.

"I heard you ask about transport to Doel?"

Caz nodded.

"My friend has a car. He sometimes takes people there. For the raves. Fifteen euros if it's only one person."

Two hundred and twenty-five rand for ten kilometers? It was crazy. But at least she could get something done. Hopefully. Here she was just wasting her time. But raves? Never mind, she would just have to bite the bullet. "Can he take me now?"

The girl produced a neon pink cellphone from the back pocket of her jeans and pushed a button. Caz couldn't follow the colloquial Flemish but the girl nodded and raised her eyebrows enquiringly.

Caz gave an answering nod.

"He'll be here in about three minutes." She smiled and returned the cellphone to her pocket.

Four minutes later a clapped-out car drew up. The bald fellow behind the wheel did not get out. The girl slipped into the front seat.

Caz struggled to get all her stuff on the back seat. Her feet were buried under papers and takeaway containers when at last she managed to sit. A pale, cupped hand adorned with tattoos was held aloft. Caz dug in her wallet and placed fifteen euros in the hand.

Off they went.

The two up front laughed and talked nonstop and barely ten minutes later they stopped at a windmill.

"Dank uw wel," Caz said somewhat sarcastically as she wrestled her possessions from the back seat.

She had barely closed the door when the car pulled away without a goodbye or a stuff-you from the two youngsters.

Anyway. Here she was.

*Erevu*
*Sint-Niklaas*

All he could do was take the train back to Ghent. Almost an hour's wait for the next one. Erevu could howl with frustration.

Fortunately he had overheard the woman speak to the conductor. Why on earth was she going to Doel? Only squatters still lived there. At least, that was what he had been told. He didn't know the place. He just knew he would stick out like a sore thumb in a deserted place like that. She would recognize him from Dampoort and if she had a single brain cell she would realize he was following her.

If only she had accepted his offer of help, he could have found out where she was heading and pretended to be going there as well. Then she wouldn't have found it strange if she spotted him at her final destination.

It was no good giving in to his frustration, however. He had to plan ahead. Focus on his mission.

Alice Auma herself had told him three things. The Ten Commandments was the only yardstick. Sinners had to be eradicated to bring about peace and prosperity. War and violence rid the world of sinners, she had said.

"But thou shalt not kill?" he had tested her.

"No, thou shalt not. Except in war. That's how wickedness is stamped out. Read your Bible."

He did. Later he learned that thousands of her Holy Spirit Movement soldiers were impervious to bullets as long as they obeyed Lakwena's commands, brought to them in the person of Alice Auma.

Alice Auma Lakwena's soldiers were eventually vanquished. Lakwena left her. She had to flee for her life and died in a Kenyan refugee camp a few years ago.

He knew why Lakwena had abandoned her. Because of Joseph Kony, Auma's so-called cousin—now the leader of the Lord's Resistance Army and probably one of the cruellest monsters ever to walk this earth.

Kony didn't wage war, let alone a holy one. He murdered, raped and mutilated as far as he went. He abducted children, forcing them to do the killing in his name. Kony didn't have a plan. He lived according to his instincts.

Kony had to be stopped. That was why it was so important that Erevu should reclaim what they had been excluded from for more than half a century. The DRC had to be freed from the stranglehold of Kony and others like him. From all the evils Alice Auma had pointed out. Only a holy war, waged by Motetela's followers, could liberate the DRC. And after that, the rest of Africa.

And the Caz woman was the key to the fulfilment of that goal.

*Caz*
*Doel*

It looked odd, the windmill from bygone days with the two nuclear energy cooling towers behind it. Two eras superimposed over each other.

Caz followed the steep path along the seawall to the windmill that had been transformed into a restaurant. She stopped to look at the sweeping vista. The Scheldt was an enormous river. On the opposite bank she could make out a building that might be a refinery. A massive boat was on its way to the port of Antwerp some distance ahead.

The wind was chilly and Caz chose a table inside the mill rather than in the extension. The stained-glass window and old walls made her feel as if she had entered a different age. One where people still wore clogs and bonnets.

The woman who came to take her order dispelled her

fantasy. Caz ordered coffee and the cheapest sandwich on the menu. In Sint-Niklaas she had been too nervous to eat, but now she was famished.

While she was waiting, she realized how tense she was. Not only because of her transport difficulties. What was she actually doing here? Who could she approach, and how?

Maybe she should simply see the outing as an adventure. Consider herself a tourist. The fewer her expectations, the smaller her chances of disappointment.

"Alstublieft." The middle-aged woman put the coffee and an enormous sandwich on the table in front of her.

She had to hand it to the Belgians: they certainly didn't skimp on servings and it looked delicious too.

"Pardon me. Do you live in Doel?" she asked in Afrikaans.

The woman shook her head. "No, in Kieldrecht."

"Did you happen to live here before?"

Another shake of the head. "I'm originally from Temse." She waved her hand at the food. "Enjoy."

"Thanks, it looks delicious. One more question: do you happen to know someone who lives here in Doel?"

"Not really. This is a temporary job." This time there was a firmness in the way she turned.

Caz tucked into the sandwich. Her stomach had long forgotten the morning's yoghurt and the packet of crisps on the train. After taking a last sip of the aromatic coffee, she sat back, replete, and looked at her watch. A quarter to three. At least she had gained a few extra hours here in Doel. She had to be at the bus stop at a quarter to seven, which reminded her that she still had to find out where the bus stop was. Enough time for that.

After she had paid the bill and visited the restroom, she retraced her steps down the steep path.

Her introduction to the town was a neglected park with wooden contraptions displaying faded comic strips of "Suske en Wiske." The long grass and collapsed structures confirmed what Tieneke had said about a ghost town.

A notice on a board some way ahead seemed to disagree: *Doel = inhabited town. Respect the residents! It is forbidden to enter or damage the houses. Trespassers and vandals will be prosecuted.*

Caz began to wander around, dazed. A dystopian atmosphere surrounded the uninhabited houses in varying stages of disrepair. There were clear signs of vandalism. Windows were broken, doors hung lopsidedly on rusty hinges, wrecked furniture lay strewn around.

Almost all the walls were covered in brightly colored graffiti. Much of it had clearly been done by true artists—gigantic depictions in fine detail, painted with a sure hand. Spray-painted attempts and the usual crude efforts by vandals formed a sharp contrast. The sum total was bizarre.

Caz approached a wall and read the words painted neatly on it.

*Later, when all the beautiful memories*
*Have taken the place of my sorrow,*
*I might be able to express*
*What now I can only say with tears.*

She was moved by the sadness of the words and the tacit aggression.

From one multicolored derelict home to another she went, the suitcase squeaking at her heels. What on earth had happened to this town? Here, where Ammie Pauwels had lived and fought for its continued existence. Evidently in vain.

"Niet kraken, hoor!"

Startled, Caz turned. Deep laughter lines fanned out from the corners of the dark-haired woman's eyes, but she looked anything but friendly. Kraken? What did she mean?

"Excuse me?"

"The houses are dangerous." Her Flemish was colloquial, but easy enough to understand. "Some are just waiting to collapse. It's not only illegal, it's also life-threatening to kraak, understand?"

"Kraak?" Caz felt like an idiot.

The woman pointed at her suitcase. "Stay over. Find a place to stay."

She meant squat, Caz realized. She thought Caz was a squatter. Caz gave a slight laugh. "No, I'm just a day-tripper."

The woman frowned. "Why are you walking around with a suitcase if your car is here?"

"No, I got a lift. I'm going further by bus."

"But I've told you you can't stay for the night. It's dangerous. Especially for a woman. There are squatters everywhere, many of them up to mischief. They start fires. Break and smash things as far as they go. Full of drugs."

Caz grew impatient. "And I'm telling you I'm going on by bus. I'm not staying the night."

The woman lit a cigarette. "Schat, there's no bus tonight. The next bus is tomorrow at six fifty-seven."

Caz began to shake her head, ready to argue, when she realized why the times had seemed so strange. The website had used a.m. and p.m. instead of the twenty-four-hour clock.

"Oh, shit." The word slipped out.

"You didn't know?"

Caz shook her head. "I thought the bus was leaving at six fifty-seven tonight." She looked around her. "Is there a B&B somewhere?"

"What does it look like?"

Caz didn't have to answer.

The woman tilted her head. "Why do I understand you, even though you're not speaking Dutch?"

"It's Afrikaans. A language that developed from Dutch, among others. I'm from South Africa.

"Africa? But you're white!"

Caz felt a slight hysteria start to rise. "There are many whites in South Africa. About five million."

"Never!"

She was beginning to feel as if she was part of a hallucination. She'd better get to the point. "You don't happen to have known an Ammie Pauwels? Apparently she lived here until 2000."

"Sorry, schat, I only moved here in 2005. Legally, mind you! I have permission to rent. A relative of yours?"

How the hell did she answer that? "I'm not sure. I want to find out where she went from here."

"Come with me." She beckoned with her hand. "We'll ask my neighbor. If she doesn't know, no one will."

Caz followed the woman to a neat house, evidently occupied.

"Wait here." She stepped on her cigarette, knocked on the door and pushed it open. "Schatske!" she called.

"Yoo-hoo," a voice replied from within.

The woman motioned for Caz to wait and went inside.

She heard voices, but couldn't make out what was being said. Seconds turned into minutes, minutes lingered on.

At last the door opened again. A thin woman with grayish blonde hair accompanied the dark-haired woman.

"You're looking for Ammie Pauwels?" the blonde woman asked.

Caz nodded.

"It was long ago. I knew her husband, not her. Just from sight. But Tobias and I served on a committee together. He died of a heart attack, in 1999. Brought on by the tension of the government's indecision. Ammie stayed on after his death, but not very long. Lived like a recluse. Protested with us only once and almost had a fit when a reporter took a photo.

"I looked in my records but I couldn't find anything more. I'm afraid I don't know where she moved to."

"Can you tell me which house was hers?"

The woman gave the address and directions to get there.

"Thanks, sorry to have bothered you." Caz forced a smile to her lips.

"I hope you find what you're looking for. Good day." The blonde woman shut the door.

"I'll show you the house," the dark-haired woman offered.

"Thank you, that would be kind." She had no idea what she would do to get back to Kieldrecht, but she might as well try to make the best of a bad job.

"What happened to leave the town deserted like this?" Caz asked as they walked along.

"In the sixties or thereabouts it was decided to build a new container dock as part of the expansion of the port of Antwerp. Doel was in the way. They said the new, bigger ships wouldn't be able to turn, which was rubbish in the end. You should see the monster ships passing here nowadays.

"Some residents fought the evictions tooth and nail. Others reluctantly agreed to sell. Then came the nuclear power station. Even greater chaos. It's a long story, but in the end the residents of Doel were evicted—the result of poor management and rash decisions.

"The power station is closing down shortly and it's going to cause outages all over Belgium. The government has thrown billions of euros into the water and they're planning to follow it up with more billions." She mentioned amounts that made Caz reel and gave some more background information before she smiled and continued.

"But I like living here. There are about two dozen residents left. Some more legal than others. Mostly we get along well. Spend time together on Sundays. Wage war against the squatters, vandals, arsonists, the raves held here over weekends. You should have heard the ruckus on New Year's Eve!"

She stopped and pointed at the ruin of a house, colorfully painted by unskilled hands and totally uninhabitable. "Here we are."

The roof seemed about to cave in. All the windows were broken. Bricks had fallen out of the walls. Over to one side stood a rusty garden chair, and further away, the remains of a vacuum cleaner.

Caz felt gripped by despair. Her mother had lived here. Here she was a wife to Tobias, whoever he was. In these streets she walked, probably without a thought for her daughter in distant Africa. Streets that must have looked a lot different then.

What the hell was she doing in this deserted, godforsaken polder town with its post-apocalyptic atmosphere? Here in the Land van Waas, where the tracks of the woman who gave birth to her had been covered such a long time ago.

Caz turned to the dark-haired woman. "Do you think the

lady who works at the restaurant might help me get to Kieldrecht? Of course I'll pay for the fuel and her trouble."

The head was shaken emphatically. "She rides a bike."

"Anyone else who might be going to Kieldrecht?"

She thought for a moment. "I'll ask Guy. Wait here, okay?"

Caz nodded, pushed down the handle of her suitcase and sat down. The bleak desolation that enveloped the town like a fog was more tangible here in front of Ammie Pauwels's house than anywhere else. It was as if she had landed in a broken kaleidoscope.

The man who stopped his car beside her a while later had intelligent eyes behind the lenses of his spectacles. His gray hair and beard were neatly trimmed. The face had strong features.

He asked her a question of which she could only make out "take" and "Kieldrecht."

She nodded. Hopefully he was asking her whether she was the person who wanted to be taken to Kieldrecht. He let the engine idle while he helped her with her luggage and then pointed at the front passenger door.

As they left the town, he tried to start a conversation, but she didn't understand his dialect. Mercifully it was only a ten-minute drive before he drew up at the bus stop and took her luggage from the trunk of the car.

She held out two ten-euro notes. He looked at her as if she had lost her mind, and declined by holding up his hand.

Moments later he was back in the car. He nodded a greeting and drove away.

A tennis ball lodged itself in Caz's throat. Not only because of the man's kindness. The events of the past hour or two had made her emotional.

While she was waiting for the bus to Sint-Niklaas, a tune kept going through her mind. When the bus came, some of the words came to her. Something like: *Say so long, Skipskop, Skipskop say goodbye*. It was a song made famous by David Kramer, telling the story of the forced evacuation of the fishing village, Skipskop, in South Africa.

Just as the residents of Skipskop in the Overberg had had

to make way for a missile-testing terrain almost sixty years earlier, more than a thousand residents of Doel had had to pack up and say goodbye to everything that once had been theirs, but no longer was. Of course they were compensated, but they were still forced to leave at the command of the people in control. Besides, the whole exercise had turned out to be pointless. It had all been for the sake of a dock that wasn't used and a nuclear power station that was going to be shut down. In Afrikaans the word "doel" means purpose. Could there be a more ironic name for a town?

*Ammie*
*Leuven*

"I am absolutely fine, Lieve. Finish up and go home. Your people are waiting for their supper." Of course she was lying. Her tongue was still lazy, her ears rang and one eye felt as if it was drooping, but Lieve's well-intentioned fussing exhausted her even more.

"Fine? I find you collapsed on the living-room floor and now you're fine? Miss Ammie, I know the doctor said it was only a very light stroke, but it's a danger sign you can't simply ignore."

"I'll have tests done tomorrow. You can't do anything more for me tonight. The doctor was satisfied. Go now, Lieve. Please. I just want to rest."

Lieve gave a protracted sigh. "Very well then. The phone is next to you. If you feel at all unwell, just press number one to dial my number. Okay?"

"Okay, Lieve." Ammie took a sip of water. Her mouth was dry.

Lieve kept hovering.

"Goodnight, Luc." Luc? She had wanted to say another name. "Lieve." Her tongue found the right name. "Goodnight, Lieve."

*Erevu*
*Ghent*

"I've been there, Nkoko. There's nothing there. Doel is as dead as can be."

"Then she probably didn't realize it was a deserted place." Erevu's frustration had not abated.

Dove thought for a moment. "There are no lodgings in Doel. We must find out where she's staying tonight."

"How?"

"Jela. Jela has Caz's laptop. Her cellphone is on roaming; she can only send and receive text messages. If she's looking for a place to stay, she'll have to do it on the internet. What a stroke of luck that list of passwords was. Now Jela can look up her incoming mail via her ISP." Dove patted his shoulder. "Chin up, Nkoko, chin up."

Erevu nodded. Thank goodness for Jela and Dove. This new technology was too much for him. He was going to ban it from the Congo as soon as all evil had been eradicated and he became president.

# Sixteen

*Caz*
*Leuven*

Caz took a seat at one of the many street cafés near the Leuven train station. A place to stay was her first priority. Later she would think about the wisdom of the crazy trip she had embarked on.

She asked for the wifi code and as soon as she discovered she wasn't searching for Air B&B, but airbnb, it went more quickly. She found the perfect place close to the station, but the minimum stay was four nights. It wouldn't do, she thought. She didn't want to spend more than two nights, at most. It would give her a day and a half in the city. Enough to go to the university and maybe play tourist for a while.

A few attempts later she hit the jackpot. The place was a little further away from the station than she had hoped, but the rates were reasonable and Jennie, the landlady, looked friendly in the photo.

She clicked on "Contact host." There was no telephone number or email address, only space to send a message.

What if Jennie didn't check her messages tonight? It was almost seven.

There was no other way. Caz filled in the required information and sent the message.

*Luc*
*Damme*

"Luc DeReu." He couldn't hide his impatience at the telephone's intrusion. He had just sat down for supper and was ravenous. He hardly ever spoiled himself with steak and he didn't want it to get cold, especially as he had managed to grill it to a perfect medium rare.

"Professor, it's Lieve Luykens." Her voice sounded hesitant.

He got up from the table and crossed over to the window. "Yes, Lieve?"

"Professor, it's Miss Ammie. I wouldn't have phoned, but she mentioned your name."

"Pardon me?" Was it his imagination, or did Lieve sound tearful?

"Miss Ammie suffered a very light stroke earlier this afternoon. The doctor called it a transient ischaemic attack. She's over the worst and out of danger. Nothing to worry about. We're having tests done tomorrow. But when she said goodbye to me, she called me Luc. It was a slip of the tongue. Now I don't know what to do. You really upset her and I didn't like it when you cross-questioned me. Still, it seems you are in her thoughts."

The news of the stroke, light or not, upset him more than he would have thought. "Lieve, if her condition is really not serious, maybe I could come at the weekend. If it's serious, I'll come tomorrow. But it won't do her any good if my presence is just going to upset her again."

"It's really not serious. Except that it could be the precursor of a more serious stroke, of course. I've just phoned her again and she was well enough to be annoyed because I wanted to make sure she was comfortable. Anyway, if her condition had been serious, I would have stayed with her or forced her to go to hospital. Her doctor thinks it's a warning, but he assured me it's not dangerous in itself. He's retired and he lives nearby. He'll look in while I'm not there."

"Well, okay then. Please let me know if you think I should drive over, Lieve. Like I said, I can call at the weekend. During the week it's difficult, but if it's an emergency, I'll try my best to come. Please keep me posted."

"I will, Professor." There was another moment's hesitation. "Professor, I don't know if I should tell you, but she mentioned Elijah again."

"Did she say who he was?"

"No. Just mentioned his name."

Luc thought for a moment. He didn't want to unnerve Lieve again, but it might be worth a try. "Lieve, do you happen to know why she's afraid of her first husband? César? And their daughter? Cassandra."

Lieve was quiet for a while. "Professor, I'm not sure. Miss Ammie is quite confused nowadays. I think César was an evil man. I think she believes their daughter inherited the evilness."

"On what grounds? As far as I know she never knew the child."

"She believes it's in the blood, Professor."

The way dullness ran in his blood? Why couldn't he have inherited his father's brilliance? It had clearly been diluted by his mother's blood. From the little Jacq had told him, he only knew that she had been good and kind and had died much too young. And that she had been some kind of assistant at the university. But with Ammie as the mother figure in his life, he hadn't really wondered too much about his own mother.

"This Elijah. Do you think he was her lover?" he mused rather than asked.

"Goodness, no, Professor. That would be a sin. She was married." Lieve sounded scandalized.

"True," he reassured her. But he knew very well that love, particularly passion, didn't recognize sin.

However, if Elijah had been Ammie's lover, how could she be so sure Cassandra was César's child?

There were a number of possible answers, but he would like to hear what Ammie said.

The steak was cold when he sat back down at last, but he hardly noticed.

*Caz*
*Leuven*

Caz was just about to give up when the email came through from the airbnb landlady. She had room and Caz was welcome. Fifteen minutes later Caz was on a bus. She asked to be let off at the Ghent-Sint-Pieters clinic. There was no doubt that Sint Pieter, whoever he might have been, was a popular saint around there.

She was met at the bus stop by a pleasant young woman who identified herself in perfect English as Jennie, took Caz's case and dragged it the last hundred meters to a lovely old house, where two cats were waiting.

Caz suddenly realized how much she missed Catya. The feeling caught her off-guard, but it was soon replaced by gratitude that she had found a bed for the night.

When she sat down on the bed in her charming room, Caz was yet again on the verge of tears—this time for a different reason than in Kieldrecht. A demon and an angel seemed to be battling for the welfare of Caz Colijn. Tonight the angel had won.

*Erevu*
*Ghent*

"Leuven. We have the address as well." Dove smiled and looked up from his tablet.

Erevu breathed a sigh of relief. "Good, I'll go there tomorrow. You'll have to keep things going here. It's a pity we didn't know the Colijn woman next door was going to be out most of the day. You could have taken a look around inside. Most of Cassandra Colijn's luggage must still be there. She left for Doel with very little."

Dove shrugged. "We can't risk it until we have determined our neighbor's new routine. I think now that the old woman is dead, she'll go out more often."

"You'll have to watch her." Erevu got up and stretched. "My fingers are getting stiff, I'll take out the mvet tomorrow. Nothing like a little traditional music to remind one of one's roots, don't you think?"

Dove smiled. "I take it I must air the dreadlocks tonight? Dust off the ankle rattles?"

Erevu patted his shoulder. "You read me like a book, Dove. Like a book."

*Luc*
*Damme*

Lieve's call brought back all the questions he had been trying to banish from his mind. Who was Elijah? Who did Ammie flee with? How did she pay Josefien Colijn? And he kept wondering about the plane crash.

He entered "Mbuji-Mayi" in the search box, clicked on a few articles and skimmed over the text to get an idea of the contents. A piece of information on the website allaboutgemstones.com caught his eye. He had read the same story the previous time he researched "Bakwanga." *In the early 1980s, a young girl found an 890 carat rough stone near the town of Mbuji-Maye. It was found by accident while she was playing in a mound of tailings from the Bakwanga diamond mine.*

It was more than an anecdote, he soon discovered.

The little girl had shown the pretty stone to her uncle. The uncle had realized it was a diamond and had sold it to local Congolese diamond dealers.

Luc didn't even want to guess what the man must have got for it. Certainly nowhere near its true value. Next, it was sold to Lebanese buyers, who took the diamond to Antwerp. A few transactions later the magnificent diamond was put on display at the Smithsonian Institute in Washington DC, before the cutting process began.

It took four years to cut the biggest part of the diamond to a stone of just under 408 carats—at the time the second largest faceted stone after the Cullinan.

The stone was named Incomparable, not only because of its size, but also because of its exceptional shades of yellow and brown and its unique shape.

In October 1988 the Incomparable became the largest diamond ever offered for sale on auction. The reserve price was twenty million dollars. The closest offer was a meagre twelve million and the stone remained unsold.

In 2002 the stone was offered on eBay for fifteen million pounds, but again remained unsold.

The diamond's present whereabouts were unknown.

The staggering amounts sparked Luc's curiosity and he learned that the most expensive diamond sold to date was the Graff Pink in 2010, for forty-six million dollars.

This record price was nearly surpassed when the Pink Star drew a bid of eighty-three million dollars at a Sotheby auction, but the prospective buyer could not honor the deal.

Luc also read about the Millennium Star, considered the most beautiful diamond in the world. But what impressed him more was learning that the mother stone had weighed 777 carats and that it had been found in the Mbuji-Mayi district in 1990. Like the Incomparable.

Mbuji-Mayi, where Ammie's father died in a plane crash four months after Ammie's marriage to César Ronald Bruno Janssen. According to Lieve, Ammie had said César Janssen was an evil man. So evil, in fact, that she had been hiding from him for more than half a century.

Evil and an unnatural death, both linked to Mbuji-Mayi, known for monstrous diamonds. Interesting. Chillingly interesting.

*Thursday, 25 September*
*Caz*
*Leuven*

When she got up, Caz's muscles protested, but by the time she had had her second cup of coffee and Jennie had given her directions to get to the university's administration building, she felt better. Only the muscles in her arm had not forgotten how far she had dragged the suitcase the day before.

Her mood varied between excitement at the thought of exploring the city and uncertainty about her proposed visit to the university. Did she really want to raise ghosts from the past?

Outside the sky was overcast and there was a chilly breeze. Maybe she should have worn a jacket. But, no, then she would have to carry it over her arm when it got warmer. It was bliss to walk with only the backpack. She could even put her handbag inside.

She had been really lucky to find Jennie. She was not only friendly, but her lovely old house dating back to the seventeenth century was beautifully restored and full of character. And it was only a ten- or twelve-minute walk from the university.

Leuven, Caz discovered, had a completely different ambience from Ghent. It was less laid back, though there were cyclists everywhere, and students, dragging cases or standing around in groups, talking. Even the buildings looked starker, though when the Town Hall came into view, she noticed it had no lack of Gothic excess.

Amazed, Caz walked round the wedding-cake-like building before carrying on along Naamse Street to the registrar's office. She had picked a bad time, she realized as she watched the students come and go. Of course, Njiwa had mentioned that it was the start of the academic year.

At ten o'clock sharp she entered the administration building through the arched doorway, to the accompaniment of a clock chiming in a church spire somewhere, or perhaps even in the Town Hall itself.

Inside there was a jumble of people and voices and movement. Three enquiries later she was directed to another building in the same street. Inside it smelled of mouldy documents and stale breath. After being sent from one office to another, Caz reached a gray-haired woman who was prepared to listen to her stuttering enquiry after someone called DeReu who used to work there.

"DeReu? Yes, of course, Professor DeReu. Which of the two do you mean? Father or son? Not that either of them still lectures here. Professor Jacq DeReu passed away a long time ago and Professor Luc DeReu ... Well, he left a number of years ago. Fourteen, fifteen, if I've got it right. Yes, it was about two or three years after Professor Jacq's death."

"Do you happen to know where Professor DeReu junior finds himself now?"

With a shake of the head the woman reached for the phone. "I'm afraid I don't know, but I'll call someone who might."

"I'm sorry to be a bother."

"I'd much rather do this than deal with the students. Like lost sheep, most of them." She lowered her gaze. "Ingrid?"

The woman switched to a dialect Caz didn't understand. Through the window the sky looked a little bluer than when she had left Jennie's house—still grayish blue, but at least not pure gray any more. An airplane trailed a white line behind it, like the wake of a ship.

"That's strange." The woman put the phone down, frowning. "Inge says no one has asked about the DeReus in years, but this is the second enquiry she's had in the past few weeks. From you and another woman. Or are you Lieve Luykens who's enquiring again?"

Caz shook her head. "No, I'm not."

"Nevertheless, Ingrid doesn't know where Professor Luc DeReu is either. Apparently he went from here to Maastricht but he left there as well. We don't know where he went from there." She shook her head. "He probably decided to stay under the radar after the debacle. And rightly so. To think his father was the epitome of integrity and moral values."

"What debacle?" Perhaps it would give her a clue.

The woman snorted. "Who would have thought such an unassuming man could get so carried away that he would destroy his reputation?" She lowered her voice. "Sexually harassed one of his students. Apparently ambushed her round every corner, making indecent proposals. To make matters worse, she was an exchange student. From Suriname. Her nickname was Suri. She left before the end of the academic year.

"When it became known, the professor handed in his resignation. I must say, the girl was asking for it, the way she behaved, but one would hope a professor would be immune." She clapped her hand over her mouth. "I hope the professor isn't a friend or a relative?"

Caz shook her head. Should she try her luck with this gossipmonger? "You don't happen to know what became of Ammie Pauwels? His mother, I understand." Shit, that would make this man her half-brother. The thought nearly knocked the breath out of her body.

"Ammie Pauwels? Now, there was a piece of work! Professor Luc's stepmother, Professor Jacq's second wife. His first wife worked here at the university, but Luc was just a baby when she died."

Caz was relieved that there was no shared bloodline to further complicate matters.

"Yes, Ammie. One day, out of the blue, she left Professor Jacq and disappeared. The poor man was never the same again." She shook her head. "That was probably where the damage was done to Professor Luc." The phone rang shrilly. "Sorry, that's all I can tell you." She picked up the receiver.

Caz raised her hand in a silent greeting. The woman nodded and turned her attention to the call.

Caz walked to a restaurant opposite the Town Hall and sank down on a chair. The fountain she looked out on was in the shape of a man reading a book and simultaneously pouring water into his own head.

"That's our Fonske." A waiter stopped beside her and smiled. "The eternal student with beer for brain cells. Officially the Fons Sapientiae, Latin for 'source of wisdom.'"

Caz couldn't help smiling. "If beer is the source of wisdom, I'll take one. Kriek, please."

"What kind?"

She shrugged. "Surprise me."

The waiter double-clicked his tongue in agreement, almost as if he was calling a horse.

Caz had no sooner taken her handbag out of her backpack than the cherry beer was placed in front of her in a goblet with an ornate logo that read Lindemans.

"Alstublieft." And the waiter was gone.

The kriek was even tastier than she remembered from the single sip she had taken from Tieneke's glass. Maybe it was because she was thirsty. Maybe because it took the nasty taste of gossip from her mouth.

Lieve Luykens. Why would she enquire about the DeReus? She stared at Fonske but he offered no answer, just kept pouring water into his head.

*Luc*
*Ghent*

Luc's eyes swept over the heads of the young people who, in a few years' time, would be holding the future of his generation in their hands. He had fewer students than ever this year. And they seemed even less interested in his lectures than before.

He had updated today's lecture, but he knew in advance that none of them gave a damn about the difference between insurgents, revolutionaries, rebels, terrorists and warmongers.

In Stellenbosch a student had got up and said his father had hunted terrorists, and now those very terrs were sitting in parliament. What did one call them now, he wanted to know.

"Politicians," Luc had answered. Only a few had laughed. It had been the liveliest conversation ever to take place in any of his classes.

"Ladies and gentlemen," he tried to call the group in front of him to order. If he thought they would pay attention to him instead of their conversations, cellphones and tablets, he had another think coming. Not that the thought had entered his mind.

"A diamond of 890 carats," he spoke into the microphone. Heaven knows where he was going with that, but it worked. Especially the girls were suddenly all ears.

"A country where a little girl picks up a pretty stone in a pile of mine waste that later turns out to be a diamond of 890 carats," he continued while he groped in his mind for a link with the lecture he had prepared. "A country where a diamond of 777 carats was discovered a few years later." He paused for effect. "A country that produces the coltan your cellphones and tablets need to work. The largest producer of cobalt ore in the world, and one of the largest producers of copper and industrial diamonds." He pushed his spectacles higher up the bridge of his nose. "You'd think a country like that would be one of the most thriving in the world."

The students were silent.

"But it isn't. It is a country where there are almost more rebel groups at present than members of parliament."

"What country is it, Professor?" a thin wisp of a girl in the first row asked.

"It's the country your forefathers and mine exploited for their own objectives."

A whispering ensued, and for the first time in his life Luc knew he had the students in the palm of his hand. If only he knew what to do with that victory.

*Caz*
*Leuven*

Caz walked back to her lodgings, deep in thought. She was aware of the buildings towering above her, but she wasn't really taking anything in.

She had a biological mother, or had had one. Surely a father too. And a stepfather. And a stepbrother. But none of them had ever become family. Only the stepfather had taken the trouble to try to contact her. Lord knows why.

She used to have a father, a mother and a sister, only they turned out not to be what she had thought they were. A father-in-law, mother-in-law and a husband, who hadn't wanted her or her child.

Except for Lilah, she was alone in the world. And Lilah had her own life to lead. One that took her progressively further away from Caz. You can't see a child once a year and expect to remain a part of her life. Superficially, yes, but the umbilical cord was being stretched thinner and thinner.

Ammie Pauwels. A piece of work, according to the gray-haired gossip. Tieneke had described her as a breathtakingly beautiful woman who had caused an irreversible upheaval in the lives of the Colijns.

A woman who had led an adventurous life. Lived in the Congo. Fled from the Congo. Landed in South Africa. Had a child and left her there. Returned to Belgium. Got married. Raised another woman's child. Walked away. Remarried. Disappeared after her husband's death.

She might have been heartless, but she was certainly brave as well.

If she had disappeared, her stepson might not know where she was either.

Why would Lieve Luykens be looking for him?

She became aware of the rhythm of her footsteps. Lie-ve Luy-kens. Luc-De-Reu. Lie-ve Luy-kens. Luc-De-Reu. Lie-ve Luy ... Caz stopped and tilted her head when another sound got through to her. The music against a background of swishing bicycle tyres, the drone of cars and the rattling of buses had an unmistakable African sound.

He was sitting some distance from the bus stop where she had got off the night before. The dreadlocks covered his face. His shirt was brightly colored, the musical instrument in his hands strange for these parts. A kind of zither. A bent stick with a few strings attached to it, and a gourd for resonance. Around his ankles were strings of seeds, shells and beads, making percussion sounds as he kept time with his feet.

He didn't look up when she approached. Words flowed

from his lips in a strange singsong language. He seemed to be telling a story rather than singing a song.

On the ground in front of him lay a cap, the hollow part facing up. A few coins glistened inside it.

The nostalgia that overcame her was as unexpected as it was intense. The musician wasn't even someone from her own country, at most someone from her continent. Yet the sudden longing she felt was like a blow to her heart.

She missed her smallholding. The wild olive trees. The sound of the wind in the poplars. The crisp Overberg air. The deep blue, aircraftless sky. Catya. Even the Cape robin that left its splotches all over the house. The hooting of the owls at night. The creaking sound of blue cranes in flight. Pheasants coming to beg for breadcrumbs or leftover rice.

She missed so, so many things. Having her own transport. Independence. Familiar roads. Facial expressions she could read. A sense of humor she could understand. A sense of humor, period. Her ears were tired of Flemish and all its various dialects.

She missed Ellen's unadorned Afrikaans. She missed Ellen. Her down-to-earth nature.

The street singer began a new melody. Lamenting yet almost rebellious. Caz pulled herself together, took two euros from the side pocket of her backpack and placed the coins in the inverted cap.

"Thank you," he said softly.

He didn't look up, just nodded slightly and sang or talked on, spilling out his own longing.

# Seventeen

*Luc*
*Ghent*

"That wasn't so bad. Why does everyone call him Luc-de-Loser?"
The student was hastily silenced when her friend noticed Luc slightly behind them. The girl turned, and blushed when she saw him. The two of them disappeared down the passage, giggling.

Luc-de-Loser. It probably served him right. He *was* a loser. A pathetic figure. But he had been different today. At least he could give himself credit for that. His lecture might not have been brilliant or a roaring success, but the majority of the class had paid attention while he was telling them about the M23 rebels, the LRA, or Lord's Resistance Army, the FLDR, ADF and almost every letter in the alphabet that could spell out violence in acronyms.

Towards the end, their attention had begun to wander until he had mentioned blood diamonds. But by that time the lecture was over.

He glanced at his cellphone as he turned the sound back on. Lieve. Verdorie, Ammie. He fought his way out of the throng and dialed the moment he thought he could make himself heard.

"Lieve, it's Luc. Is anything wrong?" he asked, anxiety rising in his throat. "My phone is on silent while I'm lecturing."

"I'm sorry if I gave you a fright, Professor. No, Miss Ammie is the same. Slightly better, I think. Actually surprisingly lucid as well."

He breathed a sigh of relief.

"You won't believe me, but she asked where you are. When I said you're lecturing, she asked when you'd be visiting again."

"Really?"

"Really. I do think she'd like to see you again. Or at least she wanted to at that moment."

Luc closed his eyes and visualized his calendar. The next day his schedule was full. On Saturday he had to work on a postgraduate student's dissertation. "Unless there's an immediate crisis I can come through on Sunday at the earliest, Lieve."

"That's very kind of you, Professor, but you do understand that her mood changes from one moment to the next? She might want to see you today but by Sunday she might not."

Luc nodded as if she could see him. "I understand. I'll call you on Sunday morning. Around nine? Then you can tell me if you think I should come."

"As long as you're not upset if she changes her mind."

"I understand."

"Thank you, Professor. I hope it's a good sign."

"So do I, Lieve. So do I."

"I truly believe it's the loneliness that gets to her. The doctor was here again this morning. Except for the light stroke, which might be a warning sign, he said her health is good for her age. But, yes, I'll hear from you on Sunday morning."

"Okay, but please call if there are problems or if her condition deteriorates."

"I will."

When he returned the phone to his pocket he realized how his attitude toward Ammie had shifted since Lieve's first phone call. At first, visiting Ammie had felt like a duty he fulfilled more from a sense of curiosity than out of concern. Now it was quite different. He didn't quite know how or why. Only that his interest in her now went beyond the call of duty.

He wanted to see Ammie again, even though he barely recognized the dignified, eccentric old lady as the young woman he had known as his mother.

Someone tugged at his sleeve and he looked down. It was the slim, pale girl who had sat in the front row during his lecture.

"Professor, I'm sorry to bother you. I was just wondering. I googled, and the enormous diamonds you were talking about, those from the DRC, they're called the Incomparable and the Millennium Star, aren't they?"

He nodded.

"I see diamonds like those are worth millions."

"That's true." Where was she heading?

"I just wondered what would happen if an enormous diamond like that fell into the hands of rebels. Just think how many weapons they could buy. Explosives. Mortars and stuff. I don't know much about weapons, but you know what I'm saying."

He nodded again. "Remember, the value on the internet is mostly an estimate, and it's based on the end product. In its rough form the stone isn't worth nearly as much. Anyway, those are truly exceptional stones. I don't think it would be easy for rebels to lay their hands on stones of that caliber."

The girl let out her breath. "Thank goodness. Yes, of course." She gave him a smile. "Interesting lecture, thanks, Professor. It's a pity we don't know how our forefathers really felt about the Congo. What their lives were like. My great-grandmother lived there, but she died before I was born. My grandma was there for only a short while, as a child. She says she can't remember much. It's actually the reason I enrolled for the module. I thought I would learn more about Africa and what it's like there."

"What's your last name, Miss?" he asked.

"Sluyck, Professor. Nele Sluyck."

"Well, Miss Sluyck, if there's time at the end of the next lecture the class might want to discuss it. Some of the other students' grandparents might have told them or their parents something. We can also look at books that might provide some insight. How does that sound?"

Nele Sluyck's cheeks turned a blotchy pink. "Wonderful, Professor. Africa sounds so exotic, so mysterious."

If only the dear child knew, Luc thought as he walked to the building that housed his office. He lectured to youngsters whose grandparents had lived in the Congo. In the meantime he had access to a primary source of information he could have tapped years ago if only he had used his head.

His stepmother had lived in the Congo, while in the case of his students it was their grandparents. It put matters into perspective. He was getting old.

*Caz*
*Leuven*

Today, exactly a week ago, she had landed in Amsterdam. A week, and already she was desperately longing for her old life, which she had foolishly thought she would exchange at the drop of a hat for a life in a country with almost no crime.

And now? All she wanted to do was pick up the rest of her luggage in Ghent and fly back to her comfort zone. Even if it happened to be a discomfort zone.

Caz gazed down at the note with the telephone number Jennie had given her. Lieve Luykens's landline number had been easy to find. Especially since she lived in Leuven. Now she had the number. Jennie had kindly said she didn't mind Caz using her landline, as long as she dialed local numbers. She had also given Caz free access to the internet.

Through Lieve Luykens she might be able to get in touch with Luc DeReu. If Lieve's search had met with success after coming up against a blank wall at KU Leuven, of course.

Caz crossed to the window. Her room was airy and light

and freshly furnished, unlike her musty, dimly lit quarters in Tieneke's home.

Leuven was a lovely city that she would like to explore, but she seemed unable to drum up the enthusiasm. Jennie had given her information on the most important tourist attractions. The Begijnhof had aroused her curiosity. Also Arenberg Castle and the Abdij van 't Park, but her listlessness remained.

She wondered whether the man singing his sad stories was still at the bus stop. She had read on the internet that the instrument was called an mvet and was native to countries like Cameroon, Gabon, Guinea and the Congo. And she had been right, traditionally music played on the mvet was more about the story than the melody or the singing.

To phone Lieve or not. That was where she should be focusing her thoughts, instead of on traditional African musical instruments.

She was chasing after ghosts—ghosts that hadn't wanted her in the first place. In the meantime she was spending money she could barely afford and her translation lay waiting.

Caz crumpled up the note with Lieve Luykens's number and threw it into the wastepaper basket. Lilah would just have to accept that she was going to book an earlier flight and she would console herself with the thought that she would be seeing her daughter in less than three months anyway.

She paid a visit to the neat bathroom she shared with Jennie, walked out onto the patio and then back into the bedroom.

With a frustrated sigh she took the note out of the wastepaper basket and ironed it out with her hand. She would make just this one call. If it came to nothing, that was it.

The phone was in the living room. The receiver was cool in her hand. The buttons were stiff when she pushed them. After the third ring, she fought the urge to replace the receiver and gripped it more firmly.

An automated voice invited her in Flemish to leave a message. She found Dutch much easier to understand than

Flemish, with its dialects, probably because Hans had been Dutch and Fien had adapted to his way of speaking, but Caz followed the gist of what was said.

She left her message in English. "Good day. My name is Caz Colijn and I'd like to get in touch with Professor Luc DeReu. Unfortunately I can't receive calls, only SMSes." She gave the number, asked Lieve to send her Luc DeReu's number or to give her number to him, said goodbye and ended the call.

Caz took a deep breath and discovered that she was perspiring.

Now it was in the hands of the angels, she thought as she returned to her room. Or the demons.

*Erevu*
*Leuven*

At least she hadn't recognized him from Dampoort. But he could kick himself for arriving too late to see where she'd gone this morning. Bloody roads were jammed with traffic. He should have taken the train, but he thought the car would give him more space to manoeuvre. And then he had to pay a ridiculous parking fee to boot.

But here he was in Leuven and he had seen her come back from wherever she had been to.

As a street musician, he could watch her lodgings as well as the closest bus stop but he couldn't follow her for more than a block or two. After that he would have to change his appearance, which was difficult with the mvet. But he would think of something. He should have brought the donnu harp; it could fit into a backpack.

Now he could only hope this Caz made contact with the other old woman by email or cellphone. Jela was watching the one and Dove the other.

*Luc*
*Ghent*

Luc had just immersed himself in a postgraduate essay when the ringing of the cellphone interrupted him. He was tempted not to answer, but saw that it was Lieve. With a sigh he pushed the green button.

"Good day, Lieve?"

"Good day, Professor. I'm sorry to bother you again, but there was a strange message on my landline when I returned from Miss Ammie's. It sounds as if someone is looking for you."

"Me?" He frowned. Who on earth would know about his connection with Lieve Luykens? "Who was it?"

"I'm afraid the message is in English and I don't understand it very well. It's a woman. I could make out something about messages and she mentioned your name. She said she could only receive SMSes, not calls. And, oh, her last name is Colijn."

Luc sat up straight. "Her name? Did she mention her name?"

"Yes, she did. It's a short, odd name. Something like Kess."

Kess? Caz, maybe? Caz Colijn? But it was impossible. How would she know about him? About Lieve? Get hold of Lieve's number? From South Africa as well. Nothing made sense. "Lieve, could you please send me that number?"

"I will. Oh, and I told Miss Ammie you might come over on Sunday. She nodded and mumbled something about finishing business, but I couldn't really make out what she was saying."

"Thank you, Lieve, that's good news."

"I'll send the number, Professor. Good day."

Moments later the number arrived. It started with +27. South Africa. It had to be the translator he had spotted on LinkedIn.

He felt like the fox terrier that had caught the bus. What should he do now?

Think. Think very carefully. That's what. Lieve probably had no idea she had been contacted by someone who might be Ammie's daughter. A daughter Ammie had been hiding from for more than half a century. Because she believed she was as evil as her father.

Does a mother know that kind of thing? Can a mother sense that her child is evil?

*Caz*
*Leuven*

Caz sat at the small desk by the window, which she had opened wide. In the distance she could still hear the far-off sound of the African playing his mvet.

The email she was writing to Lilah was becoming very long. Yet she still hadn't explained that they were actually not Colijns. It would give rise to so many questions. No, first she had to find out herself what was what.

She told Lilah about Fien's death, but not about Tieneke's part in it. She told her she had been to Doel, but not why. She described the town, but kept it short when she realized she couldn't put it into words. She considered telling Lilah about her visit to KU Leuven, but let it go. She told her about the man from Africa who had made her so homesick, before she gave her the bad news.

> Lilah, my love, your mother wants to go home.
>
> I know you'll be disappointed. I was looking forward to seeing you on your birthday, but with Fien no longer with us and Tieneke not wanting me there (I can't imagine staying with her for another two weeks anyway—it would drive me round the bend), I can't really afford to stay. It's not just the money. I have a book to translate and even though the deadline has been postponed, I'm battling with the new Word program. It's bound to slow me down.
>
> Tomorrow I'm going back to Ghent to pick up my luggage. From there I'll try to get an earlier flight to Cape Town. I'll let you know when

I'll be leaving. Let me know if I should send your boots and books and things by courier or if you'd prefer to pick them up or have them fetched at Tieneke's. I don't know if you know anyone in Ghent? I certainly don't fancy hauling everything all the way back.

I'm sorry it's going to cost you money and trouble, but I hope you understand. I'll see you in less than three months.

Love you very, very much and miss you terribly.
MaCaz

Caz was tearful when she had sent the email. She felt as if she had let Lilah down, but also as if the country was doing its best to get rid of her. It was a melodramatic thought, born chiefly from the friction between herself and Tieneke, but also from her struggle with public transport, the unreadable faces of the people, the language she had more trouble following than she had anticipated and the lack of real fresh air.

She would go home and try to be less of a recluse. One good thing this trip had taught her was that John Donne had been right: no man is an island. She had made an island of her smallholding and she had to put it right. There were wonderful people in Stanford, who had tried to involve her in their activities, but she had always shied away. Once she was home, it would change. A good way to start would be by joining a book club. Books were her life, after all. Maybe she could even find a hobby. Take a few classes.

She wasn't much of an artist, but she was quite good at making things. Like the wind chimes and clay objects she had made in Pretoria and sold at a craft market to finance one of Lilah's more expensive excursions.

Caz made coffee in the kitchen and when she returned, Lilah had sent a reply.

Dearest MaCaz
I can't tell you how disappointed I am that you

want to cut your trip short. I was soooo looking forward to showing you my world. There's also something I want to talk to you about. Yes, it's a man, but don't stress now. I just like him a lot, despite a few complications. But I want to tell you face to face. NOTHING for you to worry about. Really.

I'm so pissed off at that Tieneke bitch. If she had been nice to you, you would have stayed. But I do understand. And I don't want you to stay just to please me if you're clearly not happy. As you said, we'll see each other in December. I'll try to come earlier so that we'll have more time together. It's because of my busy schedule that you've had to hang around to see me.

Don't worry about my boots and stuff. I'll arrange for a courier when I'm back.

Love you loooooooots. Keep me up to speed with your travel arrangements.

Have to run.

Your little jacaranda blossom

This time Caz couldn't hold back the tears. Why did everything have to be so hard? She really wanted to see her child. Really wanted to hear about the man in her life. What complications?

Another frightening thought struck her. What if Lilah got married and stayed here forever? But, to be fair, could she really expect Lilah, after the life she'd been leading, to return to South Africa? Go back to living in a country where one's life is permanently in danger?

Of course not. Of course bloody not.

*Erevu*
*Leuven*

At least they now knew what her plans were, though it was still not clear why she had come to Leuven in the first place.

Because she was fluent in Flemish, Jela could follow the Afrikaans of the email reasonably well. The gist of it was that the Caz woman was on her way back to Ghent and from there to South Africa.

Thank goodness, the daughter had replied immediately. Of course Jela could not read the emails this Caz sent, only the answers. But the daughter's reply had included the original mail. Very handy.

He only hoped the Caz woman would still try to contact Ammie Pauwels before she left. He had to get to Ghent as soon as possible. When she arrived there tomorrow, they had to know where they stood.

# Eighteen

*Friday, September 26*
*Caz*
*Ghent*

Strange that Tieneke had not replied to her message, Caz thought as she waited in front of the Ghent-Dampoort station building for bus number three. She would undoubtedly be relieved to hear that Caz was on her way back to South Africa.

Caz had her two euros ready when the bus stopped. By this time she knew how long it would take to get to the Ghent Bruges stop. Quite the seasoned traveller, aren't you, she mocked herself, smiling at the thought.

But she would probably never get used to relying on public transport. Not that she would dare to drive a car over here, even if she had one at her disposal. The courteousness of the local drivers totally intimidated her.

In South Africa she considered herself a good driver compared to the rest, but here she would be terrified of making a mistake. Driving on the right side of the road further complicated matters. Especially around traffic circles, and there were hordes of them.

She got off at the stop and went into the corner shop. Chocolates for Tieneke and a bottle of wine for herself. On the spur of the moment she took a six-pack of kriek to the cash register. Tieneke liked it, after all. Maybe it would improve her mood.

Babette recognized her and smiled. "You've been away for a few days?"

Caz nodded and returned the smile. "I was in Doel and Leuven, but I'm going back home shortly." See, she told herself, it wasn't so hard to open up to people.

Babette gave her her change. "I'm glad you were in time to see Fien before she passed on."

Caz nodded, at a loss what to reply.

"I see the two tenants in Tieneke's rental home left early this morning. I was under the impression the older one was going to stay longer. Tieneke said something about a month and it definitely hasn't been that long."

"Tieneke's rental home?"

"Yes, the house next door that she rents out. Clever to do it on a weekly basis. Erdem of the B&B on the corner has to have the linen washed three, four times a week as the guests come and go. On the other hand, I suppose he makes more money."

Tieneke owned two adjoining houses. That was news. Goes to show what you can do if you lead a sober life. Valuable assets, considering Tieneke didn't have a job. Property couldn't be cheap. Especially if you converted it to rand.

"I must say," Babette continued, "personally I don't know whether I'd like African tenants. Two men, besides. But it's Tieneke's decision and money is money. I know her grandmother, who left the house Tieneke lives in to Fien, would turn in her grave. She wouldn't have approved of black neighbors, not even temporarily."

And Caz had thought racism didn't exist in Belgium. Well, well.

"Like Fien, she lived to a ripe old age. I remember Fien's

mother well. I was pertrified of her. Cranky, like you wouldn't believe. My mother told me Fien and Hans lived with her at first, but a year or so into the marriage the atmosphere became unbearable. That was why they left for South Africa. The old lady couldn't stand Hans. Maybe because he was a Dutchman."

Now she had a clearer picture of Fien's parental home. Also a victim, it seemed. Caz put the chocolates and wine into her backpack and hooked her fingers through the six-pack of kriek.

At Tieneke's home she pressed the doorbell and faintly heard it ring inside. All the curtains were drawn, as usual. Next door as well. No movement this time. Not in the house on the right either, but she had never seen movement there.

She still found the rows of attached houses odd. The rectangular strips of garden at the back, separated by neatly clipped box hedges and ending against the back walls of the garages, as well.

They were quite impractical too, especially in a country known for its copious rains, cold winters and snow. You had to walk the length of the garden to reach the garage, and if you wanted to pick up someone in front of the house, as Tieneke had done, you had to drive halfway around the block to get to the front door.

Caz rang the bell again and turned to look at the shop. Babette was smoking outside, her eyes on the passers-by. No wonder she knew so much about everybody.

There was still no reaction from Tieneke. Caz's fingers hurt from the weight of the kriek. Tieneke might be at the back or in the bathroom. Or asleep. Caz waited a while before trying again.

Still no reaction.

Damn. She had texted Tieneke, telling her she would be there just after lunch. It was three now. Could Tieneke have gone out? But why not send a message to say when she'd be back?

Caz put down the kriek and rubbed her aching fingers

before pressing the bell again. Still no reaction. She looked over her shoulder again, but Babette had gone inside.

What now? There was no restaurant close by where she could sit and wait. Not that she knew of anyway.

Caz took out her cellphone. No, no message from Tieneke. She hoped her phone wasn't on the blink. Lately the battery didn't last long and she thought the phone felt warmer than it should.

She sent another text message. *Tieneke, I'm here at your house. When will you be home?*

Caz frowned. She could swear she'd heard a sound inside the house just after she had sent the message. *Tieneke?*

Yes, there it was again. A soft ping. It sounded as if it were coming from Tieneke's bedroom right above the front door.

Bloody hell. Tieneke had gone somewhere and left her cellphone at home. That would explain everything. She should have let Tieneke know last night that she was coming, but she didn't think it would be a problem to wait until this morning.

Caz consoled herself with the thought that Tieneke cooked supper every night at five and ate at half past six on the dot. She had kept it up even after Fien's death. A two-hour wait at most. But where could she go?

Or did Tieneke leave on purpose because she didn't want Caz to stay the night? But why not say so? Maybe getting other lodgings for the night wasn't a bad idea anyway. Yes, it might be the best solution.

Caz walked past the shop, to the house on the corner opposite the bus stop. Maybe she would be lucky, like in Leuven.

It took a while after she had rung the bell, but at last there were footsteps. The same man who had welcomed his two guests the week before opened the door.

"Good day?"

"Hello. I believe you rent out rooms?"

He nodded. "But only through airbnb."

Was she imagining it or was he looking her up and down? She remembered there had also been a kind of screening process before Jennie had accepted her. She'd had to send a copy of her passport by email and provide reasons for her visit. Fortunately she had a copy on her laptop as part of her communication with the travel agent on the subject of extra medical cover.

"My sister lives further down the street, but she's not home. I urgently need a room for the night. You don't happen to have one available?" Oh shit, it's Friday, she realized. Weekend.

"I do, but the minimum stay is two nights. And we'll have to go through airbnb. I don't want to end up being blacklisted. They send me a lot of clients." She seemed to have passed the initial test.

"That's okay." Maybe she should just stay there until she managed to change her flight.

"Very well. The name is Erdem." He pushed the handle of her suitcase into the slot and picked it up. "You're lucky. I had a cancellation, so I can put you in the room with the roof terrace. The other one is rather small."

"I'm Caz. Thank you so much, Erdem." Only now did she realize he had quite a dark complexion. Turkish? Could be.

He pointed at the kriek. "Shall I put those in the fridge?"

"That would be nice." To hell with Tieneke. She wished she had moved in here long ago.

Erdem showed her the kitchen and the coffee and breakfast cereals, put away the kriek and led her up a flight of stairs. The room was modern, airy and tidy, the terrace sizeable.

"Can I bring you anything to drink? Coffee? A Coke?" he asked kindly after he had put the suitcase on the bed.

"Anything cold would be lovely, thanks."

When he left, Caz walked out onto the terrace and saw a table and chairs and a few potted plants.

The Coke Zero Erdem brought a few moments later was ice cold. When she had quenched her thirst, she took out her cellphone again to let Tieneke know she had found a place to stay overnight. Maybe Tieneke had been at home and just didn't feel like having Caz stay over. Anyhow, even if she wasn't home and had left her phone behind, Tieneke was bound to get all the messages when she returned.

For the time being she could just relax.

*Luc*
*Damme*

The moment he reached home, Luc got into the shower, then put on a pair of jeans and pulled on a fresh shirt. He rolled up the sleeves. It was wonderful weather for the time of year.

Unlike other evenings, he immediately poured himself a glass of wine and sat down on his patio with the cellphone in his hand. It was a spare phone with an extra SIM card he had never used before. Maybe he was being overcautious, but rather safe than sorry.

He still didn't understand how Caz Colijn had got onto Lieve, but the fact remained that she did. And she was looking for him. If she was looking for Ammie and found out that Lieve was Ammie's carer, why would she ask that he contact her? He could only assume that she didn't know who Lieve was, didn't know where Ammie was, but that she knew Ammie was his stepmother. How did she know his name? And where did she get Lieve's number?

It was no use speculating. The point was: should he contact her or not?

If not, he should put the bloody phone down. If he was going to, he should decide on an approach.

He took a sip of wine. In vino veritas, they say, but wine couldn't give answers or make decisions on his behalf.

*Received message from LL but Luc DeReu not available*, he typed tentatively in English. Okay then, how would she interpret it? She would certainly ask herself how the so-called messenger knew about Lieve's message? Did it matter? Probably.

*I am LDR's colleague*, he continued. *Why do you want to contact him? Maybe I can help?*

He thought for a while about an alias, decided on *TU*. The small screen turned black while he hesitated. After the third sip of wine he pressed the send button and immediately regretted it.

Complications. He wasn't a man for complications and

this could only turn into a complication. Couldn't he just have left it? Verdorie, what now?

Half an hour later, just as the rice was coming to the boil, his phone beeped. In his haste to pick it up, the spoon fell from his hand and drops of the curry mixture he had been stirring spattered over the floor. He hardly noticed.

*It's personal. Would be glad if you could give him the number so he can contact me himself. Thanks. CC.*

Luc chewed on his upper lip. How should he proceed? He raked his fingers through his hair. He was badly in need of a haircut. He had planned to go before the opening ceremony but didn't get round to it. His hair grew as though he shampooed with manure.

*Know Luc very well*, he finally replied. *He's out of reach at present. Would like to help. TU.*

He sent the message and watched the screen as if he had suddenly grown deaf and wouldn't be able to hear the sound of the phone. Ten minutes later there was still no message. Only the smell of burned rice.

The rice! Verdikkeme!

*Caz*
*Ghent*

How could she tell a bloody stranger she wanted to find out whether her birth mother was alive? She didn't know Luc DeReu from a bar of soap, let alone his colleague.

Wasn't it a bit too kind to stand in for a friend and colleague in a personal matter? Must be a woman. Men aren't usually so willing to offer help on behalf of someone else.

But something didn't make sense. Unless TU was a girlfriend trying to find out whether DeReu was cheating on her. Had she caused trouble for the man? Lieve Luykens would probably have said it was a woman who had left the message for DeReu.

Damn. She should have let it go. Maybe this was a sign to let sleeping dogs lie. On the other hand, if *she* had received a message like that, meant for the man in her life, she might also have been concerned. Not that she had any personal experience of being in a close relationship.

A knock on her door made her look up. "Caz?"

"Come in, Erdem."

He put his head around the door. "I'm going to Ghent and I'll be going past the Korenmarkt. I can drop you there, if you want. You must be hungry, and there aren't any restaurants around here. Only takeaway joints."

Caz made a quick decision. "That would be nice, thanks."

He smiled. "I'll pick you up at the front in five minutes, okay?"

"Thanks." She ran her fingers through her curls, applied some lipstick and sprayed perfume on her wrists. It would have to do. She would take a shower later.

When they drove past Tieneke's house, it was pitch dark. Not even a chink of light showed through the drawn curtains at the windows on either side of the front door. Strange. Tieneke always left the light on in the hallway. Even during the day.

Caz shivered when she thought of that awful little hallway. With the perpetually drawn curtains, apparently to shield them from people looking in, it was like a gateway to depression.

*Luc*
*Damme*

He had felt like dumping the blackened pot along with the rice. Luckily he didn't. Now it was almost clean again after a heavy bout of scouring and scrubbing. A short soak with a bleach solution and it would be good to go again.

The floor was gleaming. He'd run the mop over the entire surface. Now he was ravenous. An omelette, he decided. The curry mixture meant for the rice could serve as filling.

Bloody cellphone. Bloody woman who started something, then simply withdrew. As if he had time to waste.

Better to concentrate on his work. After his partial breakthrough with the students today he wanted to go through his lectures for Monday again. With the thrill of success still fresh, he wanted to try to put some life into them. Try new, exciting approaches.

He probably shouldn't expect youngsters to be as moved by the absurdity and tragedy of greed, ambition and the lust for power as he was. They didn't understand that kind of thing. Not in its practical form, anyhow. He had to make it real for them so that they could understand their own greed and ambition. Understand where the lust for power came from. Recognize that its seed nestles in each of us. Realize how it can escalate once it germinates. Only then might they begin to understand why those three factors were responsible for the greatest tragedies and crimes against humanity.

The omelette turned out perfect. The curry mixture had drawn a little water but it wasn't too bad. Actually quite delicious.

Content, at least physically, he took out his laptop.

Moments later he was staring despondently at the title of his lecture on the screen. *Joseph Kony as strategist and militarist, seen against the background of the failed Operation Lightning Thunder of 2008.*

Yes, indeed. A topic that would make every student sit up and take notice. They probably couldn't wait to hear how a monster they'd never heard of had warded off an attack planned with surgical precision by an entire alphabet of acronyms. In a country none of them was ever likely to visit.

Luc inserted a footnote: *Who is Joseph Kony?* And a second one: *Why and how did he orchestrate one of the worst ever reigns of terror in countries like the DRC and Uganda? Why has no one been able to stop him?*

He deleted the second part of the footnote and wrote a third footnote to himself: *In the title you give away the outcome of the operation. If it were a novel, would you have wanted to continue reading, knowing the conclusion?*

He jumped when the cellphone at his elbow announced the arrival of a text message. *CC*, he read on the screen. Verdikkeme. Just as he was making headway. With a sigh he opened the message.

*I don't know Luc DeReu at all. But I had hoped he would*

*know whether my birth mother, his stepmother, was still alive. Her name is Ammie Pauwels. I think even a good friend of his won't be able to help me with that. But thanks for the offer. CC.*

*Caz
Ghent*

There. She hoped she had reassured the woman that Caz Colijn held no threat for her.

Caz had just paid for her pea soup and kriek at a restaurant situated some way out of the crush when her cellphone pinged again. *Why do you want to know? I see from your number you're in South Africa.*

Caz frowned. The tone was almost rude after the earlier friendliness. A jealous, suspicious lover? *Presently in Belgium. For a short while. Only found out here I didn't grow up with my biological parents. Think it's logical for anyone to try and find out whether the biological parent you've just found out about is still alive. LDR was the sensible place to start. Sorry to have troubled you.*

Now *she* sounded peeved, she realized after she had sent the message. Be that as it may. She got up, slung the strap of her handbag over her shoulder, waved at the genial owner who was trading jokes at one of the tables, and headed for the Korenmarkt bus stop.

If TU still hadn't got the message that it was an innocent enquiry, it was her problem. Or his. Maybe DeReu was gay.

When Caz got off at the stop, she noticed that the shop was closed and Tieneke's place was as dark as before. But it was quite a distance away, so maybe she was wrong. She was certainly not going to walk all the way over there now. A shower and bed. That was all she could manage.

Her cellphone pinged again just as she got into bed. Maybe Tieneke had just come home? She stretched and picked up her reading glasses from the bedside table. TU. *Ammie is alive, but she's old, senile and in poor health. Where in Belgium are you?*

Caz felt as if she couldn't breathe. Her birth mother was alive. She had realized it was a possibility, but having it confirmed struck her like a blow to the head. Somewhere in this same country there was a woman named Ammie Pauwels who knew she had given birth to a child, had bartered over her, then abandoned her. Senile or not, at some level she had to know it. *Ghent,* she typed when she had regained her breath.

There was a long pause before the next message came through. *Can you meet me Monday morning in Leuven?*

Her heart was beating so fast and her fingers were trembling so badly that it took an eternity before she could type the two simple words. *Yes. Where?*

*At Fonske. Statue opposite town hall. 10:00.*

This time she managed to type faster: *Know where it is. Will be there.*

*This is no promise to take you to Ammie, but we can talk. Okay?*

*I understand. How do you know her?*

Long pause.

*Through Luc. I have his permission to act as I see fit.*

I thought he wasn't available, she wanted to say, but decided against it. She would try to unravel everything on Monday. *Thanks,* said her last message. There was no reply.

*Luc*
*Damme*

He had painted himself into a corner, Luc realized immediately. Hopefully she wouldn't notice. If she did, he would just say he was the only one who had contact with Luc, and act mysterious.

*If* he decided to speak to her on Monday. It was always very busy in the vicinity of the Fonske statue, so he should be able to see which way the cat jumped before deciding whether to meet her. If he was there ahead of her, he should be able to identify a woman arriving on her own and standing around. He could send a text and look for someone with a beeping phone. He would just have to remember to put his own phone on silent mode, in case she thought of the same plan. And he had to remember to take his spare phone, not his normal one.

Luc smiled at himself again. He read way too many cloak-and-dagger stories. Still, he was serious about protecting Ammie. If it turned out to be unnecessary, he would simply own up.

Now he just had to ask Laura if she would be willing to switch classes. It shouldn't be a problem. He had done it for her before.

First and foremost he had to talk to Ammie to find out what he could about her daughter. Watch another cat jump.

With a bit of luck he could sleep at Herman's place. He was one of the few colleagues from Luc's KU Leuven days who had been sympathetic and had remained a friend.

Luc had already switched off his reading light when his phone rang. The one he'd used to contact Caz Colijn. It wasn't a message, but a call. He groped for his glasses. By the time he had them on his nose, the phone had stopped ringing. The caller wasn't CC, as he had listed Caz Colijn. It was a private number.

Could be a wrong number, but the coincidence bothered him. Why would someone phone him tonight of all nights on a number he had never used before today?

*Erevu*
*Ghent*

If he had known what he now knew, he would never have sent for Dove.

And yet he could never have handled things on his own. Besides, the boy's knowledge of cellphones and technology was indispensable. How else would they have found out the Caz woman had tried to contact Ammie Pauwels's stepson? Professor Luc DeReu. That was the connection. The old woman must have remarried and this professor was her husband's son.

To think it had been so easy. To think the old woman was still alive! It was more important than ever to follow the Caz woman's trail. Back to Leuven.

But Dove had saddled them with other problems. Thanks to him, they had to vacate their lodgings hastily. Bloody Dove with his rash behavior. His lack of caution.

It meant they were solely dependent on technology to follow the Caz woman's trail. They would have to remain very far in the background.

Maybe he shouldn't have phoned DeReu's colleague—the one who had sent the message. But he had hoped the person would answer with a name. It would have helped just to know whether it was a man or a woman, but a name would have been first prize. He or she had probably been asleep. But it shouldn't be a problem. He had made certain his number wouldn't show.

He wondered how Dove felt in his hideout tonight. It was a dump, but the best they could find in the available time. Anyway, he was too angry with the boy to care. The fact remained, they couldn't be seen together. They would use their tablets to remain in contact but they'd limit it to the minimum. Especially now, after the boy's indiscretion. That was why he had taken over the cellphone monitoring. He was the decision-maker, after all. There hadn't been much time, but Dove had shown him what to do.

If only he knew how the boy's mind worked. What had he thought he would accomplish? Couldn't he just have ... Still. They would simply have to pull it off. Success was within reach. At last.

# Nineteen

*Saturday, September 27*
*Caz*
*Ghent*

On Monday she would find out where she came from, but to agonize about it all weekend was no use, Caz decided after a restless night. It would be much more productive to try to find out what had happened to Tieneke. Hopefully it would chase away the shadows of the muddled dreams that were still occupying her thoughts.

There was no change at Tieneke's house, Caz saw at once. The curtains were still drawn, the hallway light was still switched off. Tieneke hadn't answered any messages and the sound of the cellphone was still audible when Caz sent a new message.

Caz had thought she had an explanation figured out. Tieneke had gone away for the weekend. Left early Friday morning. Forgot her cellphone, and by the time she discovered it, she'd gone too far to turn around.

A tidy, logical explanation. Except for the hallway light.

The bulb could have blown. Yet a sense of unease kept gnawing at Caz.

In the neighboring house on the left all was still quiet, but from the house on Tieneke's right Caz heard voices and the sound of a radio. It was the first time she had noticed any sign of life there.

She knocked hesitantly.

An overweight man with a deep suntan opened the door. He gave her the once-over before turning on a jovial smile. He was wearing a green vest and ridiculously bright trousers. A silver chain glinted around his neck and a tattoo wiggled on his biceps.

"Can I help you?"

"Good day. I'm looking for your neighbor, Tieneke Colijn. You didn't happen to see her yesterday?"

The man pulled a face as if he had just bitten on an olive stone. "We don't know anything about those neighbors and we don't want to either. Talk about stuck-up and grumpy! No, we didn't see her. Anyway, we only came back last night from a month's holiday in Italy."

That would explain the dark tan.

"Thank you. Sorry to have bothered you." Caz turned to go. She felt his eyes on her until she entered the shop.

"Good morning! Is Tieneke still not home?" Babette asked when she came in.

Caz shook her head. "Can you remember when last you saw her?"

Babette put down the damp cloth she was wiping the counter with. "Yes, I tried to figure it out last night when I saw you at the door. Then I remembered it was Thursday afternoon, shortly before closing time. I saw her Polo drive past. Usually she stops at the front door to drop off her shopping in the hallway before she parks the car round the back, but not this time. She drove past. That night the lights in the house were on. I live in the apartment over the shop and my balcony looks out on the back gardens.

"That was how I saw the tenants of the rental home leave yesterday morning. I was having coffee on the balcony.

They were driving a hatchback. I could see there was a lot of luggage inside. I didn't even know the two of them were together. The older man moved in quite a while before the younger one."

"Maybe they also went away for the weekend. Maybe the older one gave the younger one a lift somewhere." And maybe she just didn't want Tieneke's disappearance to have any connection with the two men. It would present too many awful possibilities.

"I have spare keys if you want to take a look. Not for the front door. But for the padlock on the big garage doors and the door from the garage to the garden. For the French doors too, giving entry to the house from the garden. Of course you can only get in if the garage door is locked from the outside. If Tieneke has left in the car, in other words. It's an arrangement we made a while ago in case Fien had a problem while Tieneke was out."

Caz weighed her options. Tieneke wouldn't like it if she entered without permission. But she could collect her luggage and be off as soon as she found a flight. That Tieneke would like.

Of course there was also the "what if," so typical of someone who came from a country where one immediately expects the worst if someone isn't where he or she is supposed to be.

"If she takes exception to my letting you in, I'll tell Tieneke you were just worried." Babette obviously knew Tieneke better than Caz had thought.

Caz nodded. "I think I'll take a look after all, thanks. She could have fallen or something."

"As I said, if the garage is locked from the inside, you won't be able to get in. Let's see. Wait here and I'll fetch the keys. They're upstairs in my apartment." Now Babette also seemed worried.

*Luc*
*Damme*

Luc found it hard to focus on the dissertation, and not only because the student had tried to mask ignorance and scanty research with a pompous academic style.

That phone call late last night was bothering him. If it had come through on his normal phone, he wouldn't have given it a second thought, but he had never used that particular SIM card before. He bought it once when he thought he had lost his phone. Soon afterwards he had found the phone where it had fallen into the gap between the seats of his car.

Something else bothered him. Why didn't the number show? Why had the settings been made private?

Did he read too many thrillers, or could someone have tried to find out who Caz Colijn had been texting?

No, he was being silly. That would mean her phone was being monitored.

He tried again to focus on his work, but without any luck. At last he set the dissertation aside. With a sigh, he drew his laptop nearer. He googled the name Caz Colijn. There was still only the LinkedIn profile. He didn't really know how LinkedIn worked. Only that you could leave a message there for members of your network. Or so he thought. Where you went to read those messages was anyone's guess.

It took him a while to create an alternative email address and set up a LinkedIn profile for TU. Then he sent a request on behalf of TU, asking Caz to accept him as a member of her network.

He could only hope she would see the connection between TU's request and the TU of the messages and accept.

He reached for the dissertation again, but left the laptop open, watching it with an eagle eye while he read. It was like waiting for milk to boil. It never happens while you are watching. He knew it, but he couldn't help himself.

*Caz*
*Ghent*

Caz rattled the keys dangling from her finger and gazed at the garage door. The bolt wasn't shot and there was no padlock hanging from it. She tugged at the door handle but the doors remained closed. Locked from the inside.

It could mean only one thing. Tieneke's car was in there. Surely she wouldn't have driven round to the front door and come back to lock the garage door from the inside?

There might be an outside chance though. Perhaps precisely because Babette had keys. Fact was, she couldn't reach Tieneke if she happened to be inside the house, maybe lying at the foot of the stairs, injured. Neither could she get to the luggage she had left there.

A feeling that something was drastically wrong grabbed hold of her. At home she would have gone to the police or the security company and raised the alarm. Here she didn't know what the hell to do.

Babette didn't know either. "I suppose we could dial 101. It's the police emergency number."

Caz considered it, then shook her head. "I don't know whether this qualifies as an emergency. Even if her car is still in the garage, she could have taken a bus, or a train."

"Perhaps we should get a locksmith to open the front door. In case something happened to her inside the house. With your permission, surely it wouldn't be breaking in? You were Fien's foster child?"

So that was how Tieneke had referred to her. It probably wasn't far from the truth. Most likely it was exactly what she was. She had just assumed she was adopted, but who knows whether the process had been legal? In the end it probably didn't make much difference.

"I must say I thought it was terrible that for so many years you made no effort to contact the foster mother who raised you. But from the way you worry about Tieneke, I can see you have a good heart."

The bile that pushed up in Caz's throat was an emotional rather than a physical reaction. What other stories had Tieneke dished up as the truth? Still, it wasn't important now.

"I think I'll risk Tieneke's anger, rather than regret it later. Can you recommend a locksmith?"

"I can. I'll call him."

*Luc*
*Damme*

He was a bloody fool. She had told him she was in Ghent. Obviously she had to be staying with relatives if she only found out here that Ammie was her biological mother.

Luc typed *www.1207.be* into the search box. The page opened quickly. *Colijn. Ghent.* Two Colijns, T and J, the same number. As easy as that.

Luc found the street address in the directory. One visit to Mr. Google and he would know exactly where it was. In the street-view photograph he would be able to see exactly what the house at that number looked like. But why would he want to do that? He had arranged to see Caz in Leuven so that she wouldn't know they were in the same city. He had no intention of taking her to Ammie either, unless Ammie wanted to see her—which at this point was most unlikely.

He sat back in his chair and gazed up at the centuries-old wood of the ceiling. What did it feel like to know your biological mother had abandoned you and never contacted you again? He couldn't imagine it. He couldn't imagine that Caz Colijn could be kindly disposed toward the woman who had given birth to her either.

Ammie's safety was his responsibility now. Exactly how that had come about he didn't know, but that was how it was. He would have to suss things out very carefully.

Last night's call kept bothering him. Or was he paranoid? Had a switch been flicked in his mind that made him see himself as Jack Reacher or Rebus? Or was something else wrong? Early senility maybe?

It had all begun when he saw the woman with the curly gray hair and assumed the dark-skinned student as following her. Maybe he had burst a blood vessel and was close to being certifiable.

Or maybe his life was just so dull that his imagination was taking over, even outside the world of books and movies.

*Caz*
*Ghent*

The locksmith was there within an hour.

"You're sure you're in a position to give me permission to enter?" he asked as he unrolled his tool kit.

Caz nodded. Of course she wasn't sure, but she was willing to chance it and suffer the consequences if necessary.

Barely a minute later the front door was open. The fellow would make an excellent burglar.

Caz switched on the light in the hallway. It worked. The bulb had not blown. It made her very uneasy. Tieneke wasn't someone to deviate from a pattern. Well, at least she wasn't lying at the bottom of the stairs.

"Tieneke?" she called, though she sensed there was no one in the house. There was no reply.

"Could you come with me, please?" she asked the locksmith, suddenly afraid of the dimly lit house.

He looked at his watch. "I can't stay long."

Nothing in the kitchen gave any indication of what had become of Tieneke. Everything was neat and tidy, as usual. Not a single glass or cup out of place. A cabinet door was slightly ajar, but it was the one that didn't close properly. In the living room she saw nothing out of the ordinary. The cushions might not be as meticulously arranged as usual, but that was all.

The French doors to the back garden were locked, and the key was not in the lock.

She unlocked the door with Babette's set of keys and walked through the garden to the garage. Her suspicion was confirmed. The Polo stood in its usual place, white and shiny. Next to it was a bicycle.

"How do you account for this?" she asked after she had locked the French doors again.

"Excuse me?"

She looked at the locksmith. "We found the French doors that lead to the garden locked and without a key. The car is locked in the garage. There was no key in the front door. If Tieneke left through the front door, why would she take the key of the French doors along? The Polo is in the garage, but she might have taken a bus somewhere. Or a train. Still, why would she have taken the key of the French doors?"

The locksmith pursed his lips and shrugged, glancing at his watch again.

"Will you come upstairs with me, please? I'll pay for the extra time."

He nodded. A man of few words.

The stairs creaked in the usual places. In the bathroom the door of the medicine cabinet above the hand basin was slightly open. In the mirror she saw the reflection of the locksmith behind her.

She had never used the cabinet, so she couldn't tell if anything was missing, but it appeared as if all Tieneke's toiletries were still there. Surely she would have taken some of the items along if she had left by train or bus on Thursday or Friday?

She had never been in Tieneke's bedroom. When she opened the door, she noticed a strange smell. Almost like that of the iron supplement she had once taken.

The room was bigger than Fien's, but still not spacious.

Built-in wardrobes took up one entire wall. There was just enough room left for a chest of drawers under the window and a bedside table. Tieneke slept in a three-quarter bed, covered with a double-sized comforter. One corner touched the floor. Caz couldn't imagine that Tieneke would make her bed in such a slipshod way. Maybe she had been in a hurry.

On the bedside table lay a cellphone connected to a charger. It's easy to forget your cellphone that way. You think it's in your handbag and forget that you were charging it. It had happened to Caz on more than one occasion.

When she turned, she stumbled over a shoe that had been hidden under the corner of the comforter. A comfy but ugly orthopaedic shoe. The slip-on kind that Tieneke wore. Caz knelt and looked under the bed. There was no second shoe.

She opened the built-in wardrobe. There were five more pairs of shoes on the bottom shelf, but none matching the orphaned shoe. It didn't look as if any clothes were missing from the hanging section. On the shelves, sweaters and other items lay stacked, some of the piles slightly jumbled. She closed the wardrobe door.

Fien's bedroom smelled of mould and medicine. Combined, Caz imagined, they smelled of death. The bedside table was empty but the wardrobes and drawers contained Fien's belongings. The plant on the windowsill looked slightly wilted.

"Only the attic is left," she told the locksmith.

He sighed, but followed her up the steep staircase.

She tugged at the string that switched on the light. A pile of ironing had toppled from the top of the tumble dryer to the floor. The inflatable mattress and bedding were gone. Tieneke seemed to have removed everything the minute Caz left. She definitely didn't want Caz to sleep there again.

Caz's luggage was in the corner where she herself had stacked it as neatly as possible. The zipper of her lilac suitcase was not closed all the way. The envelope Tieneke had given her lay on the floor. It had been inside the case.

The key had kept slipping out of the envelope, so she had put it in her wallet when she packed to leave for Doel. She had left the note with the address and other details in the envelope. Not very clever. She should keep everything in the same place. What if she lost either of the two? But how had the envelope got from her case to the floor?

Could Tieneke have gone through her things? Had she changed her mind about the key to the strongbox? If so, why not keep the envelope? Not that it was worth anything without the key, but the opposite was also true.

Caz picked up the envelope. The shape of the key was clearly imprinted on the front, almost as if it had been embossed. The note with the address in Pretoria and the other details was still inside. She put it away in her handbag and turned to the locksmith, who was standing a few steps below her on the stairs. Only his head and shoulders were visible.

"I'll be okay now. I'll use the spare front door key on the hook in the kitchen to lock up. Thank you for your patience. What do I owe you?" She unzipped her handbag and took out her wallet.

Her eyes widened when he mentioned the amount, but she counted out the money and gave it to him. "Thanks again."

He nodded before going down the stairs.

On the key rack in the broom cupboard she found the spare front-door key she had occasionally used. There were three other sets of keys. Among them, Tieneke's car keys. She was certainly not going to try to figure out what fitted where now. She would leave her luggage for the time being. She'd had enough. The place gave her the creeps.

What Tieneke's reaction was going to be when she found out what Caz had done was anyone's guess. Accuse her of breaking in, most likely. But she'd worry about that later.

Caz used the spare key to lock the front door behind her.

Outside she paused to take a deep breath. She only realized now how tense she had been in there.

The missing key of the French doors bothered her. Even if there was a spare key on one of the bunches in the broom cupboard. She'd gone out into the garden a few times during her stay and she was sure there had been a single key in the lock. Not one on a bunch.

If Tieneke wasn't back by Monday she would go to the police, Caz decided.

At least she could get to her luggage when she needed to. Or when she had found the courage to go back inside. At the moment she didn't feel up to it.

If it wasn't for the key and the lone shoe, she might be able to relax. But she did feel slightly better now that she'd made sure nothing had happened to Tieneke in her home.

*Luc*
*Damme*

Hell, no, he couldn't carry on like this. He would have to re-read everything.

He looked at his cellphone to see what the time was. Not even twelve. He looked in his inbox again. No acceptance from Caz Colijn on LinkedIn. He went to the LinkedIn site, but there was no message. He was probably overreacting. Maybe someone simply happened to dial the number just before midnight last night. Someone with private settings on his phone.

Unlikely, but not impossible. He would like to make sure he wasn't being paranoid. But how?

Ten minutes later, not at all certain he was doing the right thing, he sent the message.

# Twenty

*Caz*
*Ghent*

Caz heard the sound of her cellphone but finished the kriek she was enjoying on the terrace before she went inside and dug the phone out of her handbag.

A text message from TU. Reluctantly she opened it.

*Can you meet me in an hour at De Witte Leeuw at the Graslei? I happen to be in Ghent. TU.*

Now? Today? Damn it, she wasn't ready. On the other hand, she would probably never be ready to learn more about Ammie Pauwels. The sooner she got it over with, the better.

The message was sent ten minutes ago. She looked on her watch. It was after twelve. No wonder she felt peckish. The previous night's pea soup, rich and delicious as it was, was long forgotten. With her anxiety about Tieneke, she hadn't even given breakfast a thought.

Maybe it was better to meet the woman here, on more or less equal ground. It would also save her a train ride to Leuven.

It reminded her that she still had to look for a flight home.

Tieneke's disappearance had upset all her plans, and this TU business didn't help either.

With Tieneke weighing more and more heavily on her mind, her attention was divided. Maybe it was a good thing, or she would have had only Ammie Pauwels to worry about.

The fact was, she couldn't leave without knowing what had become of Tieneke. Tieneke might not be at the top of her prayer list, but she had to know she was safe. Maybe she was a touch neurotic, coming from a crime mecca, but she had a bizarre feeling that the house wasn't as it should be. As if someone other than Tieneke had been there.

There she went again—feeding the neurosis.

Was she going to meet TU in a little less than an hour, or not? That was the question she had to focus on. The answer was a counterquestion. What did she have to lose?

*Thank you, yes. How will I know you?*

Caz made certain she had everything she needed in her handbag and took a light sweater. It was still warm, but last night it had grown cold at the waterfront. After the meeting, she could carry on worrying anywhere she chose. Or she could explore the city. It was no good sitting on this terrace day in and day out.

*Luc*
*Ghent*

Luc was already on his way to Ghent when the message came through. Just as well he didn't wait for her answer before he left Damme. Now he was hoping he could prove that he had a screw loose and that no third party was reading Caz Colijn's messages.

He parked at the Blandijn next to the Boekentoren and caught a tram. If he did manage to find a parking spot in the old city centre he would have to walk miles anyway. At least here at the university he had free parking. He just hoped his plan worked—whatever the outcome.

*Erevu*
*Ghent*

He had nearly missed the message.

Dove should have been here. He was the one who should have gone to the Graslei. Posing as a student, he would attract less attention. The Caz woman wouldn't be suspicious if she ran into Dove at the Graslei again. But he hadn't replied to the messages Erevu had left and there was no time to go and look for him at his hideout.

Erevu moved through the crowd as fast as possible, stopping some distance from De Witte Leeuw to collect himself. He didn't want to draw attention to himself.

His hand was trembling as he took out his handkerchief and wiped the sweat from his brow. It wasn't the heat that was making him perspirate. This country didn't have what it took to make an African sweat. It was the tension. He had been caught off-guard. Bloody Dove.

Somewhat calmer, he turned the corner. Without looking at anyone in particular, he tried to find a seat. His options were limited. There was one table that hadn't been cleared yet and at another table people were getting ready to leave.

He chose the table that was already vacant. He had to remain as unobtrusive as possible. Once the waiter had removed the used glasses and taken his order, he looked around him, instantly averting his eyes when he saw the Caz woman approach. It was unlikely that she would recognize him from Dampoort, and even if she did, it shouldn't arouse her suspicion. They had been at the same station and on the same train by chance. That was hopefully what she would think. Ghent wasn't a big city.

When he glanced up again, she was standing at the table that had just become available, searching the crowd. The waiter approached and spoke to her. She nodded, said something in reply and sat down. Amid the general noise he couldn't overhear the conversation.

A tall man with a thick mop of graying hair sauntered up

and stood at the waffle stand across the street. There were lots of other people too, but the man's height and hair had caught Erevu's eye. It was not only that, though. He looked familiar.

Something drew the man's attention. Something in the vicinity of the Caz woman. Maybe she herself. She was certainly eye-catching with her long gray curls.

Erevu tried to think where he had seen the man before. Then he remembered. The photo Jela had sent. It had been quite blurred, but he could swear the man standing over there, looking at the crowd, was Luc DeReu.

TU of the messages was in fact Professor Luc DeReu, Erevu instantly realized.

*Luc*
*Ghent*

Luc couldn't believe his eyes. The attractive woman with the long gray curly hair was smiling at the waiter as he put a kriek in front of her. Lord knows, if it hadn't been for bloody Caz Colijn he would have seen it as a sign. He would strongly have considered asking her whether he might share her table. There were no others available.

But he wasn't here to chat up one of the few women who had recently caught his eye. Unfortunately not. He had to find out who in this crowd was Caz Colijn. And whether the person who was intercepting her messages was anywhere close. If there *was* such a person, mind you.

He turned his back on De Witte Leeuw and pretended to be studying the selection of waffles on the board. He keyed in a smiley, held the phone to his ear with his thumb on the send button and turned back to De Witte Leeuw. He sent the message and crossed the street, pretending to be talking on the phone. His eyes swept over the people at the tables. The curly-headed woman picked up her phone and looked at the screen.

Was it possible? Luc was so surprised that he nearly failed to notice the man who also took his cellphone from his shirt pocket.

*Caz*
*Ghent*

Caz frowned. A smiley? What did TU mean? Was the woman making a fool of her? Or was there a hidden meaning?

She studied the crowd but didn't see anyone standing around, smiling. The only person that attracted her attention was a tall man with a mophead and a deep frown who had his cellphone against his ear. He peered at it before putting it back to his ear and resuming his conversation.

A second smiley came through and moments later a third one.

No one seemed to be trying to identify a face in the crowd. TU couldn't have made it clearer. She might as well have texted: Caught you, sucker.

If the waiter hadn't put the kriek in front of her at that very moment, Caz would have got up and left.

Happened to be in Ghent? My arse. Annoyed, she put down her cellphone. The thing could ping all it liked. She had no desire to play games with an unstable woman who had trust issues with her husband or boyfriend.

Yet even that didn't make sense. What could anyone win in that kind of game?

*Erevu*
*Ghent*

Erevu didn't understand the three smiling faces coming through at short intervals. He didn't see anyone texting. A young girl was sitting with her cellphone to her ear, laughing. Another youngster's thumbs were flying across the keys, a bored expression on his face. He was certainly not sending one smiley after another. The professor was pacing up and down, talking on his phone. Could it be that DeReu and TU weren't the same person after all? TU was supposed to be here to meet the Caz woman and DeReu was not making a move, even though he had noticed her. But TU had also said DeReu couldn't be contacted.

There was a snake in the grass. He beckoned the waiter over, paid for the coffee he hadn't drunk yet and got up. He passed as close to the professor as possible.

The professor was focused on his conversation. "If you can't manage the research, you shouldn't have handed in your dissertation. I'm sorry, Miss, but postgraduate studies call for dedication and precision."

The professor's voice faded as Erevu walked away. He looked around one last time. Into the eyes of the Caz woman. She gave a slight nod. She had recognized him. Damn all people with good memories. He frowned and turned away.

*Caz*
*Ghent*

She might be mistaken, but she could swear it was the man who had offered to help her with the train timetable on her way to Doel. The one she had seen getting off at Sint-Niklaas as well.

Maybe he hadn't recognized her. Middle-aged white women were a much more common sight in Belgium than smartly clad black men with shaven heads.

The man and his short memory were unimportant, though. The fact remained, she had fallen for a bad joke, concocted by a neurotic. It was all she could assume. Even though it made no sense.

While she drank her kriek, she glanced at the menu. The food looked delectable but the prices were beyond her means. Even the kriek was a euro more here than just a short distance away. At least they served snacks with the drinks—even if the portions were miniscule.

When she looked up, the mophead who had been so engrossed in conversation on his cellphone was gone. New people were seated at the dark-skinned man's table.

Her cherry beer was hardly finished when the waiter appeared at her side. "Another one?"

Caz shook her head. "Only the bill, please."

"Four euro fifty."

She gave him five euros and took the slip he was holding out to her.

"I've been asked to tell you to read this, but not here." The waiter smiled and left.

Caz got up and walked away slowly, the slip of paper in her hand. What the hell now?

She stopped at a safe distance and unfolded the note.

*Change your phone and SIM. Present phone being monitored. Text only with new phone to this number.* After the number the person had written: *See LinkedIn. TU.*

The note had been written in bold but hasty capital letters. She looked around her, but she couldn't see De Witte Leeuw or its patrons from there. TU, whoever she or he might be, must have been there, watching her. The handwriting looked masculine. Maybe the black man? But no, the timing between his departure and the arrival of the note didn't match.

The only other person she had noticed was the mophead on the phone. Because of his height but, to be honest, also because she had found him attractive despite his grim face.

It couldn't have been the waiter. He had served others as well. TU must have asked or bribed the waiter to deliver the note written on the back of a till slip before he came to ask if she'd like another kriek.

She could only assume that TU was completely bonkers.

Shit, what if it was true? That her phone was being monitored? But that was academic. Where would she find another phone and SIM card?

She headed for the street café where she'd had the pea soup. It was much cheaper because it was slightly off the beaten track. Still at the waterfront, but walled in by buildings on either side. She looked around, not quite sure where the place was. Just past that cannon, if her memory served her correctly. The enormous thing was called Dulle Griet according to the plaque.

She was lucky enough to find a table at the water's edge. She knew by now that it was the Leie River, though it still looked more like a canal to her. A long boat filled with tourists went past and a few waved. She waved back at them.

"Back for more pea soup?"

The man was the owner as well as the chef, she had gathered the day before. He had proved that he had a sense of humor, calling all the women Grietjie and all the men Dullerd. She had also heard him teasing a guest, who seemed to be an old acquaintance.

"You don't happen to serve cellphones with new SIM cards?"

He stared at her for a moment, then laughed. "Did yours fall into the Leie? You won't be the first to lose a phone that way. Let's get you something to drink, then I'll see what I can do. A glass of wine?"

She needed one, but she asked for coffee instead, and the menu. It was rather limited, but everything looked appetizing.

"Were you serious about the cellphone?" the man enquired when he brought her coffee.

She nodded. "I don't know how one goes about getting one here. At home it's a big schlepp."

"Well, not here. You simply buy one with a prepaid card. It will cost you about eighty euros before calls."

One thousand two hundred rand. For a phone she was only going to use for a few days? No way.

"I have an old one, if that will help? Not all that old. I upgraded about three months ago. Give me fifteen euros for it and you can just buy a Proximus prepaid card. Or if you wish, you can sit back and I'll send one of the lazy louts who work for me to go and buy it for you. I can put it on your bill and you can pay for everything with your credit card."

Caz suddenly felt her lower lip begin to tremble.

"And now, Grietjie?"

Caz cleared her throat and tried to pull herself together. "I'm not used to people being so kind. That would be wonderful, thanks."

The owner patted her shoulder. "You just relax, Grietjie, and enjoy your coffee. I'll see to the rest."

*Luc*
*Ghent*

He still couldn't get over the fact that the curly-headed woman with the slim figure and striking face was Caz Colijn.

He understood now why he had noticed her. It wasn't only the hair and the height, or the fact that he found her attractive. It was that defiant posture you saw in so many South Africans. Shoulders back, chin up. A sharpness of gaze too, as if they took in more than the average person—paid more attention to what was going on around them.

But if the woman turned out not to be Caz Colijn, if she had just happened to get a message from someone else at the same time he was sending his, he was in trouble.

She would think he was crazy. Or a pervert. Maybe she would think it was one of the weirdest pick-up lines she had ever come across. To make it worse, his cellphone number was on that note.

But there had been no alternative he could think of. Surely three messages, one after the other, made the possibility of a coincidence too remote? No, it couldn't have been by chance. She had looked at her messages three times. And she didn't seem very happy.

He hoped and prayed she would get another phone and not decide someone was playing a trick on her. And he hoped she would text him from the new number, or he wouldn't be able to contact her.

Which could be a disaster. They had to change the place and time of Monday's appointment in Leuven to mislead the person who was monitoring her phone.

For now he just had to presume it was indeed Caz who had received the note. To keep wondering about it was not productive.

Whether the man sitting near her was the one who had access to her phone was even less certain. He had heard no cellphone sounds, yet the moment Luc had sent the first smiley, the man had taken his cellphone from his shirt pocket and looked at it. It was probably set to vibrate, not ring.

He had looked closely at the phone and pressed buttons again immediately after the last two smileys had been sent.

His studies had taught Luc not to assume anything was true just because it seemed logical. At most, there could be a strong suspicion that the man was watching Caz and monitoring her calls. Why he had Caz in his sights was a mystery.

The fact that the man was black didn't mean he was from the Congo, but if he was, it could have something to do with Ammie. But how did he know about Caz?

The whole business was a conundrum. All he knew was that Ammie wouldn't have lived under an assumed name for fifty-three years if she hadn't felt threatened.

# Twenty-one

*Caz*
*Ghent*

On her way home Caz couldn't believe she had nearly broken down in tears. Everything had just become too much for her: the shock of finding out about Ammie Pauwels, seeing Fien again after so many years and then Fien's death, Tieneke's attitude and now her disappearance, and an unknown person who thought her phone was being monitored.

One random act of kindness was all it took for the house of cards that was her fragile emotions to cave in.

When she let herself into Erdem's house, she heard movement in the kitchen.

He turned from the stove, where he was stirring something in a pot. The kitchen smelled of exotic spices. "Hello, Caz. Did you enjoy your outing?"

Caz nodded. "Hi, Erdem. I need to ask you something. I have to stay longer than I anticipated. Is my room available?" Although she had the keys to Tieneke's home, she would rather use the last of her nest egg than move in there.

"Let me see." He took out his smartphone and got busy with his thumb. "The week is open. There are bookings, but I can put the guests in the other room. First come, first served. On Friday afternoon I have people who specifically asked for the room with the terrace. I could move you to the smaller room then."

"Wonderful, but I don't think I'll be staying that long. If I could stay until Friday morning at the very latest, it should be fine. I'll pay until then. If I leave any sooner, it'll be my loss."

"If you leave earlier and I get another booking, I'll refund the money. Okay?"

"Thank you, that's kind. Sleep well."

"Caz, I can see something is wrong. Can I help?"

Where did she begin to explain? "My sister has disappeared and I don't know what to do," was all she finally said.

"Babette mentioned something but I take everything Babette tells me with a grain of salt. Would you like me to call the police?"

Caz thought for a moment. "I think so. If she's not back by tomorrow morning. I wanted to wait until Monday, but something isn't right." She told him about the key and the shoe. "Still, the front door key wasn't in the lock. So she must have gone out through the front door. I don't know what to think any more."

"Rather be on the safe side, Caz. I only know your sister by sight but she has a reputation for being a difficult customer. I can understand that you don't want to annoy her, but you don't want to blame yourself later."

Caz nodded. "You're right. Yes, I think I should have the police come round tomorrow. I don't know how it works over here."

"Leave it to me, I'll sort it out tomorrow. Sleep well."

"Thanks. You too," she replied.

For the second time that day Caz had to fight back the tears. People usually cried when they couldn't find help. She, on the other hand, cried when people were willing to help her. It spoke volumes about her life.

*Luc*
*Damme*

Luc checked LinkedIn for the umpteenth time and swore. Caz still hadn't accepted his invitation. And without a new number for her he couldn't change the date and venue of their meeting in Leuven.

Thankfully Laura had agreed to swop classes with him when he'd phoned her earlier. She had sounded a bit stand-offish. Hopefully only because he was bothering her on a Saturday night.

Herman had confirmed that Luc could sleep at his house the next evening, but added that he would have to entertain himself. Herman was spending the weekend with the love of his life—the umpteenth one after his divorce—and would only be back on Monday morning. Luc could collect the spare key from the neighbors.

He would phone Lieve tomorrow morning, find out whether Ammie had changed her mind and, if not, he would drive through. The day after he would meet Caz Colijn face to face for the first time. Hear her voice. Find out if her eyes were really as blue as they looked from a distance.

And what would she see? A dry old stick with too much hair on his head and too little on his pale chest?

Verdorie, what was he thinking? What did it matter how blue her eyes were? What her voice sounded like? What she thought of him? It was completely beside the point.

He had to focus on Ammie. Make sure he asked the right questions the right way.

Luc switched off the computer. Time would tell.

*Caz*
*Ghent*

In her room Caz saved TU's second number under TU2 on the new phone. She texted Lilah, giving her the Belgian number and telling her to use it if she wanted to call. She was too tired to explain why she had a new phone. Besides, the child would only worry.

Tomorrow she would decide whether to give TU the new number. She was too confused to make any decisions now.

In the shower she remembered that she had to let Lilah know she was staying longer, though still not until the eighth.

After her shower she sent Lilah an email. She replied almost at once that she understood.

The rest of her inbox didn't produce anything worth mentioning except a few bills. The end of the month. There was also a LinkedIn request.

She hadn't used LinkedIn for a long time. It was a nuisance to keep getting requests from total strangers to join her network. Initially her profile had helped her professionally but after she had translated a few sample chapters for a well-known author and had been appointed his official translator, she had been working directly with publishers. Actually she might as well end her membership.

"See LinkedIn," she remembered the note had read, so she took another look at the request.

She laughed when she recognized the name, and went to View Profile.

The applicant's profile photo was an old book cover with the title *Till Eulenspiegel* printed over a colorful drawing of the wandering prankster from medieval times. The profile name was Tijl Uilenspiegel. Well, well.

The profile details were sparse. Only the essentials needed to open a profile seemed to have been supplied. The summary read: Searcher for truth. Experience: None.

TU had a sense of humor, or else he was one sandwich short of a picnic.

Studied at KU Leuven, was the only other information supplied. That had to be how he or she knew Luc DeReu.

She added Tijl Uilenspiegel to her network before switching off the computer.

Lying in bed, she remembered Tieneke quoting Tijl Uilenspiegel. Was everything that had happened recently her own fault? In some cases, maybe, but hell, she didn't ask to be born. Nor to be given away either.

Yet it was no one's fault but her own that she was on a quest to find the woman who had given her away. She had no idea why she was doing it. She just knew she had to.

*Erevu*
*Ghent*

Erevu didn't want to admit it to Jela, but he was worried. He hadn't heard from Dove. He knew he had been harsh with the boy. Maybe too harsh, but Dove had caused them a lot of problems.

According to Jela, the Caz woman had sent her daughter an email to let her know she was staying a while longer.

Hopefully she would look up Ammie Pauwels soon and they could follow her. At least they could rule out Tieneke and Fien Colijn's house. Dove's search hadn't produce any results.

Luckily he knew where the Caz woman was staying. She had let her daughter know she'd found lodgings close to her sister's home. It was comfy and also handy because there was a bus stop across the road. It had been easy enough to guess where the place was. Before the Caz woman arrived in Ghent, he had often watched people come and go at the house opposite the bus stop.

Dove had made a thorough search of everything in the Tieneke woman's home, except, of course, the suitcase and backpack Cassandra Colijn had taken to Doel and Leuven. They would have to be searched as well.

Unfortunately, he didn't dare search through her stuff at that Turk's place. There was always someone around. If not the Turk, his brother or other guests. With that Babette woman in the neighborhood, he couldn't go near the place anyway. She was much too nosy.

But the opportunity would come. If Caz Colijn was waiting for her sister to return, she had a long wait ahead.

# Twenty-two

*Sunday, September 28*
*Caz*
*Ghent*

Caz knew from the brightness behind the thin curtains, but also from her internal clock, that she had overslept. Not that it mattered. There wasn't much to look forward to this Sunday.

She was by nature an early riser. Early morning was the best time of day for her when she was at home. That was when she scattered table scraps for the pheasants, fed Catya and, wind permitting, sat on the veranda with her morning coffee. How she missed it.

Here she heard nothing but city sounds. Not a single bird chirping. Only traffic, a barking dog and a general buzz, interspersed with some siren or the other.

The thought of coffee got her out of bed. Her muscles weren't aching any more.

Erdem was busy at the coffee machine and glanced over his shoulder. "Sleep well?"

"Like the dead, thanks."

"Coffee? I've just made."

"Lovely, thanks."

He took out another mug and poured for both of them. "This morning, on my way to the shop to buy milk, I tried to look through your sister's windows. Pressed the doorbell as well. She still hasn't come back, it seems. Shall I inform the police?"

Caz added milk to her coffee and nodded. "Yes, I think it would be best. If she turns up later today, so be it. After coffee and a shower I'll be ready for them."

"I'll phone in half an hour. They probably won't come out at once anyway, maybe not even today. I don't know how seriously they'll take something like this or how busy they might be."

"Thanks, Erdem."

Caz sat down on the terrace. It was slightly overcast but not cold. Here and there bits of pale blue sky were visible. On the opposite side of the street an old lady was walking her dog. Possibly the barker she had heard before. From the spacious terrace the area looked less built-up than at street level. At least she could breathe here.

She had no idea why she kept feeling so short of breath. Maybe the fresh air of the Overberg had spoiled her. Or maybe she just didn't take to city life.

But breath or no breath, she had to take a few decisions today. Much would depend on what the police had to say, but it wasn't just Tieneke's disappearance that weighed on her mind.

She kept wondering about her assumption that TU was a woman. The strong handwriting and the alias made her wonder.

Man or woman, what did it matter? The crucial question was: should she let TU, or Tijl Uilenspiegel, have her new number? Should she keep the appointment in Leuven?

It wasn't just a case of letting TU have her number or not. The real question was whether she wanted to find out more about Ammie Pauwels and meet her.

She wished she could simply forget about Ammie Pauwels and mothers who gave away their children. What did she stand to gain? Yet an atavistic urge was driving her on. A primal instinct, which kept goading her to find out where the hell her roots lay. Maybe the ancient urge of the baby animal to smell its mother. She couldn't explain it any other way, but in the end, she knew, nothing good could come of it.

It was clear that Ammie Pauwels had never regretted her behavior of fifty-three years ago, or she would have contacted Caz as she had contacted Fien about two stupid curio objects. Before she became old and senile and infirm. And that was another factor dooming this quest of hers to failure. What could she possibly achieve?

Caz finished her coffee. Moping wouldn't do her any good. Finding Tieneke was her first priority now.

*Luc*
*Leuven*

Luc found a parking spot a short distance from Ammie's apartment and sat in his car. In the park children were laughing and chasing each other.

Lieve had said Ammie was having a lucid day, and was looking forward to his visit. That was at nine this morning.

He couldn't help wondering what had brought on the complete about-turn after her previous reaction.

How should he approach her? The list of questions he wanted to ask was long and if he started with the wrong one he might not get anywhere with the rest.

How had she found it in her heart to dump her baby and head off? What did she bribe Josefien Colijn with?

No.

Why are you afraid of your daughter? Probably not either. But these were things he wanted to know. Before he met Caz Colijn.

To ask Ammie why a black man might be following her daughter might also be unwise.

Caz had not sent a new number, but neither had she left a message on his alternative phone. Maybe she didn't think he was totally crazy.

He, on the other hand, was not so sure. The entire affair seemed more and more far-fetched. A product of his fertile imagination.

With a sigh he got out of the car. He would approach Ammie as seemed right in the moment and worry about the lovely Caz later.

*Caz*
*Ghent*

Caz rearranged her backpack and sorted out her wallet in an attempt to keep her uneasiness at bay. She was standing with the envelope and the key to the safe-deposit box in her hand, uncertain what to do with them, when there was a tap on her door.

"Caz? The cops are here." Erdem's voice came dimly from the other side of the door.

That was quick. He couldn't have phoned too long ago. Instantly there was a lump in her stomach. "Just a moment." She slipped the key into the bank bag where she kept her extra euros and pushed it and the envelope into a side pocket of her vanity case.

Commissioner Max de Brabander was a serious man with a deep frown that seemed permanently etched between his light blue eyes despite the fact that he was probably not fifty yet. His mousy hair had just a hint of gray.

Caz sketched the background and told him that the uneasy feeling she had about the French doors and the shoe had made her decide to contact the police.

The frown deepened. "Why didn't you contact us yesterday?"

"I didn't want to be a nuisance. And I knew my sister wouldn't be pleased if she returned and found I had called the police. She seems to have taken the front door key, which made me feel a little less anxious about the things I mentioned. I'm still hoping she'll show up. I'm just really worried about the shoe."

Her excuse didn't go down well. It was probably understandable. The policeman didn't know Tieneke the way Caz did.

"Please describe your sister to me."

She did the best she could.

De Brabander looked at the inspector who had accompanied him. The man gave a slight shrug.

The commissioner turned to her again. "You have the key to your sister's house?"

Caz took the key from the back pocket of her jeans and held it out to him.

"No, you must open up and take us in. Did you touch or move anything?"

It sounded like a premature question to her, but maybe the police over here were just more thorough than at home. "I didn't move anything, but I must have touched a few things. Including the locks and keys."

He clicked his tongue and shook his head. "Well, let's take a look."

It was only a short distance, but they went in his car.

Inside Tieneke's home she showed the policemen the French doors with the missing key before they went upstairs to Tieneke's bedroom, where she pointed out the shoe. Was it her imagination, or did the two men exchange a meaningful look?

"Fetch the camera," the commissioner ordered his sidekick.

While they were waiting for the inspector to return, De Brabander pulled surgical gloves from his coat pocket and wiggled them onto his fingers.

"I fell over the shoe," Caz remembered. "It's not in the same position any more. It was hidden under the corner of the comforter."

The commissioner sighed, but said nothing.

The photo session turned into a lengthy affair, under the silent supervision of the commissioner.

Caz began to feel more and more uncomfortable. Were they always this serious in Belgium about someone who was merely suspected of being missing?

"Commissioner, I'll be back in a moment. I just want to get some clothing from my suitcase," she said after the umpteenth photo. "My luggage is still in the attic." It felt like a banal thing to want to do while they were being so serious about Tieneke's disappearance, but her clothing situation was turning into a crisis. And Tieneke's bedroom was freaking her out.

De Brabander shook his head. "I'd prefer you to wait. We want to go through the entire house before anything is removed. I can arrange for your luggage to be brought to you, but only later."

Now she really began to worry, but she merely said, "That would be kind, thank you."

When the inspector had finally ceased taking photos, De Brabander crouched, took a pen from his pocket and used it to lift the corner of the comforter. He used the same pen to lift the shoe and bring it closer to his eyes.

Then, just like Sherlock Holmes, the commissioner took a magnifying glass from his coat pocket, lifted the corner of the comforter again and studied the navy blue fabric.

"The way the comforter is hanging ... Tieneke is a perfectionist." Why she said it, she didn't know.

The lump in her stomach grew harder. Something was very wrong. Surely they were being too serious about someone who might or might not be missing? And why had detectives been called to the scene instead of uniformed policemen?

De Brabander looked up at her. "Mrs. Colijn, I have to ask you to leave the house, please."

"Pardon?"

"We have to summon the crime scene specialists and your presence might compromise the evidence. The house is now officially a crime scene until proved otherwise."

"But ..." She looked at him incredulously, unable to formulate the right question.

He sighed. "It appears there's blood on the comforter cover. On the shoe as well. Very fine droplets, but present."

The inspector lifted the comforter.

"Grevers!" De Brabander chided.

Grevers dropped the comforter, but not quickly enough. The smear on the white sheet under the comforter could only be blood.

Caz needed no further encouragement. She fled from the room, down the stairs and came to a halt outside, covering her face with her hands.

The inspector was beside her before she had regained her breath. "Mrs. Colijn, I'm very sorry. It was thoughtless of me."

Caz couldn't utter a word. The image of the bloodstain danced in front of her eyes.

Grevers cleared his throat. "I'm afraid we have to ask you to view a body in the mortuary."

She looked at him, dazed.

"The body of a woman in her mid-sixties was taken from the Leie in the early hours of this morning. She was wearing only one shoe. The same kind and size as the one in your sister's room."

Caz sat down on the pavement. Her legs were too shaky to support her. That was why they had responded so swiftly to Erdem's call. Why they had sent detectives and approached the matter so seriously. Surely the body in the mortuary couldn't be Tieneke?

"Babette saw her on Thursday," she muttered.

"Babette?"

Caz pointed down the street. "The woman from the shop."

As if she had heard her name, Babette came out of the shop and crossed the street.

Caz felt as if she was trapped in a nightmare. She heard the questions and answers Babette and the inspector were exchanging, but nothing registered. Tieneke dead? It couldn't be true. Not now that Tieneke was looking forward to her freedom at last, now that she had the prospect of a life without Fien.

Thoughts swirled and eddied, self-reproach searing through her. She should have known on Friday ... What good would it have done? She should have ... What?

"Maybe you should take a look next door," she heard Babette say when the commissioner joined them. "It's a rental home that belongs to Tieneke. There were people there, but they left early on Friday morning."

The commissioner said something Caz didn't follow and turned to her. "Mrs. Colijn?"

Caz got up with an effort. "Ms. I'm not married." Why it suddenly mattered, she didn't know. Maybe because to her Mrs. Colijn was Fien.

He frowned. "Ms.? It means you're not married?"

She nodded. Then realized all mature women were addressed as "mevrouw" in Belgium, married or not.

"Very well." He acted as if he was indulging a naughty child. "Ms. Colijn, I'm very worried about your sister. Nothing is certain until the identification of the Leie body has taken place, but whether it's your sister's body or not, something serious has happened to Miss Colijn. Under the comforter the bedding appears to be heavily bloodstained. I'm really sorry."

Caz could only look at him in silence.

"Do you know where we can find the keys to the house next door?"

Caz shook her head, staring at the inspector, who was cordoning off the two buildings with police tape. She made an effort to focus. "Maybe on the key rack in the broom cupboard. I think Tieneke kept all the spare keys there. That's where I found the spare key to the front door."

The commissioner disappeared back inside.

Babette put her arm around Caz's shoulder and said something comforting, but Caz barely heard.

The front-door key. Tieneke had just gone somewhere. She couldn't be dead. Caz covered her eyes with her hands.

"I'm going to give her something to calm her down," she heard Babette say from afar. "You can come and find her in my apartment when you've finished. Above the shop."

The inspector must have agreed, because Babette led her away. In a daze Caz saw her lock the door of the shop before she took Caz upstairs to her apartment and fed her sugar water in her tiny kitchen.

"I'll make some tea," said Babette.

"The balcony. I want to go out on the balcony, please." Caz said. She was in urgent need of fresh air.

Babette led her to the balcony and pulled out a chair from under the table. "Sit, girl. You look as if you're about to keel over. I'll be back in a minute with the tea."

Caz obeyed. Through the railings she saw De Brabander come out of the rental home's back door and begin to inspect the hedge.

Of course that had to be how the killer removed the body. Out through the French doors. Over the hedge. It must have been dark, otherwise Babette and the other neighbors ... But the tenants weren't necessarily the culprits. It was a wild assumption. Or was it?

Tieneke didn't just go somewhere. Tieneke was dead.

Her difficult, pain-in-the-butt sister was dead. Suddenly Caz's heart wanted to break. If she and Tieneke hadn't had those last few conversations she might have been less emotional. They would never have liked each other, but in the recent past they had grown to understand each other better. The mutual hard feelings had begun to mellow.

In the neighboring houses Caz saw people peering through the windows. Those with balconies came out one by one, leaning over the railings to get a better view of what was going on, speculating amongst each other, from balcony to balcony.

How could no one have seen or heard anything? The neighbors on Tieneke's right had been on holiday, but what about the rest?

Why was it happening now? While she was here? Had she brought death to Tieneke's door? But how? Why? What was it about?

Should she tell the detectives about TU's allegation that her cellphone was being monitored? It would be the right thing to do, but how would she explain it? She didn't know what had made TU say it. And how would she explain to De Brabander why she was communicating with an unidentified person? Someone called Tijl Uilenspiegel?

# Twenty-three

*Luc*
*Leuven*

"Good day, Luc. So here you are." Ammie looked and sounded reasonably lucid but her expression was one of distrust. As if she had not been the one to request this visit.

"Good day, Mother Ammie. Lovely autumn weather we are having."

"That's to be hoped, after the gray summer. But you're not here to talk about the weather. What do you want from me?"

"Pardon?" Ammie's direct approach caught him off-guard.

She did not condescend to repeat the question.

He sat down, facing her. "I want to ask about your health."

"It's fine. What else?"

"Just talk." Did he really have to sound so awkward?

"About what?"

Luc knew he had to pull himself together and quickly. Ammie wasn't born yesterday. "If you feel up to it, we might talk about your time in Elisabethville. One of my students said she would like to know what it was like to live there and

I thought you could give me some background." It sounded like a safe place to start. Regrettably it wasn't very convincing.

"That's all?"

He nodded, but doubted she believed him. "She's especially interested in the relationship between the indigenous people and the Belgians," he tried another angle.

"Elisabethville." The grip on her walking stick visibly relaxed and a far-off look came into her eyes. "The whites lived well. For the blacks who lived in the cité indigène, it must have been hell. I didn't realize it as a child or even as a young woman. Like everybody else, I didn't think of them as anything other than domestic or garden help. Someone to do the hard labor. To be sent on errands. To fulfil our wishes.

"Their insistence on independence was a bother, instigated by the évolués—a dirty word to many Belgians, who regarded évolués as macaques, monkeys putting on airs. It was unthinkable that they should imagine themselves equal to whites. That they could presume to get training, work themselves up in a job and accept the European lifestyle. 'Honorary whites' they were called when they met certain standards." She gave a snort.

"It was a humiliating business to qualify, I found out later, when I was wiser. 'Immatriculation,' it was called. The candidate had to get a letter of recommendation from his employer, after which he underwent a practical test to see to what degree he had been Europeanized. A commission of inquiry was sent to his home to inspect things like the tableware and linen. Find out whether he ate at the table with his wife, whether he spoke French to his children."

Luc listened. None of it was news to him, though the story sounded different from Ammie's lips than from textbooks and academic articles. More realistic. Even more humiliating. He also knew the so-called immatriculation status had had a minimal effect on the prospect of promotion and a raise in salary. Immatriculation thwarted, rather than promoted, integration with the world of colonial power, prestige and privilege. It led to a desire among the "civilized Africans" to terminate the colonial system rather than be assimilated into it. Independence became their catchword.

"There were two kinds of white people in the Congo," Ammie continued. "The incomers who arrived to plunder the wealth of the country to line their own pockets, and those who were born there or had lived there since childhood and loved the country. Not even the whites who had been born there and considered themselves part of the Congo regarded the évolués as equals or respected them for what they were. Myself included.

"I was not born there but I knew no other country than the Congo. I can't even remember the five years before we moved there. I spent two years in Antwerp when I was fifteen, sixteen. My father felt I had to learn more about the country of my birth. Belgium was still being rebuilt after the Second World War and that might have been one of the reasons why I didn't take to it, but I actually suspect it was the weather. I've never been one for misery."

"You were still Amelie de Pauw then?" Luc dared to ask when she paused.

She looked him in the eye. "I was, but she died. In 1961."

The admission itself was no surprise, yet he was shocked by her frosty tone.

Lieve got up nervously and offered to make coffee.

Ammie waited until she had gone into the kitchen before she continued.

"Jacq was wrong. What I had with Elijah wasn't whoring. It was love in its purest form."

Where on earth did that come from?

"Who was Elijah, Mother Ammie?" he asked calmly.

"Elijah?" She gave him the sweetest smile he had ever seen on her face. Then the dam wall broke. She spoke about their meeting, how stealthy they had to be so that César wouldn't find out about their relationship.

Lieve brought the coffee and something to eat.

"Thank you, Lieve, please leave us alone now." Ammie sounded preoccupied.

Lieve glanced at Luc and he nodded. "I'll call before I go."

When Lieve had left, Ammie told Luc about Elijah's friendship with Patrice Lumumba and his political involvement. The home for orphaned children. Of their adorable little son, Kembo. How it had broken her heart that she could never show him greater affection than any of the other orphans. How Elijah could not give him any special attention either. No one could know that Kembo was their son.

"Kembo means 'be overjoyed' or 'rejoice'. Elijah chose the name." She stared into the distance. "After Elijah's death no one would have believed me that he was our child. I had to leave him behind. Tabia, the woman who saved my life when César assaulted me, promised to take care of him."

He knew he shouldn't mention Caz now, but he really wanted to know why she had left one child behind with so much regret and deliberately rejected the other.

"How did Elijah die?" he asked at last, softly.

She told him a tale of such gruesome cruelty it made his stomach turn. She recounted the events so graphically that Luc saw in his mind's eye the man trapped in the headlights of his killers' vehicles, heard the shots echo.

"That's the kind of man César Ronald Bruno Janssen was, Luc. Do you understand now why I wanted nothing to do with his daughter? Just couldn't raise her? I may be heartless, but at least I'm honest. I would have hated every fiber of her with every fiber of my own being."

*Caz*
*Ghent*

It might be the last thing she felt like doing, but she would have to go to Leuven tomorrow. Meet Tijl Uilenspiegel in the flesh, find out from her or him what the hell was going on so that she could tell the police her phone was being monitored. They would think she was batty if she told them what she knew at this point.

Caz stared unseeing through the window of the vehicle. She had no idea where they were. It didn't matter. All that mattered was that they were on their way to a mortuary.

She felt nauseous. She would have to look at a dead body. Whether it was Tieneke's or not.

De Brabander had warned her that it wouldn't be a pretty sight. The body had been in the water at least two days. He added that it could have been worse. They might never have found the body. It was actually a small miracle that things had worked out the way they had.

A man whose dog had chased him out of bed to answer the call of nature was taking a walk beside the Leie when he had spotted the body floating in the water and called the police. There had been no identity document or anything to identify the body. Erdem's call had been a godsend.

When they reached the building, Caz asked to go to the bathroom. She was light-headed as well as nauseous. She reached the toilet just in time. When she rejoined the others, she was shivering, but at least there wasn't much left in her stomach that could come out. The smell of the place had a devastating effect on her.

Caz was instructed to stand on one side of a glass partition. Someone in a surgical cap and mask approached, pushing a steel trolley on which lay a body covered with a white sheet.

It felt unreal.

The sheet was removed from the face.

A burning, acidic fluid pushed up in her gullet. She swallowed again and again, then turned and ran blindly from the small room and down the long passage.

Outside she spat the sour phlegm into a flowerbed. A man's hand held out a bottle of water. She emptied it in a few gulps and wiped her mouth with the back of her hand.

"I presume it's her? Tieneke Colijn?" De Brabander sounded sympathetic.

Caz nodded. "It's Tieneke." And not. It was a dead body that used to be Tieneke.

"I'm sorry for your loss, Ms. Colijn."

How many people had heard those words from him during his career? Caz wondered. At what point had he stopped truly meaning them?

"I'm even sorrier that I must ask you to come with us to make a statement and answer a few questions. I understand how awful it must be for you, but the sooner we get the information, the sooner we can track down the murderer."

"So it was murder?" Stupid question. The bloodstains on the bed had confirmed it. Besides Tieneke is ... was not the kind of person who would voluntarily jump into the Leie.

He nodded. "There's trauma to the back of her head, but we don't know yet whether it caused her death. We'll know more after the post mortem."

With great effort Caz swallowed again. She wished there was more water in the bottle.

"If you don't feel up to it, we could wait until tomorrow, but it would really be better if we do the interview now."

"Let's get it over with. I have to be in Leuven tomorrow anyway."

De Brabander raised his eyebrows. "May I ask what you're going to do there?"

He was probably wondering what could be so urgent after she had just identified her sister's body. "It's a private matter. An appointment I must keep."

"But you're coming back to Ghent?"

She nodded. "I'll be here until about Friday. Well, that was the plan. Everything has changed now. I'll have to make funeral arrangements for Tieneke. Bloody hell, I don't even know how you do something like that. Especially not here." Suddenly the tears came, unbidden but unstoppable.

"Steady, Ms. Colijn. One thing at a time. Let's just take down your statement and clear up a few matters. But I must ask you not to make any travel plans without letting us know. Especially not plans that will take you out of Belgium."

Was she considered a suspect until proven otherwise? That would be the cherry on the top.

"Shall we go?" asked the commissioner.

Caz nodded. She just wanted to get it over with.

*Luc*
*Leuven*

Ammie paused for long moments. At times Luc thought she had retreated behind her veils, but after a while she continued. It seemed to take all her willpower to remain in the present in order to talk about the past. Bit by bit and incoherently at times, her words painted a picture in his mind.

Ammie spoke of Tabia, of her flight with Tabia's nephew, how she had ended up in Nylstroom, later Pretoria. Of the Colijns. Of malicious Josefien and her equally nasty daughter, Tieneke.

"Hans was relatively kind, but only after he'd been compensated."

"Diamonds?" Luc guessed.

Ammie nodded, but did not elaborate. "I had to wait until the child was born, but I came here as soon as I could."

In many ways Ammie was indeed a heartless person, Luc realized while she was talking, but she had loved two people in her life with all her heart. Her father and Elijah.

Her father had died under a cloud of dishonor, while Elijah had died because he had grown to love Ammie. After that Ammie was half a person. It had given rise to her cold-blooded approach to life.

Or maybe it had begun with her relationship with her mother, who, Ammie said, had done nothing but complain.

"A beautiful, spoiled woman who thought only of herself and her own comfort," Ammie summed up Hortense. "Constance, my mother's sister whom my father married a year after my mother's death, was the same, only worse.

"I suspect my father got mixed up with diamonds to get Constance to stop nagging."

Luc felt his ears prick up, but he didn't want to interrupt.

"Like my mother, Constance wanted to return to Belgium, but she was used to a life of luxury in the Congo. A beautiful villa with a string of servants. She expected to be waited on hand and foot. She didn't lift a finger, just gave orders.

To maintain a similar living standard in Belgium they would have had to be truly wealthy.

"My father earned a good salary, but not that good. In Belgium our living standards would be considerably lower. But Constance would have none of that. She played on Papa's affections. Mama, who had died of malaria, was one of the aces up her sleeve. Did Papa want her to die just like her sister, simply because he couldn't give her the life in Belgium that she was used to? It was the kind of blackmail that led to incessant arguments in our home."

Her father had been an honorable man, but the nagging and bickering had got the better of him, Ammie continued. When Constance introduced him to a local businessman with important connections, Albert abandoned his principles and got mixed up with diamonds. The man's name was César Janssen.

"I knew nothing about Papa's business dealings. Nor did I know who César Janssen was. Papa merely introduced him as a friend. It was only much later that I discovered what was actually going on."

Albert's unsullied reputation through the years had made him the ideal front man for César to exploit. To make extra sure Albert remained under his control, César began to court Ammie. He acted like a true gentleman. When he asked her to marry him, she agreed, not because she was head over heels in love with him, but chiefly to escape from her home.

"I didn't know what love was then," she said with a rueful smile. "I only found that out when I met Elijah, but by then it was too late. In the late fifties no one got divorced. I would have been an outcast. If you married an évolué besides, you might as well go and banish yourself to an island."

"Elijah was an évolué?" Luc couldn't help being surprised.

"It was only one of the things that had shocked Jacq to the core."

Luc could imagine. Jacq would probably not have admitted it, but he was definitely aware of class distinctions. Not that royal houses and blue blood meant anything to him, nor wealth either. To him, intelligence, knowledge and a certain level of civilization determined class. He would have regarded an évolué as inferior. Actually he was quite an arrogant man, Luc realized, surprised.

Ammie began to speak again. She described how César had corrupted her father more and more, making him undertake ever-bigger risks. When he no longer needed Albert, having robbed him of a consignment of diamonds, César did not hesitate to have his father-in-law, his wife and the pilot killed in a plane crash.

"I found out about it a few years after the incident. Like so many other things as well." She sat for a while with her eyes closed. "I'm tired now. Come back later this afternoon, Luc. I want to lie down for a while."

Luc called Lieve and helped Ammie to her room.

When he was satisfied that she was comfortable, he closed the door of the apartment behind him, frustrated. He hoped Ammie would be as lucid later in the afternoon. It was his last chance to find out more before meeting Caz.

Caz! He glanced at his phone, which had been on silent, and gave a sigh of relief. She had sent a new number. There was no message, but that was not important. She had a new phone and remained in contact. That was enough.

He would have to tell her face to face that her biological father had been a scoundrel of note. A murderer, who had had his wife's father and stepmother killed, and had her lover shot by corrupt police officers. Also that he was the reason why her mother hated Caz with every fiber of her being.

How did one do that? How could one look someone in the eye and give her that kind of news?

Mercifully, it wasn't the real Caz Colijn's friendship he wanted to gain. It was the woman with the long gray curls he had seen at the Graslei that he wanted to get to know. The one who existed only in his imagination.

*Erevu*
*Leuven*

Erevu breathed a sigh of relief when he saw Dove's name among the emails he was downloading. There was something from Jela as well, but Dove was more important now. He had to be in Leuven tonight.

For the umpteenth time he cursed the idiot boy. He had endlessly complicated things. But he was young. Inexperienced. He understood that the boy had panicked when the Colijn woman had caught him in the house.

They both knew that she usually put her shopping bags in the hallway before driving to the garage to put the car away. It would have given Dove enough warning to slip out before she came in through the back door. But this time she didn't unload anything.

Dove had only realized she was in the house when he heard the stairs creak. He was so startled that he dropped the jewellery box he had just picked up. She was there in moments. When she saw him, she screamed, and to shut her up he had grabbed her and clapped his hand over her mouth. She had put up such a fight that she'd cracked her head against the bedpost. The wound bled profusely. Dove lost his grip and she began to scream. It was while he was trying to silence her that he unintentionally strangled her.

"She kept staring at me, Nkoko. That was why I put her on the bed and covered her with the comforter," Dove had told him in tears on his arrival after the boy's frantic call.

Erevu sighed. The scene was etched into his memory. The blood on the walls. The body under the comforter, the pale, limp hand protruding. Dove, crouching in the corner like a naughty child who knew he would be punished—shivering, his hands covering his head.

The first time you take a life is always the worst. Erevu knew that. Every subsequent time is easier, until after a while you can approach it clinically. Decide without emotion what has to be done and how to get away with it.

But Erevu knew he had also been at fault. Because it was Dove. His Dove. That was why he had lost his head as well. He had washed the blood from the walls and the headboard, but failed to clean the rest of the room as thoroughly as he should have, and he forgot to go up to the attic. Dove's terror had been contagious.

Initially he thought of getting Dove out of there, taking him next door to clean himself up, then phoning the police himself to say they had heard a ruckus next door. But Dove would never have passed the test. He could hardly come out of the toilet.

The only option was to get rid of the body and flee. Probably the dumbest thing they could have done, but it was water under the bridge now.

They had to get out of the country as soon as possible, that he didn't doubt for a moment. But first they had to get to the old woman. Find out what she had done with the nkísi.

Erevu brought the tablet closer to his eyes to read Dove's email.

> Nkoko, with everything that has happened, there's something I forgot to tell you. To be honest, I forgot about it until I checked my cellphone diary today.
>
> Before the woman arrived and everything went so terribly wrong, I was in the attic, going through Caz's stuff. There was an envelope. Inside was only a note, but the impression of a key was clearly visible on the outside of the envelope. The note said something about a key to a safe-deposit box. I entered the most important information in my e-diary. The name of a bank, the branch in Pretoria and so on. The box is registered in the name of Josefien Colijn. The contents are described as a canvas bag with wooden objects.
>
> I'm so sorry about everything, Nkoko. Maybe

> this information will go some way toward making up for it.
> Your loving grandson.

Erevu gritted his teeth. The stupid, stupid fool! He had a good mind to ... How could Dove forget the most important thing he found?

He took a walk around the block to calm down before he replied.

> Dove, there's only one way to make up for the indiscretion you committed, not to mention the crucial information about the key which you kept from me. Send the details at once.
> You must come to Leuven today so that we can plan. Limit your luggage to the absolute minimum. Destroy the rest of your things. My mvet as well, no matter how hard it is for me. Going forward, we must travel light and leave no traces.
> I'm afraid we can no longer spare anyone. I know you have a soft spot for the Caz woman, but you can't allow sentiment to stand in your way. We can no longer hesitate about who or what has to be sacrificed. The cause is more important than human lives and the cause will suffer if we don't get the key.
> Fortunately, we no longer have to bother with the old woman. She has nothing we want, though I would have liked to look her in the eye while I extinguished the flame of her life. But it would be stupid to satisfy that selfish need. We must leave the country as soon as possible.
> Back in Lubumbashi we'll be safe, but it's a long way to go. A journey we can't undertake without the key in our possession. A journey that will have to take us to Pretoria first. Jela will be able to help.

> If I don't hear from you by tonight, I will have no choice but to regard you as one of the enemy.
> Your loving grandfather.

Erevu sat back. Could he do it? Sacrifice Dove for the cause?

Yeshua expected it of Abraham and Abraham was prepared to sacrifice his son. That's what the Bible says. If Abraham could do it, so could he. But he prayed that Yeshua would provide a way out, send him a lamb to sacrifice, instead of his grandson.

# Twenty-four

*Luc*
*Leuven*

Luc felt dizzy when he collected the key from Herman's neighbor after a light lunch and walked to the house next door.

Since he'd left Ammie, his mind had been whirling. He tried to grasp what Ammie had told him, tried to see the bigger picture, but also remember the details. Tried to interpret. Understand.

Luc put his overnight bag in the guest room and went to the living room, where he poured himself a stiff shot of Herman's cognac before he walked out onto the patio and called Lieve.

"Sorry, Professor, but Miss Ammie isn't strong enough to see you again this afternoon. She's exhausted—emotionally rather than physically, I think."

He understood. For all these years she had been bottling up secrets, trying to forget, and suddenly the scabs were being pulled off.

"I have an appointment tomorrow morning, but can I drop in again in the afternoon? After that I'll have to return home." On Tuesday morning he had to be in the lecture hall and that evening was the first VGK event he and Laura had to run. The Godparents' Evening. On Wednesday it was parents' evening. He had left almost all the arrangements in Laura's hands. It embarrassed him, but in truth she was just so much more efficient at that kind of thing than he was. Actually, she was just more efficient. Period.

"I'm sure it'll be okay, Professor. Just check again before you come."

Luc sat down on a patio chair and stretched his long legs. For the moment he didn't want to think about his conversation with Ammie. He would rehash it later. Neither did he want to think of what Caz Colijn would say. He did, however, have to decide where to meet her. Or whether to meet her at all.

He devised a workable plan and typed a message.
*Thanks for the number.*
*Meet you 10:30 at Zwarte Zusters entrance to Groot Begijnhof.*
*From there we can walk to the Arenberg Castle and have lunch.*
*Okay?*

It took a small lifetime before the reply came.
*Okay for now. Will confirm shortly.*

It would have to do, but he wondered why she was hesitant.

His thoughts turned to the man at the Graslei. He might be the one who was monitoring Caz's text messages. Then there was her conversation with the young black student. Evidently she knew him from somewhere. And Ammie had been in a relationship with an évolué.

Surely there couldn't be a connection?

*Caz*
*Ghent*

"Will you please come back in, Ms. Colijn?" De Brabander held the door of the interview room. Fifteen minutes ago, after her statement had been taken down, Caz had been asked to wait in a smaller room.

Probably for them to confer. Or perhaps to verify some of the information she had given them. She hoped it was only a formality or two that lay ahead. She was worn out in body and soul.

Inspector Grevers was with De Brabander, and two more people had joined them: a woman in her thirties, who was introduced as Agent Verhoef, and a man whose name she couldn't quite make out.

"Do you mind if our IT man takes a look at your cellphone while we're busy in here?"

There was no point in refusing, she realized. She gave the man her South African phone. They were probably only interested in the messages between herself and Tieneke anyway.

The possibility seemed to have increased that she was indeed a suspect, and not one they would soon eliminate. Nausea threatened to overwhelm her when she sat down in the same chair she had sat in before.

The man whose name she hadn't heard left the room with the phone.

"Okay, we made contact with the woman of the B&B in Leuven. She's prepared to confirm under oath that you spent Thursday afternoon and evening in her home."

It was a relief, but something in his eyes told her not to get too comfortable.

"You say you never saw the tenants in Miss Colijn's rental home?"

"That's correct." She knew by now that she had to answer audibly for the sake of the recording that was being made of the conversation.

"But you were aware that there were people next door?"

"I saw the curtains move. That's all. My sister informed me that tenants normally stayed for a week or longer." She couldn't remember whether she'd already said so. Her mind was in turmoil.

"Your landlady in Leuven mentioned she saw you with a street musician near her home. Not for long, but long enough to have a conversation. Is that correct?"

What was he on about now? "I listened for a few moments because the music made me nostalgic for Africa, but I didn't talk to the man."

"The street musician played an unusual instrument? A rather primitive one?"

"That's right. I looked it up afterwards on the internet. It's known as an mvet or stick zither."

"Can you describe it?"

Caz sighed inwardly. Where the hell was the man going with this line of questioning? "It's a string instrument. The strings are attached to a bent stick. A gourd provides resonance. Or at least I think so. I'm not an expert on traditional or any other musical instruments."

"Can you tell us whether the instrument looked more or less like this?" De Brabander nodded at the inspector who got up and took something from a cardboard box. It was wrapped in transparent plastic and sealed.

Caz swallowed against the lump in her throat when she realized what she was looking at. "To the best of my knowledge this looks like the instrument the African man was playing."

"I find it strange that you can identify an instrument you say you saw in Leuven but that was left in a cupboard in your sister's rental home in Ghent by one of the tenants."

Caz could only stare at him, speechless.

"I ask again. Do you know who the tenants were?"

Caz shook her head.

"Please answer out loud."

"No. I never saw them. My sister never even told me she

was the owner of the house next door. She just told me the rooms were rented out on a weekly basis. I didn't ask for further details."

"And you never met them?"

Caz sighed despondently. Didn't the man understand what she was saying? So far he had seemed to be following her Afrikaans well enough as long as she spoke slowly and chose her words carefully. "Not that I know of. If I did, I wasn't aware that the person or persons lived in the house next door."

"Why did you ask Miss Colijn about the rental home?"

"I said something about the neighbors being inquisitive. They peered from behind the curtains. Something like that. That was when my sister said they were temporary neighbors that changed on a weekly basis." Crikey Moses, how many times would she have to repeat it?

"You speak of your sister, but Tieneke Colijn was not really your sister, was she?"

"No, but I only found that out just before I came here. I have called her my sister all my life; it's what I'm used to calling her." Exhaustion, which affected much more than her body, impeded her thoughts, made them clumsy and incoherent.

"You were estranged from Miss Colijn even before you found out, not so?"

"Yes."

"You had no contact for years."

"That is correct." Babette must have thought fit to inform him.

"When you found out you weren't related by blood, you came here to see them. While you never did so in the something like twenty years since they returned to Belgium, when you were still under the impression that you were biologically related. How does that make sense?"

"My sister ... Tieneke phoned me. She told me that our ... her mother was dying and wanted to see me. That was also when she told me that Josefien and Hans Colijn were not my biological parents and that her mother was the only one who knew the truth."

"Ms. Colijn, what is the real reason for your coming to Belgium?" he asked as if she hadn't just answered him.

Caz gave a deep sigh and forced back the tears. This was no time to crack. "To find out who my biological parents were and to see my daughter."

"You have a daughter?"

"That's right. She lives in Paris but she's currently traveling for her work."

"Where is she now?"

Caz tried to remember, but she was too confused. "I'm not sure. The Bahamas, no ... Morocco, or maybe Dubai. One of those two. I don't remember the dates on the itinerary she gave me. I only know she'll be back in Europe on October the seventh."

"What is she doing in Morocco or Dubai?"

"Shooting."

De Brabander's eyebrows flew up.

"A photo shoot. Photographic session. She's a model."

"Could you give us her name and contact details?"

"She's actually Lila Colijn—pronounced the Afrikaans way—but to make it easier for the English-speaking world, she's known as Lilah. She doesn't use her last name. Her permanent address is Rue St ..."

"Lilah?" Agent Verhoef's eyes grew wide. "You mean Lilah who was recently on the cover of *Cosmopolitan*? Last month, to be exact?"

Caz sighed. She guessed what was about to come. "That's her."

Verhoef gave an incredulous laugh. "Ms. Colijn, that is a barefaced lie."

De Brabander's frown became a chasm. "What do you mean?"

The woman got to her feet. "Excuse me for a minute."

The commissioner looked at her questioningly.

"I know where to find a copy of the magazine."

"What's going on?" asked De Brabander when Verhoef hurried out.

Caz shrugged. She would give the agent her dramatic

moment. Lord knows, she needed a breather to sort out her thoughts.

"Your foster mother died the day after you arrived in Belgium, is that correct?" De Brabander was clearly not going to allow her the breather she needed.

"It is correct."

"And did you find out the identity of your biological parents?"

"Only the name of my biological mother and where she lived a long time ago. She doesn't live there any more."

"And your foster sister, Tieneke Colijn, was Mrs. Colijn's sole heir?"

Where was he coming from this time? "Correct."

"Do you happen to know who the beneficiary is of Tieneke Colijn's estate?"

The way he looked at her gave her the shivers. "I don't have the faintest idea."

"Any suspicion?"

"No. I honestly don't know what went on in Tieneke's life, let alone her will. As you've already said, we've been estranged for many years."

The door opened and the agent came in. She put the magazine in front of De Brabander with a flourish. "That is Lilah on the cover. The article is on page 103, with more photographs."

Caz doubted whether De Brabander had heard. He stared at the cover. At the beautiful woman with the masses of long black braids, decorated with bronze beads and feathers, the high cheekbones and striking silvery blue eyes in sharp contrast with the sepia skin tone.

He looked up, let his gaze sweep over her slowly, taking in the long gray hair that had once been blonde, the sun-bronzed white skin, the Caucasian features. At last his gaze found hers. "I take it she's your adopted daughter?"

Caz shook her head. "No, she's my biological daughter, Commissioner. And for the record, her biological father, my ex-husband, is white too. She's a fluke. A beautiful fluke."

A strange sound exploded from Agent Verhoef's lips.

De Brabander cleared his throat. "Let's leave it there for now." He paged through his notes.

Leave it for now. It. "It" that had turned her entire life upside down. Of course they thought she was lying. Like Hentie had thought she was lying. Andries. Magdel. Fien and Tieneke. A white couple could not have a dark-skinned baby. It was impossible. A sallow complexion, perhaps. But not umber.

And it had to happen in South Africa, of all places. In 1983, the heyday of apartheid. During the P.W. Botha administration. His new Constitution worth less than the paper it was written on.

In 1986 the Immorality Act was scrapped and pass laws recalled, yet Lilah was still denied entry to white nursery schools. In the mornings Caz left her with a domestic helper to go to the doctor's surgery where she had a half-day post as a receptionist. In the afternoons she studied for her translation diploma at home, with Lilah chattering at her feet in a mixture of Sotho and Afrikaans.

The domestic helper had thought it her duty to teach a black child a black language. She was a wonderful woman but certainly not an ideal candidate for daycare. She began to treat Lilah more and more like a protégée, trying to alienate her from Caz.

It had been one of the reasons why Caz had chosen translation over teaching. She had hoped to get along without a domestic helper. She would work from home and be there for Lilah.

During her pursuit to get an answer to the question of how it was possible for a white couple to produce a black child, she found out that Lilah had a predecessor in South Africa in the person of Sandra Laing, a black girl born in 1955 from a white marriage. Sannie Laing, her mother, was also suspected of adultery with a black man. The big difference was that the father believed the mother and stayed married to her. Their greatest struggle had been having the child classified white and enrolling her at a white school.

The mystery of Sandra Laing's descent was never solved.

Neither was Lilah's. The Maritz family tree, as far as Caz could discover, was lily-white, and so was Magdel's. As lily-white as any South African's family tree can be, mind you. Hans and Fien's pedigrees were even purer. None of their ancestors had set foot in Africa before Hans came to South Africa.

"Would you mind," De Brabander brought her back to the present, "sharing with us the identity of the person you plan to meet tomorrow regarding, and I quote, 'a private matter'?"

For a moment Caz didn't know what he was talking about. Then she remembered. Leuven. Tomorrow. Her contact with Ammie Pauwels. Luc DeReu's friend. She shook her head, bemused. "It has nothing to do with Tieneke's death. It's a completely different matter. As the person who's inspecting my cellphone will tell you."

"Ms. Colijn, what is the person's name? It can't be such a hard question to answer."

She gave a deep sigh. "I don't know the person's real name."

De Brabander's eyebrows shot up again. He had perfected a facial expression that portrayed surprised scepticism. "How is he or she known to you?"

"Tijl Uilenspiegel." The moment the words were out she could kick herself. She should simply have said TU.

De Brabander lowered his chin, but his gaze held hers. As if he was peering at her over imaginary spectacles."Tijl Uilenspiegel."

"It has nothing ..."

De Brabander held up his hand. "Yes, Ms. Colijn, you've already said it has nothing to do with Tieneke's murder—that's right, not Tieneke's death, Tieneke's murder. Could you tell me then what he or she has anything to do with?"

Suddenly Caz had had enough. Of detectives and dead bodies and musical instruments turning up where they had no business to be and of Uilenspiegels as well. "Yes, Commissioner, I could. But I'm not going to. Ask the man who's checking my phone."

She got up and slung her handbag over her shoulder. "Am

I under arrest or can I go home? I'm tired. Dreadfully, dreadfully tired." She looked him in the eye. "I hope you won't ever be in a situation where you have to identify your sister's body on the same day that you're accused of her murder. Believe me, it's not an agreeable position to find yourself in."

De Brabander got up too. With her chin raised, Caz looked down at him.

"You're not under arrest. But I want to be informed of your movements."

"I'm going to the nearest bus stop and from there to my guesthouse. Do you want to be informed of my movements inside the house as well?"

"You know what I mean. Are you still planning to go to Leuven tomorrow?"

"Yes."

"To meet Tijl Uilenspiegel?"

"That is correct."

"Someone whose real name you don't even know?"

Caz sighed. "That is correct."

De Brabander tried another curveball. "The estrangement between you and your foster mother and sister, what was the reason for it?"

"They disowned me because of the color of my daughter's skin. And because of their so-called logical conclusion that I had slept with a black man. It was before the Immorality Act was recalled." She didn't give a damn whether he knew about the Immorality Act. She'd had it.

The man returned with her phone.

"The thing is hot, Commissioner." He looked in Caz's direction and said something she couldn't hear.

Caz frowned. Did he mean it was stolen? Couldn't be. She'd got it brand new with her most recent upgrade. It had been registered according to the strict regulations in South Africa.

De Brabander turned to her again. "Are you aware that someone can read all your messages and listen to all your calls?"

So TU had been right, though she hadn't believed him.

"No." She wouldn't even try to explain that she had suspected it. She didn't know how TU had guessed it anyway. "Can you fix it?" she asked through dry lips.

De Brabander gave the cellphone man an inquiring look. "MSpy," came the cryptic reply.

The commissioner turned back to Caz. "We could remove the software, but I'd much rather use the phone to flush out the person who's monitoring your calls. Try to establish his or her identity. Or do you know who it might be?"

"I can't think of anyone."

"Whoever it is must have had access to your phone," the cellphone man said. "The software has to be downloaded on your phone to make it work."

Caz shook her head. "My phone is always with me."

"You take it along every time you, say, go to the restroom? Even when you're in the presence of someone you trust?"

Caz hesitated. She couldn't think straight. There were too many thoughts milling about in her mind.

De Brabander fixed her with his gaze. "If this person is an accessory who doesn't trust you, things might just get interesting. It would be better if you were honest."

Accessory? Suddenly a few things made sense to her. He believed her when she said she didn't commit the murder, that she was in Leuven, but he didn't believe that she had nothing to do with it.

Enough was enough. "I am not an accessory to anything. Please find the guilty person, Commissioner. I would sleep more soundly myself if I knew who it was and why he did it. Now I'm going home. Where's the nearest bus stop?"

De Brabander was still staring at her. After a while he nodded. "Grevers, please take Ms. Colijn to her guesthouse."

The taciturn inspector got to his feet.

"Don't worry, I'll manage. When can I have my phone back?"

"I'll let you know. And I insist that Inspector Grevers takes you home."

Caz gave in on both counts. She didn't think he was entitled to keep her phone, but there wasn't much point in kicking up a fuss about a phone she couldn't use if she didn't want some stranger to know exactly what she was saying and to whom. And she would welcome a lift home. The sooner she could wash this day away with soap and water and a glass of wine, the better.

# Twenty-five

*Luc*
*Leuven*

Luc glanced through the menu at the Thai restuarant that had been one of his favorites when he had lived in Leuven. The menu had not changed much, but the waitresses were much younger than he remembered.

It was too early for supper but he couldn't face going over Tuesday's lecture yet again. And Herman's place made him feel morbid. Exactly why, he couldn't say. Perhaps it was all that chrome and glass and blond wood.

He liked coziness. Even in her advanced age, Ammie's place was cozy. Like their home here in Leuven had been when she had been married to Jacq.

Luc struggled to reconcile the memory of the Ammie of his childhood and youth with the elderly woman in her apartment. It was as if they were two different people. Not just on the outside, in temperament as well. Or maybe he simply looked at her differently now that he was older.

Then she had been a mother, now she was a lonely old

woman. Then he had been a boy and later a young man, now he was a middle-aged man.

He wondered what Ammie remembered of the almost two decades she had been married to Jacq. Whether it was as clear in her memory as the memories of her life in the Congo.

She had brought Elisabethville alive to him. Including, unfortunately, the night Elijah was shot. To think she had known Patrice Lumumba personally.

Of course he was aware of the bomb Ludo de Witte had dropped in 1999 with his book *De moord op Lumumba*. He had studied the report of the parliamentary commission that had investigated the matter. Tried to analyze the reasons for their conclusion that Belgium was morally implicated in the murder of Lumumba. He had followed everything else that had happened as well. And all that time it had never crossed his mind that Ammie had been there. He'd had no idea that she had known the man and had lost her beloved that same night in exactly the same way. In Elijah's case, the motive for his murder had not been political, of course, but personal.

How much more was there that he didn't know about? That had passed him by because he had paid more attention to the written word than to people's personal experiences?

*Caz*
*Ghent*

It wasn't out of consideration that Grevers was told to take her home, Caz realized when he accompanied her to the front door. De Brabander wanted to make sure she wasn't going anywhere else. And without her cellphone she couldn't warn anyone. About whatever.

Caz looked down the street. There were still vehicles parked in front of Tieneke's home. Probably the crime-scene unit. The house and the area leading up to the front door had been cordoned off with police tape.

"Thanks, Inspector. Goodnight," she said when they reached Erdem's front door.

"Ms. Colijn?"

She looked at him inquiringly, her hand on the doorknob.

"Commissioner De Brabander asked that you hand me your passport."

Grevers had taken a call just after they had left. It must have been De Brabander whose suspicion had got the better of him.

"Fine, but I have to insist on a receipt. I'm sure you understand?" All she needed now was for her bloody passport to get lost somewhere in the process.

Grevers nodded.

"Everything okay?" Erdem asked behind her.

"Can you help with pen and paper, please? The inspector has to take my passport and wants to write out a receipt." Now she had an eyewitness as well. It was probably only South Africans who had such a distrust of the police.

Erdem took them to a room that looked like an office. He handed the inspector writing materials and made her a copy of the first page of her passport and her visa.

"Thanks, Erdem," she said when Grevers had finally left. "I appreciate it. I feel like a criminal even though I did nothing wrong."

Erdem gave her a lopsided smile. "I know the feeling."

"How's that?"

He rubbed his cheek. "Incomers are distrusted everywhere. Probably with reason. Here in Belgium a Turk or a Moroccan or some incomer is involved in nearly every murder. Either as the victim or as the guilty party."

"I didn't think there were many murders here," Caz said, slightly dismayed.

"Very few, compared to other parts of the world, but more than you'd think. Believe me, Tieneke Colijn isn't the only one whose body has been found in the Leie." He bit his lower lip. "Sorry, that was insensitive of me. The entire neighborhood is up in arms and rumor is rife."

Caz motioned with her hand to stop him from apologizing. "It's the truth, isn't it? Anyway, thanks for your help. I just want to take a shower and go to bed. It's been a long day."

"Oh, by the way, someone from the police brought your luggage just before you came. He asked that you make sure everything is there. I had him put it in your room."

"Thanks, Erdem. At least one good thing came from this horrid day."

When she entered the room, her belongings stood neatly in a corner. When she opened the lilac case, it was clear that someone had gone through the contents. It didn't surprise her. The police had obviously inspected everything that had been in the murder house. She was much too tired anyway to feel that her privacy had been invaded. She was only too thankful she had clothes again and no longer had to wash the essentials every night.

She remembered noticing that the zipper of the case was slightly open when she had entered Tieneke's home with the locksmith. At the time she had thought it must have been Tieneke, but now she knew Tieneke could not have been the one who had opened her case.

Caz shivered. It must have been the murderer. At first glance nothing seemed to be missing, but why then? What interest could he have had in luggage that was in the attic? And why had the envelope been on the floor?

A shower was what she needed now to try to rinse off the day and all these questions. And then she'd have to make up her mind about tomorrow.

*Luc*
*Leuven*

Luc hastened to look when a text message came through. "CC-new," the screen said. *Groot Begijnhof. 10:30.*

*See you there*, he typed hastily, as if he wanted to make sure she didn't change her mind. Which could still happen, of course.

See you there. As if it was an ordinary date with an ordinary woman. Yet it wasn't.

During this date he would have to admit that he was Luc DeReu and tell a woman that her mother hated her, that her father had murdered both her grandfather and her mother's lover. That she carried inside her the genes of a murderer and those of a heartless woman.

No, this date was anything but ordinary, and neither was the woman.

*Caz*
*Ghent*

Caz could not get comfortable in her bed. It had been a hellish day but, strangely enough, it wasn't identifying Tieneke's body or knowing she was suspected of murder that was preventing Caz from falling asleep.

She was worried that she had indirectly involved Lilah. It was the last thing Lilah needed in her life. Now that she was on the crest of the wave.

She would have to let Lilah know about recent developments, but how she was going to break the news, Caz didn't know. Hey, my little jacaranda blossom, your mother is suspected of having murdered her sister ... oops, foster sister, and maybe her foster mother as well.

Lilah didn't even know yet that "those two" weren't family after all. Caz had put off telling her until she had more details.

There was only one solution and it would simplify a few other matters as well. Caz would let Lilah know she had decided to stick to their original plan after all. Of course she wouldn't tell Lilah her passport had been confiscated. Nor that she had to arrange Tieneke's funeral. There would be enough time to explain everything when they saw each other. Hopefully the nightmare would be over by then and everything sorted out.

Her return flight was booked for October 15. Two weeks from now. De Brabander ought to be convinced of her innocence by then. Now that she thought of it, she was booked on a daytime flight. If she remembered correctly, she would land in Johannesburg in the evening and her flight back to

Cape Town was only the next afternoon. If she rented a car and slept over in Pretoria instead of Johannesburg, she could be at the bank in Silverton when they opened their doors, find out what was in the safe-deposit box and be at OR Tambo in time for her flight.

The publisher of the book she was translating lived in Pretoria. Annika might be able to recommend affordable accommodation.

October in Pretoria. Jacaranda time. It would be quite fitting for her to close the book on the past in Pretoria, where she had parted ways with Fien and Tieneke. Where the jacaranda blossom had floated down and came to rest in Lilah's hair.

Out of the blue, Caz remembered the day she had burned the potatoes. Lilah was still Lila then. She must have been about five. Caz was struggling with an assignment and had forgotten about the potatoes on the stove. When the sickening smell got through to her, it was too late. The potatoes had been burned to a cinder.

She had plucked the pot off the stove and upended the charred remains on the breadboard to cool down.

Lila was watching her keenly. "Why are the potatoes black, Mama?" she asked, a serious expression on her little face.

"They burned." She was annoyed with herself and spoke curtly. "Look at the mess. Completely useless."

"Did I burn too, Mama?" Lila asked, looking up at her with those strange, wise eyes.

She had turned ice cold, grabbed Lila and held her close. "No, my love, you didn't burn."

"Then why am I black?"

Caz still remembered the dismay she had felt. "To me you're not black, Lila, you're just Lila."

"You said Lila means purple. Am I purple?" the child asked earnestly.

"Do you like purple?"

Lila nodded.

"Well then, from now on you are purple. Until you decide you like another color better. The color of your skin doesn't define you, Lila. You are defined by what you are on the inside."

Those might have been wise words for the moment, and they had satisfied Lila, but in reality her words were proved wrong. In the eyes of society Lila had always remained the black child of a white mother.

Caz didn't give a hoot about the gossip that she had broken the law and, Lord forbid, slept with a black man. More "sympathetic" people, wanting to give her the benefit of the doubt, speculated that she had been raped.

That had also been Andries's unshakable conviction and therefore Hentie's and Magdel's as well.

It was Hentie who had planted the seed. He had tried to persuade her to admit she had been raped by terrorists the night she had gone for a walk and returned breathless and bewildered. He would never blame her, he said. He loved her. She could tell him the truth.

The more she denied having been raped, the less he believed her, and the harder he pleaded for her to be honest. He said he realized it wasn't her fault, understood why she had remained silent. He believed Andries and Magdel would also understand.

Of course he shared his theory with Andries and it was immediately accepted as the truth.

Andries had the solution. The child would be sent overseas for adoption as soon as she had been weaned onto a bottle and was old enough to travel. Foreigners raised children of all colors and flavors, were his exact words; they would snatch her up. He undertook to personally make sure she was placed with good parents.

She had to grit her teeth. "Pa, 'the child' is my child. And even if Hentie refuses to believe it, she's his child too. His flesh and blood. I'm not sending my child away to be raised by strangers in a strange country," she told him, repeating it so often that it became a refrain.

After about four weeks she realized it was futile. She packed everything she owned that could fit into the trunk of her car and told Hentie to file for divorce.

He begged her to stay.

"It's our child and me, or nothing, Hentie," was her ultimatum.

Andries came to speak to her. At first he asked her politely to stay and let the child go. Then he berated her. "A woman who has lain with a kaffir isn't welcome on this farm anyway!" was his parting shot.

She had looked him in the eye, turned, put her daughter in her carrycot and walked to her car. Hentie came running, in tears as he pushed five hundred rand into her hand before storming off.

Caz was too blinded by tears to pull away immediately. She was tempted to throw the money through the window. Fortunately she didn't. She had a child to look after and she didn't have much money of her own. Pride bowed before pragmatism.

Magdel approached and, through the open window, placed two hundred rand on her lap.

"It's better this way, Sandra. God bless you," was all she said before returning to the kitchen.

Caz still didn't know how she had got to Pretoria. Of the five, six hundred kilometers she drove she didn't remember a thing. Only the fury, the humiliation, the powerlessness.

When she stopped in front of her parental home she thought she would at least have a temporary refuge.

Andries or Hentie or Magdel must have warned Josefien she was on her way. She was at the car as Caz got out.

"There's no room here for you and your bastard child," she said without greeting.

Caz lifted her baby daughter out of the carrycot. "Mother, this is your granddaughter," she said, stupidly thinking Fien's heart would melt when she saw how lovely the little one was.

Fien backed away. "She's even darker than I imagined!" She hurried back to the porch where Tieneke was standing.

Moments later a jacaranda blossom floated down, landing on the curly black hair, and "the child" got her name.

If De Brabander knew about the pain and humiliation, the helpless anger she had felt that day, he would lock her up without further ado. What he probably wouldn't understand was that she had felt no hatred that day. There had been no time or room for hatred. From that moment on, everything had been focused on survival. Hatred would have been a waste of energy and she needed every bit of resolve to find a place where she and her daughter could stay.

That night she had cried her eyes out in a third-rate hotel room. It was the last time she had succumbed to hopeless tears. She had no energy to waste on tears either.

Caz took a few sips of water from the glass on her bedside table and tried to get comfortable again.

Now she had to rally that same resolve and get some sleep. Tomorrow was going to be a difficult day. But surely it couldn't be much worse than today.

*Luc*
*Leuven*

When a phone rang, Luc was baffled for a moment. It wasn't his cellphone, neither was it Herman's landline. At the second ring he realized it was his spare phone. The one he had used to contact Caz. He had brought it along in case she used that number instead of the one he had given her on the note he had sent with the waiter.

This time it wasn't a private number, but it was still a number he didn't recognize. After the fourth ring he pressed the green button.

"Good evening?"

There was silence on the other end.

"Hello? Anyone there?"

"Good evening. This is Commissioner De Brabander of the Ghent police. Who am I speaking to?'

The policeman must have dialed the wrong number. "DeReu. Luc DeReu."

"Oh? Mr. DeReu, I'm phoning in connection with a text message that was sent from your phone to Cassandra Colijn's phone.

A lump formed in Luc's throat. "Yes?"

"I didn't expect to find you. The contents of the message indicated that the sender was a friend of Luc DeReu's. Can you explain, please?"

"Commissioner, that is a private matter."

"Mr. DeReu, Cassandra Colijn's foster sister was murdered and I'm the investigating officer. In a murder case nothing is private."

"Murdered? Her sister? Good grief!"

"It's been on the news, since we're looking for two men who might be able to tell us more, so I can give you the basic information.

"Tieneke Colijn's body was found in the Leie this morning, but it's estimated she was murdered in her home on Thursday afternoon, barely a week after the death of her mother, Josefien Colijn. Her mother's death occurred the day after Cassandra Colijn arrived here from South Africa. I ask you again, why did you pretend to be someone else?"

The messages they exchanged made everything clear. The police were probably just trying to tie everything together. Anyway, he had nothing to hide.

"Caz phoned the landline of the woman who cares for her biological mother, Ammie Pauwels, and left a message. She asked Lieve to tell me to contact her. I found it strange. I haven't been able to work out how she knew about Lieve without knowing about Ammie."

"You'll have to start at the beginning and explain everything, including who Lieve and Ammie Pauwels are."

It took Luc a good half-hour to explain and then to answer De Brabander's questions.

"Should I take it that Caz Colijn is a suspect?" Luc asked when the conversation seemed to be drawing to a close.

"Family members are always the first suspects if there's no clear alternative."

An evasive answer. He wondered what De Brabander's reaction would be if he told the detective Caz Colijn carried the genes of a murderer.

"Is your appointment with Ms. Colijn still on?" asked the commissioner.

"She hasn't canceled."

"Mr. DeReu, if I were you, I wouldn't tell her the whereabouts of Mrs. Ammie Pauwels. Make sure you and Ms. Colijn are always among people. Keep your eyes open. I expect you to give me feedback on the entire conversation. And I want to meet with you as soon as possible. You don't happen to be coming to Ghent in the near future?"

The man was probably under the impression that he lived in Leuven. Possibly because the appointment was to take place there.

"I work in Ghent. At the university. History department. I'll be back there on Tuesday. I'm in Leuven at present because my stepmother is unwell." He didn't have to give the entire game away.

"That makes it easier. I'll phone again to set up a meeting. Goodnight."

Luc ended the call. It was only when he switched off the phone that he remembered that it wasn't the phone he normally used. Now he would have to hang on to both phones, even though Caz would be using his regular number.

He was lying in bed when he realized that De Brabander didn't know about the last few texts on his regular phone. It meant that De Brabander was unaware that the time and place of their meeting had changed. It was probably not important. He was certainly not going to call the man to tell him.

The bed in Herman's guest room was hard, but that was not why sleep wouldn't come. Luc lay wondering about Caz. The attractive woman with Africa in her posture, her walk, her gaze. With a murderer's blood in her veins.

Didn't she have a little too much bad luck in one go? Coming to Ghent and having first her mother die and then her sister murdered?

To think he had almost decided to take her to see Ammie. The way things were going, he didn't even know whether he wanted to meet her himself.

# Twenty-six

*Monday, September 29*
*Caz*
*Leuven*

Caz woke up early. Erdem's internet connection was fast and she was an expert by now at finding train routes on the NMBS website. She wrote down what she needed to know and studied the map of Leuven, just to make sure she knew which way Groot Begijnhof lay from the station.

To find out what to expect, she googled "begijnhof." Google complied. It was a medieval city within a city where pious women who didn't belong to a conventional monastic order lived.

It sounded a bit like the kind of life she would have wanted if she had lived in medieval times. Only the piousness would have been a bit of a problem. She wasn't so sure about a bunch of old maids living together either.

With time on her hands, she sent Lilah an email about her change of plans. Then she took a fresh outfit from her case and began to get ready for the day. A day in which she would hopefully find out more about Ammie Pauwels, the woman who had carried her under her heart for nine months. She would rather not speculate about what she would hear.

Under the shower Caz was suddenly reminded of Ellen's words when she had spent the night with her after the break-in.

"Only a few years ago I would have had to pee outside and sleep under the kitchen table," Ellen commented drily when Caz put down towels for her in the guest room.

"Not in my home, or Lilah would have peed outside and slept under the kitchen table all her life." Caz grinned.

"Hmm. It's always going to be strange."

"What?" Caz asked.

"The white lily and the black rose from the same flowerbed."

Well, hopefully she would find out today how that flowerbed had come about.

When she was dressed and ready, Caz took a quick look to see whether Lilah had answered. She had, and she was over the moon. Caz just hoped Erdem could put her up until the eighth.

She glanced at her watch and jumped up. She had to get to the station in time.

The bus ride to Dampoort was familiar by now. She almost wished there was something new in her surroundings to take her mind off what lay ahead. Today she might hear why her birth mother left her with Hans and Josefien Colijn. Why she didn't want her own child. Caz wasn't sure if she was ready to hear it. Or if she would ever be ready.

The platform where she waited for her train was busy.

At precisely 08:40 the train, direction Ronse, arrived at Ghent-Dampoort, Track 1. At precisely 08:48 Caz stepped off the train at Track 5, Ghent-Sint-Pieters, and walked to Track 7, where she found even more people waiting for the train. Probably commuters between Ghent and Leuven.

At 08:53 on the dot she boarded the train, direction Welkenraedt, to Leuven.

An hour and many thoughts and doubts about the day

ahead later, she was in Leuven. Oh, the miracle of punctuality and a system that ran like clockwork!

But now she had to find the Groot Begijnhof. She had half an hour to get there. According to the bus timetable she could take Bus 1 or 2. Bus 1 stopped first. A number of other passengers climbed aboard, but she managed to get a seat.

*Luc*
*Leuven*

Luc was standing some distance away from the Fonske statue. If he could get confirmation that Caz's South African phone was being monitored and she was being followed by the African man from the Graslei, at least he would know where they stood.

He felt a little stupid wearing Herman's cap, but covering his hair and wearing dark glasses had been all he could think of by way of a disguise. Just in case.

So far no one had drawn his attention. No one looked as though they were keeping watch. There was a black man, but not the one from the Graslei, who had been an older man with a shaven head and very neatly dressed. This one was in his thirties and in casual clothes.

The clock had struck ten a minute or so ago. He would wait a little longer.

Luc's gaze swept over the people near Fonske again, and then went wider. One man caught his eye, only because he also stood still, looking around. Medium height. Sturdily built. Mousy hair. Face in a serious frown. On his belt a kind of radio.

Police, or just security?

Luc drew a sharp breath when a tall black man came around the corner. He was wearing a hat but Luc could swear it was the man he had seen at the Graslei. Same height, same age. Neatly dressed.

Luc took the spare phone from his pocket and pressed the button to send the message he had already composed.

He had chosen the words carefully so that Caz wouldn't be confused when she got it. *A little late. See you in a while. TU.*

Sure enough, Mr. Graslei stopped to look at his phone.

A movement to the right, where the man with the radio was, caught Luc's eye. The man was also looking down at his phone.

What now? The man with the mousy hair typed something and moments later the phone in Luc's hand vibrated. Puzzled, he looked down. CC, it said on the screen. *Fine.*

Luc's eyes went to Mr. Graslei. Over a distance of fifteen meters their eyes met. The man turned on his heel and hurried away.

Luc's gaze flew to the man with the mousy hair. Their eyes met as well.

He had Caz's South African phone, Luc realized immediately. He had to be the detective. It could wait. Luc set off in pursuit of the man with the hat, who looked over his shoulder and stepped up the pace. Luc walked faster as well but a moment later a firm hand gripped his arm. He looked over his shoulder.

"De Brabander. Where's Ms. Colijn?"

"Commissioner, there's no time to explain. I must follow that man." He motioned at Mr. Graslei who was merging with the crowd on the square.

Luc pointed in his direction. "There, at the Town Hall. The black man. I think he's monitoring Caz Colijn's phone."

"Where is Ms. Colijn?"

"Groot Begijnhof. Zwarte Zusters entrance."

"Go there and wait for me." The detective dashed off in pursuit of Mr. Graslei, who had just vanished around a corner.

*Caz*
*Leuven*

Most of the passengers got off at the Town Hall stop. Only she and a woman with an almost unnaturally thick mane of blonde hair remained, until an elderly man and his wife got on board. The bus driver apparently decided to wait for a young man in a suit who was running towards the bus, briefcase in hand, cellphone at his ear.

Caz looked through the window and marveled again at the Gothic architecture of the Town Hall. How had they managed to build it? All those statues. So many of them. The details were so fine, it confounded the eye.

Cars and bicycles flew past. A motorbike had to swerve when a cyclist cut in before him. The cyclist gave the biker with the dreadlocks a dirty look.

Caz glanced at her watch when the bus pulled away. Ten past ten. She should be at her destination in less than ten minutes. Another ten minutes and she'd be meeting Tijl Uilenspiegel. Whoever he might be.

*Erevu*
*Leuven*

The bloody professor had tricked him. Erevu turned into a side street, stood panting with his back to the wall. He expected the man to come jogging past any minute, but nothing happened.

His cellphone beeped. Dove. He glanced quickly at the message. *CC didn't get off at town hall. Direction Naamsepoort.*

It had been an enormous relief when Dove had sent word, shortly after receiving Erevu's message the night before, that he was on his way to Leuven. He had also sent the information about the bank where the safe-deposit box was. They were a team again.

Erevu peered around the corner. No sign of the professor. But there was another man who stood looking around, his hands on his hips. Erevu ducked back behind the wall, took off his hat and put it on the pavement. A pity, it was an expensive hat.

He texted hurriedly. *Let me know where.* He walked to the next corner and chose another side street, going in the general direction of Naamsepoort.

What was going on? Why didn't the Caz woman go to Fonske? Had they made an alternative plan? How?

A good thing Dove had been following her from the Martelaereplein bus stop and had sent word earlier that she had her backpack with her. The key to the strongbox had to be inside. She had to be carrying it on her person, or they would have found it in her luggage. They had to get that key today. Their flights were leaving from Brussels tonight and without the key all would have been in vain.

Hopefully Dove had got rid of the woman in the blonde wig who was evidently following the Caz woman.

*Zwarte Zusters Street, Begijn. Blondie out of action.* The message came moments later, just as Erevu was leaving Pater Damiaanplein. According to the map of the city he had picked up at the tourist office, he could reach Zwarte Zusters Street via Redingen Street.

*On my way. Prof probably too. Stop him, delay as long as possible and keep him in sight. He'll go down Naamse Street or maybe Schapen Street.*

Hopefully. And hopefully Dove would intercept the professor. It would give him a chance to get the backpack. Today the spirits of his ancestors would have to come to his aid.

*Caz*
*Leuven*

Caz came to a halt in front of the entrance to the Groot Begijnhof. The old buildings breathed an atmosphere of timeless peace and tranquillity, but there was also something mystical about them.

In the courtyard, with its cobblestone pathways, it was cool and green. The surrounding walls looked centuries old. No wonder. The Begijn village dates from the thirteenth century, she read on the information posters.

A picture of a woman writing, clad in something like a nun's habit, caught her eye and she read through the rest of the information. She could imagine herself at a time when women resided in this serene semi-village inside the bigger city. There was an unusual silence between the high, unplastered walls of the buildings. For the first time in a long while she actually heard birds. Somewhere was the sound of running water.

She looked at her watch again. She didn't know how punctual TU would be, but she probably had another ten minutes before he would arrive. She followed a cobblestone pathway and found herself in a narrow alley between old buildings with niches and arched doorways. Whichever way she looked, it was a postcard in the making. Geraniums and other flowers made splashes of color on the old redbrick walls. A bicycle propped beside a grayish blue door looked almost staged for effect.

She turned round and went back to the entrance. It was not a day for sightseeing. To pass the time and calm her nerves she focused her attention on the information posters.

*Luc*
*Leuven*

Luc was irritated when the youngster with the dreadlocks and John Lennon glasses stopped him. Not only because he was pressed for time. The fellow had actually parked his motorcycle at the Pomp van 't Groot Verdriet, before asking in faultless English whether Luc was familiar with the layout of the campus. When Luc explained that he was in a hurry, the fellow fell into step beside him, uninvited. He seemed in no hurry at all.

After a lengthy search on his cellphone to find the right name, it turned out he was looking for Hogenheuvelcollege. It was only a short distance down Naamse Street and on Luc's way to Zwarte Zusters Street, so he couldn't very well refuse to show the fellow where to go, but Luc found it hard to reign in his impatience.

"Here it is." Luc pointed at the entrance to the complex. The fellow certainly didn't look like a suitable candidate for the Economics and Business Science departments. On the other hand, appearance meant very little nowadays. Still, something about the student bothered him. Or was he just hypersensitive about any dark-skinned person who crossed his path?

"Thank you very much. Could you also tell me where the university library is? I would like to go there later."

"On the Ladeuzeplein. It's quite a walk. Maybe you should take your motorcycle. Just make sure you're considerate and park it in a legal parking bay, not in front of any of the historic sights that tourists might want to photograph."

"Sorry, it never crossed my mind. But how do I get to Ladeuzeplein from here?"

"The easiest route is through Sint-Donatuspark and across Hooverplein. It's about a ten-minute walk. If you take your motorcycle, mind the one-way streets. The GPS on your cellphone will help you." Luc wondered why the youngster hadn't used it in the first place. It was the way young people operated nowadays. Everything was done electronically.

The man with the dreadlocks nodded, but didn't leave. "I understand the library was badly damaged in the Second World War?"

"In the Battle of Leuven, yes. In 1940." Luc looked at his watch. There was no time for small talk. He could just make it, but he'd have to hurry. When he looked up at the smiling student, something jogged his memory.

"What are you planning to study?" Luc asked on the spur of the moment.

There was a slight hesitation. "History. And Political Science."

Definitely not at Hogenheuvelcollege. And if this wasn't the fellow who had carried the banner in front of the Aula in Ghent and later followed Caz, his name wasn't Luc DeReu. The dreadlocks had initially misled him. Did Caz send him? But why?

Luc remembered De Brabander's warning last night. Could Caz be hand in glove with both these African men? Had she set a trap for him? Again: why?

He would simply have to find out.

*Caz*
*Leuven*

Caz turned sharply when she heard footsteps behind her.

"Caz, I presume. Well, well, we've run into each other on a few occasions." The man held out his hand. "TU."

Automatically she took his hand and looked at him, amazed. Surely it was too much of a coincidence. Ghent-Dampoort station, both on their way to Sint-Niklaas. Then again at the Graslei.

His smile was white against his dark complexion. There were fine drops of sweat on his forehead.

"You're TU?" Stupid question. How else would he know about TU and that she was there?

"The very one. Shall we walk?" He motioned toward the area she had earlier explored.

A student came from the front, his attention on the cellphone in his hand. Caz waited until he had passed.

"The path is narrow, you lead the way," TU suggested before they set off.

Where the path led into the alley between the buildings he fell into step beside her.

"How do you know Luc DeReu?" she asked and hoped the suspicion she felt wasn't showing.

"We met at a seminar on colonialism. Had an interesting conversation. My ancestors were victims, while some of his forefathers had been enforcers. Life is strange."

She expected him to mention Ammie Pauwels, but they walked in silence through the narrow streets.

Midway onto a bridge he stopped. The canal it spanned had to be the source of the soft murmur of water she had heard. Down below some dry leaves were whirling in the flow. Red brick buildings rose up high on either side of the canal, their walls green with moss. Creepers clung to the walls in places. She felt chilly and rubbed her arms; winter was in the air. She steeled herself against what was coming. Information on how and why she had been given away. Who and what her birth mother was. Hopefully also some information on her biological father.

The man turned to her. "That backpack looks heavy. Can I carry it for you?"

Was he playing for time? "Don't bother, thanks. I'm used to it." She tried to keep her voice even but an instinct inside her was vibrating more strongly by the second. It wasn't a good vibration. The Begijnhof is a residential quarter for students and lecturers, she had read. It was the middle of the morning at the start of the academic year. There was no one else around.

She took a step back. "Maybe we should go?" Her voice was shaky.

The man sighed and shook his head. "It could have been so much easier."

His words had barely registered when he stepped forward and his fist struck the side of her head.

# Twenty-seven

*Luc*
*Leuven*

Luc was a few minutes late. There was no sign of Caz. He sat down on a bench from where he could watch the entrance. He considered calling De Brabander, but saw that the number the commissioner had used the night before belonged to a landline. It wouldn't be any good. The detective had Caz's phone, but he didn't dare send a message while Mr. Graslei was monitoring it.

He texted Caz on her new phone to hear where she was, but got no reply.

By the time he realized she was ten minutes late, worry had begun to gnaw at him. She might have got lost or missed a train, but surely she would have let him know?

Moments later Luc jumped up when De Brabander came hastening towards him. Despite the cool morning, sweat was pouring down his temples.

"Did you see him?" the commissioner asked breathlessly. "The African?"

De Brabander nodded.

"No. I thought you were following him."

"I did, but he got away."

"Verdorie."

"You can say that again. Besides, Agent Verhoef, who was following Ms. Colijn, has lost her too. Verhoef was almost run over by a student on a motorcycle. When she jumped out of the way, she fell. When she looked up again to see where Ms. Colijn was, she was gone. And of course she didn't know where your new meeting place was. Unfortunately she didn't tell me straightaway. She looked everywhere, without success."

"The student on the motorcycle. Did he have dreadlocks?" Luc asked.

"Why do you ask?"

Luc gave him a brief account of the young man on the motorcycle. Also that he suspected it was the same fellow he had seen in Ghent. First at the Aula and then talking to Caz.

"Damn! It must be the same bugger who almost ran over Verhoef. She did mention something about dreadlocks. There was also an incident here in Leuven last week when an eyewitness saw Ms. Colijn in conversation with a street musician with dreadlocks. Though apparently he was an older man."

Luc frowned. "You still consider Caz Colijn a suspect?"

De Brabander nodded. "I suspect the man who was at the Fonske is her accomplice. His appearance matches a description a woman in the Colijns' neighborhood gave of an older African man who moved into Tieneke Colijn's rental home before Ms. Colijn's arrival. There's also a younger black man who's involved. Maybe the one who stopped you, though the description I have said nothing about dreadlocks."

"A wig he and the older man both wear?"

De Brabander nodded. "Could be."

Luc frowned. "I'm just wondering. Say the youngster who stopped me was deliberately trying to delay me? Wanted me to be late for my meeting with Caz?" It would mean … he looked at De Brabander. The commissioner seemed to have come to the same conclusion.

"If it turns out she's not part of the conspiracy ..." De Brabander pulled his radio off his belt. "Start looking, take the left side," he ordered and broke into a jog as he barked orders into the radio.

Luc rushed off, but the alleyways winding among the buildings were like a maze. The chances of finding Caz were slim.

*Caz*
*Leuven*

The water was icy. On one hand it was her salvation. She must have been unconscious when the man lifted her over the railing, because she didn't remember how she ended up in the river. The cold must have shocked her back to consciousness. She had been disoriented underwater, and had swallowed a lot of water, but she had managed to kick herself up to the surface.

The temperature could still be her downfall, however. She was shivering from head to toe and there was nowhere to climb out. On both sides double-storey buildings with high foundations rose from the river bank.

Some distance from the bridge she finally managed to find a handhold by digging her fingers into a groove between the bricks. Her fingers seemed on the point of breaking, her head felt as if it was about to explode and she had double vision.

Her cries for help had had no effect. Her throat was raw. If only she knew which direction to swim in, but she was so cold, she had no idea whether her muscles would obey. Her calves cramped from treading water.

"Help me! Help me, please!" she screamed again, hoarsely.

When she looked over her shoulder she thought at first that the person she saw on the bridge existed only in her imagination. Her double vision made the image hazy. "Help!" she shouted again.

"Hold on!" a man shouted. The voice sounded familiar.

De Brabander, perhaps? But what on earth was he doing here?

Whoever the hell he was, she hoped the man could get her out of this freezing nightmare. She tried to move her lifeless fingers. A brick shifted slightly and she lost her grip. Her legs were too cold and stiff to win against the pull of the water.

She tried to swim back to the wall. The river was only a few meters wide, but her arms were too weak.

She turned to look at the bridge but she couldn't make out what the man was doing. And then she couldn't stay afloat any more.

*Luc*
*Leuven*

Luc checked the message that had just come through. It had been sent to his spare phone. From Caz's phone.

*Bridge across Dijle. C in water. DB.*

He tried to find his bearings. He knew the Dijle River forked, looping round the medieval buildings of the Groot Begijnhof and joining up again further along. As far as he knew, there was only one bridge across each of the streams forming the loop.

He began to run, not sure exactly where the nearest bridge was. He peered over a waist-high wall between two buildings, trying to find his bearings. Dry leaves drifting on the water showed that the current was reasonably strong. The water had to be freezing cold.

He looked up and down but couldn't see a bridge, nor anyone in the water. Only the high vertical walls that guided the river through the medieval town. There were very few places where she would be able to climb out. There was the occasional downpipe that might provide a handhold, but most would be too high to reach. The rest was mossy bricks. He knew that a few houses had stairs down to the water's edge, but evidently not around there.

He ran on, around buildings, down the next alley. He

reached another space between buildings and peered over the wall again to try to spot someone in the water. No one. No bridge either. The third time he found a wall where he could peek over, and spotted two heads in the water, some distance from each other. One had to be De Brabander. He sprinted for the next viewing point.

He was just in time to see De Brabander reach Caz, grab her by the hair and lift her head out of the water.

Luc looked up and down the river. There was a staircase into the water some distance downstream. De Brabander wouldn't be able to see it from where he was.

"Commissioner!" he shouted.

He had to shout three times before De Brabander heard him and looked up.

"Stairs! Downstream! Right!"

Caz seemed to be unconscious.

The detective tried to keep her head above water but kept losing his grip.

He would either have to jump in and help or think of something else. No, it wouldn't be any good if all three of them were in the water.

He called the emergency services and explained as well as he could. By the time Luc ended the call, De Brabander seemed to have a firmer grip on Caz's head and was closer to the stairs.

Feeling totally helpless, Luc watched the detective struggle and finally reach the bottom of the stairs. After he had caught his breath, he succeeded in dragging the unconscious woman's dead weight up the bottom steps.

He could hear De Brabander wheeze and sneeze, but at least they were out of the water.

Long moments later he heard the sound of a boat engine. Luc breathed a sigh of relief when the vessel came into view and he recognized the paramedics on board by their jackets.

His legs felt shaky from the adrenaline rush, but he kept watching until Caz and De Brabander were both inside the boat. He held his breath as a paramedic began to exert rhythmic pressure on Caz's chest while the boat sped off in the direction they had come from and disappeared around a bend.

Luc sat down on the first bench he could find and lowered his face into his hands.

What a great Jean-Claude van Damme Luc DeReu would make. What a milksop he was.

Mr. Graslei, he suddenly remembered. What had become of him?

Luc jumped up. Around the next corner he found the bridge the detective had mentioned. De Brabander's shoes, watch, cellphone and radio lay where he must have thrown them down before jumping into the water.

As he bent down to gather up the commissioner's belongings, a female voice spoke behind him.

"Leave it!"

Luc straightened up and turned.

A woman in a lopsided blonde wig was regarding him sternly. Her elbow was bandaged and her trousers were ripped at the knee.

"Agent Verhoef?" he guessed.

She frowned and nodded. "And you are?"

"Luc DeReu. These belong to Commissioner De Brabander. I was going to keep them safe for him."

"He said on the radio he was going into the water. Where is he?" She limped closer.

Luc gave her a brief summary of the events. "I want to try to find out where the man has gone who was presumably following Ms. Colijn."

"Help is on its way. We don't know how dangerous he is or whether he's armed." She winced as she put her weight on her injured leg.

"Stay here and wait for them. I won't try anything funny. I'll just see if I can catch a glimpse of him." Luc hurried across the bridge, not waiting for an answer.

On the far side of the next bridge that crossed the second loop of the river, he spotted something. A paperback novel. Afrikaans title.

Luc stopped to get his breath. Every time he had seen

Caz she'd had her backpack with her. This must have fallen from it.

He left the book where it had fallen. The reinforcements Verhoef had summoned would take care of it.

A few meters further, the fluttering of a few folded tissues caught his eye. Near them lay a comb and lipstick. Just before Volmolen Avenue intersected the path he found a broken perfume bottle. The floral scent rose up to meet him when he bent down to inspect it.

He continued on his way. At the next intersection he looked left, then right. He chose to go right, where there was less movement than on the Naamsepoort side. After a while he found a handbag that had been tossed aside. Still further on he found a few credit cards. He picked them up.

Mr. Graslei didn't seem to know the story of Hansel and Gretel. Or he had been in too great a rush to care whether he was being followed. Or maybe it didn't matter to him, because he knew he would not be caught. Which might mean he had transport from a certain point.

Luc stopped when his cellphone began to ring. The normal one.

Lieve, he saw. Damn it, it had totally slipped his mind that he still had to get to Ammie. There was still time before his appointment. Maybe Ammie wanted to cancel.

"Professor..." He heard at once that Lieve was distraught.

"Yes, Lieve?" An awful premonition came over him.

"It's Miss Ammie. The doctor is with her. Can you come at once?"

# Twenty-eight

*Caz*
*Leuven*

Caz came to as she was being loaded into an ambulance. Her head felt as if it was going to explode. Her throat was burning, her ribs ached and she felt terribly nauseous. The double vision had cleared somewhat, but the faces of the people bustling around her were still hazy.

The paramedic asked a few questions, which she answered with great effort.

"Concussion," she heard him tell his colleague. Something about the possibility of secondary drowning. Also something about relatives.

After a short ride she was wheeled into the hospital on a trolley.

She tried to protest, but no one listened.

De Brabander appeared at her side.

"Who did this to you?" he asked, his long strides matching the trolley's speed. His clothes were wet, his hair had been towel-dried. A foil blanket was draped over his shoulders. His knuckles were white and hard where he held the blanket together.

"African man. TU."

"TU?" De Brabander shook his head. "TU is definitely not a black man."

How would he know? The pounding in her head was driving her crazy. "My backpack. He took my backpack?"

"Must be. Be grateful. If you had fallen into the water with a backpack, you wouldn't have been here now."

"He wasn't TU?" Had he said so or had she thought it?

"No. Do you know the black man?"

"No, but I've seen him before."

"Where?"

"Graslei and ..." The headache blanked out the rest. "Can't remember now."

"Why do you think he attacked you?"

"I don't know."

The trolley came to a halt. "Okay, I'll take your statement later." De Brabander disappeared.

A woman with a stethoscope around her neck bent over Caz and shone a flashlight in her eyes.

"Hmm. Bed rest for you, ma'am. We'll keep you overnight," she declared after she had held the stethoscope to Caz's chest.

Caz was suddenly too tired to argue.

She didn't have the strength to figure out what had happened to her and why. She only knew it hadn't been an ordinary attack with robbery as the motive. The man hadn't cared whether she drowned or not. If he wasn't TU, how did he know about TU? About Luc DeReu? About far too many things?

Too tired. Too much pain.

*Luc*
*Leuven*

"DeReu," Luc answered his phone from the back seat. With his own car parked near Martelaereplein, it had been easier to take a taxi to Ammie's apartment.

"De Brabander. What happened to you?"

"Rushing to get to my stepmother. It sounds as if she might have suffered another stroke."

"Sorry to hear that."

"Is Caz okay?"

"Ms. Colijn has sustained a concussion. She has an ugly swelling on her temple. She will be kept in hospital overnight to make sure all is well."

"Do you still see her as a suspect?"

"More than ever. This looks very much like a case of two conspirators who have fallen out. They must have some connection. But I'm still looking for proof. Verhoef tells me you tried to follow the attacker."

Luc told De Brabander about the items Mr. Graslei had tossed out of the backpack.

"I picked up the credit cards, but left the rest."

"Well done. I'll call again later. We must collect the stuff on the path as soon as possible. Hopefully there'll be fingerprints. Give me the route again?"

Luc complied, ending the call just as the taxi came to a halt. He paid and hurried to the front door.

Lieve's eyes were red when she opened the door. "Thank goodness you're here, Professor. The doctor has just left."

"Mother Ammie?"

"She's asleep. Luckily it was another light stroke, but it's not a good sign. I arranged for a night nurse. Is that in order?"

Luc nodded. "Thanks, Lieve. You're a treasure."

"Let me make you a nice cup of coffee. In the meantime you can look in on her if you wish."

Luc nodded and went to the bedroom. Ammie looked small and shrunken against the pillows. Her breathing was even, but behind the eyelids, crisscrossed by light blue veins, the eyes were moving rapidly.

He was about to turn and leave when her eyes fluttered open. She raised one hand slightly.

Luc approached. "Mother? How do you feel?"

"As if I'm dying." She was lisping and the words came

with great effort, but she seemed lucid. "And I am. That's why you must be honest with me. Why do you want to know all these things now? It's not only about your father. Or the students."

"We can talk later. You have to rest."

"Later I might be dead. I want to know."

Verdorie, what if he caused her to have another stroke? He couldn't think of anything to say.

Ammie's fingers fumbled with the sheet. "It's got something to do with Cassandra. Did she find out? About me?"

"Mother ..."

"Fien swore she wouldn't tell her. I paid her extra." Her knuckles were white where she was gripping the sheet. "I thought if Casssandra doesn't know, the evil in her might never surface."

"She doesn't know about César," Luc admitted when he realized he was upsetting her even more by keeping the information from her. "She has only just found out about you. Apparently Josefien Colijn told her your name on her deathbed."

"She's dead? Fien? Only now?"

Luc nodded. "A week or so ago."

"Where is she? Cassandra?"

Luc averted his eyes, considering what to tell her, what not.

"She's here? In Belgium?"

Did old age and infirmity make her clairvoyant?

"She is," he admitted.

Ammie closed her eyes. Her breathing had quickened and her lower lip was trembling.

"Mother Ammie, please don't be so upset." Damn it, he should never have come to her room.

Ammie opened her eyes. "Does she want to meet me?"

"I don't know. We haven't discussed it. I haven't met her in person. I was going to, today, but something happened." Hardly "something." But it was better than saying your daughter nearly drowned, presumably at the hand of her accomplice in a murder.

"She's in Leuven? At this moment?"

Luc nodded.

Tears welled up in the old eyes, spilling over and trickling down her wrinkled cheeks.

"Mother, please don't upset yourself," he repeated helplessly. "I'll tell her you're not well and can't see her. If she asks."

Ammie shook her head. "Not now. Must feel better first."

If Ammie got better at all. If by that time Caz wasn't in prison for murder. But he refrained from voicing his thoughts.

*Erevu*
*Brussel*

Everything had gone according to plan. This morning, before he went to Fonske, he returned the car he had rented under an assumed name. He paid the bill with the same stolen credit card he had used at the guesthouse and destroyed the card.

After his run-in with the Caz woman, he met Dove at the prearranged spot near Martelaereplein. Dove had already returned the motorcycle he had "borrowed" this morning. They fetched their luggage from storage and here they were at the airport. In time for Dove's flight that would be leaving in a little more than two hours. First for Amsterdam and then on a Kenya Airlines flight to Nairobi before going on to Johannesburg.

He himself was only leaving at eleven tonight. On Etihad Airways. He would stop over in Abu Dhabi and arrive in Johannesburg the day after tomorrow. Dove had thought it better if they weren't on the same flight.

At least Dove seemed his old self again. He was taking initiative. After telling Jela to do the same, Dove had erased everything on the two tablets they'd used to communicate with each other and reset them to factory standards. This morning he got rid of them.

Yesterday Dove got them both new phones and SIM cards. He took the old ones apart and threw them away piece by piece on their way to the airport.

He even insisted that they didn't save each other's new

numbers on the new phones, but memorized them. Both phones were set not to display the number when they made calls. The boy had been thorough, he had to give him that. Now Dove just had to learn to mask his anxiety.

Despite a few obstacles, they had beaten the odds. Except in the most important matter. The bloody key. It had not been in the backpack.

Anger and frustration pumped through his veins. She must have left it in her room at the guesthouse. It was the only possibility.

Erevu worked out the times again. "I could be back at nine."

Dove shook his head. "It's too risky. Especially going at it alone. The people in that street know what you look like, Nkoko. Please, listen to me. It's disappointing that we didn't find it, but Caz is going back to South Africa with the key. We know where the bank is and we know when she'll be going there. We can wait for her and get what is ours the moment she leaves the building. If that doesn't work, we know where she lives. All it requires is a little more patience. Don't let panic spoil it all."

This morning Jela had sent an SMS about the email the Caz woman had sent her daughter, telling her she would be landing in Johannesburg on the evening of the fifteenth and would be flying to Cape Town the next day. That she would be spending the night in Pretoria to finish some business, but would be back home the evening of the sixteenth.

It was not hard to guess the nature of the business she'd be doing.

But Dove didn't know that since then the Caz woman had literally and figuratively been through deep waters and would hopefully never catch any flight again.

He didn't want to tell Dove the Caz woman's body was probably at the bottom of the Dijle. He would have liked to make certain she was well and truly dead, but there had been no time. DeReu or a student or tourist could have turned up at any time. She had been out like a light, that he knew. He had seen her sink.

So near and yet so far. No, he simply had to get that key. A long road lay ahead, even after they were in possession of the nkísi. And the sacred mission was waiting.

*Luc*
*Leuven*

"Good day. De Brabander. I believe you're actually *Professor* DeReu?" His voice sounded wary on the phone.

"Please call me Luc, Commissioner. It's easier." Luc had just reached his car. He ran his hand over his tired eyes. Early tomorrow morning he had to be in Ghent. He had no other option, but he couldn't help feeling guilty. As if he was leaving Ammie to her fate. Despite the night nurse and Lieve's assurance that the doctor was an acquaintance who lived nearby and that she herself would be on stand-by.

To make matters worse, Caz was in hospital. Where she might not have been if he hadn't allowed himself to be side-tracked by that kid with the dreadlocks. Fool that he was.

"Professor, I need your help."

Luc gave an inward sigh. He was not going to be called by his name. Sometimes the decorum in this country exhausted him. "I'm on my way back to Damme, Commissioner. It's where I live."

"Would you mind making a small detour?"

"Where to?"

"Brussels airport. You'll be taking the Brussels ring-road anyway."

It was indeed not far out of his way, but how much time would it take? It was four o'clock now and the traffic would be a nightmare. "What do you want me to do there?"

"Help me spot someone you'll recognize more easily than I will."

Mr. Graslei. "It sounds like a shot in the dark."

"It is. My reasoning is that the man who stole Ms. Colijn's backpack has found what he was after and now wants to get away as quickly as possible. Back to Africa."

"What do you think was in that backpack that he wanted so badly?"

"Probably money or some kind of payment for services rendered."

"What makes you think he isn't a Belgian citizen or legal resident? Or that he won't be flying from Amsterdam or any other international airport in the EU?"

"Sometimes one has to hazard a guess and follow it up. The chances are slim, but they exist. We found a number of items from the backpack. We found the backpack as well. Ms. Colijn has already identified it as hers. Even if there are fingerprints, which I doubt, it will take a while to get results, and his prints won't necessarily be in the system. We're still waiting for feedback on the prints in the rental home and Ms. Colijn's house.

"Another thing. There are several flights to Johannesburg, and others connecting with flights going there, but those that might be possibilities are leaving just after six and around eleven tonight. If he's on the early flight, he should already be at the airport. Two hours ahead of departure. With Ms. Colijn in hospital, you're the only one who can identify him."

"And if he's not there, or if he's on the later flight?"

"Then we'll see."

"Why flights to Johannesburg, exactly?" Luc frowned.

Something wasn't right. De Brabander was clearly not acting on a mere hunch. Did someone tip him off? Who?

"I have my reasons. You must still give me Ms. Colijn's credit cards anyway."

True. With all the fuss about Ammie, Luc had forgotten. "Okay, but I can't stay long. Where shall we meet?"

*Caz*
*Leuven*

The headache was more bearable, but her thoughts were still fuzzy. Just as well she had taken the extra medical cover her travel agent had suggested.

Luckily there hadn't been much cash in her wallet: thirty euros at most. The money was missing, but at least she still had her laptop. Or she would have it, as soon as the fingerprint experts had finished with it. A few other things had also been found. She didn't know yet what they were, but if Luc DeReu had her credit cards, as De Brabander had said, it would make her life considerably easier.

If only she could sleep and get a good rest, she might be able to figure out what had happened. But she hadn't been able to. If it wasn't De Brabander appearing at her bedside, it was a nurse who kept waking her up. Apparently standard procedure with concussion patients.

De Brabander had said something about a young man. Black. Someone had mentioned something to him about a meeting she had with the young man. At the Graslei.

She tried to focus, to break through the pain and fuzziness. Young man. Black. Graslei. Njiwa? But they had met by chance. Surely Njiwa couldn't have anything to do with the man who attacked her?

Damn it, her thoughts were too jumbled to even try to make sense. Her head was aching too much. Caz tried to relax. Tomorrow she might be able to think again.

*Erevu*
*Brussels*

"I'm going through, Nkoko. Please don't take any unnecessary risks. Stay here. We'll get that key. We have a plan."

Erevu nodded. "Yes, we have a plan. Go well, Dove."

"We'll see each other on October the fourteenth, in Pretoria, Nkoko. Remember. No contact until then. If there's a problem, we contact Jela. Only if we have to."

Erevu nodded again. "No contact."

He wished Dove would go through security now. Luckily the line was short. His time was running out. He was definitely not leaving that key behind. He put his arms around his grandson and embraced him.

Dove smiled and headed off.

Erevu followed him with his eyes. There went his future. The future of the Congo after his grandfather had taken the first steps to save the country from ruin. There was still a long way to go but already they were closer to their goal. The nkísi, the vessels containing his forefathers' spirits that his uncle had made so many years ago, were within reach for the first time in decades. It was an important step forward.

Mama Tabia had complicated things for them. She had never thought any further than getting even with the man she detested. But at least she had kept some of the diamonds. The stones had enabled her to send him and his half-sister to school in Belgium.

She thought she was doing them a favor by giving them a European education, all the while trying her best to follow the traditional ways herself. In a way it was a good thing. He could hold his own in any company. He spoke five languages: Flemish, Congo-French, English, Lingala and Swahili. He didn't have to take a back seat to any white person. Yet the heartbeat of Africa pulsed through his veins. Tradition was of the utmost importance. That was why he had returned to the Congo after completing his high-school career and obtaining an education diploma.

His half-sister, on the other hand, had become a true European and stayed on in Belgium. Even married a Belgian.

He couldn't depend on her, never mind confide in her. No, he could trust no one. Even Dove and Jela didn't know everything, especially not what the full magnitude of the nkísi heritage was or what it could mean to the Alice Auma Lakwena Holy Army. AALHA. His dream.

Dove waved from beyond the security gates. He was through. Erevu raised his hand in a salute and turned.

A taxi would be fastest.

*Luc*
*Brussel*

The final call for a flight to Amsterdam was being made when Luc saw the detective standing in the appointed place.

De Brabander noticed him too and came walking towards him.

"I think I saw him, but I can't do anything if I'm not sure it's him." The detective didn't waste time with preliminaries. "He's not the only black man around, but he's the only one who answers to the description I have. He went outside. I asked Grevers to keep an eye on him so that I could wait here for you. Come." Luc fell into step beside him while De Brabander spoke to Grevers on the radio.

"Taxi rank? Stop him. Delay him." De Brabander cursed. "No, I can't bloody well be sure before DeReu has identified him. Just stop him!" He broke into a run.

Luc followed suit.

*Erevu*
*Brussels*

It was the radio in the man's hand that made him realize he had unwanted company.

Erevu knew he shouldn't run. The man looked unsure, and running would attract too much attention. He lengthened his strides. He had just reached the taxi when he saw the man hurrying towards him.

He jumped in. "Ghent!" he said.

The taxi driver turned to look at him. "Ghent? That's a long trip. Where in Ghent?"

"Just go!"

The man with the radio knocked on the passenger window.

"Go!" Erevu ordered firmly.

The driver hesitated and looked from the man at the window to Erevu. He put the car in gear and began to pull away.

The next moment someone hammered on the trunk. The driver stepped on the brake.

"No! Go!" Erevu shouted.

Police identification was slammed against the driver's window. "Out!" came the order. "Get out at once. Slowly. Put your hands on your head."

The driver switched off the engine and obeyed.

Erevu gave a deep sigh and remained where he was for a moment. There were three people around the car now. He ducked his head to see who was standing at the driver's side. The man with the mousy hair looked familiar.

When he recognized DeReu he knew the game was up. DeReu—the only person except the Caz woman who could identify both him and Dove.

With the instinct of someone who knew how to betray and had been betrayed before, Erevu knew in an instant the true reason for Dove's nervousness, his sudden efficiency at wiping out tracks, his insistence that Erevu stay where he was.

He had been prepared to make Dove a sacrificial lamb for the sake of the cause. He had been grateful when it proved not to be necessary, but he had been foolish not to realize that Dove, in turn, was ready to sacrifice his grandfather.

Dove, Dove, Dove. Now everything was truly lost. Dove would wait for the Caz woman and she would never show up. She couldn't have survived that well-aimed blow and the cold water, with nowhere to get out. She was a woman. A white woman. They knew nothing of survival.

It was the mousy-haired man, whom he now recognized from the morning's confusion, who opened his door.

Erevu raised his hands in a defensive gesture and got out. He would have to keep his wits about him like never before.

The second time he was ordered to place his hands on his head, he complied. His eyes met DeReu's.

"Is he the one?" asked the mousy-haired man.

DeReu nodded. "He's the one."

# Twenty-nine

*Luc*
*Ghent*

If he reached Damme before midnight he'd be lucky. Luc had made his statement, providing details of the two occasions he had seen the black man.

He had not laid eyes on De Brabander again after the commissioner had asked him in Brussels to go to the police station in Ghent. Apparently the commissioner had sent a message asking Luc to wait for him.

At least the night nurse had called to say Ammie was sleeping peacefully.

He breathed a sigh of relief when at last the door opened.

"I apologize for making you wait, Professor." De Brabander sat down at the table and linked his fingers. Short, stubby fingers, Luc noticed. "I must ask you to be present at an identity parade tomorrow. You'll have to officially identify the accused from a line-up of five men with more-or-less similar features. Believe me, it won't be easy finding four others."

"I won't be free before the afternoon."

De Brabander nodded. "I'll arrange it to suit you."

"Thank you."

"Does the name Erevu Matari mean anything to you?"

Luc shook his head. "Is that the man's name?"

"According to his passport, yes. We found something interesting in his hand luggage. A primitive harp, which could mean he's a musician, and a wig."

"Dreadlocks?"

De Brabander smiled. "Correct. The chances are good that he was the street musician Ms. Colijn met in Leuven. DNA tests will hopefully determine whether more than one person wore the wig. The young man on the motorcycle for instance."

"How did you know he'd be at the airport?" Luc was too tired to beat about the bush. "It couldn't have been a lucky guess."

De Brabander gave a slight smile and took a cellphone from his shirt pocket. "I had Ms. Colijn's phone with me." He pushed a few buttons and turned the screen so Luc could read the message. *Brussel-Jhb. Etihad. @airport.*

"Private number, of course."

Luc frowned. "Who could have sent it? Surely not Matari himself."

"If Babette from the corner shop identifies Erevu Matari tomorrow as the man who rented a room from Tieneke Colijn, I guess it was the young man who stayed there with him. Presumably the same one who tried to delay you in Leuven and thus also the one you saw in conversation with Cassandra Colijn at the Graslei."

"Matari's accomplice?"

"To what degree we don't know, but yes, I believe we can speak of complicity. I don't know whether he deliberately betrayed Matari or whether he didn't know we had Cassandra Colijn's phone. If the message was meant for Ms. Colijn there are a few pertinent questions she'll have to answer, of course."

"Why would he betray Matari—if it was deliberate?" asked Luc.

"Presumably to buy time to get away. Possibly with whatever it was Matari took from Caz Colijn."

"What happened to the young man?"

"My guess is he's on a plane right now."

"Guess? Doesn't this Erevu know?"

"Erevu isn't talking. He's insisting on his right to remain silent and he's refusing legal representation."

Luc thought for a moment. "So he's protecting the man who betrayed him?"

"I think he's chiefly protecting himself and only by default the young man. It's possible he's also protecting Cassandra Colijn."

"How is she?"

"Fine, in the circumstances. She will probably be discharged tomorrow morning. We hope she can give us more information." De Brabander scratched his chin. "I want to thank you for getting us out of that tight spot at the Dijle. Pointing out the stairs. Calling the emergency services and getting them to send a boat."

"It was all I could think of doing. You are the hero who dived in, who put your life on the line."

The detective snorted. "My life was never in danger. It was hardly heroism. I just didn't want my chief suspect to drown before I could lock her up."

Luc laughed, but De Brabander didn't move a muscle. Clearly the man was absolutely serious.

"You still suspect her?" Luc thought of Caz with the young man at the Graslei. With the older man in Leuven. The information sent to her phone. It was a stupid question, actually.

De Brabander got up. "Let's see what tomorrow brings."

Luc looked at his watch. Tomorrow was almost here and he still had to drive home. Spending any more time on his lecture was out of the question. He would simply have to face the students' yawns and bored expressions tomorrow. Still, it was certainly better than being in Cassandra Colijn's shoes. Guilty or not guilty.

*Tuesday, September 30*
*Caz*
*Ghent*

Caz felt self-conscious about her eye, which was a curious shade of blue, and swollen almost shut. Her temple was so sensitive that she could barely run her fingers through her hair.

But those were only a few of her numerous aches and pains. Her entire body, every muscle and sinew, ached. Her nails were broken to the quick, her fingertips were raw and her hands were covered in cuts.

She supposed she should be grateful she wasn't worse off. The doctor who discharged her told her rest was the best medicine. Not that De Brabander seemed inclinced to give her any.

Grevers had fetched her at the hospital but, instead of taking her to Erdem's house, he had brought her to the interview room at the Ghent police station.

"Good morning, Ms. Colijn. How are you feeling this morning?" De Brabander asked as he entered the room. She could see it was just a perfunctory question.

"Good morning, Commissioner. I'm alive. Thanks to you."

"Part of my job. Besides, anyone would have done the same in the circumstances." He downplayed the matter with a wave of his hand. "Please sit."

She had scarcely taken a seat when De Brabander began bombarding her with questions about the man at Groot Begijnhof. He was after every detail of the assault and what had led to it. Where she had seen the attacker before. What her impressions of him were.

After what seemed like the hundredth question, he looked at her pensively. "Okay. You saw him at the Ghent-Dampoort station and he was on the same train to Sint-Niklaas. You saw him again at the Graslei, and for the last time at the Groot Begijnhof, when he posed as TU. Have I got it right?"

She nodded.

"Do you think he could also have been the man who was making music at the bus stop in Leuven?"

"I don't think so. The street musician had dreadlocks. His clothes were also different."

"But the rest? His features? Build?"

"The build, perhaps, but he was sitting. He looked down while he was singing and his dreadlocks covered his face. And I didn't really take notice. I was carried away by the music."

"Did you ever see the attacker near Tieneke Colijn's house or rental home?"

"No."

"The street musician? Or someone with dreadlocks?"

"No."

The commissioner sat back. "You say the attacker told you he was TU, the man you exchanged messages with?"

"That's right. He also said he met Luc DeReu at a conference on colonialism, but he didn't say anything about Ammie Pauwels, while that was the purpose of the meeting. How did you know the black man wasn't TU?"

"Because it seems Professor DeReu himself is TU."

Caz looked at him, surprised. "Tijl Uilenspiegel is Luc DeReu?"

The commissioner nodded.

"Then why did he pretend to be someone who knows him? Why the silly alias?"

"You'll have to ask him that yourself one day. My interest is in Erevu Matari, who told you he was TU."

"Erevu Matari?" She frowned, puzzled.

"The man who threw you into the Dijle. We have him in custody."

Caz felt a rush of relief. "Then why am I being cross-questioned?"

The relief faded when she saw the suspicion in De Brabander's eyes.

"Just a few routine questions, Ms. Colijn. I'd like to know more about a young black man you're apparently friendly with."

Caz frowned. How did he know about Njiwa?

"Luc DeReu saw the two of you talking. It's no use denying it." He had misinterpreted her silence.

"Luc DeReu? But I've never seen the professor in my life. I met Njiwa, the young man at the Graslei, before I even knew about Luc DeReu." Was DeReu out to get her deeper into trouble than she already was? Why?

De Brabander shrugged. "You'll have to ask DeReu for an explanation. Fact is, he didn't make it up. What did you call the young man?"

"I don't know his real name, but his nickname is Njiwa. It means Dove. I met him in Amsterdam the day I landed." She took a sip of water from the bottle in front of her before telling De Brabander what she remembered about Njiwa.

De Brabander chewed on his lower lip. "You say he helped you update your WhatsApp?"

"Yes, he was very helpful. Not that I use WhatsApp, but it was nice of him anyway."

"Did it ever strike you that he might not have been updating WhatsApp? That he might have downloaded the mSpy software on your phone?"

How could she have been so stupid? "No, it didn't. I actually forgot about the episode. I've just remembered, though—he also put his number on my phone. In case I get into trouble somewhere."

De Brabander put his hand in his coat pocket and took out the phone. "Under what name?"

"I don't know, I never looked. I never phoned him."

De Brabander pressed a button on his phone. "Did you make a list of Ms. Colijn's contacts?" The tip of his shoe tapped on the floor. "Look under N for Njiwa.

"Nothing?

"D for Dove?

"Bring me the list."

De Brabander ended the call. "You never saw the so-called grandfather?"

"No."

"All the coincidences around your meetings, it never struck you as strange?"

"It did, but stranger things happen. Besides, in Amsterdam I had just landed from South Africa. He could have been on the same flight, for all I knew. We both happened to be going to Ghent, but to different areas. And, as you certainly know, Ghent isn't so big that you can't run into someone by chance. Especially a student in a neighborhood with the most popular pubs. That was what I thought."

"Student?"

"Yes, he said he was enrolled as a first-year student. He wanted to be in politics. He said something about saving the Congo. He grew up there before his mother brought him to South Africa to live with her and attend school."

De Brabander frowned and made a few notes. He got up when someone knocked, took a document from the person and placed it in front of her.

"Can you identify any name here that might belong to the young man?"

Caz went through the list of her contact numbers. She hadn't realized there were so many numbers on her phone, but they were all familiar. She shook her head. "He must have pretended to add his name. Or he keyed something in and deleted it again. The point is, if Njiwa planted the mSpy software on my phone, there must be a connection between him and the man who pretended to be TU. How else did he know about TU? Luc DeReu?"

De Brabander was quiet for a while. Caz drank some more water. Her mouth was dry. Maybe from the painkillers she had taken before coming here, but more likely from stress.

"I read the article in *Cosmopolitan*," the commissioner surprised her a few moments later. "The interview with your daughter. I see she attributes her success to her mother, who sacrificed everything for her. But she doesn't mention your name."

Caz didn't know whether she could trust this new train of enquiry. "Lilah doesn't want the public to know she has a white mother. We have both had enough of prejudice and judgment, assumptions and accusations by tactless people who don't know what they're talking about. Lilah knows I'm a very private person. Media attention is the last thing

I want. Besides, it has nothing to do with anyone else who I am or what the color of my skin is. Lilah is the star."

De Brabander looked at her thoughtfully. "It must have taken a lot of grit to raise her."

"It wasn't easy. For either of us, but especially for her. She had to prove herself to the third power to get where she is today. Firstly, she's a woman in a society that is still much more patriarchal than we'd like to admit. Secondly, she was born black under apartheid laws and thirdly, she has a white mother. Now that a black government is in power, ironically enough, it's problematic all over again. She's had to overcome and make peace with all these factors and everything that comes with them."

"It's an extraordinary situation." The commissioner nodded as if he understood. "But for a white woman to have a black child couldn't have been a walk in the park either?"

Caz grew suspicious. "No, it wasn't. It was a big responsibility. My child's happiness was at stake. Her future. As the grown-up and her mother, I had to manage the 'extraordinary situation' to the best of my abilities. There was no textbook."

"Nor any help either, as I understand? You said you were rejected by your mother and sister—as you thought of them then. At a time, I take it, when you needed them most."

Caz shrugged. "At least I didn't have to consider their opinions. We could lead our own lives without interference."

"And your daughter's father?"

"We got divorced shortly after Lilah's birth. He and his parents refused to believe he was Lilah's father." She wished he would stop, or get to the point.

De Brabander leaned forward. "No wonder you hated your foster mother and sister. They were your last resort. On top of that, you found out a few weeks ago that they had been lying to you and deceiving you."

Caz realized she had been led into a trap. She knew the knockout blow was about to be delivered.

"No wonder you wanted to take revenge. No wonder you wanted to wipe them off the face of the earth when you found out about everything. A murderous rage must have taken hold of you. Literally and figuratively."

Nothing she could say was going to make this man change his mind. She kept silent.

"But you needed help. And in Africa money can buy anything. Even killers. You can get away with it too, like Shrien Dewani presumably got away with it."

She was surprised that he knew about the honeymoon murder, but she allowed him to continue.

"All you had to do was go for a walk while Josefien was being murdered—possibly while Tieneke was taking a break. The rest was done for you. After Josefien's death, Tieneke was in a vulnerable state and you could convince her to leave everything to you. Then you just had to make certain that you were in Leuven when Tieneke was killed and you could lay your hands on everything that belonged to the Colijns."

Caz's jaw dropped. "I beg your pardon?"

He fumbled in the inside pocket of his coat, unfolded a document and placed it in front of her. *Last will and testament of Martien Colijn*, she read through narrowed eyes.

"According to this, you're Tieneke Colijn's sole beneficiary."

He wasn't lying. She knew it from the victorious light in his eyes. "This was the real purpose of your trip to Belgium, wasn't it? Money—and vengeance, of course. It's quite clear that everything was carefully planned. You just had to play on the affections of your foster sister to get her to change her will while she was still upset about her mother's death."

He smiled grimly and pushed the document even closer to her. "Go ahead and read."

"I can't see without my glasses. They were in the backpack." She didn't want to read it anyway. He wouldn't have shown it to her if it couldn't serve as another nail in her coffin.

He picked up the document and glanced at it. "She changed her will the morning before she died. Significant, I'd say."

Caz looked down at her ragged fingertips.

"In a note to you she says she plans to spend as much of her money as possible in the years ahead but, seeing that she has no heir, you may have what remains."

Caz swallowed against the lump in her throat. There had been no "years ahead" for Tieneke.

"She also says you mustn't for a moment believe she thinks she owes you anything. She and her parents more than earned Ammie's stuff."

Caz was still silent.

He put the document down. "Can you tell me what she meant by 'Ammie's stuff'?"

She didn't think it would be wise to tell him it was uncut diamonds. She had no idea how Ammie Pauwels got hold of the stones or how they were exchanged for cash, but De Brabander wouldn't believe her. What use was it anyway to make trouble for a senile woman in her eighties? Caz sighed inwardly. "Bribe money."

"How's that?"

"My birth mother bribed the Colijns to raise me."

"And yet, all these years later, that money is still part of the estate? Shouldn't the remaining money have gone to you when you left your parental home?"

"I didn't know about it. About the bribe money or that I wasn't their child. Not until Tieneke told me."

"And she did so a while before her death." He shook his head in mock sympathy. "Lied to and robbed as well. One can understand your murderous rage." She saw no understanding in his cold gaze.

"And you can prove this, Commissioner? That I hired her killers—I presume you're referring to Njiwa and Erevu Matari—to take back what was rightfully mine?"

"Prove? No, not yet. But the day will come that Matari will break his silence and speak the truth, and we find Njiwa. Hopefully sooner rather than later. Then the game will be up for you."

A shiver crept down Caz's spine. "Why would Matari attack me, try to kill me, if we're in cahoots?"

"You had a disagreement. Possibly about payment for

services rendered. He was looking for what was due to him in your backpack, found it and off he went. Unfortunately he gave it to Njiwa, who betrayed him."

But Matari didn't get what he was looking for. And she didn't bring anything along that anyone ... the key! It was the only thing that had come into her possession since her arrival in Belgium. It was the only thing the man could have been after. That was why the envelope ...

"Your laptop," De Brabander interrupted her bewildered thoughts. "Will you give us permission to look at it? It would save me the trouble of getting a search warrant."

"I have nothing to hide."

"Good. Your password?" He moved the document with the contact numbers towards her, along with a pen.

She wrote down the password.

De Brabander got up from his chair. "There will be an identity parade this afternoon between three and four. Inspector Grevers will fetch you. I hope you'll give the matter some serious thought and tell me what it was Matari was after. What Njiwa got away with. It could help us find him. That is, of course, if you want your sister's killers to be found."

Caz didn't bother to reply. She was also not going to mention the key that was in the strongbox. With all the suspicion hanging over her, she had to make sure before she got herself even deeper into trouble. If she was ever allowed to go back, mind you, and didn't end up in prison.

The only thing that cheered her up somewhat was that they had to have proof before they could arrest her. And of course there was none.

When she got to her feet, she had a dizzy spell and had to hold on to the chair. When she had regained her composure, she looked at De Brabander.

"Commissioner, I realize I'm in no position to ask favors, but won't you please find out whether Tieneke's landline is monitored as well?"

She could see she had caught him off-guard. Fine. Now he knew how she felt when he was throwing curveballs and setting traps.

"A listening device?"

"Something that can read a number that was dialed from there."

De Brabander's frown deepened. "I could do it, but why?"

"It might explain a few things."

"Like?"

Caz hesitated only a moment. Without providing motivation she wouldn't get very far. "There was a burglary at my house in South Africa. I'd like to know whether it has any connection with the events over here. If there's a device, I can tell you more. If there isn't, I don't have to waste your time with it."

"I can't see how a burglary in South Africa could have anything to do with Miss Colijn's murder. It would be better if you told us the truth instead of trying to throw us off the track."

His "track" of course, she realized, being the search for evidence that would unmask her as the mastermind behind everything—and bugger the rest.

# Thirty

*Caz*
*Ghent*

Caz put thirty euros in the pocket of her jeans and stuffed the rest of her extra euros back into the side panel of her vanity case. It was little enough. She paused with the key in her hand.

What if De Brabander got it into his head to go through her things again? This time through all her things? The envelope, especially, would arouse his suspicion.

She felt slightly silly when she took an unused bar of Pears soap from its box, wrapped the key in cotton wool and stuffed it in the box, along with the folded envelope.

She made sure the key was firmly wedged and did not rattle inside the box. It was too light to fool anyone into thinking that the soap was still inside. It wasn't smart to keep the key with her for the next two weeks anyway, even if it was more or less hidden.

Maybe she could mail it home. But then she wouldn't be

able to go to the bank before flying back to Cape Town from Johannesburg.

Annika. She would send it to Annika. By airmail it should reach her in Pretoria before Caz arrived. If the postal staff in South Africa didn't go on strike again. A courier service, perhaps? Registered post?

Erdem could help her. Also to find a bigger, stronger box and another envelope to put the original one in. He probably wouldn't mind mailing it for her. A gift for a friend, she'd say.

She could teach Nancy Drew a thing or two.

*Luc*
*Ghent*

Luc jumped up when his cup tilted and the lukewarm coffee spilled on his thigh. "Verdomme!" It wasn't painful, just a nuisance. His spare trousers were at the dry cleaner's. He'd been planning to fetch them today. And he was already late.

He pulled off the trousers, dried off his thigh and stood shivering in front of his wardrobe. He had ripped the only other decent pair and hadn't had time to take them to the seamstress to be fixed. His only remaining option was jeans.

A few of the younger lecturers wore jeans to class, why couldn't he? A tweed jacket would give it a more formal look. Only the fabric was different, after all.

He was much too tired to worry about the students' reactions. It was after one when he had finally got to bed, and then he couldn't fall asleep.

Luc changed quickly and grabbed his briefcase and keys. He wanted to look in on Laura before his first lecture. Coffee would have to wait until afterwards.

As he drove to work, he was haunted by yesterday's events. Caz in the river. Caz on the boat, water being pumped out of her airways. Ammie struggling to speak. The look Erevu Matari had given him when he got out of the taxi.

After his late-night conversation with De Brabander, Luc understood slightly better. In that moment when their eyes had met Matari must have realized he had been betrayed. Whether deliberately or not.

Or had Matari suspected before then that he had been betrayed? Was that why he was trying to flee in a taxi?

When De Brabander phoned him earlier this morning to inform him of the time the police line-up would take place, he said Matari had definitely been booked on the Etihad flight to Johannesburg via Abu Dhabi. His luggage had already been weighed in. The detectives were waiting for it to see if it would reveal anything, but it might take a while. Why he was at the airport so early was unclear.

Evidently Matari was still not talking. De Brabander now thought it was chiefly to protect Caz, that she had something on the man.

Luc didn't know about that, but his life didn't revolve around Caz Colijn. Though lately it certainly felt like it did.

He had to stop thinking about yesterday's events and concentrate on his job. He began to go over all the points he wanted to raise in his lecture. The traffic wasn't too bad and he was in time to see Laura, just as she was about to enter the lecture hall.

There was something very cool and aloof in the way she looked him up and down. "We do what we can to help each other, Luc. There were no problems," was all she said when he thanked her for taking his classes.

He had no idea why she was being so curt, but Luc didn't have the energy to focus on it. He was just in time for his own lecture.

It went surprisingly well. A few times he spontaneously digressed from his notes to provide background. The students were attentive, asked questions. Not everyone, of course, but quite a few. Especially the pale one, Nele Sluyck, was a livewire.

The day that had begun on such a false note was getting better, especially when Lieve sent word shortly after his lecture that Ammie had had a good night and felt better, though she was very tired and her speech was still slightly slurred.

Her tears when she had found out that Caz was in the

country had caught him unawares. Did Ammie regret her decision all those years ago? Now that she was staring death in the face? What he would do if Ammie wanted to meet Caz, he didn't know.

Just as he didn't know whether Caz was an accomplice in her sister's murder.

But for now he had to focus on the departmental meeting that lay ahead.

*Caz*
*Ghent*

Grevers arrived at a quarter to three to pick her up, as arranged.

"Wasn't Babette supposed to come as well?" she asked as they drove past the shop.

Grevers nodded. "Agent Verhoef is fetching her."

Caz assumed they were deliberately keeping them apart before the line-up.

Maybe she should go over to Babette's shop sometime and hear exactly what she had told De Brabander about her and Fien and Tieneke.

"Commissioner De Brabander wants to see you before the line-up," Grevers said when they stopped at the police station.

Caz gave an inward sigh, but nodded. She felt she knew the inside of the interview room like the back of her hand by now.

De Brabander came in just as she was sitting down.

"Good afternoon." He sat down to face her. "We found a monitoring device in the Colijns' home telephone."

Caz felt like giving him a smacker on the lips. Or maybe just a smack.

He looked at his watch. "We don't have much time, and I don't think there's necessarily a link, but could you tell me briefly about the burglary at your home in South Africa?"

Caz kept it as short as possible.

"What was stolen?"

"TV, music centre, computer and a few other electrical and electronic items. There was quite a bit of vandalism."

He nodded thoughtfully. "I take it the laptop in your backpack is new?"

Caz nodded. "I'm a translator. I can't be without a computer. Speaking of which, when can I have my stuff back?"

"I'll see if I can return everything after the line-up. I'd also like to know what's missing from your backpack. But back to your computer. Are you the only user?"

"Yes."

"You gave no one access to your previous laptop?"

"Definitely not."

"I understand from the IT guy that there's a document on your computer with a list of all your passwords. An unprotected document."

Caz felt her cheeks flush. Everyone warned against it but she had never thought anyone would have reason to hack her computer. "I'm afraid that's so."

"The list was on your old computer as well?"

She nodded.

"So anyone who could work out the password of your previous laptop would have access to any of the internet accounts and websites where you are registered?"

Caz shifted slightly in her seat. "It was an oldish computer. Windows 7. It wasn't secured with a password. It was too much bother for me to have to log on every time I used it."

De Brabander didn't seem surprised. "According to the IT guy, anyone who knew your password could read your email on your service provider's page. And you generously provided the password to anyone who bothered to look."

"Someone reading my mail is the least of my problems. I don't have secrets, but a second user? When a computer is stolen in South Africa and by tikkoppe besides, as the police seem to think, it is reformatted and sold as soon as possible. Thieves don't keep it to intercept someone's email."

"Tikkoppe?"

"Metamphetamine users. In South Africa, mostly young people. It's a serious problem, especially in the Western Cape."

"I see. Anything else that was out of the ordinary?"

Caz was about to say no, when she remembered the inactive alarm. She explained briefly.

"If you did activate the alarm, it must have been someone who knew how to deactivate an alarm system," De Brabander came to the logical conclusion.

She nodded, but her thoughts were elsewhere. What if someone was using her computer? Surely he would have been more interested in emptying her bank accounts than reading her emails? Why hadn't he done so yet? He'd had about three weeks.

Fortunately her nest egg couldn't be touched, unless she went to the bank in person and filled out forms. Even though her cards were in the red at present, she was creditworthy. She would have to change all her bloody passwords as soon as possible. Her email addresses as well. What a mess.

"The IT guy came up with a theory. If the burglary in South Africa is linked to the events over here, a third person in possession of your computer might be involved. Presumably someone in South Africa. This person would have been able to follow most of your movements, thanks to your emails to your daughter and others, like your landlady in Leuven."

Slowly the implication got through to her. "If Matari and the street musician are one and the same person and he's in contact with the third person, he could have found out I would be in Leuven that day and where I was staying. That's why he was at the bus stop near the B&B." But why had he been following her?

"It's possible." He looked at the clock on the wall and got up. "Let's see whether you can identify Matari. Wait here a moment. I'll go and find out whether Professor DeReu is done."

Caz didn't reply. She tried to think of all the emails she had sent and received since the burglary. There must have been hundreds. She subscribed to a number of blogs for translators and language practitioners, as well as Network24, which kept her up to date with current affairs on a daily basis. Dealings with the bank and the usual spam. Correspondence with Annika and other publishers. The travel agent.

Otherwise she mostly wrote to Lilah.

Thank goodness she hadn't let Annika know she had sent her a parcel for safekeeping. She had been planning to do so as soon as she got her laptop back.

Erdem must have mailed the parcel by now. It could have been a disaster. She might have put Annika's life in danger.

The door opened. "You may come through."

She followed De Brabander down a passage to a room with a glass panel.

"It's a one-way mirror. They can't see you. Please wait until the end of the parade before you make your final decision known."

Five men filed in. All black, three tall and two slightly shorter. Two of the taller ones and one of the shorter ones had shaven heads. One by one, according to the numbers they carried, they were ordered to step forward and turn sideways so that she could see their profiles. First left, then right.

When they were all back in line, De Brabander looked at her. "Do you want them to go through the procedure again?"

She shook her head. "Number four."

He raised his eyebrows. "Are you sure?"

She looked at the man with the shaven head again. "I'm sure."

"Quite sure?"

Caz took another look. She tried to look past the smooth scalp, studied the features. The build. "Dead sure," she answered firmly.

"Okay. Wait a moment." He said something into a microphone that she couldn't follow.

The five men filed out.

She looked enquiringly at De Brabander.

"Give us a few minutes."

The clock on the wall said it was three minutes later when the five men filed back in. This time they all had dreadlocks.

The procedure was repeated.

The dreadlocks made it harder. No wonder she hadn't recognized him as the street musician.

"Once again?" De Brabander asked when she didn't give a number immediately after they had gone through their paces.

"No. Number two."

"Certain?"

She nodded.

"Thank you, Ms. Colijn. We can go." He bent over the microphone. "You are done." Someone asked a question. "No, the hats were only for Professor DeReu."

He allowed her to lead the way. "Could you please wait in the interview room again? I'll be with you in a moment."

Caz obeyed. She didn't really have a choice.

*Luc*
*Ghent*

"I'm sorry it took a while, Professor."

Luc looked up when the commissioner entered.

"Was he correctly identified?"

"We have to wait for Babette. We'd like to ask you to work with a police artist to compile an identikit of the young man. Apparently Ms. Colijn knows him as Njiwa, so that's how we'll refer to him in future."

"How does she know him?"

"Evidently ran into him at Schiphol. Tell me, if a student is interested in politics, specifically the politics of the Congo, what subjects would he enroll for?"

Luc gave it a moment's thought, then listed a few subjects. "And my own subject, of course."

"But the Njiwa fellow isn't a student of yours?"

Luc shook his head. "Definitely not. I would have recognized him."

"Fine, let's go through."

"Will the identikit take long? I have to meet a colleague at five. We have to discuss the final arrangements for a function that's taking place later tonight." He wished he could use the story of the identikit as an excuse to get out of the Godparents' Evening, but he couldn't do it to Laura.

"I'll take you to the artist at once. Let's hope it's quick."

Luc wondered how Caz had fared. It would be a disaster if their identification of Matari didn't correspond.

*Caz*
*Ghent*

Caz looked expectantly at De Brabander but his expression gave nothing away.

"I have to go through the identification procedure with Babette. After that, I hope you'll be able to help us compile an identikit of Njiwa. Would you mind waiting a while longer?"

She was fed-up, but could hardly refuse. "Commissioner, just a moment. I'm trying to work out why Matari followed me the first time I went to Leuven—that is, if he was the mvet player. Also why he followed me when I was on my way to Doel. I think you're concentrating so hard on what he wanted from me yesterday that you're forgetting that he and Njiwa have been following me since I arrived here." Or the detective might be so convinced of her guilt that he was focusing only on catching her out and providing himself with a reason to arrest her.

"Doel?"

"Yes, he followed me to Sint-Niklaas, as I told you, but I didn't mention that I had actually been heading for Doel. After Sint-Niklaas I didn't see him again. Until he popped up as a street musician in Leuven the next day. But I didn't recognize him."

"What were you doing in Doel? And in Leuven?"

"Tieneke told me that Doel and Leuven are two places where my birth mother used to live. I went to Doel to find out whether anyone still remembered her. In Leuven I went to the university, because Ammie Pauwels's ex-husband had worked there, also according to Tieneke. That's where I found out not only he, but also his son had lectured there."

De Brabander gnawed on his lip, deep in thought. "That's how you got hold of Luc DeReu's phone number?"

"No, but apparently a Lieve Luykens had asked about him earlier. I looked up her number and left her a message that I would like to get in touch with Luc DeReu."

"Do you know who Lieve Luykens is? How she's connected with DeReu?"

"No idea, but she was good enough to contact him and give him my number."

The detective's eyes went to the wall clock. "I'll be back in a moment."

Caz sat gazing at the tabletop.

They had followed her in an attempt to get to Ammie Pauwels. They must have thought Ammie had whatever they were looking for. It was the only logical conclusion. When he went through her things in Tieneke's house the day Tieneke was killed, Matari must have seen the envelope. The imprint of the key was clearly visible on it. Inside the envelope were directions to a bank in Pretoria. He must have realized then what the key would unlock. After that, Ammie Pauwels was no longer important, only the key. He must have suspected she would keep it in her backpack. That was why she was assaulted at the Groot Begijnhof.

She should have had concussion a long time ago. Apparently it had shaken her brain cells into action.

If only she could find out what the connection was between Ammie, Matari and the key, she might get somewhere.

# Thirty-one

*Luc*
*Ghent*

"Sorry to interrupt."
Luc looked over his shoulder when De Brabander spoke behind him. Figuring out facial features was more difficult than he had anticipated.

"Do you happen to know of a connection between your stepmother and Matari?"

"A connection with Ammie?" Luc shook his head. "Unless it has something to do with the Congo. Ammie left there as a refugee in 1961. Which makes Matari too young. He could hardly have been born."

"Interesting. According to his passport he is indeed from the DRC. Okay. I'll see you later." He walked away, turned again. "By the way, Ms. Colijn found out at KU Leuven that Lieve Luykens enquired about you. She got hold of Lieve's number to get in contact with you. But she doesn't know Mrs. Luykens is your stepmother's carer."

When the detective had left, Luc sat staring at the four

examples of noses in front of him. He couldn't recall the shape of Njiwa's nose. And he had no idea what could possibly connect Matari to Ammie. Or how Matari could have known there was a connection between Caz and Ammie.

Ammie might be able to throw light on the matter. If she was lucid. If she remembered. If she didn't soon suffer a more serious stroke.

At least the Lieve puzzle had been solved.

*Caz*
*Ghent*

She had been waiting almost an hour, her thoughts tormenting her, her arguments growing more and more muddled. As soon as she thought she had a solution to one problem, she remembered something else.

All she knew was that she shouldn't give De Brabander any more ammunition than he already had. She couldn't tell him about the key and the safe-deposit box. It would only strengthen his suspicion that she had hired hitmen. He would probably assume the box contained whatever she had promised Matari in exchange for murdering Tieneke, and that was why he was after the key. She couldn't give any explanation as to how two complete strangers from Africa knew about the bloody strongbox and what was inside it. He would never believe her that it was only two pieces of African art. Or that Tieneke had voluntarily handed her the key.

"Ms. Colijn? Would you come with me, please?" The pretty girl peering around the door was the friendliest face Caz had seen all day. "I'm Elke Behrens. We're working on an identikit and we'd like your input."

At least it was something to do. Caz followed the girl and, at her invitation, sat at a table scattered with identikit printouts.

She picked one up and held it out to Caz. "Professor DeReu helped us get to this one, but he had an appointment before he was completely satisfied. Do you reckon it's a good likeness?"

Caz took the sketch, but shook her head. "I'll need my reading glasses. They were in my backpack."

"I'll see if I can find them." The girl hurried out.

Moments later she returned triumphantly with Caz's spectacle case. "It was still in your backpack."

"Thank God for small mercies. I've been struggling since yesterday." She put on the glasses and studied the identikit closely. At first glance it resembled Njiwa as she remembered him, but some of the details didn't look right. "The nose. The nostrils aren't so big. The entire nose is finer. The lower lip isn't so full either."

The girl sat down at her computer, worked for a while and printed out a copy.

"Better?"

Caz nodded. "The chin isn't quite right either. It's too heavy. I don't really know how to explain it."

Half an hour later Caz had a picture in her hands that looked almost identical to Njiwa. Or the way she remembered him. "I think we're there now."

"Wonderful." The girl got up with a smile. "Coffee?"

"That would be heavenly."

"Okay, go back to the room where you waited before, and I'll bring the coffee. Sugar? Milk?"

"Milk, no sugar, thanks." Coffee would indeed be heavenly, but she wished she could go home, pour herself a glass of wine and begin to write down the thoughts that were whirling through her head. Try to create order in the chaos she had been dumped in.

*Luc*
*Ghent*

Luc was on time, yet Laura seemed to be on the warpath.

"Laura, what's the matter? Why are you looking at me as if the cat dragged me in?" Luc was too tired to beat about the bush.

Laura threw him another look.

"Out with it, Laura. We can't work like this."

"Very well then." She rearranged the notes on her desk although they looked perfectly symmetrical. "I've always respected you and dismissed the rumors as gossip, but lately I don't know what to think any more."

He sat down to face her. Where was this coming from? "Think about what?"

"Your appearance has always been impeccable, but recently ... The other day I saw the way that little student looked at you, the fluttering hands as she talked to you. The scales fell from my eyes and I noticed the change."

"What change, Laura?" he asked, confused. What little student was she talking about?

"Your new glasses. The longer hair."

"Heavens, Laura, I had my eyes tested in the summer holidays and I needed new glasses." He hadn't been too sure about the frame the optometrist's receptionist had helped him pick out, but glasses were glasses. "I'm in need of a haircut. It's on my to-do list. Are you chairperson of the fashion police now?"

"Don't be sarcastic. Look at you today. In denims!" She spat out the last word as if it was an expletive.

Luc shook his head. "I can't believe new glasses, an overdue visit to the barber and a pair of jeans could upset you like this. You were annoyed with me before the jeans, which, by the way, I'm only wearing because I spilled coffee on my good trousers. What's your point?"

"Luc, the academic fishbowl is small here in Belgium. We know what happened at KU Leuven. I've always assumed the stories were exaggerated. I also presumed that, though you might have been guilty of indiscretion, you clearly saw the error of your ways and learned from it. Everyone makes mistakes, I thought, and I can forgive you as long as there isn't a repeat. And now ... this." The chubby hand waved in his general direction.

Luc suppressed the anger building up inside him. "'This' being glasses, hair and jeans?"

"The general effect. You look ... what do you call it ... sexy." Her voice dripped with displeasure.

"Me? Sexy?" He burst into laughter.

Laura blushed a deep red. "There's a student in your life again, am I right? That pale little one who looks at you as if you have descended from heaven. I saw you talking on campus. And she's not the only one looking at you like that. After your lecture today I overheard three female students talk. How they couldn't understand that students from previous years called you drab and boring. One of them called you a ... a ... hunk!"

Luc stared at her, dumbfounded.

"Don't act all innocent. You provoke naive young girls into having dirty daydreams about you."

His annoyance changed to cold fury. Luc got up slowly, bent down and leaned with his hands on the table. His face was barely a meter from Laura's. "Laura, let me make it clear to you. I left KU Leuven under a cloud because of biased, petty people like you. I kept quiet and took the beating because the student concerned gave up her studies and left anyway. I thought the sooner the whole thing died a quiet death, the better for everyone. Until today I thought it was the right decision but, damn it, I'm not going to allow you to insult me and accuse young girls of having 'dirty daydreams' about me. Maybe you would have been married today if you'd had a few daydreams yourself."

Laura gasped, but he gave her no chance to interrupt.

"The student I had a relationship with was in her late twenties. She was a postgraduate student, not an innocent young girl. I was in my thirties, not a dirty old man. We were both single. Yes, I suppose our relationship contravened the code of ethics, but I was in love.

"The things she accused me of were a pack of lies. She deliberately set out to win my affections and when it came to the assessment of her dissertation, she blackmailed me. If I didn't give her a cum laude pass, she would charge me with sexual harassment. The reason? She was aiming for a post at a university in the Netherlands, but her academic record didn't meet the required standard.

"She tried to use me as a stepping stone to get the post

she was after. I gave her dissertation the grade it deserved and she carried out her threat.

"Yes, we had a relationship. Yes, we had sex. There was no hint of harassment. Not from my side, anyway.

"And just so there's no misunderstanding: I have no wish ever to get involved with a student in any capacity other than that of a lecturer again. Especially not at my age. I want to be a good lecturer. I want to spark the students' interest in contemporary history. Help them think further than dates and rebellions and riots and wars. If I happen to look more approachable with my new glasses, longer hair and jeans and it makes them take part in class discussions instead of sitting there like dummies, then it's a good thing."

He was slightly out of breath when he straightened up. "The glasses are staying. I'll have the hair cut at the first opportunity. If I want to wear jeans, I will."

Laura covered her mouth with her hand, jumped up and rushed from the room. But not before Luc had noticed the tears in her eyes.

Instantly he felt like a louse. Couldn't he have taken a gentler approach? Where had his usual composure disappeared to?

Verdomme. That's what happens when a man allows women into his life. First Lieve Luykens convinced him to visit Ammie, thereby complicating his life no end. Now Laura, with this attack on his integrity. Not to mention Caz Colijn—a woman who created chaos wherever she went, who was possibly the mastermind behind a murder and, to crown it all, had drawn him into the mess.

*Wednesday, October 1*
*Caz*
*Ghent*

Last night she had been so exhausted and her headache had been so severe that she hadn't even considered inspecting the contents of the backpack. The most important thing was that she had her laptop back.

With breakfast and a few painkillers inside her, she was prepared to face the world again. Provided she remembered to avoid mirrors. The swelling in her face had gone down, but she still looked like someone who had come second in a bar fight.

Caz unpacked everything on the bed and ticked off the items on De Brabander's list despite the difficulty the task presented to her injured fingers.

Her wallet was not among the items, but except for the cash and Lilah's photo, everything that had been in it had been found: all her cards and fortunately also her driver's licence.

The bottle of Red Door perfume had evidently broken but the cordless mouse had survived. Her sunglasses and the Belgian cellphone, even her lipstick and comb were there. Also the thriller she had bought for Lilah but had begun to read herself.

De Brabander's people had been thorough and the residents of Leuven seemed to be exceptionally honest.

Caz walked out on the roof terrace. It faced away from the main street, overlooking a side street, but if she peered around the wall, she could see the bus stop. Yes, the car was still parked opposite the stop. She could swear it was Grevers behind the wheel, this time with his cellphone against his ear.

She had seen the car while she was enjoying her first cup of coffee on the terrace. Kind of them to keep an eye on her, she had thought like a fool. It only struck her later that Grevers was watching Erdem's front door and therefore her movements. Well, he could watch as much as he liked.

Today she was tackling her laptop. Sore fingers be damned.

She would have to upgrade her antivirus program. Get a new email address. Change a bunch of passwords.

Hopefully she would be able to focus better than yesterday. She thought she had managed to figure out last night how the whole Erevu-Njiwa thing fitted together.

They found her because of Tieneke's call, broke into her house in Stanford in search of whatever was in the bank, but found nothing. From there they physically and electronically followed her, hoping she would lead them to the contents of the safe-deposit box.

They had been the tenants next door. They searched Tieneke's house and realized that the key held the answer. Tieneke surprised them and was fatally injured during a scuffle, after which they had to make her body disappear. They would keep searching for the key until they found it.

There were a myriad questions she would like the answers to. How did they know about Ammie Pauwels and what did they know about her? How did they think Caz could lead them to Ammie? How did they know about her connection with Fien and Tieneke Colijn?

In other words, how did they know about things that happened fifty-three years ago? At a guess she and Matari were more or less the same age. He must have been a baby at the time.

Besides, why did they wait for more than half a century before they came looking for whatever it was they were looking for?

And the million-dollar question: What did they want the bloody stuff in the strongbox for? According to Tieneke, it was a mask and a figurine that might as well have been bought at a curio shop. Or was there more?

If she could answer the last two questions, the other mysteries might be solved.

Conclusion? She had to get to Pretoria and open the bloody strongbox. Discover what was worth a life. And she had to do it without Njiwa or the person in possession of her computer stopping her.

Because they had access to her laptop, they knew when she would be landing. She would have to leave either earlier or later. She couldn't risk letting Lilah know of her changed plans, so she would have to wait until the eighth to tell her she was cutting her visit short.

If she could find a flight, of course. If she had her passport back. So many ifs.

There was another if. If she could call on Ammie Pauwels,

she might get answers to her questions. But she would have to look her birth mother in the eye. Hear the truth—which she could never again unhear.

*Ammie*
*Leuven*

For fifty-three years she could ignore the fact that she had a daughter. She had her reasons and that was the end of it, had been her point of view. Except for the episode with Jacq. The day he found out.

She would never forget the look in his eyes. Not shock alone. Disgust as well.

"How could you, Ammie? To think how desperately I wanted another child. With you. When you told me you were infertile, I made peace with it, but I always longed for a child. Now you're telling me you have a daughter and you simply threw her to the wolves?"

"You're being melodramatic, Jacq. I made certain she was well cared for." That was her defense, but deep inside she knew he was right. Fien was not mother material. Perhaps even less so than herself.

She had moved out of Jacq's home and began to make plans for a new life. She relegated Cassandra's existence to its proper place again—behind the lead curtain she had drawn between the past and the present. Between Africa and Belgium.

She had always been good at compartmentalizing the various phases of her life. Her Congolese childhood before her mother's death. The period after her mother's death until she married César. The period from her wedding until she found out César had married her to get a hold over her father and, when he had served his purpose, had arranged for his death. The time between that realization and the moment she had looked into Elijah's eyes. The time between her meeting with Elijah and his murder. The time between his murder and the day she boarded the plane for Belgium. The Jacq epoch. The Tobias epoch. The period after Doel until the present.

She had carefully stored each of those eras in her life in a separate box. A box only she could open. She had believed the final era, after Tobias's death, would last until the day she died. But yesterday, when she discovered that her daughter was about to find her, a new box was opened.

No, she corrected herself, not yesterday. The lid of the new box sprang open the day Luc arrived. Inside that box were Luc and Cassandra, memories, and a stroke. All new to her. All connected.

How was she going to close and seal this box? Could she?

*Caz*
*Ghent*

Caz jumped at the strange sound. The Belgian phone. The name TU2 did not appear on the screen. It was a landline number. After the fifth ring she answered.

"Good day?" If it was a wrong number, hearing her answer in English would hopefully make that clear to the caller.

"Good day, Ms. Colijn."

De Brabander. Of course. The phone had been in her backpack.

"I presume not telling us you have two phones was just an oversight?"

"That's right."

"It resulted in us not knowing you and TU, or Professor DeReu, had changed the time and place of your appointment in Leuven?"

"It slipped my mind."

"That's why you could meet Matari before TU arrived."

"No. That's why Matari didn't know where and when I was meeting TU until someone, at some point, informed him. Anyway, why didn't the professor inform you of the change of plans?"

De Brabander remained silent.

"Commissioner, I'm getting a bit tired of being under suspicion." Tired wasn't the word.

"We got the results of the post mortem. Maybe you'll understand why I'm really keen to find the murderer if you realize how serious the matter is."

"So you don't think I understand that murder is a serious matter, Commissioner?"

"I hope you understand. Your foster sister didn't die of the injury to the back of her head. It wasn't simply a tussle that ended badly. After she was injured, she was strangled with brute force. Such force that her hyoid, her tongue bone, was crushed. Intentionally."

Caz sank down on the bed. Intentionally. Not by accident. Tongue bone.

"At the estimated time of Tieneke's death, Matari was playing his mvet in Leuven. Your helpful young friend Njiwa must have committed the murder."

Caz covered her eyes with her hand. Njiwa with the white smile. The pretentious private-school accent. Blue Bulls cap.

"Ms. Colijn, I'm asking you again. What was Matari looking for? Where did this Njiwa go with it?"

"Commissioner …" Caz struggled to put sound to the word. "I know only one thing. Whatever he was looking for, he didn't find it. Only my wallet, containing some cash and my daughter's photo, is missing from my backpack."

"You know where to find me if you miraculously remember what they are after." He seemed to be forcing the words out between clenched teeth.

Caz stood with the dead phone in her hand for a while before she went out on the terrace and sank down on a chair, her legs suddenly rubbery. If she hadn't already mailed the bloody key, she would have seriously considered telling him about it after all. But to confess now would serve no purpose. It would just get her deeper into trouble.

She understood why De Brabander was angry, but it was the least of her problems. Even if she could convince him of her innocence, even if he gave back her passport and gave her his blessing to return home, she was still in big trouble.

At the time of the murder Matari had been in Leuven and, ironically, she was part of his alibi. Matari might be found guilty of assaulting her and stealing her cash and wallet, maybe even of helping Njiwa to flee, but not much more. How long he would spend in prison, she couldn't guess. In all likelihood not long, though she didn't know how that kind of thing was regarded in Belgium. If he was even found guilty, of course. No one had seen him attack her or throw her into the water or take her backpack. It was her word against his.

In a few months, weeks, even, he could be free.

In the meantime Njiwa was still at large. Njiwa, who had strangled Tieneke with his bare hands until her tongue bone was crushed. Intentionally.

Even if neither of them had personally been responsible for the burglary at her Stanford home, they knew where she lived. Her laptop would have revealed it. They would come looking. Whether for the key or the contents of the strongbox. Or her.

No, even if she hadn't mailed the bloody key, giving it to De Brabander would have solved nothing. If she could, she would give it to Matari. In his hands. Tell him he could have whatever it unlocked. But even if she did, she doubted they would leave her alone. They would think she knew what was in that bloody strongbox. She would have to be silenced.

It *had* to be more than two pieces of African kitsch.

# Thirty-two

*Thursday, October 2*
*Caz*
*Ghent*

By the time Lilah's text message came through, Caz had finished her first cup of coffee. When "Happy Birthday" began to play, Caz realized what the date was.

Fifty-three. Humanly speaking, about two-thirds of her life was over. Old age and loneliness lay ahead. If her tongue bone survived the onslaught, of course.

The macabre thought caught her unawares.

Another SMS pinged. *See email.*

Finally. She'd been wondering why Lilah had been silent since yesterday. She'd presumed the email in which she revealed that the Colijns were not blood relatives after all would take a while to digest. Even though she'd sent a carefully edited version to make sure Lilah didn't get too upset. She hadn't said a word about the murder and the assault. One thing at a time.

Caz switched on her laptop and waited impatiently. Of

course Lilah's mail would be the last one to be downloaded.

> MaCaz, I know it must have been a shock to find out your birth mother abandoned you, but I have to say it's the best news I've had in a long time.
> I wanted to wait until we see each other again before I told you about Aubrey. It's the kind of thing one does face to face, but things are looking slightly different now. With you in Belgium, where you have the chance to find out certain things, maybe even where you and I come from, you need to know what's going on. You can help us.
> MaCaz, Aubrey is the man of my dreams. We're crazy about each other. He has asked me to marry him.

Caz had to get her breath back before she could continue.

*Luc*
*Ghent*

Luc put down the cellphone with a deep sigh. What was going on with Ammie today of all days? She was not usually the weepy type, yet Lieve had just told him she arrived this morning to find Ammie crying, and the tears just kept flowing. Ammie refused to say what was making her so sad.

Hopefully Lieve would phone as soon as she determined what the problem was. It couldn't be good for Ammie's health.

But now he had to focus on his lectures. He had another one in half an hour and he didn't feel sufficiently prepared. Yesterday had been a full day.

The Godparents' and the parents' evenings had both gone reasonably well, even though things were awkward between Laura and himself. But for Laura duty came first and it was clear that she had set her emotions aside. He appreciated it. How things would ultimately work out for them, he couldn't say.

What he did know was that he was fed-up with complications. That was why he had decided to cut all ties with Caz Colijn. He would do what De Brabander asked him regarding the case, but that was all. Caz Colijn would have to muddle along on her own.

When the phone rang again five minutes later he closed his eyes in frustration. He had just got going.

"Yes, Lieve? Did Ammie tell you what's wrong?"

"It's not Lieve, Professor DeReu, and I don't know whether Ammie told her anything. It's Caz Colijn here. Can we please stop playing games?"

Luc looked at the screen. *CC-new*. Of course. She could use her Belgian phone. He had given her his regular number. What an idiot! He considered ending the call, but took a deep breath instead.

"Are you there?" Her voice was husky. A sexy kind of husky.

"I'm here. And, yes, I realize the so-called game is up. I had my reasons for misleading you, making you think I was someone else." He could barely remember what they were.

"I'm not interested in your reasons. As long as we can behave like grown-ups. I'm not interested in a second-hand version of events either. I want to meet Ammie Pauwels. Preferably before someone gets an urge to chuck me into a river again."

A lump had formed inside him. "Ammie is unwell."

"And when might she be well again?"

Her sarcasm instantly infuriated him. "What, Ms. Colijn, makes you think I would consider introducing you to Ammie? Wherever you go you leave a trail of blood and chaos." He instantly regretted the melodrama, but it was too late.

"At least I don't sexually harass my students and ruin their futures. I just kill people and move on."

He gasped. Where in hell had she heard the Suri story?

"Professor DeReu, I presume you're intelligent enough to

understand that I categorically deny ever in my life having committed a murder or being an accessory to murder."

"I'm quite intelligent enough to understand that. And I categorically deny ever having harassed a woman—sexually or otherwise—or ruined anyone's career."

"If you give me the benefit of the doubt, I'll do the same."

"We don't have to believe each other. Fact remains, Ammie is not well. She's had a setback. Remember, she's eighty-two."

"I'm sorry to hear about the setback, but her advanced age also means I can't wait forever." He heard her sigh. "Look, Professor, it's my birthday today. In other words today, fifty-three years ago, Ammie gave birth to me. It is my first birthday after finding out she's my birth mother. It's the kind of day when one has more questions than usual. Such as: How could she simply abandon her newborn baby and leave? Where do I actually come from? I want to know and I want to hear it from her."

"I understand that you want to know. But I don't understand why you want to meet her. She rejected you. Doesn't want anything to do with you. Why punish yourself?" The cruelty of his words shocked even himself, but it was the truth. Perhaps it was less cruel than hearing from her birth mother how she hated Caz, that she was the bearer of killer genes.

A drawn-out silence followed.

"It's not only about me. I want her to look me in the eye and tell me why my daughter is black."

He nearly dropped the phone. He managed to catch it in time and put it back to his ear. "*What?*"

"Black. My daughter is black. It's the politically correct way of referring to the color of her skin. Are you a racist, Professor?"

Luc nearly choked. "Naturally not."

"If you're truly not a racist, there's very little that's natural about it. Racism—and I'm not talking about racial hatred, rather about the view that one's own race is superior—is actually a very natural reaction. It boils down to 'us' and 'them'.

Just like sexism: Venus and Mars. Religion: the saved and the unsaved. In fact, it's also in the nature of competitive sport. War. Any conflict or otherness."

"Thanks for the lecture, Ms. Colijn, but the fact remains that I'm not a racist. Neither am I a sexist. And though I was raised a Catholic, I'm more or less agnostic. Of sport I know just about as little as I know of war. Okay, your daughter is black and you want to ask Ammie why. You probably want to know who your father is. It's understandable, but I can find out for you." *Or rather, decide how much to tell you.*

"It's a little more complex, Professor. You see, my daughter doesn't only want to know who her grandfather is. She wants to trace her entire family tree. She wants to know how much black and how much white blood are in her ancestry. Only Ammie will know. And I want to hear it from her in person, not from you."

"May I ask why your daughter needs so much detail?"

"No." There was a short pause. "Okay, fine. She wants to have children. There's a professor of genetics who can help her work out how big the risk is of having a white child. It's important to her."

The louder tick of the wall clock made Luc look up. Damn, his lecture.

"I'm sorry, but I'm already late for class. I'll think about it. Speak to Ammie. I'll call you when I know more. Have to run."

"I can find out where she lives. I know it's in Leuven. I want to hear from you today, or I'll take matters into my own hands. Goodbye, Professor."

Luc stuffed the cellphone in his coat pocket, grabbed his briefcase, remembered the printout of his lecture notes just in time and rushed out through his office door.

*Caz*
*Ghent*

Why she hadn't realized long before now that she could phone out on her Belgian phone, she didn't know. It only dawned on her after De Brabander's call. Then she also remembered that she actually had DeReu's number, not the number of some phantom friend.

On the other hand, she had nearly forgotten her own birthday. If it hadn't been for Lilah's message, it might have passed her by entirely.

Caz didn't know how she felt about Lilah and Aubrey's strong feelings about the possibility of having a white child. They were willing to accept shades of brown or black, but not white.

Up to a point, Caz understood their view, but it wasn't as if they were dealing with a bloody congenital disease. Of course she knew from personal experience how hard it would be for them, and certainly for the child as well, but should it stop them if they really wanted to have a child? Well, at least they were prepared for the possibility, not like Hentie and herself, who had never dreamed their child would not be white.

Going by the information Lilah had given him on the Maritz and Colijn families, the professor in genetics had declared it impossible for Lilah to be black. If a freak occurrence had taken place, however, and if Lilah really came from all-white ancestry, chances were excellent that she and Aubrey might have a white child. Especially as Aubrey's mother had mixed blood herself.

Ammie Pauwels had to have the answers. Caz's threat hadn't been an idle one. She would find the woman herself if she had to. It wasn't only about her or the bloody contents of the strongbox any more. More than anything, she was fighting for her child's happiness.

Yesterday afternoon she had moved her flight forward to the thirteenth, unfortunately only two days ahead of time, but it made a difference. It would mean she had until the twelfth to discover what she could over here. And on the fourteenth she would know exactly what was in that bloody box.

Any plans and decisions would have to wait until then. But before she left here, she wanted to look Ammie Pauwels in the eye. That was non-negotiable.

*Luc*
*Ghent*

Luc was relieved to see that the students were still waiting for him in the lecture hall and he was happy to hear a group arguing about the way the Congo's independence was handled.

"What did they expect?" Nele Sluyck asked the student behind her. "The colonialists refused to train the évolués properly or allow them to progress beyond an internship. Then they suddenly say: Here you go, here's your country. Do as you please with it. Sort out your own problems. We wash our hands."

She fell silent when she noticed the others looking at her with wide eyes. She turned and blushed when she realized Luc had been listening.

"A valid argument, Miss Sluyck." He put down his briefcase and lecture notes, and leaned with his elbow on the lectern. "What do the rest of you think?"

A lively debate ensued. At times he had to intervene, but mostly he just facilitated the exchange of opinions through questions and hypothetical answers, occasionally playing devil's advocate.

Now and again, while the students were presenting hackneyed arguments, his mind wandered. He remembered Ammie's account of Elijah's murder. On the same day and at more or less the same time that Patrice Lumumba was murdered.

It must be terrible to see your beloved shot dead before your eyes. By your lawful husband, besides. At the time Ammie didn't know she was pregnant. Her conflicting emotions when she did find out must have exhausted her emotionally. Especially since she didn't know whose child she was carrying.

Today was that child's birthday. Was that why Ammie had burst into tears today of all days? Could she have been crying on this day for the past fifty-three years?

"Don't you get it?" a louder voice got through to him. "Many of the colonialists you are reviling now happen to be our forefathers. You are accusing our grandparents of those atrocities, for crying out loud."

Luc realized he would have to step in again. He would worry about Ammie and Caz later.

*Caz*
*Ghent*

Babette avoided Caz's eyes when she entered the shop, and muttered a reply to her greeting.

Caz took a bottle of sparkling wine and a six-pack of Lindemans from the shelf. Bread, cheese and ham. Erdem had butter. Not exactly a birthday feast, but she didn't feel up to going to a restaurant with her eye looking the way it did and Grevers watching her.

She wondered whether Grevers had followed her on foot. She didn't want to look over her shoulder on her way to the shop.

Babette didn't meet her gaze while she rung up the items.

"Were you able to identify the two men who rented from Tieneke?" Caz asked and hoped she didn't sound as irritable as she felt. What was up with the woman? She was the one who'd been telling tales, after all, blackening Caz's name.

"I'm sure it's confidential," came the curt reply.

Caz reined herself in. "I've been wanting to thank you for your kindness the day we found out about Tieneke. But things have been a bit chaotic since Sunday. As I'm sure you understand."

Babette shoved the change across the counter and looked up at last. Her eyes widened slightly, probably at the sight of Caz's shiner, but her gaze was filled with venom. "That was before I realized you're in cahoots with those savages. To think I felt sorry for you."

For a moment Caz was speechless. It was one thing to be suspected by De Brabander. It was completely different to understand she'd already been convicted by an outsider. Someone she had been on friendly terms with.

"Babette ..."

Babette silenced her with an angry shake of the head. "I'd appreciate it if you left my shop. Now." Something like a sob came from her. "Sparkling wine! You're drinking sparkling wine before your victim has even been buried. It's shameful."

"As far as I know, Tieneke's body hasn't been made available for burial yet. As for the reason behind the sparkling wine, it's my birthday and against all odds, I am still alive. Goodbye, Babette."

Caz left, blinded by tears of rage. Let Babette think her judgmental thoughts and to hell with De Brabander and Luc DeReu. She knew what she knew. And what she didn't know, she was bloody well going to find out. As soon as possible. Fuck them all.

*Luc*
*Damme*

After getting home late three nights in a row and spending two nights in Leuven, it was a relief to arrive home in daylight. Some of his plants looked wilted and the patio was covered in dust and dry leaves. He hadn't attended to the garden and greenhouse since Saturday and then it had been a rushed affair. It felt like an eternity ago.

Considering what had happened since then, it *was* an eternity ago.

Lieve had sent a message to say Ammie was calmer and her speech wasn't so slurred any more, but she was still miserable and refused to talk about it.

He had to phone De Brabander, find out where things stood before he could even think of making a decision about a possible meeting between Caz and Ammie. Fortunately he had a good rapport with the detective since the events at the Begijnhof and Brussels.

"No new developments, but some progress, yes." De Brabander sounded tired. "We hope to make Miss Colijn's body available to the undertakers tomorrow. The post mortem has been completed. There's no doubt it was murder, not manslaughter. We have evidence that the tenants in the house next door were involved, but we can't prove yet that Matari and this Njiwa youngster were those tenants. If Miss Colijn kept a register of the tenants, it has gone missing.

"We're waiting for forensic results. In the meantime we're looking for Njiwa. Unfortunately there were no African surnames on passenger lists of flights leaving Brussels at the time. There's no first-year from the DRC registered at the university and the single one from South Africa is white."

Luc wasn't surprised. "In Leuven he also pretended to be a student. Undoubtedly another lie. Weren't the results of the identity parade conclusive? Could Babette identify them as the tenants?"

De Brabander hesitated. "I might as well tell you. Ms. Colijn was spot-on and so were you. Babette identified Matari without the dreadlocks but not with the wig. She was only eighty per cent sure the youngster she saw next door to Miss Colijn resembled Njiwa's identikit. Apparently she never really saw his face and always from a distance.

"It means we don't have irrefutable evidence that it was Matari and Njiwa who stayed in the house next door and were involved in the murder. The mvet alone isn't enough. If they were indeed the perpetrators, and I have little doubt they were, Njiwa must have committed the murder, as Matari was in Leuven at the time of Miss Colijn's death."

"And the assault?"

"There we're on solid ground. We know it was Matari, but he's making it very hard for us with his silence. Your evidence in that regard is very valuable. But of course the first prize would be if the fingerprints on Ms. Colijn's possessions match Matari's.

"Unfortunately there's no evidence that he was the one who monitored Ms. Colijn's cellphone. The only phone we found on him was brand new and unused. Not a single number on the SIM card. Which raises suspicion, but doesn't prove anything. Besides, we have only Ms. Colijn's word that he pretended to be TU."

"Any further news about her? Ms. Colijn?" He tried to make it sound like a casual enquiry.

"We've been in contact with the Stanford police in South Africa. They're still convinced she forgot to activate the alarm and that so-called tikkoppe were responsible for the burglary at her house. They didn't take fingerprints. Bizarre, but true. Our IT man tried to identify the second user on Ms Colijn's laptop but the person has vanished into thin air and cleaned up after himself."

Luc didn't really know what De Brabander was talking about. Perhaps the commissioner was under the impression he knew more than was actually the case. Perhaps he was just tired.

"What I actually want to hear, Commissioner, is whether you think Caz Colijn is a danger to others. She wants to meet Ammie Pauwels. Among other things, she wants to know if Ammie can cast light on the fact that she, Caz, has a … an unusual daughter." He remembered just in time that it might be confidential.

"We know about Lilah. That she's black. Beautiful young woman. Truly breathtaking."

Luc wondered how he knew what the daughter looked like, but chose not to ask.

"Ms. Colijn and her daughter probably have the right to ask about their ancestry, Professor. I don't think Ms. Colijn herself is capable of physical violence. How badly she might upset your stepmother, well, that I can't predict. But it may help you to know we're having Ms. Colijn watched. So far she hasn't done anything suspicious. Walked to the corner shop once, that's all. Now you'll have to excuse me. I hope to spend tonight with my wife and children for a change."

"Of course. I'm sorry I kept you."

"No problem. Have a good evening."

Luc hesitated a moment, then typed a message. *Will speak to Ammie tomorrow. She's still not well. If she doesn't agree, I'll do everything I can to make sure you don't get to see her. But if she's willing, I won't stand in your way.*

*It's a little late, but happy birthday. Luc.*

Her reply came within moments.

*Could we please stop threatening each other? And please*

*speak to Ammie as soon as possible, it's urgent. Thanks for the birthday wish. Caz.*

Caz
Ghent

Caz couldn't believe she was brushing away tears yet again. All because a stranger had wished her a happy birthday.

She glared at the Belgian phone when it started to ring.

"Caz, hello?" she said hesitantly.

"Ms. Colijn, Commissioner De Brabander. I believe felicitations are in order."

"Pardon?"

"Your birthday. Felicitations. There's a message on your phone from one Annika congratulating you on your birthday. A few others as well, but they sound like business acquaintances."

"Oh, thanks. If it wasn't for you I might not have seen another birthday."

"I can't take the credit for that. Luc DeReu is actually the one who saved you from the Dijle."

Caz frowned. "But you were the one who jumped in?"

"That was only half the job. The professor helped me find a place to get out and phoned the emergency services, providing them with practical information. Without that, the outcome might have been different. Nevertheless. I actually called to tell you I'll soon be returning your phone. There has been no further activity on it and I don't think there will be any again. Now I must run if I don't want to be whacked on the head with a rolling pin. Have a good evening."

What had got into the man? He sounded almost cheerful. The news about the phone was good, but now she would have to thank that bloody professor as well.

She recognized the tap on the door. "Come in, Erdem."

"Hi, Caz, I had a look, as you asked. I can put you up until the morning of the twelfth. You don't have to move to the smaller room in the weekend either. The guests canceled." Erdem looked out of sorts.

"Is something wrong?"

He gave a deep sigh. "The murder. It's in all the papers and on the news. People don't want to stay in a street where a murder has taken place."

"Is that the real problem, or is it because I'm staying here? Perhaps you don't want to accept guests while I'm here?"

"The police are watching you, they follow you when you go to the shop. Detectives are calling you. I don't know what to think. But I can't allow people to stay here while this is going on. It can damage the reputation of my business."

"Should I look for other lodgings?" But where? In the house where Tieneke was murdered? Not bloody likely.

He shook his head. "Babette is talking through her hat. I don't believe for a moment that you're guilty. It's unfortunate for business, but it's only for ten days. Anyway, ten days' fixed income is better than a day here and a day there."

"I could pay you more." She was so deep in the red already that getting in deeper would hardly matter.

"You don't have to. Really. I'm sorry I even mentioned it."

Caz hoped he didn't change his mind about the accommodation or her innocence. So far he had been good to her. But she could wring Babette's neck. Figuratively speaking, of course.

# Thirty-three

*Friday, October 3*
 *Caz*
*Ghent*

Caz was at once relieved and irritated when she walked away from Tieneke's church.

It turned out to be less difficult to arrange a funeral than she had thought. Especially if people didn't seem to want you involved. The minister assured her that he and his sisters in Christ, along with the undertakers and Tieneke's notary, would handle everything. The memorial service would take place on Tuesday. Caz could just arrive. If she wished.

Earlier today, Agent Verhoef had let her know that Tieneke's body was available for burial. De Brabander had not made contact again. There was probably no need. Grevers now followed her quite openly. Without saying a word, he got onto the bus with her this morning. When she came out of the church, he was waiting outside.

Caz ignored him, sat down at the first street café she encountered, and ordered coffee.

For the umpteenth time she had the cellphone in her hand. This time she typed the message she had been mulling over since last night.

*I believe the fact that I came out of the Dijle alive was as much your doing as DB's. Thank you. I was certainly not ready yet to join the invisible choir. Caz.*

She hesitated a moment. Should she ask about Ammie again? No, this message was only meant to thank him. She pressed the send key.

Caz had finished her coffee and paid the bill when a message came through.

*DB exaggerates, but I'm glad I could help. Luc.*

The next message arrived just as she had taken a seat in the bus, with Grevers diagonally behind her.

*Ammie is prepared to see you. She won't allow me to be present but at my insistence Lieve will be. Would Sunday morning at eleven suit you? Luc*

Caz's heart gave a jolt. The day after tomorrow. In less than forty-eight hours all the mysteries might be cleared up. She would know where she came from. Who her father was. Why Lilah was black. What sin she had committed to have her mother reject her.

Her thumb trembled so badly that she pressed one wrong key after another, but at last there was a short string of words on the screen that made sense. *It suits me. Address, please.*

*Will send address Sunday. Text me as soon as you arrive in Leuven*, the reply came almost immediately.

He was probably afraid she would pitch up earlier than agreed. The man definitely had trust issues. She didn't reply, just sat there, listening to the hammering of her heart, fighting a dizzy spell. Did she really want to know the truth?

*Sunday, October 5*
*Caz*
*Ghent*

Why did her hair have to look like a bird's nest, today of all days? It had to be the wet weather.

The drizzle that had begun to fall last night had not cleared up. The rain was about all Caz remembered about yesterday. She had spent most of the day wandering through Ghent's old city but if she had to be tested on what she had seen and done, she would fail miserably. Grevers would probably fare better.

When she had changed her outfit for the third time, she realized she was going to miss her bus and therefore her train if she didn't leave at once.

She had woken at five and forced herself to wait until half past five before getting up to make coffee as quietly as she could. Erdem deserved his Sunday rest. He worked hard during the week, she had discovered. Spent hour after hour in his office.

Now she was suddenly late. And looking like a dog's breakfast in spite of all the trouble she had gone to.

Late as she was, she took one last look in the mirror. She shouldn't have. The woman gazing back at her was pale and looked frightened. The eye was no longer swollen but the colorful bruise was visible under the foundation. The curls, which on dry days looked as if she'd had a spiral perm, were frizzy today. Dark circles under her eyes betrayed a lack of sleep.

Ammie Pauwels would be proved right. Who would want a child who looked as if graverobbers had stolen her from a sarcophagus?

To hell with Ammie Pauwels.

Caz grabbed her handbag. The backpack was staying behind today.

Hastily she locked Erdem's front door. When she turned, she was just in time to see the bus leave. The next one would be there in ten minutes but it would be too late for the train. Punctual public transport had its downside too.

She was going to be dismally late for arguably the most important appointment of her life. How was it possible?

Her head jerked up when she heard a car door slam. Grevers. He must have been on his way to get on the bus with her when he realized she wasn't going to make it.

Caz strode to the car, opened the passenger door and got in.

Taken aback, he looked at her.

"How about you save me a lot of time and yourself a lot of trouble? Leuven, please."

It took a good minute before he wordlessly switched on the engine. The man had to be related to a sphinx.

*Luc*
*Damme*

His home had never been that clean. Nor the greenhouse. There was not a single weed in his small garden and not a speck of dust on the patio.

Since Lieve had phoned to say Ammie wanted to see Caz, Luc had had no rest for his soul. On Friday he finished every single piece of unfinished business. Yesterday he sallied into the hothouse and garden like a maniac, later also tackling the house, and this morning he dusted each book individually in every single bookcase.

No, he couldn't spend the entire day waiting with bated breath to hear how the meeting had gone.

Ammie might have refused to have him present while Caz was there but nothing prevented him from going to Leuven.

Should he have prepared Caz? What for? Ammie's revelation that she had killer genes? What business was it of his anyway what was said between mother and daughter?

All he could do was be close in case some catastrophe arose.

Luc had just passed Brussels when Caz's message arrived. *Address, please.*

He waited until shortly before eleven to send the address. He was nearly there.

*Caz*
*Leuven*

The woman who opened the door was about twenty years too young to be Ammie and a nervous wreck, judging from her restless eyes and wringing hands.

Caz held out her hand. "Cassandra Colijn. Please call me Caz."

"Lieve. Lieve Luykens." The hand was cold and limp, the touch brief. "Miss Ammie's carer."

So that was how Lieve Luykens fitted into the picture. If she had known it, she might have found Ammie a lot sooner. Tieneke might still have been alive. No, speculation would get her nowhere.

"Miss Colijn ... Caz ..." Lieve pronounced her name Kess. "Miss Ammie ... Please, don't upset her. She's had two light strokes in the past few weeks. She's frail."

Caz nodded. So DeReu had not exaggerated. Ammie was really unwell.

Lieve showed Caz inside and led the way. All three doors leading off the hallway were closed. Lieve opened the middle one a chink.

"Miss Ammie? Your ... guest is here."

Caz's heart was a clenched fist. For a moment she felt like turning and running away.

"Let her come inside, Lieve, and go and make us something to drink." The voice belonged to an elderly person, but it was strong. Ammie Pauwels sounded all but frail. Not senile either. Merely hostile.

Caz went past Lieve, who was still hovering in the hallway. The room was cozy. Fresh flowers on the buffet emitted a soft scent. On the floor, a Persian carpet. A woman, her white hair in a chignon, stood at the window, her ramrod-straight back turned to Caz. She was of medium height. Her elderly figure was clad in a stylish frock. Nylons and low-heeled court shoes completed the picture. One hand was resting on a walking stick.

"Good morning, Mrs. Pauwels." Caz's voice was even huskier than usual. "Thank you for agreeing to see me." It was probably not a good way to break the ice at your first meeting with your birth mother, but she didn't know what else to say. It wasn't as if you could google the proper etiquette for the situation. Besides, it was very clear that this meeting was not going to end in a tearful embrace or the killing of the fatted calf.

Ammie Pauwels turned slowly. Caz recognized her own chin in Ammie's slightly raised one. The nose was also familiar. Their eyes were the same blue, though Ammie's were slightly watery and without Caz's brown flecks. A maze of wrinkles prevented her from recognizing any further similarities.

Slowly and quite openly Ammie looked her up and down. "You're tall," she said when she had completed her inspection.

"I presume I take after my father." Ammie barely reached her shoulder.

Ammie shook her head. "César wasn't much taller than me. It must have come from another ancestor."

César. Her father's name.

Ammie looked past her. "Come, come, Lieve. Miss Colijn must be dying of thirst."

Caz looked over her shoulder at where Lieve still stood transfixed.

"Coffee or tea?" Lieve asked. Her lower lip was trembling slightly.

"Coffee would be nice, thank you." If she could get it down.

"For me too, and before you start with all the crazy names again, koffie verkeerd will do," Ammie decided for them both.

Two weeks ago Caz wouldn't have understood what she meant, but she knew by now that koffie verkeerd was milky coffee. It happened to be her preference as well. Hallelujah, she and Ammie Pauwels had something in common.

"Sit, please. It's hard to have to look up all the time." Ammie pointed at a chair facing the one that was clearly her favorite, sat down with an effort and propped her walking stick against the armrest of her chair.

Caz obeyed, and made a conscious but fruitless effort to relax. The woman confused her. The situation confused her. Besides a few shared features, there was nothing to indicate that this woman had given birth to her. She didn't know what she had expected, but she had thought there would be some kind of emotion. A feeling of recognition, at least. But except for a familiar chin and nose and a pair of blue eyes, there was nothing. A shared coffee preference hardly counted.

"Luc tells me you're a translator."

Caz frowned. How the hell did he know? LinkedIn, she remembered. "Yes. I also do editing sometimes. And proofreading."

"Editing." The corners of Ammie's mouth lifted, but it was hardly a smile. "If only one could edit one's life."

"What would you have done differently?"

Ammie linked her fingers together on her lap. "Knowing what I know now? Had you aborted."

Caz stared at her, dumbstruck.

"I take it you are the person I read about in the papers. The one being questioned about the murder of Tieneke Colijn."

It took Caz a few moments to find words. "I had no part in her murder."

"I don't believe you, Cassandra. Not because of your name, not because of the ancient curse that said no one would ever believe you. I don't believe you because your father was a murderer. I was right, after all. An evil man like him couldn't help but sire a child that carries the evil within her as well. Evil just waiting to be aroused. It's in the genes."

Caz swallowed against the lump in her throat. She could say something about nature versus nurture, but it wouldn't do any good. Not with her history of nurturing. "I suggest you start at the beginning, Mrs. Pauwels, and tell me why you married a murderer. Why you allowed him to sire so-called evil children." Ammie Pauwels wanted to destroy her with words, she could see it a mile away, and in a duel there was no place for being civil.

"I didn't allow anything. After I found out César had had my father killed to get his hands on a consignment of diamonds, he had to take me by force. And he did. Repeatedly—and reveled in it. That's the kind of man whose blood flows in your veins."

The implications left Caz stunned. She was the product of rape, albeit within marriage. It was really not what she had wanted to hear.

"César not only orchestrated my father's death in a plane crash, he also killed, in cold blood, the man I loved. He tried to kill me too, leaving me for dead."

Caz's stomach contracted. Why hadn't she let sleeping dogs lie?

"Sometimes I wish Tabia had never saved me. That I had died on the savanna outside Elisabethville. With you in my belly."

Ammie stopped talking when Lieve entered with a tray.

Like a robot, Caz took the coffee from her. She shook her head when Lieve offered sugar. She refused the cake, managing an apologetic smile. Whoever Tabia was, Ammie might be right. It might have been better if she hadn't saved her.

When Lieve had left, Caz looked at Ammie again.

"Heard enough?" Ammie raised her eyebrows.

"Why didn't you have me aborted?" Caz instinctively knew that the law wouldn't have stood in the way of this cold-hearted woman.

"Because until you were born I couldn't be sure you were César's child."

It took a second or two to digest this piece of information. "You hoped I was another man's child. The man you loved. The one César killed." She wasn't asking.

"Elijah." There was so much tender emotion in the word that Caz could hardly believe it was the same person speaking.

# Thirty-four

*Luc*
*Leuven*

Seated at the street café closest to Ammie's home, Luc had just started on his second kriek when he saw, of all people, Inspector Grevers approach. How on earth did the man track him down? And why?

Grevers stopped when he saw Luc. His surprised expression revealed that Luc had not been his quarry after all.

He approached. "Professor DeReu. This is a surprise."

"I could say the same, Inspector. Take a seat. What are you doing in Leuven?" The moment he asked, he remembered De Brabander telling him that Caz was being watched. Of course.

Grevers sat down. "Cassandra Colijn is giving me gray hairs. Imagine! Instructing me to bring her here. What she's doing here, heaven knows, but orders are orders." When the waiter approached, he asked for fruit juice.

"And your orders are?" Luc asked.

"First I had to follow her to see who she made contact

with, who she might meet, make sure she doesn't decide to flee. Then came the additional assignment. I have to make sure she's safe."

Luc frowned. "Why do you think she's in danger?"

"We can't get confirmation that Tieneke Colijn's alleged murderer, the Njiwa youngster, has left the country. Commissioner De Brabander thinks he might try to finish what Matari started."

Luc turned ice cold. "Then why are you here and not where you can look after Caz?" Ammie and Lieve as well.

"A man gets tired and thirsty. And nature calls. It's been almost an hour since I dropped the woman at the apartment she directed me to. And I have no reason to think anyone has followed us or knows where we are. And you? What are you doing here?"

It was obvious that Grevers didn't know who Caz was visiting. "I have relatives here. I'll be calling on them in a while." Luc deliberately kept it vague.

When the juice was placed in front of Grevers, he drank thirstily. It had to be a helluva job just waiting for someone to move. Hour after hour.

"The changed orders. Is Caz—Cassandra—no longer a suspect?" Luc asked.

"I wouldn't say that. The commissioner is especially worried about ..." Grevers seemed to have second thoughts. "Well, about a certain document."

"Still?" Not that he had any idea what document the man was talking about, but maybe Grevers would fall for it.

"Then you know Cassandra Colijn is the sole beneficiary of Tieneke Colijn's will?" Grevers fell for it.

Luc smiled. It seemed to be enough.

"Max—Commissioner De Brabander—finds it dodgy that the will was made the morning before she died."

Luc tried to keep his expression neutral.

"Tieneke Colijn might not have been exceptionally wealthy, but she was well-off. Well-off enough to give someone like Cassandra Colijn motive to have her murdered by hitmen as soon as the will had been changed.

"But it seems Max isn't quite as convinced of her involvement any more. Personally I think he's making a mistake. Why would two criminals kill someone without stealing anything? Tieneke Colijn wasn't raped, so there was no sexual motive." Grevers finished his juice with one last gulp and began to rummage in his pockets.

Luc shook his head. "Don't worry. It's on me."

"Nice of you. Now I definitely have to heed the call of nature. I might see you again." Grevers rushed off in the direction of the restrooms.

Luc hardly noticed. If he had turned ice cold a moment before, he was now virtually frozen.

De Brabander's anxiety made terrifying sense. When she found out she had been deceived all her life, Caz came to Belgium for revenge. She had two African men who would help her. Caz discovered that her foster sister had financial means and convinced Tieneke to change her will in her favor before she had her taken out. But that wasn't where it ended. She found out Ammie had paid with diamonds to have her raised by strangers. Was that why she began the frantic search for Ammie? Was she hoping Ammie would acknowledge her as her biological daughter so that she would be first in line for an inheritance she hoped might also have everything to do with diamonds?

Luc closed his eyes. If it was true, Caz Colijn was the biggest opportunist he had ever come across. One who could think on her feet.

He might be hung up on thrillers, perhaps even paranoid, but the scenario he had sketched for himself certainly wasn't impossible.

*Caz*
*Leuven*

Lieve had brought coffee three times before Ammie's story dried up.

Caz doubted whether Ammie had told her everything simply because she had asked. For long moments Ammie had sat talking with her eyes closed, as if she was reliving the events. She spoke about her first meeting with Elijah and how they ended up in a relationship. The son born from that relationship. How Elijah was murdered. How Tabia saved her and how she and Tabia's nephew fled, ending up first in Nylstroom, then in Pretoria. Caz realized that during those moments Ammie had completely forgotten about her.

"So you see, Cassandra, I had no other choice but to leave you behind."

Caz looked at her, thinking about everything she had heard. "What I see is that I was like the canary in the coalmine. The child who was sacrificed so that you could survive."

Ammie gave a bitter laugh. "Have you thought of the possibility that I sacrificed you so César wouldn't find you? That I might have had your safety in mind?"

"No, Mrs. Pauwels, I don't think that's what you had in mind. You might have consoled yourself with that thought later, but that's all. You feared César, you knew he wouldn't stop searching for you. You admit the diamonds you bribed Fien with were stolen from him. Someone like him would not have forgiven you for that. And you would have been able to bring him to justice—he tried to kill you after all. Had your death certificate issued. And of course fleeing with a child is harder than without one. Especially if you're using an assumed name.

"I was the sacrificial lamb so that you could escape César's vengeance. You didn't care what would happen to me. You knew what Fien was like, yet you chose to leave me in the care of a woman who was so greedy that she was prepared to raise someone else's child—a child she didn't want—in exchange for money."

For a moment Caz saw something in Ammie's eyes, but she couldn't make out what it was. She knew it wasn't regret.

"You must remember, Cassandra, that I wasn't accountable for my deeds at the time. I was an emotional wreck. Sick in body and soul."

Caz shook her head. "I'm sorry, Mrs. Pauwels, but actions speak louder than words. One's integrity is revealed by the way one acts under pressure. You put your child on the altar in order to shake off your old life and make a fresh start. From the word go you couldn't face raising me yourself. That was why you convinced yourself I was César's child. To ease your conscience."

There was steel in Ammie's expression again. "The evidence was there. The frizzy blonde hair, the lily-white skin. I was terrified, yes, I did fear for my life, but I was especially afraid of a child who is the product of a man who was a monster and a woman who had forgotten what a conscience was. Because that I was, I don't deny it. Yes, Cassandra, I was afraid of you. I didn't want to see either César or myself reflected in you, not to mention a combination of the two of us. Are you satisfied now?"

"Satisfied? Satisfied to hear that in your eyes I could be nothing but an abomination? But I'm not, you know. I'm a person with integrity and good values. Perfect? Anything but. But I did everything in my power to be the best possible mother to my child. And believe me, it wasn't learned behavior. The woman you left me with didn't know what love or compassion was. I had no example of what it means to be a good mother. Only instinct.

"Where it came from I don't know, because it was evidently not genetic. But something inside me knew the right, the honorable way. I had options when my unusual child was born. Even though we ..."

"Unusual?"

Caz hardly noticed she had been interrupted. "My husband and parents-in-law might have rejected my child and me but my father-in-law was a decent man in his way. He undertook to make certain that my daughter was adopted by good people. I believe he would have kept his word, but my moral compass told me it wouldn't be the honorable thing to do and my natural maternal instincts made me fight for my child.

"Psychopaths have no conscience. What one calls someone without the most basic maternal instincts I can't say. I only know you answer to that description, if there is one."

Ammie snorted. "If that's the case, you should absolve me. Then it wasn't a conscious decision but a pathological condition. But you're wrong. My love for my first child was instantaneous. There was nothing harder than letting him go, but I had to. For his own sake and for Elijah's. It was the greatest sacrifice of my life."

"So you were experienced in the art of abandoning children by the time I was born."

"Desensitized, perhaps."

"How did you know your first child was Elijah's?"

"Kembo was brown. A deep toffee brown."

Caz gasped for breath. "Elijah was black?"

"Not quite. His father was Belgian, his mother was born from a relationship between a Somali woman and a Belgian man, but he had a reasonably dark complexion, yes. That was why his father had left him at the mission station as a child. His mother, brothers and sisters had sallow complexions, at most. His dark skin was an embarrassment to the family."

Caz began to laugh. It was a laugh born from a deep ache. About the irony of life. About the jester's hand that dealt the cards.

"How would you feel if I told you my daughter, your granddaughter, is a different kind of brown from your son, Kembo. The color of molasses. With silvery-blue eyes. A lot like yours and mine, except that hers are ringed with gold."

Ammie turned pale. She remained silent for a long time before she shook her head. "That doesn't mean anything. César's mother was a woman of loose morals. She died of syphilis before I met him. Of course I only found out long after the wedding. Nonetheless. He was quite sallow himself. His hair a bit frizzy." She gave a small, triumphant smile. "He also had brown flecks in his clear blue eyes."

Just like you. Ammie didn't say it, but the unspoken words hung in the air.

Caz knew it was checkmate. If she could believe Ammie. She got to her feet. "Only one more question, Mrs. Pauwels. If César was possibly of mixed race, how certain are you that Kembo wasn't César's child?"

Ammie gazed at her.

"Think carefully about how certain you can be that I am not Elijah's daughter. Especially now that you know your granddaughter is black. Thanks for your time and the enlightening conversation. Please don't get up. I'm sure Lieve will show me out."

Caz had progressed a few steps when Ammie laughed. She turned to look at her.

"At least there's no doubt that you're my daughter. You're every bit as ruthless and coldblooded as I am."

"I don't think so."

"You think wrong. You've just proved it. You want me to have doubts. You want me to wonder for the rest of my days whether I had made a mistake. To question everything that happened in the past fifty-three years and wonder what it would have been like if I had accepted you as Elijah's child and raised you myself." Ammie shook her head. "It's cruel, Cassandra Janssen. It's terribly cruel."

"I am not a Janssen. Evidently not a Colijn either, but definitely not a Janssen. I know it in my core. And God knows, if I ever get the chance, I'm going to prove it." Caz hesitated a fraction of a second. She knew she was exposing herself to hurt, but pressed on. "You've been watching me for two, three hours. Is there really nothing that reminds you of Elijah?"

Ammie shook her head. "Nothing. Not a single feature or mannerism." Everything about her spoke of conviction.

Caz couldn't help but believe her.

The eyes that had seen so many things in eighty-two years closed. The head leaned more heavily against the backrest. "Go now. I'm exhausted."

Caz was at the door when Ammie spoke again.

"Bring your daughter. Arrange it with Luc."

Caz turned, surprised. Ammie's eyes were still closed and she was breathing deeply and evenly. Had she talked in her sleep? Or had she meant it?

*Luc*
*Leuven*

Luc had just paid for his lengthy lunch and was wondering what to do next when his phone rang.

Lieve.

He hastened to answer. "Lieve?"

"Miss Colijn has just left, Professor."

"Is Mother Ammie okay?" His throat contracted. "Should I come? I'm close."

"Miss Ammie fell asleep in her chair. She looks quite calm. There wouldn't be any point if you came."

"Did it go well?"

"I can't really say. I wasn't allowed to be present. The few times I took in coffee and refreshments I couldn't gather much. They stopped talking as soon as I entered."

"But you could sense how it was going?" He tried to curb his impatience.

"Well, it's very clear they didn't hit it off, Professor. I don't think there's any question of reconciliation between mother and daughter. Like two boxers in a ring, that's how they were."

Luc sighed. He supposed one couldn't really expect a happy ending. Yet he had secretly hoped there would at least be some compassion on Ammie's part. Forgiveness on Caz's. He was such an idealist.

In the past hour or so he had managed to control his dismay at Grevers's news and the panic it had roused. He was still not at ease, but he conceded that he might have overreacted.

"There's something I find strange, Professor," Lieve's voice interrupted his thoughts.

"Yes?"

"Miss Ammie. She was lucid and remained so all afternoon. Despite her recent stroke. Despite the veils that have dropped down so often in the past two years. It's as if she used every grain of determination and strength to keep up this conversation. She was like her much younger self until she fell asleep."

"Can you stay until she wakes?"

"I'll stay. But she mustn't sleep too long, or she'll have a hard time tonight. And she must eat something. They hardly touched the cake I served. Wouldn't hear of having lunch either. I must see to it that she takes her medication too."

"Thanks, Lieve. I'm sorry to ask this on a Sunday but I'll pay you overtime, of course."

"Don't worry, Professor. Miss Ammie pays me well and she doesn't mind paying overtime. I'll call if there's a problem. Otherwise I'll let you know how she is tomorrow."

"Thanks, Lieve. Mother Ammie can thank her lucky stars for you."

"I'm just grateful you're back in her life, Professor. I don't think I know a lonelier person. She desperately needs someone who cares about her."

Better late than never, he thought, but he drove back to Damme filled with self-reproach.

*Erevu*
*Ghent*

He profited from his self-appointed silence in more ways than one. He now saw things more clearly. What he saw very clearly was that Dove couldn't have devised the act of treachery by himself.

Jela must have instructed him. He should have guessed it when Dove suddenly became so efficient at covering tracks. The tablets, cellphones. No numbers on the new phones. He bet the number Dove gave him to memorize was false. The details of the bank in Pretoria as well. He bet if he phoned Jela, he would get no reply.

There was only one way the mvet that De Brabander had rubbed under his nose could have "stayed behind" in their lodgings. He had kept a lookout the morning after the woman's death while Dove loaded the car before they left for his hideout.

Dove must have left it behind deliberately. With the full

knowledge that the Caz woman would recognize it after Leuven.

By the time they left there, Dove had already decided to make his grandfather the scapegoat for the stupid thing he himself had done the day before. To think he had bent over backwards to save Dove, only to be betrayed by the boy.

Dove had only told him about the contents of the envelope because he needed help to get the key. When his grandfather failed, Dove cast him aside.

If the Caz woman had drowned in the Dijle, Dove would have fallen flat on his face, but apparently she was alive and kicking and surely still in possession of the key.

Erevu realized his fate would still have been sealed even if he had got the key. Right from the start, the plan had been for him to take the fall. He can guess why. It was because Jela's dream differed from his own.

Never again would he underestimate the treachery committed by one's own blood.

# Thirty-five

*Monday, October 6*
*Caz*
*Ghent*

Caz could kick herself. That was what one got from tempers and arguments. She and Ammie Pauwels had been so intent on crossing swords that she had never asked Ammie about the contents of the strongbox. How the hell could she have forgotten?

Three questions were all she had to ask. Who is my father, what is in the strongbox and who is Erevu Matari? And she'd forgotten two of them.

Why couldn't she have forgotten the question about her father instead?

She was the daughter of a murderer. Murder was in her genes. That was Ammie's firm belief and that was why she wished Caz had never been born. Great! Exactly the kind of thing you expected to hear when you went in search of your roots.

Yesterday she was too upset to do much of anything.

Grevers drove her home in silence. She held herself together until she got back before she succumbed to tears.

Afterwards she had felt like a zombie. Today she looked like one. Last night she didn't sleep more than an hour at a stretch. When she did doze off, she was tormented by nightmares.

The only thing that kept her going was the prospect of seeing Lilah in two days' time, but before that happened she still had to attend Tieneke's funeral.

Today she would pull herself together. Decide whether she wanted to contact Luc DeReu about Ammie Pauwels's request or wait until Lilah arrived. If Ammie had really meant it, of course, and if Lilah was prepared to meet her grandmother. God save her poor child from a grandmother like that.

*Luc*
*Ghent*

Lieve's call caught him between lectures. Luc sat down on a bench under a tree.

"How is she, Lieve?"

"She looks rested. Physically, anyway. But I can see she's worried about something. She stares into the distance for long lapses of time. But she's lucid." Lieve gave a nervous laugh. "She asked what I thought of Miss Colijn. What could I say? I said she's an attractive woman, that she resembles Miss Ammie. Well educated, as far as I could see. 'She's a hellcat, but at least she's strong,' was all she said but she looked ... I don't really know ... almost satisfied."

Hellcat. Strong. What exactly did Ammie mean by that?

He stayed seated after he had ended the call. It was good to hear that Ammie looked rested. He certainly couldn't say the same of himself. The information about the will preyed on his mind. As did his paranoia.

Ammie was now far more involved than before. Caz knew where she lived. The only thing that set his mind at rest was that Grevers was watching her. But it was cold comfort. It wouldn't take much for someone like Caz to pull the wool over Grevers's eyes.

If only he knew who and what Caz Colijn really was. One moment he was convinced she was an archvillain after Ammie's wealth, the next he regretted his mistrust and believed she only wanted Ammie to tell her where she came from. Felt sorry for her, pitied her for finding herself in such a mess.

He wished he could meet Caz face to face. Talk to her. Try to figure out who she really was. A con artist, or someone who had studied at the school of hard knocks and was just trying to get by?

Maybe Ammie's curse had worked. Or maybe he found it so hard to believe Caz precisely because she was a slippery customer.

*Tuesday, October 7*
*Caz*
*Ghent*

Caz was surprised when she entered the church ten minutes before the start of Tieneke's memorial service. About thirty people were already seated. Mostly women. Some dressed soberly, others informally. The majority didn't look like regular churchgoers. Why she should think that she couldn't really say.

The minister looked somewhat grim-faced as he took up his position behind the pulpit and announced that, consistent with Tieneke's wishes, there would be no interment. Her will stipulated that, like Fien, she was to be cremated.

In the parts of the sermon Caz could follow, the man said good things about Tieneke. He praised her for her dedication to her mother over many years. He deplored the fact that she had come to such a violent end and earnestly pleaded with the Lord to have the guilty parties brought to book.

Caz had no desire to attend the tea after the service. She didn't know a soul and everyone seemed to be avoiding her. No, not avoiding, looking straight through her as if she didn't exist.

On her way to the bus stop, someone held her back by the arm.

"Miss Colijn?"

She recognized the notary from Fien's funeral. What his name was she didn't know. She had never been introduced to him.

"My sincere condolences. Tieneke was taken too soon."

Caz nodded.

"I would like to hear when it would suit you to come to my office. We have to talk about Tieneke's will."

The will debacle had completely slipped her mind. "Mr. ... er ..."

"Kuyper. Jan Kuyper." He held out his hand for Caz to shake.

"Mr. Kuyper, as implausible as I find it, I understand from Commissioner De Brabander that Tieneke changed her will in my favor. I presume nothing can be settled before the investigation has been completed?"

"That is indeed so. There must be no question of blood on the hands of the heir. But as you probably won't be staying in Belgium indefinitely, we might as well complete the formalities while you're here. If it suits you, we can go to my office right now. I made a tentative appointment for you for after the funeral. Unfortunately I didn't have a contact number to confirm whether it suits you or not."

Caz hesitated only a moment. "Fine." The sooner she got it over with, the better.

The short drive to his office took place in silence.

The notary's office was cramped and airless. Caz sat down, wishing he would at least open a window. She felt short of breath.

He reached for a file on his desk and drew it nearer.

"The detectives have probably showed you the copy of the will they requested. Are you familiar with the contents?"

"Commissioner De Brabander told me I'm the sole beneficiary and that Tieneke left a note declaring that she owes me nothing but has no other heirs."

He nodded. "Good. The inheritance is made up of the two

residences, a savings account, a cheque account as well as a few investments. The only outstanding debt is a pharmacy bill. The estimated value of the bequest, which includes a valuation of the two houses, is about six hundred thousand euros."

"*What*? It's ... it's ..." She tried to do the conversion. "... something like nine million rand?"

"I'm not sure what the exchange rate is. Of course there are a few deductions we won't go into now. But, providing the murder investigation is concluded to everyone's satisfaction and the inheritance comes your way, I have to ask what you have in mind with regard to the fixed assets. The houses. Their contents."

Caz was still trying to catch her breath. "Sell them, I suppose? Actually I haven't the foggiest, Mr. Kuyper. I don't know what Tieneke's wishes were. And I don't know what made her change her will. We weren't close. Do you happen to know what she would've liked me to do?"

He looked at her pensively for a moment, then leaned forward as if he had come to a decision. "Let's start at the beginning. Tieneke was effectively in control of her mother's financial affairs long before Fien's death. Tieneke would automatically have come into everything her mother owned, unless, of course, you laid claim to part of the estate. That didn't happen.

"In her previous will Tieneke had made provision for Mrs. Colijn—for her care and so forth. But there was another bequest. One that had no longer been relevant for quite a while." He hesitated slightly. "There had been someone in Tieneke's life who would've been the main beneficiary of her will, but died about two years ago. In her grief at the time Tieneke had neglected to change her will."

Caz's jaw dropped. "There was a man in Tieneke's life?"

Kuyper cleared his throat awkwardly. "You must understand this is confidential, Miss Colijn. Fien had no idea. No one did, except their closest friends. But no, there wasn't a man in Tieneke's life. It was a woman. She was childless as well, so ..."

"A woman?" And she had thought nothing could surprise her any more.

Kuyper nodded. "The woman's relatives had cut all ties with her on religious grounds, so Tieneke obviously didn't want them to benefit from her will. Tieneke and Elaine had a few good years together even though it was in stolen moments. I hope you won't condemn her because of it?"

"For being in a gay relationship? Good grief, no, of course not. But I must admit it's a shock. Well, a surprise, actually." Tieneke in a clandestine relationship. Regardless of her lover's gender, Caz would never have suspected it.

"With her friend's background in mind, Tieneke wanted to make the rental home available to women in the same position as Elaine had been. Gay women who, for whatever reason, had nowhere to go. It's hard to believe that even today people are rejected on the basis of their sexual preferences, but believe me, it happens. Be that as it may, Tieneke couldn't implement her plan while Fien was still alive. You probably know how ... conventional Fien was."

The man had a talent for euphemism. Caz nodded.

"With Fien's death, everything changed. Tieneke had to update her will. As an interim measure, she made you the beneficiary—merely so that she wouldn't die intestate. It was supposed to have been only until she could set up a trust and establish the safe house. We designed a workable plan, but we hadn't got to the finer details yet. Tieneke hadn't signed anything either. With her premature death, everything was left up in the air. Of course, if you do inherit, you are completely within your rights if you choose not to go ahead with the project."

It was all too much, too soon. Caz tried to gather her thoughts, to make sense of what she had heard. "Mr. Kuyper, I'm a bit overwhelmed, but can this project go ahead without my involvement?"

"As far as the transfer of the rental home is concerned, you would only have to sign a few documents. But you must understand that it would take a chunk of about two hundred thousand euros out of your inheritance. That's more or less the value of the house. And I'll have to find a way to finance the project."

"Mr. Kuyper, how can I be worse off? The money was never mine to start with."

She thought she could see a glint of approval in his eyes. "Do you intend to take occupation of the other house? Tieneke's house? Temporarily or permanently?"

Caz shook her head. "No." She would prefer never to set foot in that house again.

He leaned forward. "Miss Colijn. I know where Fien and Tieneke's money originally came from. We discussed it at length the last time Tieneke was here. Despite Tieneke's note, I am convinced in the end she would have wanted to compensate you for the injustice done to you. Without short-changing herself while she was still alive, of course, and not with all of her estate either. As her executor, I suggest we handle the matter in the following way. That is, if you approve.

"We keep Tieneke's house, renovate it and furnish it the way Tieneke and I had been planning to do with the rental home. We sell the rental home, because it would frankly be easier than trying to sell a house where a murder took place. With the proceeds we finance the project. You get the investments, which comprise about a third of the estate. If your information regarding the exchange rate is correct, it would mean that about three million rand would be coming your way."

Caz gave a slight laugh. "Mother Fien would turn in her grave. And not only because of the money coming to me. Homosexuality, like so many other things, was an unforgivable sin in her eyes. 'Conservative' really doesn't cover it."

Kuyper smiled. "She was cremated. No grave to turn in."

This time Caz laughed out loud. She was amazed she still knew how. "Well, I bet those ashes are quivering."

"Do you agree?"

"I do. If you're sure Tieneke really would have wanted me to benefit."

He nodded. "As sure as I can be."

"Then you may draw up the documents. I hope to fly back in a little less than a week. Everything will depend on the murder investigation, of course, but my visa expires in a week or so."

"Agreed. I'll put everything in writing as soon as possible. Your contact details?"

Caz wrote them down.

"Tieneke would have been proud of you, Miss Colijn."

Caz smiled, but she doubted it. At most, Tieneke might be heaving a sigh of relief, wherever she was.

"Can I take you home?"

Caz shook her head. "I'll take the bus, but thank you."

When he held the door for her, Caz hesitated. "Mr. Kuyper, I don't know how things are done in Belgium, but aren't you almost too involved in Tieneke's plans? For someone who is merely her notary and executor, I mean?"

"My daughter is also gay. My ex-wife rejected her. I've met a few of my daughter's friends who have had the same experience, including Elaine. A number of them attended the service this morning. There comes a time when one has to do something. Reach out a hand. It's what Tieneke wanted to do, and I would like to see it through. Thanks to you, we can go ahead."

"What would happen if there's evidence that I have blood on my hands?"

"Do you?"

She shook her head.

"Well, don't worry about it then."

Caz wished she could be so sure.

When she left the building, Grevers was leaning against a lamppost.

# Thirty-six

*Wednesday, October 8*
*Caz*
*Ghent*

What a wonderful bodyguard and shadow she had. Grevers was asleep in his car. He nearly jumped out of his skin when Caz tapped on the window.

Grevers fumbled with the key in the ignition before opening the window.

"Good morning, Inspector."

He nodded, mortified.

"I just want to inform you I'm meeting my daughter at the Graslei in an hour's time. On the bridge near De Witte Leeuw. We're going to have breakfast and for the rest of the day I'm in her hands. She'll be staying at my guesthouse too, the one over there that you are watching.

"It would really mean a lot to me if you could leave us alone. It's her birthday today and I haven't seen her in ten months. We want to enjoy ourselves without someone trailing behind us. You can phone me if it makes you feel any better, but I hope you won't.

"I'm getting on the bus now. Don't follow me. Leave me alone today. We can talk again tomorrow. Okay?"

He stared at her, astonished. Caz pointed a warning finger at him and crossed the street to where the bus had just stopped.

Grevers remained in his car.

Attaboy. Good dog.

*Luc*
*Ghent*

It was hard to believe. The same Ammie who had wanted nothing to do with her daughter now wanted to meet her granddaughter.

Luc wished Ammie had kept refusing to see Caz. It would have made life so much easier. For him anyway. His seesawing thoughts about the woman was exhausting.

The truth was, whether she was virtue personified or evil incarnate, Caz wasn't his responsibility. Ammie was.

Luc picked up his phone and dialed.

"Good morning, Commissioner. Luc DeReu."

"Good day, Professor. To what do I owe the pleasure?"

"Cassandra Colijn. She eventually met my stepmother on Sunday."

"I'm aware of it, yes. Grevers took her there. We checked the address."

"According to her carer, Ammie has got it into her head that she wants to meet her granddaughter. I haven't heard from Caz yet, but apparently Ammie told her to arrange it with me. Ammie wants to see her on Friday. The granddaughter. Caz will presumably accompany her."

"And?"

"I'm worried Caz may be after my stepmother's money and that she's in danger." He blurted out the words.

"Is your stepmother exceptionally wealthy?"

"I can't say, but she's wealthy enough to pay for a private carer, and she lives in a spacious apartment in a good neighborhood. She wants for nothing."

"Is your stepmother convinced that Ms. Colijn is her biological daughter?"

"It seems so. Lieve, the carer, says it's obvious. I've only seen Caz from a distance, so I can't say." All he could say was that she had Africa in her walk and hair that made one's fingers itch to touch it.

"Well, what's your problem, Professor? As her biological daughter, Ms. Colijn is surely entitled to be her mother's heir? Wouldn't you say so?"

Now the man probably thought he himself was after the inheritance. "But, Commissioner, you suspect that she had Tieneke murdered to get her hands on her money."

De Brabander kept silent for a while. "I can't remember telling you that but, seeing that you seem to know about it anyway, that aspect of the case has more or less been resolved."

"How's that?" He hoped he hadn't created a problem for Grevers.

"Cassandra Colijn undertook to sign away two-thirds of Tieneke's estate for a charitable purpose and there's no reason to think she won't stick to her word. The amount she's signing away comes to about four hundred thousand euros. I can hardly imagine she would do so if she had Tieneke murdered for her money."

Luc was speechless.

"In sceptical moments I have wondered whether she might be doing it precisely because she knows she's been caught out and wants to allay suspicion, but overall it doesn't make sense. Yes, you might be out of an inheritance yourself. No, I don't think Cassandra will have her birth mother killed for her money. Yesterday afternoon she asked that her passport be returned to her. Her visa expires shortly, and I have no further reason to keep her here. Now you'll have to excuse me."

Luc said goodbye and sat gazing through his dusty office window. He had so many questions, but with Caz on her way back to South Africa, he would probably never learn the answers. He would never find out whether Africa was in her eyes as well.

*Caz*
*Ghent*

Caz saw Lilah from a distance. Her first instinct was not to hurry towards her, but rather to take her in with her eyes, make Lilah her own again.

She was not the only one watching the lithe black woman with legs that went on forever. You couldn't miss her, and not only because she was tall and striking. The way she walked revealed an energy that seemed to rush through her veins. Her smile radiated an unmistakable inner joy.

"MamaCaz!" she cried over a crowd of heads when she saw Caz. She waved excitedly and, despite her killer heels, broke into a run. Her braids bobbed up and down, her short flared skirt fluttered around her thighs.

Caz hurried towards her and, laughing, they fell into each other's arms.

"I missed you so much!" Caz hugged her child so tightly that she was short of breath herself.

"And me!"

"Thirty-one today. Congratulations, Lilah."

"I'm getting old." Lilah let her go. "Champagne. French. That's what we need."

"Your birthday. Your call."

Seated at a restaurant after Lilah had tried to order Veuve Clicquot but had to make a different choice from the wine list, she gave Caz the once-over. "Fuck it, MaCaz, that must have been a helluva shiner if it still looks like that." Lilah frowned.

"You know just how to make a girl feel gorgeous." She should have known Lilah would see right through the thick layer of make-up.

"It's a knack I have. Don't you dare tell me you walked into a door. What the fuck is happening in your life that turned you into a murder suspect with a black eye?"

"How do you know about ..." Caz stopped when Lilah held up her iPhone.

"It's called the worldwide web. If you google 'Colijn' to try to find out something about the family tree, you hit on a murder your mother didn't tell you about. The online newspapers are full of innuendoes I can decode because I know who they're talking about. I've been waiting for you to tell me, but all I've heard is the wonderful news that I'm not a twig of the Colijn family tree after all."

"I would have told you. Tomorrow, after your birthday."

"That makes me feel so much better. Out with the truth. The whole truth and nothing but the truth."

The breakfast and the champagne were almost forgotten by the time Lilah was satisfied that she knew enough about everything that had happened.

"I know you've sugarcoated a lot of it, but I won't insist on more detail on my birthday. I'm just happy you got out of it more or less in one piece. Let's concentrate on the living instead. We must find out when Grandma Ammie can see us."

"You want to meet her?"

"Definitely. Maybe she'll clap a hand over her mouth and shout: 'Elijah! You look just like Elijah!' But more important is that we find out who this loser Erevu Matari is. And why the hell he's so interested in this curio shit. And she'll have to explain why she wants to make my saintly mother out as a murderer. Fuck that. She has me to deal with now."

"Okay. I'll contact Luc DeReu and see what he says. What would you like to do the rest of your birthday?"

"Bruges. I want to show you Bruges. Take you on a canal cruise. Eat a loooong, late lunch at a place where they have Veuve Clicquot. Spend time with my mother."

"And when are you planning to tell me about Aubrey?"

"Sometime during our loooong lunch. Let's get going. I rented a car, a BMW cabriolet, no less. Today we're letting our hair down. But first, please send that bloody professor a message."

Caz obeyed. Half an hour later, as Lilah was letting down the hood of the cabriolet, the reply came.

"Friday morning. Eleven." She looked inquiringly at Lilah.

"Sounds right to me. Now we're going to forget about everything, Lucy Jordan. It ain't Paris, but it ain't a bad alternative."

*Friday, October 10*
*Caz*
*Leuven*

The two days with Lilah had flown. Yesterday Caz signed some documents at Jan Kuyper's office, where she learned that the estate had provisionally been frozen. Then she and Lilah left for Brussels, where they explored the old city on foot. In the afternoon they went to Antwerp.

They had more or less caught up with everything that had happened in the past ten months. Caz knew that Lilah and Aubrey had met at a fancy charity reception where he was the speaker and she a guest of honor. Something to do with raising funds for emergency relief to children in African countries. She also knew it was love at first sight and that for the first time ever Lilah was serious about a man. Serious enough to consider accepting Aubrey's hand and having her genealogical descent traced for his sake.

Caz thought Aubrey sounded manipulative and bigoted, but she couldn't share her thoughts with Lilah. Definitely not before she had even met him.

"Here we are," Lilah said as she drew up in front of Ammie's apartment building.

Lieve looked less nervous than the last time, but her eyes widened and her hand flew to her mouth when she laid eyes on Lilah. "Ooooh," was all she managed to get out.

"Good day, Mrs. Luykens. MaCaz told me how kindly you treated her, so nice to meet you." Lilah was the picture of innocence.

Lieve was still speechless when she escorted them into the living room. "Miss Ammie," she croaked at last.

Ammie was at the window again, standing with her back to them. She turned. Ignoring Caz, she gave Lilah the same treatment she had given Caz the previous Sunday. She looked her over carefully before their eyes met.

"Grandma Ammie?" Lilah took the lead.

Ammie's eyebrows lifted a fraction.

"I'm Lilah. Your granddaughter," Lilah continued calmly.

"You're terribly tall. Much taller than her." Only her head moved slightly in Caz's direction. Ammie's eyes remained fixed on Lilah.

"A mere one point eight three meters in my socks, but I prefer high heels. Much more elegant, don't you think? The height is probably part of my black heritage. Congolese, I hear? Tall, lean people. I was an excellent athlete at school. We blacks have more muscles than brain cells, they say."

Caz knew it would have sounded like sarcasm if she were the one who had said it. Lilah's words were filled with laughter, though. Laughter that had to be contagious, because a moment later Ammie's eyes began to twinkle and she didn't quite manage to stifle a smile.

"I must add, my father is white as snow, but also nearly two meters tall. In the wedding photos he towers over MaCaz and it was clearly before flat shoes got their evil claws into her. Oh, and his father was even taller. Tall genes, that's what I have."

Caz looked at Lilah, frowning, Ammie forgotten for a moment. "Wedding photos? Where did you see my wedding photos?"

"MaCaz, did you really think I wouldn't search every nook and cranny for clues about my father? And a shoe box at the top of your wardrobe is not a very clever place to keep your secrets out of a teenager's reach."

"What did I teach you about respecting the privacy of others?"

"It was before the lesson had sunk in." She turned to Ammie, who was watching them with a hand clasped over her mouth. "Well, Grandma Ammie, do I look like Elijah, or more like the wicked César?"

If a pin had dropped it would have sounded like a hammer blow. All the humor drained from Ammie's features. At last she looked at Caz. "I want to speak to my granddaughter in private."

"I have a right to be told as well."

Ammie clicked her tongue. "It's not the only thing I want

to speak to her about. But fine. I don't know. She doesn't resemble either of the two. Satisfied?"

"Is that the truth?"

Ammie held Caz's gaze. "It is."

Caz sighed. She should have known it wouldn't be so easy. Nothing was ever easy. Not for her or for Lilah. "Fine, I'll leave you alone. But before I do, I want answers to two questions."

This time it was Ammie who sighed. "Well, take a seat. But keep it short." She sank down in her chair and Caz and Lilah followed suit.

Caz waited until Ammie looked at her. "Tieneke told me about a safe-deposit box in a bank in Pretoria that has some of your possessions in it. She gave me the key and said I could do with it as I pleased. But that was before we found you. I'll try to return the items to you, of course, but what are they? Please don't tell me they're nothing but an African mask and a figurine. I have good reason to think there's more to it."

"I don't want them back. I have no use for them. At the time I just felt it would be a shame to let them go to ruin." Ammie intertwined her fingers on her lap. "It is indeed a mask and a figurine, but I only found out in 1983 that they were valuable, so I asked Fien to put them in safekeeping. Apparently they'd been in her garage for more than twenty years before I contacted her."

How ironic, thought Caz. She grew up with the stuff lying in the garage and now she wanted at all cost to know what they were.

"What makes them valuable?" she asked.

"They were made by a well-known Congolese artist. He only became famous long after the objects came into my possession. Any art dealer specializing in African art would pay a few thousand euros for each of them. The artist's name is Aron Matari."

"Matari?" Caz's heart began to race.

"Yes, Tabia's nephew. The one who helped me flee. I told you about him on Sunday."

She had mentioned him, Caz remembered, without saying his last name, only referring to him as Aron. "How old would he be now?"

"He was a good ten years my junior. About eighteen at the time. Possibly about seventy-two by now."

"Did he have any children at the time?"

"No, but there was a son later, Arondji. He must be in his forties now. There was an exhibition of Aron's work in Antwerp. That's where I met the boy. Why all the questions?"

"Well, here's the second question: Do you have any idea who Erevu Matari might be?"

Ammie was quiet for a long time. Her eyes were restless. "When was he born?"

"I can find out." Caz didn't wait for Ammie to agree before she sent De Brabander a message.

Lieve peered around the door. "Coffee?"

"Not now, Lieve. Leave us alone." Ammie didn't look at her. Her eyes were glued to the phone in Caz's hand.

"Who do you think he could be, Grandma Ammie?" Lilah broke the silence after Lieve had left.

"Erevu. It means sly. Cunning. Shrewd." She didn't seem to notice that she hadn't answered Lilah's question.

Caz jumped when the phone pinged. She brought the screen closer to her eyes. "Born at Lubumbashi. June, 1961," she read aloud.

Ammie gasped. Her hand flew to her heart

"Grandma Ammie, who is he?" Lilah asked urgently.

Ammie struggled up from her chair so hastily that she nearly fell. Lilah hurried to her side and helped her regain her balance. Her bewildered eyes flew from Caz to Lilah.

Caz had also jumped up. "Mrs. Pauwels, what is it? What's wrong?"

Lieve opened the door and seemed uncertain about what to do next.

"He must be Tabia's son." Ammie's voice was croaky; her face wore an expression of fear. "Aron's son warned me against him. How do you know about him?"

"He might have something to do with Tieneke's death."

"Tabia's son," Ammie repeated. "Tabia's son by César. She wouldn't have given him the name without good reason. Tabia knew things. He was the product of a brute and a woman with magic powers."

Ammie looked up and pointed at Caz. "Your half-brother." Her eyes closed and her legs gave way. Lilah helped her to sit down.

The watery eyes fluttered open. "Go away! Go away! Lieve, who are these people? Lieve? Take them away!"

Caz tried to get through to her. "Ammie, Mrs. Pauwels! Please, tell us what you know."

"Lieve!" Ammie cried shrilly.

"Please! Let her alone, please!" Lieve pushed Caz and Lilah away. "Please!"

Caz was shaking all over when they came to a halt on the pavement outside. "Bloody hell."

"Fuck, that was intense," Lilah said. She was also trembling. "What just happened?"

"Let's just go." Caz headed for the car. "I'll phone Lieve later to hear if Ammie is okay."

"Kess! Kess!" Caz turned. Lieve came running towards them.

She stopped, breathless. "Miss Ammie. She insists that I tell you one more thing. She says ..." Lieve made the sign of the cross and muttered something, her eyes turned skyward. "She says the mask and the figurine. She says they are magic objects. Talisman stuff. Something about kissy."

"Kissy?"

"Something like that. I have to go back. The doctor is on his way. Oh, and she also said it has something to do with the ancestral spirits. Holy Mother Mary, keep us from evil." Lieve turned to go. Moments later they heard the front door slam.

Caz looked at a wide-eyed Lilah.

"Holy shit."

"Amen. Lilah, I need wine. Real wine. South African wine. A lot of it. Now."

"I agree." Lilah grabbed her mother's elbow and steered

her to the car. "And getting drunk isn't an option. It's a given."

*Luc*
*Ghent*

"I can be there in ninety minutes, Lieve." Luc covered his eyes with his hand. His heart had nearly stopped when he saw he'd had five calls from Lieve while he was in a group session. Fortunately everything seemed to be under control.

"There's no need, Professor, really. Unless you *want* to come, of course, but I don't think there's much point. The doctor gave her a light sedative and she's asleep now. It wasn't another stroke. Just a panic attack."

"What triggered it, Lieve? What caused her to panic?" If he got his hands on Caz Colijn now, he couldn't vouch for her life.

"It had something to do with a name. Tarie or something. And magic objects. Pagan stuff. She also said something about Tabie and César's son and that he must be the devil himself."

"Tabie or Tarie?"

"No, Tarie is the son, I think. Tabie is the mother."

At last the penny dropped. "Lieve, did she say Tabia?"

"Yes, Tabia. That's right. She makes magic and the son is sly and cunning. Tarie is Kess's half-brother."

Another penny. A disturbing one. "Lieve, the son—it's not Matari, is it?"

"That's right. Matari. Revu. Now I remember."

Erevu Matari. "Lieve, call me the minute Ammie wakes up or if anything happens. I have to go now."

"She's calm now, Professor. Don't worry."

Luc said goodbye and called De Brabander's number. Busy. He tried again. Still busy. He phoned Caz, but the phone just rang. He left her a message, speaking between clenched jaws: "Call me urgently."

To think De Brabander had wanted to return her passport.

*Erevu*
Ghent

And people called this place a prison. Bah! They should go to the Congo to see what prison was like.

He was a child the first time he had landed in one. For stealing a loaf of bread. Not because there was no food at home. Just because the bread looked good. White man's bread.

Mama Tabia got him out. That was when she decided he had to come to Belgium. His father's country of origin. Here he had to live on white man's food. How he had missed fufu, bananas tasting of the real thing, coconut milk. And warm rain.

He was a young man of twenty-five the second time he went to prison. In Uganda, while searching for Alice Auma Lakwena. There he learned how you get what you want in prison. Also how to get out. In Africa money talks and violence buys respect.

It had been worth it. He had found Alice Auma.

And he was going to reap the fruits as soon as he got out of here. With the nkísi in his possession, the spirit of Lakwena would come back and command the Alice Auma Lakwena Holy Army. He had intentionally chosen an English name. The whole world would sit up and take note of AALHA. The Congo was only the beginning. It was time for the whole planet to be rid of sinners.

He had thought Jela was with him, even though she had a different mission in mind. The mission of Kamau Kambon, and now of his son, Obadele Kambon.

The Kambons with their unique terminology. Father and son, both professors from Ghana, who believed that white people were aiming to exterminate all black people in a total genocide and had been doing so for centuries. Who were calling on all Africans to eliminate all whites.

About the liberation of Africa, he and Jela did not disagree, nor about re-Afrikanization. It was about dewhitenization that they disagreed. At an ideological level it sounded like a good idea, but in reality it was foolishness. They needed the white man's skills and knowledge on too many levels to eradicate whites at random. Once the expertise they needed had been fully assimilated, the ultimate goal could be pursued, but that would not happen in his lifetime, and possibly not in Jela's either. Dove's? Maybe.

A world without white land-grabbers. A world where people from Africa could define for themselves what civilization entailed.

For that to happen, they couldn't entirely rely on the Mongo ancestral spirits who were also the Tetela's forefathers. Alice Auma had proved it. They needed a white spirit to punish its white children for the robbery and the scorn with which they had treated, and were still treating, Motetela's children.

But first he had to get the nkísi. The nkísi, which would prove who and what he was.

*Caz*
*Leuven*

Lilah exhaled the smoke of her long menthol cigarette and took a sip of her wine. "Here we are," she sighed, "sitting at Abdij van 't Park in Leuven on Oom Paul Kruger's birthday. Two half-breeds with murderous genes."

Caz burst out laughing—a helpless laugh that took possession of her entire body.

"Hey, it's not that funny," Lilah said with a worried look in her eyes.

Somewhere during her fit of laughter Caz discovered that she was no longer laughing. She had burst into a flood of tears. She took the handful of tissues Lilah held out to her and tried to wipe her cheeks, but the tears kept coming.

So thin was the line between laughter and tears. Between funny and not funny. Joy and sorrow. Courage and despair. Valor and fear. Almost indistinguishable.

How many more times would she be pushed aside by a mother of sorts? Ammie, Magdel, Fien, now Ammie again. But that wasn't all.

Of course she had realized that there must have been a racial mix somewhere for her to have given birth to Lilah, but she had never thought it would be a father or grandfather. An old transgression of the immorality law on the Maritz side, perhaps, or one of Magdel's forefathers in days gone by who had fallen out of the family tree.

Now it turned out that she herself was of color. Despite her white skin. Whether Elijah was her biological father or not, whether she was the granddaughter of a woman of ill repute or not. Until Lilah had said it so comically, it hadn't really dawned on her. A half-breed. That was what she was.

It didn't turn her into anything or anyone other than Caz Colijn, but it was still a shock. An idea she would have to get used to.

Lilah let her be until she stopped crying. Caz blew her nose.

"Better?" Lilah asked, and pushed her refilled wineglass across the table.

Caz swallowed and nodded. "Sorry, probably a build-up of hysteria."

"You've been through a tough time. It's good that the pressure cooker's valve has blown."

"I'm so tired of thinking, so tired of trying to find out what's going on. Tired of unraveling. Tired of being a murder suspect. Tired of hearing that Ammie Pauwels thinks I'm the embodiment of evil. For the rest of the day I'd like to forget about genes, and background, and race, and worries."

Lilah raised her glass. "Ammie who?"

The lump was back in Caz's throat. "Lilah, I just want to tell you, you're truly exceptional. Not because you're beautiful or smart or funny. Or because you're black and have a mother who is white but has just found out she isn't. You're just exceptional, full stop."

"I'm your daughter, MaCaz. With a mother like you ... how could I be anything but exceptional? And by the way, we're multiracial, not just plain black or white. Multiracialism is also an identity."

Looking out on the lake over which the deck of the restaurant was suspended, Caz allowed the silence to lengthen. "I think Ammie is right," she said at last. "I have murderous genes. If I thought anyone wanted to hurt you, I would kill him with my bare hands."

"No, that's not murderous genes. I feel the same about you. But I do think there's a spell on you. It must originate from those kissy things Grandma Ammie carried with her while she was pregnant with you. Your kind of bad luck doesn't come naturally. Perhaps we should consult a witch doctor the next time we're in Cape Town together."

"Witch doctor isn't a politically correct term." The reprimand came automatically, though she knew, as always, Lilah was masking gravity with humor. It was a defense mechanism. One she sometimes took too far.

Lilah grinned. "I don't have to be PC. I'm black ... multiracial."

"Lilah." Caz peered over the rim of her glass like a schoolteacher over her spectacles.

"Okay. Let's be both politically and ethnically correct. We'll get a sangoma. Not one of those who can lengthen a man's penis. Aubrey already ..."

"Too much information! Especially for an old hag who hasn't had sex in years. Spare me, Lilah."

"Years? Sheesh, MaCaz, that's not healthy. If fifty is the new forty, as they say, you're at your peak."

Caz shrugged.

"There must have been sex somewhere along the line?"

She knew Lilah was trying to distract her from the things Ammie had said. And, yes, maybe they could just sit back and play at being mother and daughter, like they used to before this hornet's nest was uncovered. Before she heard she had a black half-brother who was probably an accessory to her foster sister's murder. Before she ... Enough!

"Pretoria, 2004. Before I decided to go to the Cape. It lasted three months."

"Then he found out about me?"

"Then I told him about you. Proudly. It was his reaction that made me decide to take a month's leave and find somewhere else to live, shake the dust of the north off my feet. I arrived in Stanford and saw the estate agent advertising the smallholding. The rest is history."

Lilah sighed. "Was the sex at least good while it lasted?"

"Average."

"Hell. And before that?"

"Shortly after you went overseas the first time. Two months."

"Then he found out."

"Hmm. No loss. Great sex, but the man wasn't exactly a nuclear physicist."

"And before that?"

"Nada. Only your father."

Lilah mused for a moment. "We must find you a man before you're over the hill. Not to marry, just for fun. This time intelligence is a prerequisite. You deserve a smart man."

"He must be taller than me," Caz played along.

"And something for the eye."

"And unmarried."

"And he must be able to handle the fact that your daughter is black."

"And that I have murderous genes. That I might even be bewitched."

"Sheesh, MaCaz, it's a tall order."

"Never mind, maybe my peak will soon be over. Cheers."

# Thirty-seven

*Saturday, October 11*
*Caz*
*Ghent*

Caz couldn't remember when last she'd had a hangover, but she knew she had definitely never had such a bad one.

She looked up with bleary eyes when Lilah breezed in, holding two glasses of orange juice. "Come, get yourself out on the terrace. You need fresh air. And vitamin C."

"Toilet," Caz mumbled, dragging herself out of bed and into the bathroom. She realized she had left her toothbrush behind. Fetched it. Stumbled back to the bathroom.

Lilah put out her cigarette when Caz came out onto the terrace. "Welcome to the hereafter. Come, drink your juice so that you can get your strength back. And take two painkillers, while you're at it."

Caz sank into a chair and gulped down half the orange juice. It was too sweet and not cold enough, but it helped against the dry mouth. She swallowed the tablets with an effort.

Lilah had her iPhone in her hand. "Here's an update. It's not kissy-something, it's nkísi. Nkísi are spirits. Or objects, like figurines or a variety of other thing that contain spirits. They are linked to the ancestral spirits.

"Wikipedia is a bit muddled, but it looks as if these nkísi become nkísi nkondi once the spirits are activated. This is done by hammering metal tacks into the object. They reckon this is where practices like voodoo originated. Nkondi originally meant hunter, but nkísi nkondi are used for various purposes, like vengeance, the swearing of an oath or to provide protection."

"Lilah, I don't have the mental energy. Not this morning. And by the way, how the hell did you get us home after all that wine?"

"Sheesh, you really overdid it if you don't remember. In the first place, I drank a lot less than you and I stuck to water for the last hour or two. The pasta also helped."

Caz had only a dim recollection of food.

"Do you remember we're going to Damme today?"

Caz made the mistake of shaking her head. She shut her eyes tightly. "No, I don't remember. Why Damme?"

"We googled Tijl Uilenspiegel and we came across Damme. The Belgians claim it's where he's buried."

Caz shuddered to think why they had googled Tijl Uilenspiegel. Especially after Lilah's decision that she needed a man in her life.

"Oh, and I found your phone in the car, where it must have fallen out of your handbag. You didn't even notice it was gone. There are a few missed calls. From TU2 and DB. Whoever they may be."

"Oh, shit. De Brabander. The detective." Caz sat up. "Where's my phone?"

"I put it next to your bed a while ago. I'll fetch it."

"Never mind, I'll get it." Gingerly Caz got to her feet, fetched the phone and moved to the corner of the terrace. No Grevers, she noticed while the phone was ringing.

"Ms. Colijn, at last."

"Good morning, Commissioner. Sorry, I mislaid my phone. I've only just seen you've been looking for me."

"Yes, initially to tell you you may have your passport back. Then to tell you unfortunately that's no longer possible now I've learned that Erevu Matari is most likely your half-brother."

Caz's heart sank. She should have phoned him, told him herself what she had found out. Immediately. But she had been in such a bloody state and ... No, damn it. What business was it of anyone? "How did you find out if I heard it only yesterday myself?"

"Professor DeReu phoned me with the interesting scrap of information. And of course we don't know whether you really found out for the first time yesterday."

Caz chose to remain silent. Her mind wasn't as clear as it could be.

"Ms. Colijn, when are you going to tell me what you're hiding? What is it that you're not telling me?"

That there was a spell on her and that she had the key to a strongbox in a South African bank, which contained wooden objects imbued with ancestral spirits? Objects you could hammer nails into to activate the spirits in order to take revenge or seek protection? No, surely she couldn't tell that to a detective born in a country that supposedly invented French fries?

"Ms. Colijn?" he reminded her that she hadn't answered.

"Commissioner, whether we're related or not, I don't know Erevu Matari from Adam and I give you my word that yesterday was the first time I heard he might be my half-brother. I was not involved in the murder. That's all that's important. I want to go home. My flight has been booked for the fourteenth. Could you please arrest me for whatever it is, or return my passport? I don't want to play this game any more."

There was a long silence on the other end. "It'll be on your conscience if you allow a murderer to go free. The way things look now, he might be sentenced to a few months in prison. There's not enough evidence. But okay, you may have your passport back. I'll ask Grevers to bring it to you. If he's allowed to intrude during your daughter's visit, of course."

"As long as it's before eleven. We're going out."

"So noted, but it will depend on Inspector Grevers's schedule. If he can't make it before eleven, he'll leave your passport at your guesthouse. Your phone as well. We removed the spyware. Good day, Ms. Colijn."

Caz couldn't care less about his bad mood. She considered listening to DeReu's message, but decided against it. Bloody snitch. Her brain was too fuzzy anyway. To find out whether Ammie had got over her distress as well. Besides, Ammie had chased them away. She doubted a call to enquire about the state of Ammie's health would be welcomed.

"And?" Lilah asked when she turned.

"I can have my passport back, but I think the detective is cheesed off with me. Most likely because he doesn't have enough evidence to arrest me. I think he's still convinced I'm the mastermind behind Tieneke's murder."

"Well, he's wrong. Besides, a life without enemies is boring. Cheer up. Take a shower, put on some make-up. We'll paint the town of Damme red."

*Luc*
*Damme*

Thanks to his cleaning spree last Saturday there was little to do today. Outside it was misty, with an occasional light shower, alternated by slivers of blue sky and a few rays of pale sunshine doing their best to break through the clouds. Hopefully the blue sky would get the better of the drizzle in a while.

His frame of mind wasn't exactly sunny either. According to Lieve, Ammie was back where she had been before. Behind veils. She seldom spoke, slept a lot, barely ate. The doctor reckoned the cause was psychological rather than physical. If she was no better by Monday, the doctor wanted Lieve to make an appointment with a psychiatrist.

The matter of Matari being Caz Colijn's half-brother was

now in De Brabander's hands. He would have to determine whether there had been a conspiracy or not. What the connection was between the two.

Caz Colijn had ignored his message. She probably didn't want to admit she had pushed Ammie over the edge. Or maybe she didn't want to face the fact that she was related to a murderer. Okay, alleged murderer. Well, actually, alleged accomplice of an alleged murderer.

Whatever the case, he was definitely not going to call her again. It wouldn't be wise anyway. He was way too angry. He might say something that was better left unsaid.

It wasn't just about Ammie either. He was tired of racking his brains about the woman. Tired of trying to work out why he should care about her at all, except where Ammie was concerned.

He was a fool, but even fools sometimes had insight into their own foolishness.

He blamed the year he had spent in South Africa. The country—problems and all—had got under his skin. The splendor, the natural beauty, the weather and, yes, the people as well. Their approach to life, which was so much less conventional than over here.

Caz Colijn represented that incomprehensible and romanticized longing that had stayed with him after his return. A longing not only for the country and its people, but for the man he had briefly thought he might be if he could break his ties with the nonentity he had become.

Moments later, when the sun broke through the clouds again, Luc put on his windbreaker and went out. A long walk might clear his head. Get rid of the worst of his frustration.

*Caz*
*Damme*

"You have no idea why we've come here, right?" Lilah asked as they covered the last few kilometers to Damme.

"Something to do with the professor?"

"The prof? Hell, no, why would it have anything to do with him?" Lilah glanced briefly at her. "Does he live here?"

Caz shook her head. "I have no idea where he lives, but I assume it's in Ghent. He lectures there, I believe."

"So?"

"His alias was Tijl Uilenspiegel. That's where TU comes from." Hopefully it would satisfy her.

"I see."

"What do you see?"

"Last night you rattled on about Tijl Uilenspiegel who said the things that happen to you are your own fault. When I asked who the hell Tijl Uilenspiegel was, you told me about the medieval trickster and all the stories about him. Then you said you'd like to meet Tijl Uilenspiegel. So I googled and read about Damme. And I teased you and said we could visit his grave. That's when we decided to come here." Lilah glanced at her again. "Actually I thought you were going on about the storybook character. That it was the trickster himself you were after. But now I'm wondering."

"Of course I was talking about the storybook character." Had to be.

"You remember that, but you don't remember the rest?"

"I remember now. Let it go, will you? Look at the beautiful scenery. The canal on one side, the avenue of trees on the other. Oh, and look at the windmill!" She meant what she was saying, though she was also trying to change the subject.

"And there's a canal boat."

"Lamme Goedzak," Caz read out the name of the boat. "Tijl Uilenspiegel's friend, if my memory serves me right. Lilah, this place speaks to me."

"You said it about Bruges too."

"Yes, but this is different. Bruges is a city. Damme is a village."

Lilah turned right onto the bridge over the canal.

Caz looked down the street as they got out of the car. The medieval houses and street cafés with their steep, rusty-red tiled roofs on either side, the flags fluttering in front of the sedate town hall, everything struck a chord with her.

It was exactly the right place to forget about cold-blooded mothers, evil fathers and enigmatic nkísi and ancestral spirits. At least acting like a tourist was less harmful than succumbing to alcohol.

While Lilah was collecting brochures at the tourist office, Caz glanced at the books on the shelf. Wherever she looked, she saw Tijl Uilenspiegel.

"Pick one," Lilah spoke behind her. "You spoiled me with Afrikaans books and CDs, I want to buy you a book to remind you of today."

She selected one by Henri van Daele. The illustrations were too modern for her liking, but the quotation on the cover was the deciding factor.

*"Let us drink to the lark that sings the song of freedom!" said the skipper.*

*"To the cock, that crows the war cry!" said Uilenspiegel.*

She found it suitable for someone from a continent where the cock's crow so often drowns out the lark's song.

*Luc*
*Damme*

After coffee in Lapscheure, Luc decided to walk back. It was no good. If he had to keep walking to improve his mood, he would end up in Knokke.

An hour and a half later, perspiring inside his rain-soaked windbreaker, Luc was back in Damme. Not ready to go home, he stepped into a small restaurant. It was too stuffy inside for his overheated body, so he ordered a kriek and sat down on the veranda.

Totally unfit, that was him. He used to walk for two or three hours without breaking a sweat. He liked cycling, but today it wouldn't have been enough of a challenge.

"Alstublieft." The glass of kriek and a book were placed in front of him. "Thanks for this. A thrilling read. Something to eat?"

"Not just now, thanks. First I'll quench my thirst." He smiled at the woman who was the life and soul of the restaurant.

One of the few people he lent his books to, precisely because she always returned them promptly.

"Shout when you're ready."

Just as he was raising the glass to his lips, he noticed the woman approaching in the distance. He forgot to take a sip. He gazed at the breathtakingly beautiful creature, taller than tall, with the figure of a supermodel, a bubbly laugh, and African braids that bounced as she walked. She put her arm around the shoulders of the woman by her side and kissed the top of her head.

That was the kind of spontaneity he'd so often seen in South Africa.

It was only when he raised his glass again that he glanced at the companion. Just in time he stopped the glass from slipping through his fingers. That hair could belong to only one woman. Only one known to him, at any rate. He swallowed hastily, grabbed the book, opened it near the middle and held it in front of his face while trying to peer over the top.

Caz Colijn in Damme. Probably with her daughter. Was it bloody well possible?

Evidently. And they had to go and pick this restaurant. He slumped lower in his chair and raised the book to hide his face. He didn't think she knew what he looked like, but he wasn't going to take a chance.

After all the dithering about a possible meeting with her, it was the last thing he wanted to happen now. His thoughts would just start seesawing all over again.

The next time he took a cautious look, Caz was seated with her back to him, a good distance away. But the daughter looked him in the eye and smiled. A breathtaking smile.

*Caz*
*Damme*

"Are you sure it's not too cold? I can skip the smoke."

Caz shook her head. "I'm not cold and I know you want that cigarette after all the walking we did. I'm just glad we could find a place under cover—the only one it seems. It looks as if it's about to start raining again."

"We smokers have an eye for a place that's sheltered from the wind and weather. More or less, anyway. What are you drinking?"

"Anything but wine. I'll try a kriek. Lindemans, if they've have."

"Is it my imagination, or have you become quite a kriek connoisseur?"

A friendly woman in an apron came out, placed the menus in front of them and took their orders.

Lilah picked up the menu. "MaCaz, don't turn round." She kept her voice low. "But I spy with my little eye ..." Her eyebrows bounced up and down.

"What do you spy?"

"A possible candidate."

"For?"

"You. Slouched down in his chair at present, but he looks tall enough. Snazzy glasses. About your age. Still has all his hair. That earns him double points. On the thin side, so chances are he won't have a beerbelly. And ... drrrumrrroll ... he's reading. Not a newspaper, not an e-reader, a real book. Lee Child, no less, even though it's in Dutch." Lilah clasped her hands melodramatically. "A match made in heaven, if he happens to be unmarried."

"Belgians read, Lilah. Real books. In Dutch. And if the I-spy man is such a hunk, he'll be married. And even if he isn't, what do you suggest I do? Go across and say: Hi, I'm Caz. I haven't had sex for ten years and I'll only be in Belgium a few more days. So how's about a roll in the hay? That is, if you don't have a problem with the fact that I'm multiracial and possessed by ancestral spirits."

"Hmm. I see your point, but it's a good thought. By the way, he's drinking kriek too. If only he would lower the book slightly, I could see if he's really such a dish."

Caz rolled her eyes, but wished she could look over her shoulder. Lilah had roused her curiosity. The poor man. His ears must be ringing.

The kriek arrived. Lilah suggested they should wait until they were closer to home before they had something to eat and Caz agreed.

They spoke about Tijl Uilenspiegel, his grave, the artwork all over the town depicting him and his friends, the museum dedicated to him, all the names of restaurants linked to the odd trickster from the Middle Ages. But Caz remained annoyingly aware of the man's presence behind her.

"Take a look when we leave," Lilah whispered urgently when at last they got up from the table.

As if she wouldn't have anyway.

Caz caught him at the moment he peered over the top of the book. Gaping at Lilah, she supposed. But no, he was looking at her. Their eyes met and locked before he hastily lowered his gaze.

Lilah had been right. Not a dish, exactly, but there was a certain sexy quality about him. He looked kind of familiar too. His hair was longish in the neck, but fashionably styled on top. If it wasn't the mophead from the Graslei, she would eat her scarf. She averted her eyes and headed for the exit.

It was weird. Really weird.

Caz looked up when Lilah dug her elbow into her ribs, motioning with her eyes at the man. Caz shook her head, annoyed. Yet she couldn't stop herself from taking another look. Straight into his eyes.

He gave a slight nod, raised his book and carried on reading.

Suddenly she knew. It was bloody Luc DeReu who was hiding behind Lee Child. He was the one who had been at the Graslei and had seen her talk to Njiwa. Who had sent the smileys while pretending to be busy on his phone. And he knew exactly who she was.

Tijl Uilenspiegel, indeed. The kind of man who turns one's life upside down and then walks whistling into the sunset.

A reckless feeling took hold of her. "Wait for me." She pulled her new book from its bag, turned on her heel and strode to his table.

He looked up at her, clearly embarrassed.

"Would you mind signing your biography for me?" she asked with a feigned smile, opening the book at the title page.

He sat motionless for a moment before he put Lee Child down. Retrieving a pen from his inside pocket, he took the book from her. "With pleasure."

His silver hair slid forward as he bent over the book and began to write. He returned the book with a lopsided grin. "Alstublieft."

"Dank uw wel." Caz returned to Lilah, who was staring at her, flabbergasted, and linked Lilah's arm with her own. "I reckon we can tick Damme off the list, don't you agree?"

Lilah looked down at her and then over her shoulder before they started for the cabriolet. "Well, I never. Are you going to tell me what happened there?"

"In the car. Just keep walking and help me if my legs give way. They feel like jelly."

"You're in love? So soon?"

"No, I'm livid. Have been for a long time. Now more than ever."

*Luc*
*Damme*

He should have gone over right at the beginning, introduced himself and improvised from there. It had been an excellent opportunity to determine whether she was the witch or the fairy godmother. But no. The coward in him took over and was stupid enough to be caught.

Goodness knows how she had known who he was.

As the BMW drove away he closed his eyes and drew the moist air deep into his lungs. He could detect the scent of flowers. It smelt like her. When he opened his eyes, the cabriolet was crossing the bridge. It turned left in the direction of Bruges and disappeared from view.

*Caz*
*Damme*

"What are you saying? The prof? Luc DeReu? That was him?"
"Yep."
"How do you know?"
"I've seen him before. I just didn't realize it."
"Why are you angry with him?"
"Because he's hand in glove with De Brabander. Telling tales behind my back, making me look even more suspect than I already do. And that after he blatantly lied to me. Pretended to be a friend of Luc DeReu's. One day he's nice, the next he suspects me of all kinds of things. Including being a danger to Ammie. Besides, it was clear he knew me. Hiding behind a book. Why? Bloody coward."
"Okay, but when was he nice?"
"He congratulated me on my birthday." She sighed. "And apparently he helped save my life. When Matari threw me into the Dijle."
"Ah. Saved your life. And that's all?"
Caz kept silent. Lilah's sarcasm didn't deserve an answer.
"What did he write, damn it?"
Caz took a deep breath and opened the book. "To Caz. Pleased to meet you. Tijl Uilenspiegel."
"That's all?"
"That's all." Lord knows why she was upset. Lord knows why the silver hair falling over his forehead had stuck in her memory. That and the picture of the lean hand holding a pen in such an intimate way.

# Thirty-eight

*Sunday, October 12*
*Caz*
*Ghent*

De Brabander kept his word. Her passport and her phone were delivered to the guesthouse.

Erdem looked slightly relieved when she took her leave. Nevertheless he put his arms around Caz and gave her three kisses on alternate cheeks. He sounded sincere when he wished her everything of the best for the future.

"Okay. Amsterdam, here we come," Lilah said as they drove away.

The day was misty and cool. They had crossed the border into the Netherlands by the time Lilah was able to let the top down.

"We'll have lunch at the Zaanse Schans. It's the quaintest place. Windmills galore. Then we'll take the city streets. And tonight we're staying at a decent hotel. Herbergh Something-or-the-other. There are several restaurants to choose from. Oh, and in the morning the cabriolet will be returned to the rental people and we'll take the shuttle to Schiphol. From there I'll take the Thalys to Paris."

"My superefficient daughter. I could never have imagined you'd be so organized."

"Neither could I, but I must admit I learned from Aubrey. Every minute of his day goes like clockwork and pity the poor soul who throws a spanner in his works."

Sounded like a control freak, thought Caz. A businessman, Lilah had said a few days ago when Caz asked how Aubrey made his living. Import and export. "When do I meet the remarkable Aubrey?"

"In January, if it's okay with you. We have reservations at one of the hotels in Hermanus from the fourth to the eighth. Then on to Cape Town for four days before it's back to the salt mines and the freezing cold."

"Of course it's okay, but why stay at a hotel?"

Lilah glanced at her. "It's better that way, MaCaz. Believe me, Aubrey can be quite demanding."

It didn't sound promising, but Caz decided to reserve judgment until she had met the man. She was certainly not the world's best authority on men. And she was biased. No man could ever be good enough for her Lilah.

*Luc*
*Damme*

Luc tried to read, but he could not concentrate. He kept smelling flowers. His thoughts kept returning to those forty minutes at the restaurant. If he had done this, if he had acted like that. Over and over he reviewed the events and changed the outcome.

Caz resembled Ammie after all, he had realized last night. Especially the Ammie he had known as a young woman. The nose, the chin, something about the mouth. That beautiful mouth.

Luc closed the book and pulled a Jean-Claude van Damme DVD from the shelf. Ten minutes later he switched off the DVD player. The man irritated him no end.

At his wits' end, he logged onto the internet. Read every Belgian newspaper he could find. Read a free quota of Network24 reports on events in South Africa. The country was still plagued by crime. There were few murders in Brussels and most were related to drugs or failed love affairs. And yet, Caz's foster sister was murdered here, in Ghent. And in Leuven, Caz was assaulted and could have died. Did she drag violence along with her like a comet its tail of gas and dust?

That was what she was in his life. A comet shooting past. One of those rare ones that made its brief appearance in the night sky only once every decade or even century.

Thank goodness she was on her way back. Hopefully his life would return to normal.

The disappointment he felt because he would never get to know the woman who had caught his eye at the Graslei was nothing but foolishness.

*Monday, October 13*
*Caz*
*Amsterdam*

The hotel shuttle dropped them at the airport at eight. Lilah helped Caz weigh in, and with the lilac case now at 22.9 kilograms and very little hand luggage, there was no problem at all. She even got a window seat.

The farewell was tearful, but December was just around the corner, they kept assuring each other.

Caz followed Lilah with her eyes as she walked away with long strides and bouncing braids. Heads turned as far as she went, but Lilah seemed oblivious. Caz felt as if her heart would burst. With pride, but also with longing, already tugging at her heartstrings.

She waved when Lilah looked over her shoulder and wiggled her long fingers in a final farewell. Caz was left to her own devices until she had to go through the security gate.

She would look for a gift for Annika before she went to find the right gate.

On the plane Caz took out the Tijl Uilenspiegel book.

She had no wish to sit and brood about things she could do nothing about. Hopefully the book would distract her.

After an initial struggle she got into it. Flemish was easier on paper than on the ear.

Every so often she looked through the window. Tried to guess where they were as they flew over African plains and deserts.

Hours later, the lights of Johannesburg flickered far below the wing of the plane. Caz's ears ached during the landing but not as much as when she landed in Cape Town.

So far, Van Daele's book had been a disappointment. The Tijl Uilenspiegel she remembered from her childhood wasn't nearly as inconsiderate, borderline mean and arrogant. Maybe it was the translation. Maybe she was just older and hopefully wiser. Maybe she was just better able to put herself in others' shoes today and that was why her sympathy lay mostly with his victims, rather than with Tijl.

Van Daele's Tijl was a know-it-all who stepped all over people, didn't trust anyone, and took no responsibility. He messed with people because he thought himself superior and cleverer and went his merry way.

But in the end she wasn't sure whether she was passing judgment on a fictional Tijl or bloody Luc DeReu, whose unbidden image kept popping into her mind.

Her luggage wasn't first to emerge, but neither was it last. The angels were smiling on her today. And hopefully tomorrow too. No, she didn't want to think about tomorrow. Not even speculate about the answers she might get, or about exactly what the nkísi would be.

She walked unchallenged through the green zone and began to look for directions to the car-hire counters. She still had to find out from Annika where she had arranged accommodation for her. She would switch off the roaming function on her phone in a while and call Annika. First she had to rent a car.

"Surprise!" a voice behind her cried out moments later.

Caz turned. "Annika!"

"If you weren't so bloody tall I would give you a proper

hug. Would I allow my favorite translator to muddle along on her own? Let's get you home. I have a lasagne in the oven and a bottle of wine on ice. You're staying at my place. I want to hear all about your trip and that parcel you sent. I'm dying of curiosity."

"You're a darling," Caz managed to get a word in. Annika liked to talk, Caz recalled. Not that she minded. The sound of Afrikaans was music to her ears.

*Tuesday, October 14*
*Caz*
*Pretoria*

At half past seven Caz was raring to go. She'd had three cups of coffee. Her luggage was in the trunk of the car. Her backpack was packed. She had kept out her handbag. The key was in the pocket of her jeans.

Last night she let Lilah know that she had arrived safely, but so far there had been no reply. She didn't want to bother the child again. She was probably up to her ears in work after her short break.

She had told Annika that she had mailed her the key because she was afraid she might lose it during her travels. She explained that the key would open a safe-deposit box that contained something she had inherited, but that she didn't know what it was.

"Are you sure you won't have breakfast?" Annika asked.

"I couldn't, even if I wanted to. I'm too tense."

"Okay, I'll tell you what, we'll take the scenic route to kill time. Let me show you all your old stomping grounds on our way to the bank."

Caz nodded, relieved. Anything was better than just sitting there, waiting for the hands of the clock to move.

Annika shoved her handbag under the driver's seat before she got in. "Put yours out of sight as well. The joys of living in our dearest country." She gave a wry smile.

At the security gate to the townhouse complex she waved to the guard, who acknowledged her with a broad smile.

Caz hardly recognized the city where she had grown up and spent a large part of her life. Even though the jacarandas were in full bloom.

Her heart grieved for the Hatfield she remembered. Sunnyside, where she had taken long strolls with Lilah in her pram, had changed unrecognisably. Sadly, not for the better.

She shook her head when Annika asked whether she would like to go to Meyerspark to see her former home.

A few minutes before opening time, Annika pulled into a parking lot in Silverton.

To Caz the centre looked as if it could belong in any other African country. Fenced off by a green palisade, papers fluttering in the breeze. On the other side of the fence, the fronds of a palm tree rustled softly. The place looked deserted, except for a number of minibus taxis. A few people emerged from one and strolled inside.

"I'll wait here, Caz. I have a few calls to make and an email to reply to. Thank goodness for smartphones."

"Are you sure? It might take a while."

"Not long enough for me to do anything more productive than what I can do on my phone."

"Will you be safe?" Caz couldn't help asking.

"I'll lock the doors and keep my eyes open. I'm used to the city, you country bumpkin."

"I must say, it's like another planet to me."

"You're lucky down in the Cape. Go on in."

Caz heard the sound of the doors being locked and saw the lights flash the moment she shut the car door behind her.

A huge Shoprite sign kept watch over the entrance to the mall. Some of the smaller stores were still closed but inside it was already bustling. Cleaners, people with cellphones at their ears, Shoprite customers—some going in, some already on their way out, carrying their shopping in plastic bags. So different from Ghent or Leuven.

The door of the bank opened as she approached, yet she wasn't the first client to enter.

She was second in line at the enquiries counter. She kept

looking around her. Was Njiwa watching the mall in case she came earlier to avoid him? Would she see him in time? Here, where he wouldn't be conspicuous because his skin was dark? Where she was the one who drew glances instead?

At last it was her turn.

"Good morning. I don't really know how it works but I want to get access to a safe-deposit box. I presume the manager ..." she began in Afrikaans.

"Sorry, I don't speak Afrikaans." The woman was unapologetic, but not impolite.

Caz switched to English. "I presume the manager has to accompany me to my safe-deposit box?"

"The safe?" The woman frowned. "No one can get to the safe."

"No, not the bank's safe, I mean the personal strongboxes. Where clients keep their valuable possessions?"

"Sorry, I don't understand what you mean. The safe belongs to the bank."

Caz stifled a sigh. "Could I please see the manager?"

"Do you have an appointment?"

"No, I flew in from Europe last night, so I was unable make an appointment."

A shake of the head. "Sorry, but without an appointment I can't help you. You can make one but it will only be for tomorrow."

"I'm on my way to Cape Town. My flight leaves in a couple of hours. Please, I must see the manager."

The woman sighed. "What's your name?"

"Cassandra Colijn. The box is in the name of Josefien Colijn."

"I'll see what I can do. Please wait here." She waved towards a row of chairs against the wall.

Caz sat down on the edge of a chair. Five minutes later the woman was back.

"The manager can squeeze you in between appointments. His assistant will call you."

It was a full thirteen minutes before she was taken to a booth with four orange plastic chairs and a round melamine table. The manager was a man in his early forties with a drawn face and fine veins on his cheeks.

"Good morning, ma'am. Barend Stols," he said. "How can I help you?"

"I would like to remove the contents from my mother's safe-deposit box and close the account. She was Josefien Colijn and she recently died ..." She fell silent when he began to shake his head.

"We haven't had any private boxes for years, ma'am. If we ever had any."

Caz took Tieneke's note from her handbag and showed it to him. "The branch moved to this location, I know, and according to this note the boxes were transferred here."

"Mrs. Colijn, it's donkey's years since the branch moved here." He looked at the note again. "This dates back almost eleven years."

"But what could have happened to the box? It contains my mother's property. Left at the bank for safekeeping."

He raised his hands and got to his feet. "I'm sorry, ma'am, I can't help you. There must have been some communication between the bank and the person who rented the box, but it's not information I can access. It was long before my time."

"But ..."

"I'm sorry, you'll have to excuse me. I have an appointment with a client. It's a pity people don't keep their personal information up to date. It happens all the time with estates. Try your mother's attorney. Or the executor. They might know more."

The notary was in a country where banks remain in the same spot for centuries and had no information other than a note and a key in an envelope that he had kept safe. The executor of her so-called mother's estate had been murdered. Thanks for nothing.

"Thank you for your time," was all she said. She would have to take up the matter with one of his seniors. Someone who actually cared about the repercussions when a bank allowed a client's strongbox to get lost.

With an irritated gesture, Caz draped the straps of her handbag over her shoulder and pushed the note into the same pocket where the key was.

When she walked out through the revolving door, she wasn't nearly as annoyed with the bank as with Fien and Ammie Pauwels. Couldn't they have handled their bloody affairs better?

Njiwa would probably be waiting for her here on the sixteenth, guess that she had come sooner when she failed to arrive, or think that she was coming later and wait a few more days, but what would happen then? He would go straight to Stanford, probably strangle her as well and still not get what he was looking for.

She had to find out whether the box really contained nothing but "two wooden objects" before she could decide what to do next. Whether to let De Brabander know what Matari and Njiwa were after. What he could do about it from Belgium was a different matter. At least he might stop believing that she was the kingpin who refused to give her accomplices their due. Besides, she had to know what was in the strongbox before she could decide how to outwit Njiwa. Or whether she should just hand him the bloody mask and figurine.

They might have value as items of African art and Ammie might have carried them with her on her flight through Africa, evidently to protect her child and herself, but she was certainly not prepared to sacrifice her life for the sake of money and sentiment. Njiwa could take his bloody nkísi and go, as long as he left her alone. Not that she could see it happen, but she supposed there was a chance.

But for now she could do nothing. Make no plans. Just wait for her tongue bone to be crushed as well. In vain.

Unless ... Moerdyk. Would Moerdyk know?

Caz jumped back, startled, when a minibus taxi came racing towards her and braked sharply. She was berating herself for not watching where she was going when the sliding door was flung open in front of her. Someone grabbed her arm, yanked her handbag from her other arm and tried to drag her inside. Caz gripped the doorframe and held on.

The taxi began to move. Shouts sounded from various directions. Caz lost her balance. Her knees grazed the tarmac while she tried to break free from the painful grip on her arm.

Hands grabbed her from behind and wrenched her away from the minibus. Her eyes met those of the man who had been trying to drag her into the taxi. It was Njiwa, but not the Njiwa she remembered. His face was twisted with rage. He shouted something and the taxi pulled away with screaming tires.

"Sorry, Madam, sorry, Madam. Eish. You hurt? Bad man, very bad man." Caz looked up at an old man who was gently trying to lay her down on the tar. His face showed suffering but his gaze was clear.

"Tsotsis. Bad tsotsis."

Caz tried to suppress her tears of fear and rage. "Thank you. Thank you so much." Her knees burned like fire.

He shouted something in an indigenous language.

A woman in a traditional shweshwe dress kneeled by her side. "Ma'am? Can I call the ambulance? The police?"

Caz shook her head. An ambulance was unnecessary. The police wouldn't help her, just slow her down. She had no strength for endless explanations that would lead nowhere.

Annika's car drew up beside her. "Bloody hell, Caz, are you okay?" she gasped.

"I'm fine. This man saved me." She turned, but the old man was gone.

"What happened?" Annika asked the black woman.

"They tried to steal her. The tsotsis."

"The man who saved me, where is he?" Caz asked anxiously.

Annika looked around. "What does he look like?"

"Black, elderly. Dressed in overalls, I think."

"He left, ma'am. Ran back to the taxi he was just getting into when he saw what was happening. Will you be all right now?" the woman asked.

"I'll be okay. Thank you, you've been very kind."

"No problem, ma'am. Eish, what is this country coming to?"

With a wave of her hand, the woman walked away, her back straight.

"Fuck it, Caz. What happened? I saw that fucking taxi race towards you. I shouted to try to warn you, then I heard the commotion." Annika's voice was shrill. She had to be scared out of her wits, because Caz had never heard her swear before.

"It's a long story." Caz tried to get up, but her knees refused to cooperate. Annika helped her to her feet and she limped to the car. Njiwa must have figured she would come earlier. He had probably been waiting for days. The taxi was almost certainly one of those that had already been there when she went into the bank.

"Something to do with the key?"

Caz nodded. Her hand went to the pocket of her jeans. The key was still there. Regretfully so, actually. He might as well have taken the damn key that didn't unlock anything anyway.

Annika had just switched the engine on when there was a knock on the window.

Caz looked up, startled. A security guard. She opened the window a chink.

"The other taxi driver. He saw the taxi that's not allowed to pick up people here. He was here yesterday as well. The driver wrote down the registration. I called the police. They're on their way. You must wait."

Caz sighed and looked at Annika, who shrugged.

"I can't. I have to get to the airport. I'm flying to Cape Town." She was still en route on an international flight and had to be there two hours ahead of time.

He shook his head. "You must wait."

# Thirty-nine

*Caz*
*Cape Town*

Caz sat down on her suitcase to take the weight off her knees. She was in pain, despite Annika's effort to take her to a pharmacy where her wounds were attended to while waiting for the police. She was convinced all her previous aches and pains had also decided to kick in again. She was a bloody wreck.

Hopefully the guys from the long-stay company were on their way with her car. Without her cellphone her hands were tied, but Annika had informed them of the time of Caz's arrival and where she would be waiting.

Thank goodness for Annika. She had cut the interview with the police short. The police had assumed Caz had just been in the wrong place at the wrong time. An incidental victim. The two men in the taxi must have seen her enter the bank and thought she had cash on her person.

Caz didn't enlighten them. What could she tell them? The man had wanted to kidnap her because he was after the nkísi she had inherited? He had most likely murdered a woman six thousand kilometers away? Unfortunately, she didn't know his name. Neither did she know where the nkísi were.

Besides, she and the policeman had found it hard to understand each other. The other taxi drivers kept interrupting to rant about the new taxi stealing their clients. A babble of voices ensued.

She had given all her details and a case docket was opened. Robbery and attempted abduction. For what it was worth.

At last she was home. Well, almost.

A drive of nearly two hours lay ahead before she'd get to Stanford, and she still had to pick up Catya at the cattery, but she would be home well before sunset. She wasn't keen on arriving after dark, though common sense told her Njiwa couldn't possibly already be waiting.

She remembered she would have to pick up her house keys from the security people. Her own set had been in her handbag. How convenient for Njiwa. She would have to replace the locks, probably a futile exercise, but one more item on a long list of things that needed to be done. Thankfully she had left the remote with the security people as well.

While the woman at the pharmacy had been tending to her injuries, Annika had made sure that Caz's South African cellphone was blacklisted. When she had been ministered to with plasters and antiseptic ointment, Caz had reported her credit cards stolen. Annika had had a similar experience and knew the drill.

She had a spare phone at home, but she would have to get a new SIM card. During the flight to Cape Town she realized that both her cellphones had been in her handbag. Still, her most pressing problems were more or less sorted out. For the time being.

She was thankful her passport had been in her backpack and her car keys with the guys at the long-stay parking.

After a while someone drove up in her Camry. It might

be a rustbucket, she thought, but at least she had her own transport again.

It was good to be back. Despite everything. She knew the roads. She had her independence back. She knew how things worked over here. She could read people's facial expressions and body language. She knew she wasn't safe, but she could at least make plans in flawed but familiar surroundings. Take precautions. Hopefully.

*Wednesday, October 15*
*Caz*
*Overberg*

Caz had just fed a furious Catya and made herself a cup of coffee when her landline rang. She limped to the study. It had been a long night but she had finally fallen asleep, the panic button clutched in her hand.

"Ms. Coolen?"

"Caz Colijn speaking."

"Captain Dlamini. I'm calling about the incident at Silverton.

"I have some good news and some bad news. A patrol car spotted the taxi and tried to pull it over. The taxi sped off, but lost control, left the road and overturned. We arrested one of the passengers. He had the house keys you described—on a silver whale-tail keyring—in his possession. But I'm afraid we didn't find your handbag. I'll fax some photos to the Stanford police and you can try to identify him. They'll be in contact."

"Who is he?" She held her breath.

"According to the passport I have in my possession, David Verstraeten." His tongue tripped over the surname.

Caz sat down. Damn it, they had the wrong person.

"Where's he from, according to his passport?"

"He has a South African passport, but I see he was born in the DRC."

Perhaps they didn't have the wrong person after all?

"Will he go to prison?"

"As far as we can ascertain, it's his first offence. His fingerprints aren't in the system. I don't know whether we'll get very far with the attempted abduction charge. The eyewitnesses disappeared before we arrived on the scene and the security guard didn't see what happened himself. We'll have to wait and see what the prosecutor decides."

An overworked prosecutor in a judicial system drowning in a deluge of crime couldn't be expected to make handbag theft a priority.

She thought for a moment. At least the man seemed to know what he was doing. He sounded sympathetic.

If Dlamini and De Brabander pooled their knowledge, they might find out the truth. In the meantime it might buy her enough time to try to find out what had happened to the bloody strongbox.

"Captain, a young black man followed me when I was recently in Belgium. He goes by the name of Njiwa. I can't be sure whether he's David Verstraeten until I've seen the photos, but it was Njiwa who tried to drag me into the taxi. A detective in Ghent by the name of De Brabander is looking for this Njiwa in connection with ..."

"Why is this not in your statement?"

How could she explain? "I was shocked. I had to catch a plane. Everything was in such a muddle."

"Well, let's see first whether you can identify Verstraeten. Once you've identified him, we can take it further. I'll contact you shortly."

She had to be content with that.

*Luc*
*Ghent*

Luc was hardly aware of the throng of students. Since Lieve phoned earlier that morning, he'd been unable to get Ammie out of his thoughts.

It turned out that her lethargy wasn't the result of age or

the stroke. There was a psychological reason, the psychiatrist had said. Ammie was mentally cutting herself off from reality because of something she refused to face.

Lieve was in tears. "She was so lucid on the two occasions her daughter was here, Professor. How could she just regress like that again? Sometimes she doesn't even seem to recognize me."

Ammie's daughter. Ammie's bloody daughter, who as good as robbed Ammie of her soul.

Like Lieve, he had also thought Ammie would be better a day later. Or maybe a few days later. But the psychiatrist thought that kind of withdrawal from reality could last a long time. It might even be permanent. And it was all that woman's fault.

Ammie had been right. A hellcat.

"Luc!"

He stopped when he saw Laura approach.

"Good day, Luc." She was slightly out of breath when she reached him.

"Good day, Laura."

Laura seemed embarrassed. "Luc, I've been wanting to apologize for the things I said. About what happened in Leuven and about your appearance."

"There's no need, Laura. Forget it." He meant what he said, yet he appreciated her willingness to clear the air.

"No, I was wrong. I'm ashamed to admit it, but I was … well … a bit jealous."

"Laura, don't …"

"No, I have to. I really enjoyed the time we spent together after the academic procession. Just talking to you. I now know I read too much into your kindness. I understand. I'm not an attractive woman. Nor am I exciting, but I'd like to be your friend. Sometimes you're probably lonely too. I'd like to make up for my rash pronouncements. Why don't you join me for supper on Friday evening?"

Luc looked at Laura. No, she wasn't attractive or exciting, but she was intelligent and sincere. Someone with integrity.

"That would be nice, thanks, Laura. I'll bring wine." Definitely not South African wine, he told himself.

Laura gave him a broad smile, a slight blush on her cheeks. "Would seven suit you?"

"Seven is fine." It was time for him to regain his equilibrium and Laura was just the one to help him with it. They might even become more than friends in the end. Be there for each other when necessary.

Beauty and excitement weren't the be-all and the end-all in life, after all. On the contrary, they could be destructive. Ask Jacq DeReu.

*Caz*
*Overberg*

Moerdyk junior expressed his condolences when Caz informed him that both Josefien and Tieneke Colijn had passed away, but she realized he had no idea who she was talking about.

"I believe your grandfather looked after their affairs. I contacted your secretary about six weeks ago. She'll know more."

"Thanks for letting us know. I'll wind up their affairs and send the final account. You can claim against the estate."

Caz suppressed a sigh. A claim against an estate in Ghent that was provisionally frozen? She could kiss another small fortune goodbye. "Fine," she said, "but there's another matter." She told him about the missing safe-deposit box. "I'm at my wits' end. Can you advise me?"

"I might get an answer while I'm winding up the estate. I must admit, though, that I'm not up to speed with my grandfather's affairs. His system wasn't exactly user-friendly. He was also reasonably unorthodox. Old-school. The affairs of the clients he still personally took care of until recently are a particular mess. Of course those were the cases my father sent my way when I joined the business. But if I run into a blank wall, I'll ask my grandfather. He's eighty, but he's still sharp."

"That's kind of you." He'd probably bill her for asking his grandfather, she thought after she had given him her contact details.

The Cape robin hopped from one bookshelf to the next, leaving his streaky white visiting cards.

"Little hooligan," Caz muttered, but even the robin made her feel at home. Everything would be back to normal as soon as Catya forgave her. Since she fetched her from the cattery, the cat had been giving her the cold shoulder.

As if she could read her mind, Catya sauntered up to Caz, meowed, and hopped onto her lap.

Caz held the soft body against her and, to her surprise, the cat did not protest. She even began to purr.

Now she was really home. In her own fucked-up country. On her own fucked-up continent. But home.

*Ammie*
*Leuven*

Of course she remembered. October the second, 1962, October the second 1963, 1964, and every year that followed. She didn't want to, but she did.

And then Fien had mentioned in her letter that a grandchild was on its way. Of course it had touched her. Made everything real again. Could that have been why she had subconsciously wanted the truth to be revealed?

Jacq had thought she was the best thing ever to happen to him. He wasn't a demonstrative man, but she knew his love for her was deep. So much deeper than hers for him.

She didn't deserve his love. He loved a phantom. It was unbearable.

A grandchild. And she was black.

Had she made a mistake? That would be equally unbearable.

The only thing that was bearable was hiding behind her veils. If only the veils weren't so transparent.

*Caz*
*Overberg*

It was late afternoon and the locksmith had just left when Moerdyk junior called.

"I think I have good news, Ms. Colijn."

"About the box? What happened to it?"

"There's a sealed strongbox in our own safe, marked the property of Josefien Colijn."

"I can hardly believe it!"

"Neither can I, but my grandpa was still prepared to bend the rules to accommodate his clients. When I asked him, he remembered quite clearly. Evidently the bank manager at the time was instructed by Mrs. Colijn to give the box to my grandpa when the private strongboxes had to be removed from the bank. Mrs. Colijn asked my grandpa to keep it for her. He took delivery of it, also of the second key. The one you have and the one in our possession are both required to open the box. If your key fits, I can let you have the box."

"Mr. Moerdyk, I'm in the Overberg and I urgently need that box. I can't make a trip just to bring you the key. Do you have a courier? I'll fax you my mother and sister's death certificates, as well as my mother's handwritten note with the details. Also my sister's will, appointing me as her sole beneficiary. I can have it all verified at the police station and provide you with an affidavit if it will help."

"I don't know. Let me talk to my grandfather first. It's his responsiblity, so I'll let him decide."

"I'd appreciate it." Caz had the idea Junior would be only too relieved to rid himself of Grandpa Moerdyk's knotty responsibilities. She hoped so.

Caz had not heard from Lilah again after Schiphol, though she might have sent a message before Caz inserted her new SIM card in her spare phone. It was a shock to discover how many numbers she had lost. According to the fellow at the cellphone shop it was probably because she had stored the numbers on her phone instead of her SIM card.

She couldn't do anything about the loss of the Belgian phone, so De Brabander and Luc DeReu's numbers were gone. Not that she particularly wanted to phone the professor, though she would have liked to find out whether Ammie was okay.

She had no wish to speak to De Brabander either. She'd had quite enough of his mistrust but she would only be able to address the issue once she knew what was in the strongbox. Hopefully. He needed to be informed of Njiwa's whereabouts and his true identity, but once she had identified Njiwa on the photos, Dlamini would surely inform De Brabander. The Stanford police had asked her to come in the next morning.

Today she wanted to email Lilah. She missed her terribly. She didn't really know what to write without sending the child into a panic.

It ended up being chiefly a thank-you letter for spoiling her during the few days they had spent together.

Lilah's reply came in the evening, just as Caz was about to switch off the laptop before going to bed.

> It was lovely to spoil you a little, MaCaz. Tried to call yesterday, but your phone said the number does not exist.
>
> It's chaos here. I'm dead on my feet. Will write a proper letter soon. Tomorrow I have a shoot in Istanbul. Look after yourself. Love you very, very much and miss you lots. L.

*Phone working again*, Caz texted, but got no reaction. Lilah had probably gone to bed.

*Thursday, October 16*
*Caz*
*Overberg*

Dlamini called just as Caz arrived home after picking out Njiwa's photo among four others.

"Stanford has sent the results. You correctly identified the man we have in custody, but I must warn you he's going to plead not guilty. He says he wasn't the one who stole the handbag. It was one of the other passengers in the taxi. He just picked up the keys and was planning to give them to the driver before he got out."

"He and the driver were the only ones in the vehicle, Captain," Caz protested.

"Not at the time of the accident. Two men died, including the driver. Another is in a critical condition in hospital. Verstraeten himself has only a sprained wrist and a few bruises and scratches. He was the only one wearing a seatbelt.

"So we have just your word that Verstraeten and the driver were the only ones in the taxi when your handbag was stolen. Bear in mind that the situation was stressful. Your observation of what happened in those moments and what you saw might have been impaired."

"I looked into his eyes, Captain. He was definitely the one who had deliberately made my acquaintance in Amsterdam and followed me around in Belgium. The detective in Ghent had an identikit drawn up. If you contact him, he'll send it to you."

"Identikits have put innocent people in jail. According to Verstraeten he's never heard of a Cassandra Colijn. He doesn't know why you're saying he goes by the name of Njiwa. He was in Belgium, but never in Ghent. He thinks you're confusing him with someone else. He says white people think all blacks look the same."

"He's talking rubbish, Captain." She could tell him she of all people knew better, but this wasn't about Lilah. And it wouldn't do any good. "Besides, why do you think the taxi tried to get away from the patrol car?"

"It could be because the driver or the taxi didn't have the proper licence. Or because he had picked up passengers at another taxi's pick-up point. The competition is stiff."

Dlamini might have been kind up to now, but he didn't seem to believe her. She supposed she couldn't blame him.

Most people would be fooled by Njiwa's private-school manners—she certainly had been.

"The other men, were they just ordinary South African passengers?" Caz changed tack.

"Funny you should ask. All four in the taxi were originally from the DRC. Verstraeten is a South African citizen, but not the others. One was an illegal immigrant, one has a visa that expires next week and the taxi driver had a local work permit."

Shit. Did that mean Njiwa wasn't alone in this thing?

"The two deceased as well as the man in hospital had tattoos. They vary in size and design but correspond in that the word 'Afrikanize' or 'Afrikanization' appears in them. Afrika with a k. Does it mean anything to you?"

Caz grew ice cold. "No, but it doesn't sound good."

"Verstraeten says he doesn't know any of the other men."

Verstraeten was probably lying through his teeth on all counts. "Captain, there's something very sinister going on here. Please, just contact the detective in Ghent. De Brabander. I beg you." Should she tell him about Tieneke's murder? He might take her more seriously, but she'd also have to confess that De Brabander suspected her of being the mastermind behind it. No, De Brabander could tell Dlamini himself. Maybe there had been new developments in the meantime.

Dlamini sighed. "Ms. Colijn, I really don't have time to do another country's policework as well. I can't even handle the crimes in my own jurisdiction. But, okay, give me the man's number."

"Unfortunately I no longer have it. But anyone at the Ghent police station could help you. If you'll just …"

"I'm sorry, there's another call for me. I'll see what I can do."

Bloody hell, it was like pulling teeth. Hopefully he would call De Brabander. For now she had to focus on the strongbox.

Caz called Moerdyk junior.

"I'm sorry, I should have phoned, but things are crazy," he apologized without sounding sorry. "My grandpa agrees that it would be best for us to close the Colijn file and get it over with. It sounds as if he's had several problems with the account over the years."

Rather with Fien Colijn, Caz guessed. "That's excellent news. Thanks for your trouble. When can I expect the parcel?"

"To tell you the truth, it's already on its way. It should be delivered tomorrow."

Caz thanked him again and ended the call in a daze. Tomorrow. Tomorrow she would find out what the hell it was that had more value than a human life.

# Forty

*Friday, October 17*
*Caz*
*Overberg*

Although she knew that the parcel couldn't possibly be there before late afternoon, Caz was on tenterhooks all day.

She phoned Dlamini. David Verstraeten, he told her, had been charged and released on bail. He had to report at the police station every day before eleven. Dlamini hadn't had a chance to call Belgium, but he would do so as soon as he could find the time.

If Njiwa had gone to OR Tambo directly after getting bail, he could be here by this afternoon, she realized as she put down the phone. But he needed an ID to fly.

She phoned Dlamini again. Asked whether Verstraeten was in possession of an ID document or a passport. Dlamini sounded annoyed but confirmed that he was.

Caz found it even more impossible to focus on the translation than the day before. At this tempo she would never meet the deadline.

Frustrated, she googled Afrikanization. Almost all the websites she found required of her to register before she could get past the homepage. Membership was reserved for "Afrikans (black)." The Abibitumi Kasa Afrikan Language Institute that popped up at regular intervals was no exception. On their guest page they proclaimed: "reAfrikanization + Dewhitenization = Total Afrikan Liberation."

She simply didn't have the stomach for such blatant racism, so she went into the garden and pulled out some weeds. Watered the plants. Fed the fish in the fishpond a second time. Catya as well. Catya fled up a tree. Caz swept the veranda at the side of the house. Washed the glass panes in the door leading out on it. And the glass panes in the front door. Polished the brass doorknob. Swept the front veranda as well.

Just after three she heard a vehicle approaching on the gravel road. She went out onto the front veranda to wait for the courier.

The man looked grumpy about the heavy parcel he was expected to carry inside and put down on the kitchen table. His mood lifted somewhat when she put a ten-rand note into his hand.

Caz sat down on a kitchen chair and gazed at the thickly wrapped brown-paper parcel. She waited until the drone of the car had died away and nothing but the sound of birds and rustling leaves were audible. A sudden weakness in her knees kept her seated a little longer.

At last she got up, took the kitchen scissors and cut through the tough packaging tape.

She tore off the brown paper to reveal a gray metal box with two keyholes. A key was taped to the lid of the box with wide brown adhesive tape. She cut through that as well and tried to remove the sticky residue. To no avail.

The key resisted when she inserted it into the slot and she struggled to turn it, but finally the first lock was open. Caz put her own key in the second lock and the box clicked open.

All she had to do now was lift the lid.

A musty smell filled her nostrils and caused her to sneeze.

The canvas bag inside was worn and dirty. She took it out and put it beside the box. The canvas had hardened and she struggled with the rusty buckles, but at last the bag was open.

Her hand found the figurine first. It was covered in dust. Fien must have taken the things straight from the garage after who knows how many years and put them in the box. It spoke volumes about her attitude towards Ammie. Fien had been fanatic about cleanliness.

The figurine was bigger and heavier than she'd expected. No nails had been hammered into it. If Lilah's information from the internet was correct, the nkísi had not been activated to become nkísi nkondi. Thank God for tiny mercies. At least a dormant spirit was preferable to an active one.

She had been unfair in her flippant judgment on what she thought would be kitsch curio's. The craftsmanship was truly superb. Not her kind of art, but exceptional nonetheless. Comical, in a way. Odd proportions. Two enormous buttocks, a grotesquely distended belly. Big head and big breasts. The body was supported by short legs. Small feet. Short arms and stubby hands.

The eyes and bulging navel had been fashioned from mirror shards. They gave her the shivers.

The upper part of the belly was covered with a labyrinthine pattern. Not carved out of the wood, but fashioned by means of raised bumps, as if something inside the wood was trying to escape. Almost like carbuncles. Caz shuddered again.

She put down the fertility figure and took out the mask. Though it was stylized, she recognized the nose and chin at once. It was a good likeness of Ammie, but also of her own face in the mirror. The objects were nothing like the items usually found in a curio shop. They were beautiful works of art.

The intricate pattern on the figure was repeated in a similar series of bumps on the cheeks of the mask. When she ran her finger over one of the bumps that looked more worn than the rest, it turned into a small crater. Fine dust coated her fingertip. Whatever had been hiding underneath seemed to have escaped.

Caz rinsed her dusty hands under the kitchen tap and moistened an old dishcloth. Carefully she wiped first the mask and then the figurine. She rinsed the cloth a few times before she was satisfied that the items were clean.

Okay. That was it. A mask and a figurine and nothing else.

The canvas bag. Caz winced at the thought of putting her hand inside. Rather not. She spread a newspaper on the floor, turned the bag upside down and shook it. Dust billowed out and she sneezed again. She heard something roll away. A small stone, she saw when she retrieved it from under the table and put it on the newspaper.

She struggled to undo the buckles of the two side pockets and shook the bag again. Only dust and a little sand fell out.

Caz heaved a sigh of relief. Whether Njiwa and Matari wanted them because they were nkisi or because they had great artistic value, at least the two items were no more than what they purported to be and there was nothing else in the box. Nothing illegal.

She would call De Brabander herself and spill the beans. She would find out whether he had heard from Dlamini that Njiwa had been arrested and released on bail. That his name was David Verstraeten. With a bit of luck they might even have exchanged fingerprints.

How things worked internationally she didn't know, but hopefully Njiwa would be imprisoned for life, and Erevu too. She doubted Njiwa would take the rap for Tieneke's murder without implicating Erevu Matari.

Erevu Matari. If Ammie was right, he was her black half-brother. She tried to recall his features. She couldn't recall anything that reminded her of Lilah, except perhaps the tall, slim figure.

As soon as she had spoken to De Brabander and set the wheels rolling, she could carry on with her life. Try to make peace with her roots, discover the identity of her real father and help Lilah unravel their complicated ancestry.

Caz crouched and folded the newspaper around the dust and sand. The pale pebble caught her eye. A little larger than a chickpea, and not completely round. Angular, with rounded edges and flattened curves. Almost like two pyramids with their bases fused together.

She left the newspaper on the floor, picked up the pebble and got to her feet. She hardly noticed her protesting knees.

Caz put on her reading glasses, turned the pebble this way and that, and held it against the light. It was translucent rather than transparent. She bent over the mask and laid the stone in the hollow that used to be a bulge. It was a perfect fit.

A much bigger stone lodged itself in her stomach.

No, she was being silly. It wasn't possible.

She counted the bumps on the mask. Noticed that some were bigger than others. Fourteen on one cheek and the same number on the other. She counted the bumps on the figurine. Twenty-five.

Fifty-three in total.

She took the loose pebble from its nest and studied the hollow closely. Inspected the other bumps again. Ran her thumb over them. A fine powder stained her thumb.

Clay that had pulverized over the years. The mask and figurine were made of wood but the bumps had been covered with clay, then painted or treated to resemble wood.

She studied the gleaming stone again and sank down in the nearest chair.

If this stone was an uncut diamond that had fifty-two companions, she was knee-deep in shit. De Brabander would assume that she had promised the diamonds to Matari as payment for getting rid of Tieneke.

Her only experience with diamonds was the stone in her engagement ring she had saved for a rainy day and finally sold to send Lilah on her first trip abroad. The diamond had been just under a carat. She guessed that none of these stones was less than one, or even two carats.

Still. There were a lot of diamonds and she assumed they were worth a lot of money, but enough to kill for? Especially in their rough form?

Caz's hand trembled when she picked up the figurine again. She turned it round and round. Horizontally, vertically, diagonally. Finally she fetched a strong flashlight and shone the beam into every nook and cranny.

She found the first sign of a seam in a groove just above the buttocks. It was so fine that she would have missed it if hadn't been for a slight discoloration of the glue. At closer inspection she noticed that the seam went between the legs, around the protruding belly, between the breasts, over the head and around the back.

From her tool kit she retrieved the small screwdriver she used for repairing her spectacles and began prodding at the seam. The glue was old and the top layer turned to powder under the onslaught. After that it grew harder.

When it began to get dark, she switched on the lights, sat back down and proceeded with caution.

Just after nine, the two halves of the figurine that slotted together like a three-dimensional puzzle separated. Cautiously she wiggled them apart. The wood, about a centimeter thick, had been carefully hollowed out to accommodate six clay balls. She dislodged one from the buttock of the figurine. Another one from the other buttock. More from the breasts, the head and finally the pregnant belly. The hollows in which they rested had been smoothly finished.

The smallest sphere was the size of a smallish chicken egg, the largest one bigger than a tennis ball.

Her mouth felt like sawdust and she remembered she hadn't had a thing to eat or drink since the parcel arrived.

She poured herself a glass of wine, took two big gulps, found a steak knife and sat back down.

She chose the largest of the clay balls because it was the easiest to grip. At first the serrated blade glanced off the hard clay but once she had made a nick in it, it was easier.

It took ages to remove most of the unbaked clay. The last bit she washed off under running water.

The object in her hand was not as round as it had appeared in its clay shell. It was narrower on one side, though not exactly oval. The surface was multifaceted, with varying gradients. Deep in the heart of the stone was a shimmer of lilac.

Caz gulped. It was the kind of stone people would kill for. If she wasn't mistaken, the reason why Ammie's father had been murdered was lying in front of her. Her grandfather. Lilah's great-grandfather.

And there were five more stones. Smaller, but still bloody humongous for diamonds. Because that's what the stones had to be. It was the only thing that made sense. Besides, there was an aura around the stones. A kind of palpable energy. However silly that might sound.

*Ammie*
*Leuven*

It was the eyes that haunted her. Cassandra's eyes. Lilah's eyes. Elijah's. César's.

Kembo's eyes.

Doel. That photograph. She had pleaded with them not to publish it, to give her the negative. The photographer said the paper would choose. He had taken several. There was only a slim chance that the one on which she appeared would be published. But it was. Thankfully without a name. It was the only ray of light in the darkness, yet she knew she had to leave.

She nearly made it, but you don't pack up the home you had lived in for fifteen years in a matter of days. The day the removal van was due to arrive …

*2001*
*Ammie*
*Doel*

The knock on the back door made her blood freeze in her veins.

Ammie peered through the kitchen window, through the geraniums on the windowsill. She couldn't really see from that angle, but her first reaction was relief. It wasn't César.

The man was too tall. The posture too young. But it wasn't one of the Doel residents either.

The cap was low over his eyes, covered by the hood of his jacket. His hands were in his pockets. His clothing was too scant for the chilly autumn weather.

When he looked up, she noticed his brown complexion. He was in his forties, she guessed. Despite the overcast weather, his eyes were hidden behind dark glasses. The smile on his lips told her he had spotted her. He approached the window.

"Good morning, ma'am. May I come in? I bring a message from a distant place." She had forgotten how different Congolese French sounded from Wallonian French.

She shook her head. Backed away.

The squeal of brakes in the street outside startled her, until she realized it had to be the movers. She rushed to the front door and opened it just as the driver was raising his hand to knock.

While the movers were carrying out her possessions, she returned to the back door. He was still there. He raised his hand. Smiled.

One of the movers entered the kitchen and picked up a box.

"Could you wait a moment?" she asked. "Stay here?"

He gave her a strange look, but put down the box and folded his arms.

Ammie opened the back door, but remained in the doorway.

The caramel-skinned man took a step closer.

"I have a message from Tabia."

The name shook her.

"She's ill. She won't live long. She asks for the nkísi. To protect her the way they protected you."

"I don't have them any more." Behind her she heard the mover shuffling his feet impatiently.

"Where are they?"

"I don't know."

He took off his dark glasses. The scorn in the blue gaze was unmistakable. "You're lying."

"Ma'am, will this take long?" the man behind her asked.

"Just another moment, please," she said over her shoulder before she turned back to the dark skinned man with the blue eyes. "Who are you?"

"They say my father was a good man. Until he got mixed up with a white woman. They tell me it's because of her that my father died when I was a child. They tell me she is my mother. I tell them a mother is the one who cares for you. Who raises you. Not a woman who throws you away. You know who I am."

Ammie knew but she didn't want to know.

"My name is Kembo Elijahsi. My father was Elijah, but I'm telling you you're not my mother. Tabia was closest to a mother to me. I'm telling you Tabia saved your life. Save hers now."

"I don't have them any more. If I had them, I would give them to you. I left them behind." The tears were warm on her cold cheeks.

"Where?" Kembo stepped even closer, a slightly menacing figure. "The city of purple blossoms?"

She nodded, her body racked by sobs.

"Ma'am?" The mover pushed past her. "What's going on here? You're upsetting the lady. I'm going to call the police. Scumbag!"

"Wait! Kembo!"

But Kembo had already vanished around the corner.

No! She didn't want to remember. She didn't want to think of the implications. She didn't want to feel the growing doubt. Couldn't she just be taken in her sleep?

*Caz*
*Overberg*

Midnight came and went. Caz lay in bed but sleep eluded her.

All she could think of was the objects that she had returned to the strongbox, which she had shoved under her bed with a huge effort.

Why did Tabia give those two objects and their contents

to Ammie? Did she even know about the enormous diamonds Aron Matari had hidden in the nkísi? But why, if Tabia didn't know about the stones, would he have given the diamonds to Ammie? Without telling her about them? She would certainly not have treated them so recklessly if she had known. She said she had them locked away because of their artistic value. Twenty-three years after she had left them behind in Africa, along with her child.

All these questions were academic. She was stuck with the consequences of whatever had happened.

Even if she threw away the nkísi, diamonds and all, as she felt like doing, Njiwa and Matari would still be on her tail. For the rest of her life. No matter where she went.

Should she give them the lot and beg them never to contact her again? Promise to tell no one that she knew now why they'd had no qualms about killing Tieneke when she had stood in their way?

No, even if she handed over the nkísi and the diamonds, they wouldn't allow Caz Colijn to stay alive—whether they wanted the diamonds for personal gain or for more sinister reasons.

Chances were slim that anyone would believe the story, but surely there had to be someone who could help her?

The South African Police weren't an option. She knew there were wonderful, honorable men and women among them. Captain Dlamini was probably one of them. They might even be the majority, but how the hell was she going to know who the honest ones were while so much corruption was going on? There was too much at stake. She couldn't even begin to imagine what that pile of shiny stones was worth.

De Brabander? Even if he believed her when she told him that she had never offered Njiwa and Matari the diamonds as payment for services rendered, what could he do from Ghent to protect her? He would have to go through official channels and that brought her back to the South African authorities.

Who knows what would happen if she told them she was in possession of a pile of uncut diamonds. For all she knew, she would end up in prison herself, but even if it didn't happen, it would be a time-consuming exercise. In the meantime Njiwa was out on bail.

Should she contact the De Beers company? She had no idea what they would do if she came to them bearing diamonds. Who would she go and see anyway? She didn't know how this kind of thing worked. There was something called the Kimberley process, but what it entailed she didn't know. If she wasn't mistaken you need a licence for the possession of uncut diamonds. Where would she get one? Besides, the diamonds came from the Congo. She shuddered to think of the consequences it might have for Ammie. She was the one who had smuggled the stones out of the country, whether she knew about them or not.

Could someone in Antwerp, the diamond capital of the world, help her? She and Lilah had gazed in awe at thousands of diamonds of all sizes and colors on display in shop windows in the diamond district. They had also passed the entrance to the block where the world's biggest diamond bourse can be found. Caz had stared at a number of hyper-orthodox Jews in dark suits, hats, long beards and sidelocks.

Should she simply walk in at the nearest diamond trader, ask to see the boss and tell him: Here, take these diamonds, I don't know what to do with them?

Not a bad option, but how the hell would she get the diamonds there without landing her arse in jail?

Somewhere in the future she would probably say she should have done this or that—if she survived, of course—but at the moment she had no idea how to take it from here.

She would have to think creatively. To be able to do that, her mind had to rest for a while for the panic to subside.

Caz wrapped both hands around the alarm remote. It was her talisman. If the panic button worked.

Njiwa was in Pretoria. Tomorrow he would check in at the police station in fulfilment of his bail conditions. She had to believe it. She also had to believe that he would keep doing so until he appeared in court. That he would go to prison. Even if it was only for a few months.

She needed time to make plans.

Preliminary plans as well as long-term ones.
Not that she had the foggiest what those plans could be.

*Saturday, October 18*
*Luc*
*Damme*

Maybe he had been a little overly optimistic, Luc thought as he cleaned a pump in the greenhouse.

The evening with Laura had been quite pleasant. He noticed that she had gone to trouble with the food. Flowers in a vase, candlelight. Everything exactly right. She had made an effort to look pretty too.

He truly appreciated her attempt to put things right between them. And she had succeeded. The initial tension between them had been allayed by the wine. They spoke about the university, the VGK, her proposed research tour.

He told her about his new approach to his lectures and how it was being received by the students. And about his hydroponically grown vegetables. She was very interested. That might have been the reason why he had shared his witloof recipe with her.

He knew that if he had made the slightest move, he could have shared her bed. The temptation had been there. He had wondered whether he shouldn't just succumb to what she so clearly wanted to happen and get it over with.

But he couldn't. Not with the image of Caz Colijn that kept coming between himself and Laura. He didn't understand it. He was furious with Caz. Every day Ammie remained in her cocoon, he grew angrier. And she hadn't even asked after Ammie's health. Not a single SMS since she left. Yet ...

*Caz*
*Overberg*

Caz woke up with a start and a scream that stuck in her throat when she felt the foot of the bed give way.

The meow told her it was only Catya who had jumped onto her bed, but her heart kept thumping in her chest.

It was a clear, sunny day. She had bloody well overslept.

Catya nestled against Caz and meowed more loudly. The poor cat was probably starving. So was she. She had forgotten to eat last night.

An hour later both their tummies were full and Caz had taken a shower.

She had to shake off last night's panic and think rationally. First, make certain that the stones were indeed diamonds. She couldn't just assume they were. She sat down at the computer.

Even a perfunctory search on the internet made her realize she was in possession of a few hundred carats' worth of stones, whether they were diamonds or not. But the shape looked right. An eight-sided threedimensional object is an octahedron, she learned. If the stones turned out to be high-quality diamonds to boot, they'd be worth millions. But only an expert could tell.

A more refined search took her to a simple test to determine the density of a stone. You weigh it dry, then weigh it suspended in water, and divide the dry weight by the second number. The resultant "specific gravity" value will tell you what kind of stone you are dealing with.

Her kitchen scales were probably not perfectly accurate, but at least they were digital. The most difficult part was to fix a length of wire around the stone and suspend it in water without touching sides or bottom. She made her calculation and got a result of 3,5.

The value put it more or less on a level with malachite and titanite, she learned. But malachite was dark green and its crystal structure was different, whereas titanite was usually yellow and looked nothing like the stones in her possession. One after the other she eliminated stones with a density of around 3,5. Until only one remained. Diamond.

Caz closed her eyes. So be it.

Two hours later she was staring at a long list of notes she had made. Random thoughts and ideas.

She actually didn't give a damn about the bloody diamonds, but there were two issues she couldn't ignore.

In the first place, her life was less than worthless at the moment. Njiwa had killed once to get to the contents of the box. He wouldn't hesitate to do so again.

Her second concern was almost worse. If the diamonds fell into the hands of a group set on reAfrikanizing and dewhitenizing Africa, the consequences could be far-reaching. She didn't really know what the two terms entailed but it didn't take a genius to guess what they were about. The secrecy surrounding the groups that used the terms was indication enough that a Sunday-school picnic wasn't on the agenda.

It would be no use trying to hide or destroy the stones. She had to get rid of them in a way that would prove she no longer had them in her possession. Njiwa in particular had to be left in no doubt about it.

The diamonds were much too big to try to get rid of just anywhere.

South Africa was out. She could trust no one here. Not with all the corruption, mutual distrust and flawed interpersonal communication in the country. Especially while words like reAfrikanization and dewhitenization were being bandied about.

Antwerp, on the other hand, was neutral and synonymous with diamonds. At one of the diamond bourses they would know what to do. Their reputation had to remain above reproach and it meant they would follow the right channels. Yes, it had to happen there. How, she didn't know, but that she could figure out later.

De Brabander could possibly help her, but only once she was back in Belgium. The fewer the people who knew she was going to try to take a shitload of diamonds to Antwerp, the better. He would probably suspect her of all kinds of devious motives again, but she believed De Brabander had integrity. She believed she could trust him. More than anyone else, at least. Now she only had to work out how the hell she was going to get the diamonds out of the country without landing in prison.

Maybe she could take pottery classes and conceal the diamonds in new figurines. No, there wasn't enough time. She could hardly take a lesson or two and expect to be a master ceramicist. Nor could she approach an experienced potter. What would she say? Excuse me, I have a few hundred carats' worth of diamonds. Won't you cover them in clay and fire them for me?

And what would happen to the diamonds if they spent hours in a kiln at an incredibly high temperature? She didn't know and she wouldn't want to take the risk anyway.

An hour later she was staring at a possible solution on the screen of her laptop. She was going to take a massive chance but it might just work.

She would need a week or two. In the meantime she'd have to beef up her own safety. But she couldn't do it before Monday. If Njiwa stayed where he was, she might survive the weekend.

Caz called Dlamini. There was no reply. She called the police station and was sent from pillar to post before someone confirmed that David Verstraeten had checked in.

She had a day's reprieve. If she was lucky.

# Forty-one

*Tuesday, October 21*
*Caz*
*Overberg*

For the second time in less than a week a courier service delivered a parcel. It was a different courier. The parcel was about the same size as the first, and not much lighter.

Sunday was a nerve-wracking day, but luckily Ellen had been there on Monday. What her poor char could do if Njiwa appeared was a question best left unanswered, but just the presence of another living being helped calm Caz's nerves. At least they could talk about normal subjects. Lilah and their few days together. Ellen's children and grandchildren. The weather. What had happened around there while Caz had been away.

Caz unpacked the multitude of brightly colored blocks on the kitchen table. Neon green, bright pink, turquoise, purple, bright blue, sunflower yellow. A few in other colors too. Half a dozen in reddish-brown. At the bottom were two large gray blocks the size of bricks.

The tools and other accessories she had ordered, as well as a book of projects, had also arrived. She had bought the pasta machine in Hermanus on Saturday afternoon.

With all the unforeseen expenses of the past month her finances looked dire. Her nest egg had been dealt a serious blow. To tell the truth, a flimsy quail egg was all that remained. The surrounding nest was gone.

Still. A brand-new hobby, was how she should view it.

At least she had something to occupy her hands and her thoughts. To steer them away from birth mothers who left their children to their own devices and wished they had been aborted. Who fled across the African plains with potbellied ancestral spirits instead, and all the consequences of that flight.

*Wednesday, October 22*
*Luc*
*Ghent*

Luc looked at De Brabander, astounded. "Deportation?"

"It's the best option, according to the investigative judge. Like last year, there will be the usual protesters who will rant and rave because we're deporting a man to the DRC, but it's his native land, no matter how dangerous and corrupt it may be. He came here with a visa that was valid for four months, not to ask for asylum. As far as we know, but can't prove, he assaulted and robbed a woman while he was here. Possibly played a role in the killing of another woman. If there's a trial and he's found guilty and sent to prison, the Belgian taxpayer foots the bill. If he's released, he'll walk the streets until his visa expires. So Erevu Matari is being deported."

"From Belgium. But no one can prevent him from going to South Africa from the DRC." Caz. She might not be at the top of his prayer list at present, but it was unthinkable that she might become Matari's target yet again.

"If he can get a visa, no. But there's a rumor that he belongs to a rebel group that has been trying for some time to undermine President Kabila. Chances are that he'll be thrown in jail for a long time." De Brabander seemed to be weighing his next words. "It seems cruel to extradite him in these circumstances, but there's another reason for deporting him. He's a dangerous man. He's not afraid of prison. Somehow he commands respect from the other prisoners. One night there was a helluva brawl in which a prisoner lost a testicle. No one was willing to talk. The man who lost the testicle is known for ... let's say 'initiating' the new prisoners."

Luc's mouth went dry. He wasn't sure he wanted to know more about Matari. "Heard anything about Njiwa?"

"Nothing. The partial fingerprint we found on the staircase railing either didn't belong to him or else he's a first offender. In Europe anyway. Forensics didn't come up with anything usable. Neither did Matari's luggage. And there were no usable fingerprints on anything Ms. Colijn had in her backpack.

"All the blood samples belonged to Tieneke Colijn. The injury at the back of her head probably occurred when she hit her head against the headboard of the bed. A luminol test revealed the presence of blood on the headboard, as well as blood spatters on the wall that had been cleaned."

"Have you notified Caz Colijn? Of the deportation?"

The commissioner shook his head. "Not yet, but she'll be informed in due course. It will take a while for all the paperwork to be completed. I'll see to it that she's brought up to speed. Possibly by the Stanford police. When I tried to phone her last Wednesday on her South African cell number, I was told that the number didn't exist. I find it odd. Also that she hasn't contacted us to hear whether there are any new developments. Or at least sent us a new contact number. If Matari is tried over here, she'll be a witness. Her Belgian phone is dead, of course."

De Brabander got to his feet. "Thanks for looking in. I'll keep you informed about the deportation."

Luc went out, deep in thought. Winter was making itself felt, but it wasn't the only reason he felt chilled to the bone.

Ammie had still not fully recovered and, yes, he was annoyed with Caz for not even asking, but she was all alone in a crime mecca. Njiwa's whereabouts were unknown. Matari was going to be deported and once he was back in the Congo, if he managed to stay out of prison, he could go about his business as usual.

Caz would have to keep looking over her shoulder. The mere thought that she might fall victim to Matari and Njiwa's evil machinations drove the breath from his body.

*Tuesday, October 28*
*Caz*
*Overberg*

"I beg your pardon?" Caz shielded her eyes with her hand. Of course she had heard what Dlamini had said but she was hoping she had got it wrong.

"I said, David Verstraeten didn't check in this morning. He's not at the address where he's supposed to be. He's missing. I'm sorry, Ms. Colijn. These things happen."

"Have you let De Brabander know?" Panic choked her.

"Who?"

"The detective in Ghent. The one I asked you to contact."

"Ms. Colijn, do you have any idea how many cases I have? I can't remember everything. I am up to my ears in murder and rape cases that demand more urgent attention than a stolen handbag. And according to your statement, that's what this case is about."

Caz stood motionless after bidding him a curt farewell. She'd been so bloody stupid. She should have contacted De Brabander herself. Told him everything, despite the possible consequences. Even if it meant that he would regard her as the instigator, who had denied Matari and Njiwa the reward she had promised them—the contents of the strongbox. Now it was too late.

She could call Captain Dlamini back and tell him where David Verstraeten would surface shortly. She could phone the Stanford police and try to explain, even if the case wasn't theirs. And then? Even if they sent someone to wait here for

Njiwa, which was unlikely, even if they caught him, it would be the same old story all over again. Even if he was caught red-handed, he'd be charged with breaking and entering, or attempted burglary, probably be brought to book for breaking his bail conditions, but he'd soon be released again. Come and find her again. Whether it was in a few months or a few years.

Besides, Erevu Matari wouldn't be in prison long. There was also the unidentified third person. The one who had her old laptop in his or her possession. There were probably others involved too, with or without reAfrikanization tattoos.

There was no point in fleeing either. This had to end. She and Njiwa had to end it. The sooner, the better.

She was at the end of her tether. She barely slept at night. Every sound woke her. A dog barking in the distance, the donkey braying on the neighboring farm, the brakes of a big truck on the bypass, a creaking branch, Catya jumping off a chair.

Caz picked up the mask and gazed at the image that vaguely resembled her own features.

"You'll have to help me, old girl," she muttered aloud.

She went to the mirror in the hallway, held the mask in front of her face. Through the shards of glass that formed the eyes it looked as if she was wearing a death mask. As if she was looking at her deceased form.

Shuddering, she yanked the mask away from her face.

During one of her internet searches she had read that the wearer of a ritual mask loses his human identity and becomes one with the spirit represented by the mask. What did this mask represent? Why did Aron Matari create Ammie's image and give it to her?

Caz studied the mask carefully. The outer surface supplied no clues. It was when she scrutinized the smoothly finished inside that she noticed the inscription in the corner.

She put on her reading glasses and tried to make out what it said. Three words. The last one might be "Ami." She sat down at the kitchen table and reached for pen and paper. One by one she deciphered the letters and wrote them down. *Nalingi yo Ami.*

In her study, Caz typed the words in the search box. The first entry was something about a graffiti project. A few links led to a singer and a song in which the words *na lingi yo* appeared. There was a reference to the Lingala Institute—learn Lingala.

She looked up Lingala. Wikipedia cleared up the mystery: *Lingala (Ngala) is a Bantu language spoken throughout the northwestern part of the Democratic Republic of the Congo.*

Bantu? Didn't Wiki know about pejoratives?

Caz typed *nalingi yo* again, omitting *Ami*. The first link gave her *Nalingi yo—translation—Lingala-English Dictionary—Glosbe.*

She clicked on it.

*Translation and definition "Nalingi yo," Lingala-English Dictionary online.*

*Translations into English: I love you.*

I love you, Ami.

But Aron had been ten years younger than Ammie. Ammie had been married, pregnant and fleeing from her evil husband. It was a doomed love right from the start.

"Aron, wherever you are," Caz whispered as she looked at the words on the mask, "your spirit will have to help me. You're the one who made sure that Ammie survived while she was pregnant with me. It's thanks to you that I was born. Now you must keep me from dying. Njiwa is on his way."

Caz lowered her head into her hands. She was losing her marbles.

*Erevu*
*Ghent*

Erevu lay with his eyes closed. In the bunk above him a cellmate was snoring. Someone else farted and yet another one groaned. Probably from the stench spreading through the cell.

It barely registered with Erevu. He was back in Lubumbashi. The night after Noko Aron had joined the ancestral spirits. Two years ago.

He and Arondji were sitting at the fire—the funeral food heavy in their bellies, the beer light in their heads.

"I want to know about the nkísi, Arondji. The nkísi Noko Aron made for the white woman Mama Tabia told me about. The woman who was married to the Belgian who fathered me."

"It is strong nkísi." Arondji drew on a hand-rolled cigarette. "Very strong."

"How can it be so strong? It's not nkísi nkondi."

"The ancestral spirits, they listen not only to iron. They are in stone too. The right stone. The stone that the iron cannot penetrate."

"What stone? Almasi?"

"I say nothing."

"I know there are fifty-three almasi in the two nkísi. Mama Tabia's years were twenty-five and the white woman's years twenty-eight. Mama Tabia told me so just before she died. I asked Noko Aron. He said he took her to the city of purple flowers."

"That was long ago. After that she lived in the city of almasi. Across the sea. That's where I saw her."

"You saw her there?"

"A very long time ago. Tata Aron took his statues there and sold them for a lot of money. I went with him. She came. She said the nkísi are in a safe place."

"Why did your father put the almasi in the nkísi? Mama Tabia gave her enough." Erevu filled Arondji's mug and pretended to pour himself another beer as well.

Arondji took a few sips. "Tata Aron's heart beat for her. She bewitched him."

Erevu almost dropped his mug. "A white woman? A land-grabber? Your tata was mad."

"He was, but his heart beat only for that white woman. Not for others. There were a lot of almasi. Your mama gave the white woman some of her share and tata Aron too. A lot more than your mama. Tata Aron's heart was stupid but his head was smart. Smarter than your mama's. He didn't sell here. He went to the city of almasi." Arondji drank deep, then filled both their glasses.

"Where is the money now if he was so clever?" Erevu motioned at the modest home behind them. Next to the house stood a rusty pick-up.

"I have it. It's not smart to show what you've got. Like tata Aron I look after many people. People who fight against Kabila."

"You gave Kony money?" Erevu held his breath.

"La! Just our people. Kony is Ugandan. Rwandan. He is mad. Kill, kill, kill is all he knows. Killing doesn't make things right."

"I want to fight against Kabila. Against Kony. The others who are making the Congo a bad place. Will you help me?" Erevu pretended to drink deeply, then wiped his mouth with the back of his hand.

"La! Your daughter is a black white. Your grandson is a black white. Their hearts do not beat for Africa, not for the Congo. They live in other countries."

"I'm here. My heart beats for Africa. My heart beats for the Congo. Very strongly. Deep inside of me there is just Congo."

Arondji tossed another log on the fire. Green firewood. The smoke made Erevu's eyes burn.

"Get the nkísi back from the white woman. Then we can talk."

"But she must have used all the almasi by now?"

Arondji laughed. "She does not know about the almasi counting her years. When I saw her where my tata sold his statues in the city of almasi, I saw she did not know where the nkísi were. Tata Aron gave his heart to her when he gave her the nkísi. She stepped on it. He saved her life but she left him behind. She did not give him work when he wanted to be close to her, wanted to look after her. The people where she stayed chased him away. He hid, stayed until the baby come. He wanted to help her. What did she do?

"She left her child too. Just like that. She does not have a heart. Your mama hated the man who fathered you but did she leave you? No. She raised you. She took almasi when you were in prison, got you out, and sent you away. But she sent you away because she wanted the best for you. Not because she did not want you. Her heart was full of sadness during the years you were away."

"Were there more almasi? Other than the ones that counted the years?"

"That time in the city of diamonds..." Arondji poured more beer. "Tata Aron was too shy for her to see him. He wanted to give his heart to her again. He wanted to say to her: come with me, I have a lot of money. I can be your Elijah. Then I saw she did not know where the nkísi were. Then I knew her heart will never beat for him. Now he is dead. Now the nkísi must come back."

"I asked ..."

"I know what you asked. Bring the nkísi, and we can talk more. Then we can talk about president Erevu Matari. You know the white world. We need you. You can be the big man. We are behind the mask. You are our mask. We do it for Congo. For Motetela who must come back. For reAfrikanization."

"Who are 'we'?"

"Kembo and me and Kembo's son."

"Kembo?"

"The other child the white woman left behind. You remember your mama always went to the kimisionari? It's he she went to see. She took food. Later she gave him money. Tata Aron did the same after he come back from the city of purple blossoms. Kembo is like my brother, though he grew up with the kimisionari. Kembo is clever, though he did not go to school in a white country."

"Why don't you get the nkísi back yourselves?"

"Kembo tried. Someone told him where his white mother was. Someone who wanted her dead. Kembo went there, wanted to get the nkísi, wanted to kill her, but other people were there. The white woman said the nkísi were still in the city of the purple blossoms, but the people she left her child with were gone when Kembo went to look.

"You are the white mask, Erevu, though your face is black. You speak white languages. You are the sly one. You can go where we cannot go. I have money. Kembo and I have power here. You can be our power out there and share the money. But the test is for you to bring us the nkísi."

Erevu rolled over on his side. Two years ago he had been filled with hope. He had told Arondji about Alice Auma, about his dream. It was soon clear that he and Arondji spoke the same language. But Arondji didn't know that Motetela's blood flowed in Erevu Matari's veins. Arondji could believe he would only be their mask. But once he had the nkísi, Arondji would have to bow before him.

Since that night, his life had revolved around the nkísi.

Little by little, with Jela's help, he had made progress. With Njiwa's help, he had come closer and closer to the nkísi.

And then he was foiled by a white woman and betrayed by his family. This could not go unpunished.

Today he heard that he would be deported. His name was not Erevu for nothing. Sly and crafty. He would find the nkísi, but he would make sure he had the upper hand.

Erevu began to laugh. Out loud. Someone protested but was soon silenced.

Good. They knew who they were dealing with here in prison. Njiwa and Jela would also find out. As would Cassandra Colijn.

# Forty-two

*Friday, October 31*
*Luc*
*Damme*

Here he was on All Saints' Eve, on the bloody internet, getting nowhere.

He had just left Caz a message on LinkedIn, asking for a contact number, but the message didn't deliver. How dare she just vanish into thin air after creating such havoc? He would love to give her a piece of his mind. At the same time warn her that Erevu was going to be deported.

When Lieve called, he had to take care that he didn't sound as peeved as he felt.

"Professor, a miracle has happened."

"Yes, Lieve?"

"I was on my way back from mass, with 'Agnus Dei' still sounding in my ears, and I thought of a plan. See, I recognized Lilah from one of my sister's magazines. *Cosmopolitan*. She's a world-famous model, you know? I asked my sister to lend me the magazine, though I don't actually like that kind of reading matter. I took it to Miss Ammie. She was in bed by then but not asleep. Just staring into the distance. I showed her the magazine with Lilah on the cover."

"Yes?" he said when she stopped for dramatic effect.

"Professor, it was as if the Holy Virgin Mary had touched her. 'Where's my granddaughter?' she asked."

"And?"

"She said she wants to see her. Lilah. Miss Ammie is back from behind the veils, Professor. Our Miss Ammie is back."

*Caz*
*Overberg*

This time it was a soft click that woke her. Caz lay motionless until she was sure there was no one in the room.

Her hand felt around on the empty side of the bed, but the panic button had vanished in the folds of the comforter. She groped frantically. Grabbed hold of her cellphone. Continued to search with anxious fingers. Found it. She had no idea which button to press. There were four, of which three were active. Panic, which sent out a silent alarm. Sleep, which beeped but sent no alarm—only lit up the blue light at the front door. Activate, which also beeped and was silent until someone moved past a sensor and triggered the alarm.

Another sound. Dim. A kind of crunch. No breaking glass, no movement in the air around her.

The creak of a floorboard.

Around her the dark was breathing. It was dense. Untouched by streetlights or any other light from outside. The curtains were drawn. There was no moon.

She felt with her thumb, pressed each button in turn. No beep. No blaring siren. Did it mean the panic button wasn't working either? Did her signal go through? She didn't know. If it did, wonderful, but she had to assume it didn't.

The brass bedstead rattled slightly when she sat up and swung her legs off the bed. The clay tiles were cold under her bare feet. During the renovation she could save the wooden floors in the living room only; the rest were too far gone. She knew where that floorboard had creaked.

Her only advantage was that she knew her house. She had known right from the start that a weapon would not help her. She had no knowledge of firearms. She wouldn't be able to bury a knife in someone's flesh or knock someone over the head, even if she'd had the strength of a younger person. A weapon in her own hands would only end up as a firearm in her attacker's hands.

Soundlessly she moved to the doorway between the passage and the living room. A dim light was playing around the room, wandering over the coffee table, pausing on the buffet. The beam of the penlight torch lingered on the nkísi. No, the nkísi nkondi.

Caz took a deep breath and flicked the light switch.

He swung round, dressed in black from head to toe. Just like in a movie. But this was no movie. No dream. Through the slits of the balaclava, his eyes glittered.

"Good evening, Njiwa. Or should I say David Verstraeten?" The sling of a canvas bag crossed his chest from left shoulder to right hip. The bag itself rested diagonally on his stomach. It bulged slightly. Maybe a burglar's tool kit. Or a firearm.

He pushed the balaclava back to expose his face and switched off the flashlight.

"Caz." He motioned with his head at the buffet where the wooden figurine stood, nails protruding from the belly, breasts and buttocks. "I see you activated the nkísi. Or tried to."

She made no reply. Just stood waiting.

He sniggered. "Did you think a few nails were all that was needed to rouse the ancestral spirits? That you could play nganga?"

No, but she'd hoped he would think so.

"Did you think you could rouse *my* ancestral spirits to protect *you*? A white woman? One of the white robbers who tried to steal Africa from us?" He shook his head. "How misguided you are."

"I'm tired of fighting against Africa, Njiwa. Take the stuff and go."

He shook his head.

Had she made it too easy? Made a tactical error? She wasn't much of a strategist. She should have stayed in bed. Pretended to be asleep. Maybe he would have taken the nkísi and left.

"You know my face. You know my real name. I can't, Caz. There's too much at stake."

Just as she had thought.

"And if you kill me? Strangle me the way you strangled Tieneke? Do you think you won't be caught? Dlamini knows that you and I have a history. He'll put two and two together."

He nodded slowly. "Yes, I do believe I won't be caught. This may be South Africa, but it's still Africa. You see, I've got help. At different levels and from various interest groups. We're taking Africa back. It belongs to us. It's only a matter of time. These nkísi are going to give us a major boost."

"There's something you're overlooking, Njiwa. You see, you're not black either. Your grandfather, Erevu, is the son of Tabia, but also of César Janssen. A white man. One who could possibly be my father. We may therefore have the same ancestor."

"I know all that. Your point is?"

"My point is the nkísi won't favor you either. Your white great-grandfather was a traitor to Africa. Your grandfather and my mother abandoned Africa for Belgium for long periods of time. Africa is diluted in you. You have lost the true spirit of Africa and only greed and the hunger for power have remained."

Njiwa did not reply. Silently he placed the nail-spiked figurine in the canvas bag, followed by the mask that had lain beside it on the buffet. When he was done, he looked up at her again. His gloved hand reached behind his back and emerged holding a handgun. What kind it was she didn't know. It had a barrel. And it was aimed at her.

"It's a pity you woke up. It would have been easier not to know what had happened. Simply not to open your eyes again. Just another white woman killed in her bed on a farm."

He put both hands on the grip, straightened his arms. "Sorry, Caz."

Caz pressed down the light switch where her thumb had still been resting and dived sideways, away from where he was aiming.

The shot rang out even before she hit the floor. A crippling pain shot through her hip. The fall or a bullet? Caz didn't know.

It was pitch dark. Outside she heard the sound of a speeding vehicle in the distance. Inside she heard the creak of the floorboard. The door leading to the side veranda was flung open. There was the sound of running feet. Away from the front of the house, where a small eternity later she heard the squeal of brakes and a vehicle grind to a halt on the gravel.

A key rattled in the front door. The door flew open. The beam of a flashlight blinded her. "Ma'am! Ma'am! Where are you?"

"The side door! He went through there!" She shielded her eyes with her hand when another beam was shone into her eyes. "Someone switch on the lights!"

Someone obeyed.

"Is she okay?"

"Don't see any blood."

"Follow the bastard! Go look for him!" Caz screamed. Two men raced off, the veranda door slammed, but she knew it was too late. Njiwa was too cunning. Too quick.

From the emblems on the jackets of the remaining two men she realized it was the second security company who had arrived. The company who got the signal when she switched on the living room light.

The technician had shaken his head when he came to do the installation, but he had done as she had asked. The manager had agreed to follow the instructions she had provided in writing. Send armed guards without delay if the signal was received. No calls, nothing. Just hurry and enter at once.

Njiwa had known how to deal with one alarm. He couldn't have known about Plan B.

"The ambulance is on its way, ma'am."

"Thank you." She knew it could take long. But she also knew she didn't need it to survive. Only to treat the pain in her hip and back.

Two of the men helped her to her feet and lowered her onto a chair.

"Anything stolen, ma'am?"

Caz glanced at the buffet. "Two artefacts. By a well-known African artist. Aron Matari. Worth a lot of money." She saw the disdainful look they exchanged. In Hawston or Fisherhaven or Blombos or wherever they had grown up art wasn't high on the priority list. Least of all African art.

"Good evening, Captain, Ambrose here of Whale Security." Dazed, Caz looked at the security guard with the phone against his ear. "Armed robbery. The woman is okay. There's a bullet in the doorframe where she was standing moments before. Attempted murder, if you ask me." He left the room and his voice grew dim.

Dlamini. She had to let him know. No, the police would be here any moment and they could do it. At some point one had to start trusting the system. At least this was a serious offence.

*Saturday, November 1*
*Caz*
*Overberg*

Caz felt like new when she woke up and saw it was after eleven. Once the police had left, she had just about passed out, reassured by the presence of a security guard in case Njiwa returned.

The guard had left, she noticed when she entered the kitchen. His shift was over at eight. She was supposed to let the company know if she wanted them to send a replacement.

Of course her problems were far from over, but she believed she had some breathing space. Until Njiwa discovered that the diamonds in the mask and the figurine had been replaced with empty clay spheres.

Njiwa had clearly not realized that she couldn't have

hammered the nails into the figurine if it still had its original contents. Not all the way, anyway. But how would he know? No one had seen the figurine before. No one had any idea of the size of the diamonds. At most they could know that the figurine contained a number of large diamonds.

She had hammered in the nails while the rust-colored polymer clay balls with which she had replaced the diamonds were still soft. She was terrified that the figurine would catch fire when it went into the oven but to her great relief it didn't. Perhaps because she had turned the heat right down and baked it for longer instead. The wood just darkened slightly. When it had cooled down completely she had tried to pull out the nails. They didn't budge. They seemed embedded in the clay, as she had hoped.

Njiwa would only discover what she had done if he could overcome his fear of the ancestral spirits. The figurine would have to be damaged severley to get to what was inside. But if luck was on her side, he would hesitate to offend the spirits and that would buy her more time. That was how she had argued, at any rate.

Now that Njiwa had made it clear that a rebel group or several groups were involved, she knew that ancestral spirits and magical powers would not stall them. They were looking for the diamonds because they needed money—big money. To chase the white land-grabbers into the sea, it seemed.

Caz heaved a sigh of relief when she saw Lilah's name in her inbox. It was her lucky day.

> Sorry I'm only writing now, MamaCaz.
>
> Aubrey and I had a tiff and I didn't want to write to you while I was upset and tearful. With all the shoots and things that had to be finished before winter, it's been crazy anyway. I'm exhausted.
>
> I arrive December 9 and I'm looking forward to spending time with you and to a proper rest.
> Luv u
> L

Caz tried to curb her concern. Lovers had tiffs. She couldn't do anything about it and she wasn't going to interfere. Lilah would tell her what it was about if she wanted to and Caz could only offer advice if Lilah asked.

There was a bigger crisis. How was she going to make sure that the problems with the nkísi had been solved by the time Lilah arrived in less than six weeks?

She called Dlamini.

"We're working closely with the police in the Western Cape to catch him, Ms. Colijn," he tried to ease her mind. "We are watching all the border posts. In the meantime we have learned that he has a second passport. From the DRC. One consolation, if he's left the country, he won't be able to set foot here again."

"Captain, did you contact Commissioner De Brabander in Ghent?"

No reply.

"Won't you just do it, please? We're talking of attempted murder here. If you two put your heads together, you might catch Verstraeten sooner."

"What's it all about anyway? Why was Verstraeten after you in the first place?" She could hear the frustration in Dlamini's voice.

Trying to put him in the picture would be an impossible task. "As far as I understand, Verstraeten assigns some kind of spiritual value to the mask and the figurine I inherited. He says his family's ancestral spirits are contained in the objects. Something like that."

Dlamini was quiet for a while. "The people in Stanford say they are works of art," he said at last.

"They are. Apparently worth a few thousand euros."

"I can see this Verstraeten's point about the ancestral spirits, but he should have offered to buy the items back from you. Do you have photos?"

"I do." A good thing she had thought of it.

"Send them to me." He gave her an email address.

"How do you spell the man in Belgium's name? The detective?"

She spelled it out. "He's from the police station in Ghent." She spelled Ghent as well.

Three hours later her cellphone rang. A Belgian number, she noticed at once.

"Caz, hello?"

"Ms. Colijn. I received an interesting call a while ago."

"Good day, Commissioner." Her heart was in her mouth. For all she knew De Brabander had finally concluded she was the key player.

"It seems you suddenly and miraculously remembered what Matari and Njiwa, or rather David Verstraeten, were after."

"I only realized what they were after when I took possession of my inheritance here in South Africa. They must have found out about the key I got from Tieneke and known what was in the strongbox. I, on the other hand, didn't."

"Ms. Colijn, do you realize how irresponsible you were? You could have been dead! Besides, our case ..."

"Commissioner, I repeatedly asked Captain Dlamini to contact you," she interrupted him. "I wasn't aware that he hadn't done so. And my cellphone with your number on it was stolen shortly after my arrival, as Captain Dlamini might have told you."

"Ms. Colijn, surely you could have found a way to reach me?"

She ignored the accusation. No way was she going to get involved in an argument that wouldn't lead anywhere. "Erevu Matari. What's the current state of affairs?"

"Initially he was awaiting trial and then he was scheduled for deportation. But now we'll have to wait and see what happens with the murder investigation. Everything will depend on whether Njiwa is caught and what happens after that. Matari will remain here for now."

"For how long?"

"It will probably take a while. But first there are a few things I want to clear up with you."

Caz answered his questions as briefly as possible. They were chiefly about the incident in Silverton and the events of the previous night. When she ended the call she gave a sigh of relief. If Njiwa were caught it would buy her time. To enjoy a holiday with Lilah in December, to make plans, to get money. Hopefully Lilah would help finance her trip back to Belgium.

Caz peered at the bits and pieces on the mantelpiece.

Amongst a collection of candles, a few seashells and some other items, a kitsch turquoise whale with an enormous head glowed in the sunlight that fell through the window. A glaring green pregnant rhinoceros and four other similar polymer clay figures were scattered throughout the house. She would have liked to claim that her artistic attempts could be seen as deliberately stylized, but she knew the figures resembled a child's artworks. No, actually, a child's craft items. Yet she was proud of her handiwork. In more than one way.

It turned out that diamonds are able to withstand a temperature of a hundred and thirty degrees Celsius in a normal oven. Hot enough to bake the polymer clay to a rock-hard consistency.

She had bought time. She had managed to hide what had to be hidden.

Now Njiwa just had to be caught so she could get to Antwerp safely.

It was after nine when her landline rang again.

"Mrs. Colijn, this is Captain Divan de Jager from Musina. In connection with David Verstraeten."

Caz was almost too scared to hear what he had to say. "Yes?"

"The taxi he was traveling in was pulled off at a road block just before Beit Bridge. Regrettably, he managed to get away. It looks as if he might have crossed the border into Zimbabwe.

"However, now that the international guys are involved, I can assure you he won't be any threat to you. Evidently a partial fingerprint found on the murder scene in Belgium corresponds with the prints taken in Pretoria. He has to cross other borders before he reaches the Congo. I have no doubt he'll be arrested somewhere along the way."

She wanted to believe him. For her own sanity's sake, she had to believe him.

Caz was in bed when her cellphone rang again. A Belgian number, but not De Brabander's.

"Caz Colijn?"

"It's Luc DeReu." A grumpy Luc DeReu, it seemed. "I hear from the commissioner that you're answering your phone again."

Caz closed her eyes. She could call up his face surprisingly easily. The silver glint of his hair. The slender fingers folded around the pen. The lean figure she had watched at the Graslei.

"Good evening, Professor. This is quite a surprise." If he could be grumpy, she could return the favor with sarcasm.

"I can well believe you're surprised. What I can't believe is that you don't have an ounce of concern for Ammie. You come here and cause her such distress that she retreats into a mental coma. Then you simply wash your hands. And you accuse *her* of being coldhearted?"

Caz sat up in bed. "What do you mean, a mental coma?"

"Since you and your daughter left, she's been like the living dead. It's thanks to Lieve that she has emerged from her cocoon. The irony is Ammie wants to see Lilah again."

Caz wasn't surprised that Ammie wanted to see her granddaughter yet she apparently had no interest in seeing her daughter. What did surprise Caz was that she felt hurt by it.

"Well, I'm sorry to hear she hasn't been well and I'm glad she's improving. Things have been crazy here. My cellphones were stolen and I lost your number. But be that as it may. You'll have to contact Lilah herself to find out whether she wants to see Ammie again." It was Lilah's choice. At least it would give her a chance to find out more about her own roots. If anything came from it, she would be glad for Lilah's sake. There was no reason why Lilah should miss out on a relationship with her new-found grandmother just because Ammie wished that her daughter didn't exist.

"Seeing that your LinkedIn page is no longer operational, I left a private message on her Facebook fan page, but I haven't had an answer yet. I don't want to contact her on Twitter; it's too public. Could you give me a contact number or email address for her?"

"I'll send them both. I have your number now. Please remember it's confidential. I'm only doing it for Ammie's sake." She realized that she had neglected to update her LinkedIn details when she had changed her email address.

"I do know the meaning of the word discretion." There was a brief silence. "De Brabander tells me Njiwa tried to shoot you."

The sudden fury that took hold of her caught her by surprise. "Yes, but unfortunately for you and Ammie, he missed. Goodnight, Luc DeReu." She ended the call. He knew she had nearly died, yet he went on about the fact that she hadn't asked about Ammie. How was that for empathy and compassion?

*Luc*
*Damme*

Luc stared at the phone in his hand. His heart had nearly stopped when De Brabander told him what Caz had gone through. He'd called because he was worried. Because he wanted to tell her ... Well, he couldn't quite remember what he had wanted to tell her, but it certainly hadn't been his plan to lash out at her. Until he heard that sexy voice say *Caz Colijn?* The epitome of innocence. As if he hadn't been to hell and back because of her. And then the sarcasm: *This is quite a surprise.* It had been the last straw.

Luc paced his living room floor, cellphone in hand. He couldn't leave it like that.

He didn't care what she thought of him, he simply had to tell her he had been upset about Ammie, but understood her side of the story better now. After all, she had been engaged in a life-and-death struggle of her own.

He wanted to suggest she come to Belgium, where she'd be safe. She could stay in his houseboat. He'd get the police in Zandbergen to keep an eye on her. Matari was in prison and, if he had an ounce of sense, Njiwa wouldn't return to Belgium.

But more than anything he wanted to tell her he'd like to get to know her better. That she had awakened something in him that he could not for the life of him lay to rest again.

*Verdorie*, Luc DeReu, are you a man or a mouse? Just call, in heaven's name, and see what comes out of your mouth.

*Caz*
*Overberg*

Caz silenced the phone when it rang again. She didn't have the strength to be bullied any further. She sent Lilah's contact details and added a message: *Please leave me alone now*.

He obeyed. Why it should reduce her to tears again she didn't know. She had turned into a real crybaby.

Maybe because she knew he was right. She could have made an effort to find out how Ammie was doing. She knew the old lady had been upset. Yet something had stopped her.

She didn't want to care about Ammie Pauwels. She didn't want to feel the slightest twinge of emotion for the woman. More than anything, she didn't want to admit there was a part of her that understood why Ammie Pauwels had rejected her newborn baby. If she admitted that, she would also have to admit why she understood.

Her baby's skin color had been an intense disappointment to Ammie. She had known that the child could be either black or brown or white. In the end the baby wasn't the right color.

*Her* newborn baby's skin color had been a huge shock to Caz.

If she had been in a hospital, if other people had been present, she might have thought she had lost track of time and that sometime during her labor the baby had been switched—however slim the possibility.

But she and Magdel had been the only two people in the room at a time before fathers were welcomed into the intimate circle of childbirth. At Liefenleed, anyway.

Caz remembered that last powerful push. The sense of being ripped apart. The pain. The enormous relief.

She had lain back for a moment to catch her breath, her eyes closed, when Magdel's shriek pierced the silence. The next moment the baby was thrust into her arms. Arms that automatically closed around the wet, slippery bundle of limbs.

When she looked down she thought for an instant that Magdel had played a trick on her. That she had handed her one of the babies born in the workers' cottages. Then she realized it was impossible.

While she was struggling to breathe, she realized that the baby had to breathe too. Pure instinct made her insert her finger into the black baby's mouth and rake out the mucus, before giving her a pat on the back. She heard the first breath being drawn, and wondered why she had helped this child to breathe.

But when she heard the cry of life and the small mouth began to move, when the tiny fists opened and closed, the eyelids lifted and the eyes gazed sightlessly at her ... In that magical moment she realized she had given birth to a living being. One who had come out of her body. A child created out of love.

Nothing else mattered any more. Not Magdel's sobs outside the door. Not Andries's loud bellow: "What the fuck do you mean black?" Not Hentie's unearthly cry.

When Andries pushed open the door, she shielded the baby with her arms and body. "Go away! Get out!" she screamed, rocking her baby, holding her tight, covering the little ears as best she could.

"What the fuck ..."

She had looked Andries in the eye. "Get. Out. Of. Here."

For the first time since she had known him, he had obeyed a woman. He left, closing the door behind him.

There was another first that night. The little mouth had searched for her nipple and found it. When her baby began to suck, Caz had felt for the first time that she truly belonged. To her child.

Caz drew a deep breath. She felt sorry for Ammie. For

missing out on that experience. Whatever her reasons had been.

Was there a difference between pity, understanding and forgiveness? Caz wondered. Of course there was, but they were separated by a hair's breadth. She couldn't say she had forgiven Ammie or that she ever would, but she thought she could understand that moment of revulsion before love took over. Ammie had never reached that second phase. Maybe because of the Caesarean section, the hysterectomy. Maybe she had simply not been prepared to give it a chance.

But it was thanks to Ammie that Lilah was there. Whether Lilah was related to César or to Elijah, Ammie was the common denominator. Ammie's amniotic fluid had also been Lilah's beginning.

Ammie might not have been a mother's arse, but she was the womb that had borne the fruit. The harvest was Caz and Lilah, and Lilah's future children. White, brown or black.

And fuck Lilah's Aubrey if he didn't want a white child. She and Lilah came from a family tree where they had to make peace with shades. Like the yesterday-today-and-tomorrow outside her window had to make peace with its fading flowers.

Caz groped around for her glasses when the phone pinged. Lilah?

*Didn't mean to fight with you. Worried to death about you. Can we start over? I would like to get to know you, Caz Colijn. Without all the complications that have come along. Not as Ammie's daughter. Just as Caz.*

Luc DeReu. Caz just had to close her eyes to see him.

Another message came through. *How do you do? My name is Luc DeReu.*

She leaned on her elbow and switched on the reading lamp.

The soft light fell on the purple polymer figurine on her bedside table. A fat pregnant mermaid with huge boobs regarded her with beady eyes.

Beautiful her clumsy creation was not, but she was going to be a hit in Antwerp. Soon.

Caz looked down at the cellphone. She hesitated a moment before she replied.
*Pleased to meet you, Luc DeReu. My name is Caz Colijn.*
She drew a deep breath, let it out slowly, winked at the mermaid and pressed the send button.
A moment later there was a smiley. Then another message: *May I phone you tomorrow, Caz Colijn?*
*You may. Goodnight, Luc,* she replied.
*Sleep tight, Caz.*
He was over there and she was here. How could it work? Still. At this moment she wouldn't change the sweet warmth that settled inside her for the world.
Caz switched off the light and pulled the covers up to her ears.
The darkness was comprehensive, the silence nuanced by crickets rubbing their hind legs together in search of a mate, frogs chorusing out the same longing, an owl calling woefully.
A soft breeze breathed through the wild olive tree, rustled the leaves of the today-yesterday-and-tomorrow dispersing the fragrant smell of it's tricolored flowers.
In its smells and sounds, the texture of the air, Caz could sense Africa around her.
Africa, with her distinctive heartbeat and ever present heartache. Her own rhymes and reasons. Her own mysterious life-force.
Africa, the dancing shadow of times primordial and all that followed.
European intervention had swayed the dancers, warped the tune, but not the dance itself.
Africa was still dancing to her own rhythm. A rhythm Caz felt pulsing inside her. For better and for worse.

## Foreign words

The definitions below are rather simplistic and should be considered a mere indication of how the words are used in *Sacrificed*. Words from African languages are mostly from Swahili or Lingala.

Almasi: Diamonds

Cité indigène: Residential quarters of the indigenous people (township).

Daktari: (Western) doctor
Dewhitenization: Extermination of white/Western population groups.
Donnu harp: Small harp made by the Mangbethu people.

Évolué: Literally "developed person." A French word from the colonial era denoting an African or Asian person who has been Europeanized.

Fisi: Hyenas

Iboga: The bark and root of a shrub (*Tabernanthe iboga*), which have a hallucinatory effect when chewed. Sometimes used to communicate with the dead.

Kimisionari: Missionary

Liefenleed: Name of the farm. It means the sweet and bitter of life.
(Ba)Luba: The largest ethnic group in the DRC.

Macaques: Monkeys—derogatory term for indigenous people.
Mganguzi: Witch doctor
Motetela: Deity of the Mongo population group, which includes the Batetela. Motetela means "he at whom one may not laugh."

Msichana: Girl/daughter
Mvet: Traditional musical instrument.

N'Gongo Leteta (Gongo): Congolese leader and tribal chief in the nineteenth century.
Nganga: Spiritual healer who also communicates with the dead.
Nkísi: Spirits or objects inhabited by spirits, often ancestral spirits.
Nkísi nkondi: Objects inhabited by spirits that have been activated—often by hammering nails into the objects.
Nkoko: Grandfather (form of address)
Noko: Maternal uncle (form of address)

ReAfrikanization: Return to African values and eradication of the effect of colonisation and Western influences.

Scarification: Decoration of the body by deliberately damaging the skin and using the scars to create patterns in the skin.
Shweshwe dress: A dress made of a printed dyed cotton fabric widely used for traditional Sotho (South Africa & Lesotho) clothing

Tai: Vultures
Tata: Father (form of address)
Tetela: Ethnic group in the DRC.
Tsotsi: A black urban criminal.
Yeshua: Hebrew spelling of Jesus/God, preferred by some religious groups.

*Flemish/Dutch:*

Blandijn: A building complex at Ghent University.
Boekentoren: The tower forming part of the Blandijn, housing about three million books.

Gentse neuzen: Purple raspberry-flavored sweets, traditionally made in Ghent, firm on the outside with a soft centre.
Geus/Geuzen: Protestant/Protestants
Koffie verkeerd: Coffee containing more milk than coffee.
Kriek/kriek beer: Beer made of sour cherries.

Verdikkeme/Verdorie/Potverdorie: More or less the equivalent of bloody hell/damn/shucks.

Waterzooi: A Belgian chicken or fish stew with a rich sauce of vegetables and cream.
Witloof: A leafy vegetable resembling chicory that is grown in the dark. A typically Belgian dish.

*Afrikaans:*

Alikreukel: Large sea snail belonging to the class *Gastropoda*.

Backvelder: An unsophisticated country person, living in a remote part of South Africa.
Braai: To grill or roast meat over open coals; barbecue.

Galjoen: Black bream or blackfish. A species of marine fish found only along the coast of southern Africa; the national fish of South Africa.

Skollies: hooligans, gangsters

Tik: a slang name for the drug methamphetamine in crystal form.
Tikkop: Tik user

# Author's note

Though I conducted my research as meticulously as possible, the historical events depicted here should be regarded as suspect. I am no historian, neither am I Belgian or Congolese. I am merely a writer of fiction whose interest was aroused by the circumstances around Patrice Lumumba's death, but who ended up writing a totally different story from the one I had initially planned.

In some cases I twisted the facts to fit the story, in others I blatantly lied.

All the characters are fictitious. No person like Elijah ever existed, for instance. He, like César, Ammie, Tabia and others, are characters created by my imagination. The street café near Dulle Griet in Ghent does exist and the pea soup is inexpensive and delicious but the owner is fictitious, just like Erdem and the people Caz met in Kieldrecht and Doel.

Even historical figures like Patrice Lumumba have been fictionalized to a greater or lesser degree.

There is no AALHA rebel group, but there are numerous actual rebel groups striking terror in the hearts of the people of the DRC.

Contact in 1986 between a Congolese man and Alice Auma Lakwena is highly unlikely. Tragically, Joseph Kony and his LRA are very active in the DRC.

To simplify the reading experience, the names of Congolese characters do not conform to the correct naming tradition.

Caz's view of the South African situation, as well as her observations in Belgium, are her own.

The above is not meant as an excuse for facts or statements that may be wrong. I am a writer of fiction. I make a living out of lying. But I try to lie as truthfully as possible.

A book is never the sole creation of its writer. In fact, without help from so many quarters *Offerlam,* and subsequently *Sacrificed,* would never have seen the light.

People who meant a great deal to me and Caz's story and whom I wish to thank from the bottom of my heart for their contributions are:

All the people in Belgium and the Netherlands who meant so much to me and the book. There are too many to name, but I want to single out a few.

Gino Laureyssen, who set the ball rolling and his wife, Elke van den Bergh, my Dutch translator. Thank you both for your faith in me and my work..

Carine Duprez, who welcomed me into her home, cooked delicious meals, drove hither and thither to show me places, and introduced me to kriek.

Ingrid Glorie, Frank Judo and everyone involved with *De Week van de Afrikaanse Roman.*

Prof. Emanuel Gerard of KU Leuven for a delicious lunch and a wealth of information, without which I would never have made head or tail of the situation in the Belgian Congo and the period after independence. Especially the information on Patrice Lumumba was invaluable.

My sincere thanks as well to Marcel Pruwer and Chantal Pauwels of the Antwerp Diamond Bourse for giving me their precious time and affording me the great privilege of holding a handful of rough diamonds!

Many people in South Africa also helped and supported me. Once again, I can only single out a few.

LAPA Publishers, for their extensive support.

Cecilia Britz, my patient publisher, who gives me the freedom to turn flights of fancy into stories and forgives me when I start to panic.

Wilna Adriaanse, for her thorough reading of the manuscript, her understanding of how stories work, her ability to spot the gaps and her willingness to share her expertise. Without her input the story could not have reached its full potential.

Elsa Silke, who translated *Sacrificed* from Afrikaans to English and was so patient with me.

Karin Schimke who edited *Sacrificed* and advised me so wisely.

Jessica Powers for taking a chance on me and *Sacrificed*. Thanks for your insight and expertise, enthusiasm and hard work.

Samantha Buitendach, for her enthusiasm and dedication.

Beryl Maxwell, who lent me exactly the right book at exactly the right time, without which I would have known much less about the Belgian Congo.

Ernie Blommaert, the man in my life who, after more than a decade, still brings me numerous cups of tea with incredible patience, looks after house and home when I go away to write and understands that I'm sometimes absent in spirit because my head is making up stories. Thanks, Blom—for everything.

My wonderful friends, who support me when I need them and forgive me when I neglect them.

My readers. Without all the emails, Facebook messages, reactions to my blog, stars on Goodreads and various other kinds of feedback, my life would have been so much poorer.

# Bibliography

*Books (inter alia):*

Allen, Tim & Vlassenroot, Koen (eds). *The Lord's Resistance Army.*
Bennett, Ronan. *The Catastrophist.*
Eichstaedt, Peter. *Consuming the Congo: War and Conflict Minerals in the World's Deadliest Place.*
Nzongola-Ntalaja, Georges. *Patrice Lumumba.*
Van Daele, Henri. *Tijl Uilenspiegel. Trouw tot aan de Bedelzak.*

*Websites:*

One visits numerous websites in the course of one's research. Wikipeda is always a good starting point and has helped me endlessly. I picked a few other sources that I think the reader might find interesting or that can provide more information on specific aspects or places.
http://www.gentvoorbeginners.nl/
http://www.bbc.com/news/magazine-24396390
http://www.bbc.com/news/world-africa-20586792
http://www.dailymail.co.uk/health/article-1387468/Black-couple-Francis-Arlette-Tshibangu-white-baby-blond-hair.html
http://cellspyinghq.com/whats-best-way-tap-husbands-cell-phone/
http://www.forgottenbooks.com/readbook_text/The_Belgian_Congo_and_the_Berlin_Act_1000163281/181
http://www.internetstones.com/incomparable-diamond-famous-jewelry.html
http://www.johnbetts-fineminerals.com/jhbnyc/articles/specific_gravity.htm
http://www.mindat.org/advanced_search.php

*On "Skipskop":*

http://versindaba.co.za/2011/08/02/andries-bezuiden-
    hout-onderhoud-met-ronelda-s-kamfer/

*YouTube:*

*Gent-togati-stoet:*

https://www.youtube.com/ watch?v=USpiXkaGJzk

*On Doel:*

https://www.youtube.com/watch?v=3k-sivAayAo
https://www.youtube.com/watch?v=-gvvWdEPpQI
https://www.youtube.com/watch?v=iPERJf0Q3vo